THE CHICAGO CAP MURDERS

This book is a work of fiction. The names, characters and events in this book are the products of the author's imagination. Any similarity to real persons living or dead is coincidental and not intended by the author.

BookBullet.com
1300 W Belmont Ave Ste 20G
Chicago, IL 60657-3200

Editing by: Sherry Roberts from The Roberts Group

ISBN: 9781619841864

TO DEBBIE,
ALL THE BEST!

THE CHICAGO CAP MURDERS

WARREN FRIEDMAN

Dedications

For mom and dad, Edith and Morris Friedman

Acknowledgements

I would like to thank my amazing editor Sherry Roberts from The Roberts Group, who helped make this book the best it could be; Rob Price at Price World Publishing, whose consideration and professionalism guided me through uncharted territory to create this book; brothers Larry and Richard Friedman, whose contributions, advice and support were invaluable; writer and cousin Amy Friedman, who taught me how to write a novel while working as a fulltime pharmacist; first draft readers David Hochman, Ava Rubin, Dorothy Rini, Jared Klein, daughters Kelly Friedman and Courtney Friedman Ricchetti; Lauren and Laurie Kabb, my Chicago guides; and last but not least my wife Geri, whose love and support was the foundation to make this dream come true.

Table of Contents

Chapter 1

March 31, 2013

Ted Banks felt luckier than most Chicagoans. His nighttime security job at the Science Museum allowed him to enjoy all of Chicago's offerings during daylight hours. Spring, summer, and fall meant only one thing to Ted: Cubs baseball. From his family room easy chair in North Chicago, he'd watched thirty home openers. Opening day was a bonus, a day of new beginnings, the day when Chicago started the season tied for first place. In the crisp springtime air, the promise of a winning season, maybe even an incredible season, flew like a banner over the city. Each and every Cubs fan longed for a world championship, a title that had eluded them for 105 years, since 1908. Even apathetic fans desired a championship, if for no other reason than to stop hearing about the drought, or the curses.

Ted may have felt luckier than most Chicagoans in the past, but this spring his luck appeared to be running out.

Still cloudy from the injected drug, Ted's mind drifted to the absurd, wondering if baseball fans had attended the 1908 Series by foot, automobile, or horse. Over the years, Chicago had played many important games, but as far as Ted was concerned, none were as important as today's. Sweat slowly dripped down his forehead and cheeks as the game went to commercial, reaching the bottom of the ninth and the Cubs trailing the Mets, 3-2.

A voice bellowed from behind.

"Mr. Banks, you've no idea what impact you'll have on the Cubs. Win or lose, I believe you and I are going to make America take notice of our beloved Cubs. For your sake, I hope they rally, but I don't think this team understands the true meaning of a life-or-death situation."

"Come on, guys, two more runs, just two more runs," Ted moaned under the tightly wound gag in his mouth.

Fighting the ropes that bound him to the chair, Ted watched the naked actor in the erectile dysfunction commercial sip wine in the bathtub; he appeared content and confident of a long night. Ted Banks, however, feared by evening's end he would be getting the short end of the stick. As the advertisement faded back to the game, Ted stared at the screen with desperation. Max Neyland, the play-by-play broadcaster, continued.

"Here's the answer to the trivia question, "What's the translation of the Latin words Eamus Catuli? *Those are the words on the sign located across the street overlooking the right-field bleachers on Sheffield. Well, the two translations we hear the most are 'Let's go, young mammals' or 'Let's go, young bears'. That's as close to 'Let's go, Cubs" as you can get in Latin, isn't it, Ben?"*

"You bet, Max," replied the Cubs color commentator Ben Fair. *"The Cubs will bring Petronsky, Carrisquillo, and Bailey to the plate to battle right-hander Barry Jones, who has kept the Cubbies off-balance all day with his assortment of off-speed pitches to go along with his ninety-seven-mile-an-hour fastball, but he looks tired out there right now. Petronsky has taken three straight pitches as Jones is having trouble locating the strike zone, running the count on the third baseman to 3-0. Here's the windup and the pitch . . . and there's ball four."*

"Jones walked Petronsky on four straight pitches, and now the Cubs have the lead-off batter on first to start the ninth," yelled Fair.

The masked man behind Ted nudged him.

"Hey, Ted. Did you hear that? Sure gets your heart pumping, doesn't it?"

Now, like Cubs manager Doug Cahill down in the dugout, Ted began to think of all the possibilities. Should Petronsky steal? Should he be sacrificed over to second? Or should Carrasquillo hit away?

Neyland ranted from the announcer's booth. *"I mean, this guy can't bunt. Heck, he's only had four sacrifice bunts in his entire major league career. No, the man's a power hitter, and he's one of only two guys on the team who can win this game with one swing of the bat from the left side. Especially against a right-hander like Jones. But wait, here comes the Mets manager from the dugout. They apparently aren't going to let Jones face the left-handed hitting Carrasquillo. The manager is pointing to his left arm, and that means he's calling to the bullpen for big lefty Kurt Hammond."*

Ben Fair shared some stats with the audience. *"Hammond's mechanics were off in the preseason, walking fourteen batters in twelve innings. Carrasquillo might be better off if he leaves the bat on his shoulders, like Petronsky did, and tries to take a few pitches for a walk."*

Ted squirmed. "Shit!" he thought. "Carrasquillo can't hit left-handed pitchers to save his ass—let alone my ass!"

"What's wrong, Mr. Banks? Not a big proponent of the lefty-righty theory?"

Managers love playing the percentages. And the percentages say that left-handed hitters don't hit as well against left-handed pitchers as they do right-handed pitchers. Last year, left-handed batters hit .251 vs. left-handed pitchers, but hit .281, thirty points higher, against right-handed pitchers.

"I happen to love it," the voice of the intruder continued. "If this overpriced piece of garbage can't hit a lefty, he shouldn't be in the big leagues. I'm telling you, Teddie, baseball doesn't teach the fundamentals anymore. It's sickening!"

To Ted Banks, the pitches began to resemble the last few grains of sand in an hourglass.

"Strike threeee!" blared the broadcaster. *"Carrasquillo never swung his bat at any of those pitches as he heads back to the bench. Nothing wrong with Hammond's work on that at bat. Here comes Vinnie T. to bat for Bailey, which is a good move. The catcher went 0 for four today with three strikeouts. Bailey's a great hitter, but he may have come back too soon from that nagging oblique injury and he's not swinging well. Hopefully, Vinnie can keep this inning alive."*

Vinnie Thompson, a thirty-eight-year-old first baseman/ third baseman with bad knees, was a free agent pickup for the Cubs in the off-season. Every other year, he has a good year. Last year, he was outstanding.

"Thompson digs in from the right side of the plate. Hammond gets the sign. Here's the pitch—it's fouled back out of play. The guy attempting to catch the ball dropped it, and the fans are booing. From my count, there have been thirteen errors today: one on the field and twelve in the stands. Hammond is in his stretch—he throws and—there's a weak dribbler back to the mound. Hammond fires to second for one, back to first,

it's a double play! The Mets have taken the season opener from the Cubs, three to two."

"Well, Mr. Banks, the Cubs may have let you down, but I'm gonna see that you get into the Cubs Hall of Fame. They are going to remember you, and trust me, you are going to spur your beloved Cubs on to greatness this year."

Ted struggled in his chair to see the man in the shadows behind him; the man who had forced his way into Ted's apartment; who had bound him to his chair, drugged him, and gagged him; who had forced him to watch the game at the end of a nine-inch stiletto blade. Ted felt the blade at his throat then the blood running down, down, down. His attempts to scream were muffled by the warm blood gurgling in his slashed throat. His murderer's voice seemed quieter as Ted began to slip away.

"Thank you, Ted. The Cubs will win it all this year. Trust me; I'm making you a hero."

* * *

Banks's lifeless body slumped in the leather chair, soaked in blood. The killer made sure Ted was dead then placed a Chicago Cubs baseball cap on Ted's head, dimmed the lights, and headed out the door into the cool Chicago afternoon.

WARREN FRIEDMAN

Chapter 2

April 1, 2013

"Crisp."

"Whadya say?" asked Charlie Brainard.

"Crisp," continued Slats Grodsky. "A five-letter word meaning British potato chip. That's what you asked for, twenty-six down. Right?"

"How in the hell did you know that?"

"They were invented by an American chef back in the 1850s. One of his customers griped that his French fries were too thick, so to spite the complaining bastard, he sliced them as thin as possible and baked the hell out of them so the guy wouldn't be able to pick them up with a fork. The plan backfired, because the guy LOVED them. And the potato chip was born. When it was introduced in England, they called it a crisp, because French fries were called chips—you know, as in fish and chips?"

"Jeez, Slats, gimme a break. I mean, I'm only a self-educated man, not a UIC Flame grad like you."

Slats Grodsky was used to filling in the blanks when others tried to solve problems. Helping Charlie Brainard with his crossword puzzles was easy. Homicide, Eighth Precinct, where he displayed the analytical skills that set him apart from his fellow police officers, was a little harder. In his twenty-eight-year career, he had been honored more times than he had been disciplined. That ratio had shrunk, however, as his thirst for alcohol had outpaced his need to quench injustice.

The Eighth District, one of Chicago's twenty-five police precincts, was Grodsky's fourth precinct assignment in the last six years. If nothing else, he had met many of Chicago's finest in that time span. The district, also known as Chicago Lawn, contained Midway Airport. Built in 1923 and christened Chicago Municipal Airport, it earned the title "World's Busiest Airport" by 1932. It was renamed Chicago Midway Airport in 1949 in honor of the World War II Battle of Midway. With the dawn of the "Jet Age," Midway with its shorter runways fell out of favor. But after years of expansion and remodeling, it became the fastest growing airport in North America and was the forty-seventh busiest airport in the world. With growth, however, came crowds, and with crowds came crime. Slats Grodsky's inaugural day in the Eighth District nearly eleven months ago began with a homicide investigation in the men's bathroom near the baggage claim area, located in the lower level of the newer terminal building. The murder of an apparent homeless man had yet to be solved.

"Brainard! Where's your report on the Marathon Gas Station beating?" screamed Sam Pearson, the precinct commander.

"Have it for you soon, sir!"

"That's what you said three days ago. The DA wants that report ASAP, and I want it on my desk today!"

"Sorry, sir. My computer's down, and I haven't been able to . . ."

"Today, Brainard. Am I making myself clear, ass wipe?"

Charlie Brainard, the young, good-looking African-American who made detective in less time than anyone in the Wentworth-Calumet area, the detective whose hatred for criminals led to more busts in the last two years than any officer in the Eighth District, was scared to death of Commander Pearson. Maybe it was Pearson's gruff demeanor. Maybe it was Pearson's six foot five, 275-pound physique that towered over Charlie's five ten, 180-pound frame. Or maybe it was because Pearson was Charlie's father-in-law.

"Does your wife know her father talks to you like that?" Grodsky asked.

"Are you kidding? My wife talks to me like that!" Brainard responded.

Apparently, Charlie was afraid of his wife, too. That might explain why he volunteered for overnight stakeouts, rather than his insistence that he needed the overtime to pay for his Personal Seat License (PSL) and season tickets for the Bears games. You had to have a PSL to get season tickets. It was a one-time purchase but a hefty one. Grodsky thought it was ridiculous to pay thousands of dollars for the privilege to buy tickets. The tickets themselves were $200, not to mention food, beer, and parking—that's about $4,600 per year! . . . the phone rang.

"Eighth Precinct. Grodsky."

"Slats, it's Rocky. We need your help, unless you gotta problem working on something without sexual overtones."

Do I need to take this crap forever? Slats thought, acknowledging that his fame as the "Cop Who Cracked the Bermuda Love Triangle" was going to follow him to his grave.

Rocky, an old friend from the police academy now working out of Chicago's Seventeenth Precinct, continued, "This looks like it could be a Hitchcock. Does that interest you?"

Slats checked his watch. It was 9:30 a.m., April 1.

"Oh, I get it. April Fool's Day to you, too, Rocky!"

"No April Fool's joke, Slats. What, you think everything I say's a joke?"

"Rocky, what the hell are you talking about? Can you just give it to me in a simple declarative sentence?"

"Hitchcock, buddy, Alfred Hitchcock, as in a mystery."

A mystery. Rocky Parma had a mystery.

"Right. So what happened?"

"Come to 512 North Rogers Avenue, Slats. I'll explain when you get here."

Chapter 3

April 1, 2013

Slats Grodsky joined the Chicago Police Department long before a college degree was a mandatory requirement for Illinois police officers. He graduated in four years with a bachelor's degree in criminal justice from the University of Illinois Chicago, but history was Grodsky's true passion. His summa cum laude standing, reflected by a 3.89 accumulative grade point average, verified his academic excellence in areas above and beyond criminology, law, and justice.

Most who knew him agreed, that with a timeline of major world events etched into his brain, Slats had *Jeopardy* knowledge. It won him countless bar bets. And, even more, it gave him a secret weapon in the pursuit of felons. Sure, he knew dates and places, kings and presidents, the staples of the amateur historian. And he had developed mastery of the grand themes of history, the sweeping theories of eras and empires. But unlike the armchair students, he merged an understanding of these elements with a detailed knowledge of murder, mayhem, and crime through the ages. Early in his career he had solved a case by drawing on his knowledge of crimes of centuries gone by.

Today's recruits and young police officers were eager to take advantage of the modern tools of crime solving. And though he, too, respected forensic data, he differed from those who put their faith solely in technology; those with a blind devotion to winning cases by using the fruits of DNA, retinal imaging, fingerprinting, tire tracking, microscopic fiber identification, and the rest of the arsenal of the crime lab.

Slats and his generation were instrumental in shaping the modern qualifications of a Chicago police officer. In the past, anyone who met the minimum height and weight requirements and could wield a nightstick or shoot a gun was a viable recruit. Now, a CPD trainee needed at least four years of college, four years of active duty in the United States armed forces, or a combination of the two; plus a written exam, followed by drug test screening, background checks, medical exams, and psychological exams. Once the applicant was accepted as a Chicago police officer, he or she entered the academy, which consisted of 780 hours of coursework required by the State of Illinois and the city of Chicago. Passing the State Certificate Exam and proving residency in the city of Chicago were the last major hurdles for the recruit to become a CPD member.

As a young recruit, Slats was not only the brightest of his class, but the most physically fit. The POWER (Peace Officer Wellness Evaluation Report) test was the standard by which all candidates were measured prior to entering the academy. The three most vital areas of concern were aerobics, strength, and flexibility; they were measured by a one-and-one-half-mile run, a one-time maximum bench press, one-minute sit-up test, and a sit-and-reach flexibility test. These minimum requirements were no match for Slats's athletic prowess. A two-year, two-way starter at halfback and linebacker for his high school football team, and an Illinois State High School finalist in the eight hundred meters, Slats had retained his conditioning by running six miles a day during college. In fact, his mark of 7:47 in the 1.5-mile run, well below the 13:46 required for his age bracket, was still the fastest recorded time by any CPD recruit. Twenty-eight years of pounding the pavement, the torn medial and lateral meniscus on both knees, and the arthritis in his left hip had ended his jogging days. Slats was relegated to moving around in his 1997 Grand Prix, which was what he was driving now, on his way to meet Rocky Parma.

Grodsky's twenty-one-mile trek started by hopping onto the Kennedy Expressway and merging onto the Eden Expressway before exiting onto West Peterson Avenue. He drove eastbound down the four-lane avenue separated by a grassy median for about a half-mile before stopping at the intersection of North Kilbourn Avenue, one of a few thousand one-way Chicago streets.

Slats passed seven drivers in a row engaged in cell phone conversations. It may not have been a world record, but it was a record for Slats, no doubt about it. He frequently amused himself with accumulating trivial, unsubstantiated data. Maybe it was his police training, or the mindless ramblings of an inner self, or both. He would wonder how many steps it took to get from his desk at work to his parking space in the garage, and then pace it off. Or how many people were eating Big Macs in the world at exactly noon, Chicago time, all across the world. Today, apparently, the obsession was cell phones.

Slats found North Rogers Avenue and turned into a logjam created by the police cruisers at the area's three-way intersection. Eight squad cars had responded to the 911. Two cars blocked entrance to the street. Patrolmen stood by their vehicles diverting traffic to alternate routes.

Slats flashed his badge to one of the officers approaching his car as he eased his vehicle toward the other side of the intersection.

"Can you tell me where I can find Rocky Parma?" Slats asked.

"Yes, sir; he's in the brown house over there. I'll move my car so you can get through."

The officer was pointing to a two-story house, the fourth house on the south side of the street. The police had cordoned off the crime scene in typical fashion. Besides the roadblock, two cops were rolling yellow tape around the dwelling, while another stood sentinel at the front door. Three patrolmen were talking to onlookers on the street and taking notes.

Slats parked his car, flashed his detective badge to the officer standing guard at the door, and stepped into the house, sizing it up with a glance. To the left, a staircase led to the second floor. The living room-dining combo was to the right and, beyond that, a den. A hallway connected the front door to the kitchen. Off the hallway and before the kitchen were three steps down leading to a side door, a small bathroom, and another staircase continuing to the basement. It was here that Slats found Rocky Parma.

"Slats!" yelled Rocky. "Over here."

"Hey, Rocky," Slats retorted. "What's going on? What are you doing up North? You were in the Twelfth last time I saw you?"

"Yah, Slats, that's right. I was. But you know what? I'm getting too old for this shit. My cousin Bobby Davis works up here and called me when this gig opened up. There are not as many murders up here as there were in the Twelfth. After twenty-eight years, it's cushier, and I've earned cushier. So I transferred last year. Best thing I ever did."

Slats reached down and patted Rocky's belly. Back when he was in his twenties, Rocky had a six-pack abdomen. Now he had a keg.

"Did they ban exercise in the Seventeenth, or are you taking up sumo wrestling?"

"Okay, okay. I've put on a few pounds. But I'm still as pretty as ever."

Rocky had a leather-skinned face only a mother could love.

"Yes, Rocky, you are."

Slats turned his head, looked around the stairwell, then turned back to Rocky.

"What happened here?"

They both went up the steps and headed through the kitchen toward the den.

"The victim is a security guard named Ted Banks. Worked night shift at the Science Museum. His wife died of cancer ten years ago. Has two daughters, one in Chicago, one in Vegas. Lived alone, but was a pretty well-liked guy, according to the daughter here in town. She was the one who found him in the den. He was in his leather chair, apparently watching TV. She said he was a big Cubs fan, so he was probably watching the game. Coroner said he'd been dead for about twenty-four hours, so that makes sense. The TV was on WGN, which broadcasts the games. There's no sign of a struggle. Mr. Banks was found bound to his chair with his throat cut. That was the wound that killed him, but he was also bleeding from a blow to the back of the head. I figure he was probably knocked out or dazed so he could be tied up."

"Was there blood found anywhere else?" Slats asked.

"No," Rocky continued, "it appears he was attacked in his chair."

"Did you find the murder weapon?"

"Nope. Killer must have taken it."

"Any sign of forced entry?"

"Nope. His daughter said he was always forgetting to lock the side door."

"Funny, the guy spent a lifetime making sure the museum was locked down and didn't lock down his house. Who else knew the door was open?"

"Shit, from what we've been told, everyone. But there's no sign of anything missing. He didn't have any jewelry or cash in the house. Nothing in the house was disturbed. No one was looking for anything. Robbery doesn't appear to be a motive."

"Enemies?"

"We're talking to neighbors, bosses, coworkers, family, and we're getting reports that all say the same thing—everybody liked this guy; doesn't appear anyone hated him enough to want him dead."

"Any girlfriend or lover?"

"No, Banks didn't date after his wife died. He was a loner in that regard. There's no jealous boyfriend or girlfriend or crazed lover, if that's what you're getting at."

"So this is a random killing?"

"I told you, a real Hitchcock, isn't it?"

Slats slowly walked around the chair, circling the remains of Ted Banks. With his right hand covering his mouth and chin and his left hand resting on his hip, Grodsky absorbed the scene. Banks was wearing a bloody Chicago Bulls sweatsuit, white crew socks, and a Chicago Cubs baseball cap.

"Were you able to pick up any prints?" Grodsky asked Parma.

"They must have worn gloves. This place is clean as a whistle."

"So nothing's stolen, nobody hated the guy, no angry girlfriend."

Grodsky walked to the window and stared at the garage behind the house.

"Guy drove a beater, Slats. It's still there. Not that either."

What then? Grodsky wondered. Why is Banks dead? What possible motive could there be to kill this man? Yes, it is a mystery, Slats thought. But as he turned around and stared at the dead man again, there was one thing that looked out of place after all.

"Rocky, you said he was struck on the back of the head. Do you know what hit him?"

"Not sure, Slats, but it could have been a gun butt. Why?"

"Well, it must have been a pretty substantial hit to make his head bleed. Don't you think a severe blow to the head would've knocked his hat off?"

Rocky looked at the back of the hat.

"You know, Slats, now that you mention it, there's no indentation on the back of the hat. And it's on his head straight as an arrow. A blow to the head should have at least knocked it off-kilter, if not off entirely."

"Exactly. Now, Banks here is either woozy or unconscious after he's struck. I don't think the first thought he has after regaining his awareness is to put his hat on straight."

"And if he's tied up, impossible," Rocky blurted in.

"It's more likely," Slats continued, "that the killer placed it on him once he was tied up."

"And that means . . .?" Rocky asked.

"Could be a calling card, or could be ab-so-lutely nothing," Slats said absent-mindedly.

The two ex-classmates headed for the front door.

"Thanks for calling me, Rocky. Hey, I forgot to ask. How're Shirley and the kids?"

"They're all good, Slats. Shirley's as feisty as ever. All the kids live out of town, though. That sucks. Every kid in the country moves to Chicago, but my kids? They want to be somewhere else. Hey, sorry about you and Julie. What was that, three years ago? Four?"

"Eight."

"Eight? Shit! Where has the time gone? You okay now?"

"If you're referring to my . . ."

"No, no, Slats, I didn't mean that. I'm asking, you okay?"

"Yah, Rocky, I'm okay. Great, in fact. Thanks for caring."

The two headed back outside. Standing by Slats's car, the friends seemed to run out of things to say. Finally, Slats pulled out his car keys with one hand and thrust out his other. "It was great seeing you, Rocky. Call me if you find anything else."

Rocky took his hand. "I will, Slats, I will. You be good."

Slats cranked up the Grand Prix, waved again at Rocky, then headed for home. Though he had been sober for almost a year now, he was anything but good. His life had taken a torturous path through hell and back, losing his wife, Julie; his daughter, Ava; and his lofty position on the force to a different force—the force of alcohol. After years of therapy and rehab, he knew what he needed to do: restore bonds with his fellow officers, cope with his demanding profession, and win back the respect of his ex-wife, Julie, and his daughter, Ava. He wanted back in his daughter's life. Once upon a time, in his child's eyes, he had been the world's best dad. Relapse after drinking relapse had stripped him of that title, leaving him on the outs, not even invited to Ava's wedding. As he had poisoned himself with spirits, so too had Julie poisoned their daughter with stories of his drunken exploits. They were mostly true, but he was different now, trying to change.

Slats looked at his reflection in the rearview mirror. No wonder people asked if he was okay. He looked like day-old toast. But it wasn't always this way. Once, he was the toast of Chicago.

Chapter 4

The Bermuda Love Triangle

June 1996

Biatelli's Ristorante connected past to present on Taylor Street in the heart of Chicago's Little Italy. The decades-old, faded signage above the door; the unwashed windows facing the street; and the homey interior décor strewn with red-checkered tablecloths and pictures of immigrant Italians adorning the walls were similar to Italian restaurants found in almost every city in America. Intermittent screams from the kitchen area, mostly in Italian, only added to the ambiance.

At the turn of the twentieth century, mass migration by Europeans brought Jews, Greeks, and Italians to the neighborhood. And though other ethnic groups eventually left the area, the Italians stayed. By the 1940s, the neighborhood was a thriving Italian community with more than eighty thousand inhabitants. Close to a thousand food-related businesses such as restaurants, grocery stores, and bakeries lined the streets. It was during this time that Anton Biatelli opened his restaurant.

Several businesses and homes were bulldozed in the 1960s during the construction of the Eisenhower Expressway and the University of Illinois Chicago campus, displacing residents from the area and driving the population into decline. But Biatelli's remained, fueled by the loyalty of remaining Italians, the influx of twenty-five thousand students, and the patronage of the Maravelli mafia family.

Known for its history of Prohibition Era gangsters, Chicago entertained the most notorious: Al Capone, the Genna Family, Hymie Weiss, Bugs Moran, the North Side Gang, Tony Accardo, and Sam Giancana. Most of the Chicago family's roots were in bootlegging. The Maravelli family was no exception. Affonzo Maravelli obtained a license to produce industrial alcohol in 1925, and, following the lead of other mobsters in the business, redistilled gallons of it to be sold as drinking alcohol. Outlasting their rivals, the Maravellis eventually segued into drug trafficking, loan sharking, gambling, extortion, and protection services. High on its list of businesses to protect was the favorite restaurant of the family, Biatelli's.

In 1946, Clemencio, the eldest son of Affonzo, lived above the restaurant with his wife, Maria, and their seven children: three boys and four girls. The quarters were cramped with two bedrooms for the seven children, but Affonzo had insisted that Clemencio, heir apparent and eventual Don through the '70s and '80s, live on the premises to run the daily business meetings held in the restaurant's back room. When Clemencio became Don, his eldest son Lorenzo lived there with his family until his untimely death, at which point Lorenzo's brother Damarco, next in line, inhabited the second floor with his family. The bond between Biatelli's and the Maravelli family had become so close that the restaurant's overhead expenses, including its protection, were taken care of for life, guaranteed by Clemencio. Of course, this was in exchange for meals provided to the immediate family of the Don. All others in the Maravelli family were expected to pay for their own meals out of duty and respect to Anton Biatelli.

Now, Clemencio Maravelli's son Damarco was the Don. Lorenzo had been gunned down years earlier in a turf war as the family struggled to retain its position in the waste disposal business among the Chicago clans. Were it not for the heroic efforts of Bruno Discenzo, six members of the Maravelli family including Damarco would have died that day as well. Due to his bravery, taking out the enemy while catching four bullets in his torso, Bruno was promoted to a top position in the organization. Though Clemencio's youngest son Mark Anthony was now the consigliere, it was Bruno whom the family most heavily relied upon to be the "fixer."

Affonzo, Clemencio, and Damarco were the names most associated when discussing the Maravelli family, but it was Bruno Discenzo's name that struck fear into the hearts of their enemies. Bruno's life and exploits were well documented. Hiding in a closet, he watched his sister being raped and murdered along with his parents and brother during a botched burglary. He was placed in an orphanage at the tender age of seven, with a heart hardened to the world. Fighting and bullying other children, defying the simple requests of teachers and taskmasters, Bruno was bounced from one orphanage to another until the age of ten, when he escaped to the streets.

Sleeping in the basement of Our Lady of Pompeii Church, he survived by begging and stealing. He flew under the radar until he stole a hubcap from the wrong person: Clemencio Maravelli. Caught trying to fence it to a junkyard under the protection of the Maravellis', the youngster was taken directly to Clemencio, who immediately took a liking to the handsome boy and his brash attitude. Clemencio insisted that Bruno live with his oldest sister, Sophia, and her husband Carmine, a lieutenant in the family. The couple, unable to conceive, had been desperate for a child of their own after three miscarriages.

Everything Bruno could want or need was at his disposal: a mother and father who loved him, a warm bed, a life of privilege, enrollment in the finest private schools, a generous allowance bigger than any of his classmates', and the structure and guidance of a family.

Despite the surroundings and trappings of his new family, Bruno remained steel-eyed and cold. Unimpressed with money, Bruno considered money only as a means to an end. Unable to form close friendships, though friendly to those near him, Bruno was obsessed with one thought: retribution. He was driven to erase the face that was burned into the back of his memory, the face of the murderer who had ripped his family apart.

In 1978, at the age of eighteen and at the insistence of his adopted father, Bruno joined the Air Force. Originally trained as a cook, he volunteered and was accepted into the Special Forces. By twenty, he was leading his platoon in special ops behind Afghanistan lines, training rebel troops who were fighting the Russians. At the end of his tour, he was recruited to join the CIA, where he became one of the organization's top European assassins.

When the CIA disbanded his position, in 1994, Bruno headed back to Chicago with a skill set that was extremely useful for the Maravelli family business. Rising to the top of the organization, Bruno became known as "The Eliminator."

In his spare time, Bruno could be found in Biatelli's kitchen, practicing his culinary skills and expanding the restaurant's menu, a blessing for the seventy members of the Maravelli family who were expected to eat at Biatelli's at least twice a week.

It was on one of those days, in the summer of 1996, that Bruno was eating with his bodyguard Eddie and complaining about the future of Little Italy.

"I'm telling you, this neighborhood is going to shit. I'll bet you within ten to fifteen years Little Italy won't even be on the Chicago map anymore."

"Bruno. Whatta yah talkin' about? You're so fuckin' dramatic. We're always gonna be here. No one's gonna mess with our community, capiche?"

Bruno didn't answer. His eye had caught sight of a killer blonde at one of the front tables. She was with two friends. They looked like students at the university.

Bruno was instantly smitten.

He motioned to one of the waiters exiting the kitchen and pointed to the girl's table.

"Hey, Emilio, bring that table a bottle of the Fuligni Brunello di Montalcino Riserva, 1989."

* * *

Engrossed in conversation, Didi Lecate and her friends Kate and Alexa were surprised by the arrival of the fine Italian red wine.

"Compliments of the gentleman at the far table," Emilio stated, tilting his head toward Bruno as he displayed the wine label to the young ladies.

The girls politely nodded in their benefactor's direction as the waiter placed the glasses on the table, then poured a sampling of the wine in Didi's glass.

"Excellent," she said, giving her approval. Emilio poured the wine for the others at the table.

"Can you believe that?" said Kate. She leaned forward. "He's a little old to be hitting on us, don't you think?"

"Uh, yaaaah," replied Alexa.

"I dunno, I think he's cute; well-built, too. And look at that suit; gotta be Armani. He must be a lawyer or something," said Didi, raising her glass to Bruno.

"Well, I'll stick to my own age, thank you very much," said the twenty-one-year-old Kate.

"It's only a bottle of wine, for Christ's sake," retorted Didi.

"Does it comes with a condom?" asked Alexa.

The girls continued their banter, giggling their way through lunch. As their table was being cleared, Emilio leaned in and whispered to Didi.

"Girls," said Didi, "it appears our check has been taken care of. We really have to thank the gentleman."

The girls wound their way between the tables to thank Bruno. Standing as they approached, Bruno covered his heart with his hand. Didi took the lead, acting as spokesperson for the group.

"Mr. ….?"

"Discenzo. But please, call me Bruno."

"Well, Mr. Disc . . ., I mean Bruno, it was very kind of you to send us the wine and take care of our bill."

"Honestly, it was my pleasure."

"Do you own the restaurant?" Alexa asked.

He laughed out loud. "Well, I do make a few suggestions to the chef from time to time; however, no, this establishment does not belong to me. But I do enjoy the food and eat most of my meals here. And I can tell you with absolute certainty, this establishment is rarely graced with young beautiful women such as yourselves. So, when it is, it is my civic duty to make sure you come back again."

Not wanting to be late for their next class, Kate and Alexa quickly extended their hands to thank him then excused themselves. At the door, Kate turned, "Coming, Didi?"

Bruno said, "Why don't you stay, Didi, is it?"

The corner of Didi's lip curled as she studied her pursuer. Sleek black hair combed straight back highlighted a creased forehead hiding an old scar. Dark blue hypnotic eyes dotted the handsome face with movie-star trimmings—Elvis-long sideburns and Errol Flynn-styled mustache and goatee.

"Sure, just for a few minutes. See ya, girls."

"Please, sit with me for a while. I must know more about you because you are absolutely the most beautiful woman I have ever seen. Are you dating anyone?"

Didi was taken aback. Bruno was a fast mover. "Excuse me?"

"I'm sorry for being forward, but I'm headed for Bermuda in a couple days and wondered if you might be willing to accompany me. I have to see more of you. Have you ever been there?"

"No, I've never been, but Mr. Discenzo!"

"Separate rooms, of course!"

"I have to work," Didi said. "I don't attend the university like my friends. I work at a salon down the street."

"No problem. I can take care of it for you; make sure they give you the time off. Where do you work exactly?"

"Are you crazy? I can't go to Bermuda! First of all, I don't even know you. Second, I can't get time off from my job at Mario's! And third, my parents, my God, they'd never let me go."

"Mario's. I know the place. As for your parents, they can come, too. Seriously, a few days, a few weeks, whatever it takes. I want to get to know you, and I'd enjoy showing you the island. If you learn anything about me today, you'll realize I'm not going to take no for an answer."

Didi frowned. Everything was moving so fast. "I don't know. I'll tell you what, I'll ask for time off, okay?" she answered, if for no other reason than to end the conversation.

"Good, good. May I have your number, so I can call you later?"

Didi took out a pen and, searching for paper but finding none, wrote her number on a napkin. They exchanged polite good-byes, and she headed out of Biatelli's to take the six-block walk to Mario's.

Didi soon found out about the man she had been talking to. As she entered the salon, Mario, the owner and namesake of the salon, said, "Didi, why didn't you tell me you were dating Bruno?"

"What the f . . . I'm not . . ."

"He said you wanted to spend some time together. Of course, you can take the next few weeks off. Jennifer can take your clients until you get back. Take as long as you need."

Mario had never talked to her with such respect. Something, or someone, had made him obsequious. Bruno was obviously a powerful person who got what he wanted, when he wanted it. Maybe a politician, she thought.

Stunned by Mario's kindness, she headed home to try to figure this all out. She was even more shocked when her cell phone rang.

It was her mother bubbling about the trip to Bermuda.

"Hi, honey. What's going on? Can you believe we're all going to Bermuda? I just talked to Dad, and they've given him a two-week leave of absence. Didi, what's going on? Are you having an affair with the mayor or somethin'? Who is this man? I can't wait 'til you get home so you can tell me all about him."

"Mom, I . . ."

"Oh, it doesn't matter, sweetie. Isn't this exciting? Last-minute surprises are the best. What do they call that?"

"Spontaneous, Mom. What did Dad say?"

"Are you kidding? We haven't been out of town since Cousin Howie's wedding in Gary, Indiana, four years ago. Your father's thrilled. He said we've never even won two dollars on a lottery ticket. And now we're going to Bermuda for free! He can't wait to meet this gentleman."

"Mom, I have to tell you . . ."

"Dear, I have to go. Save it for later at dinner, okay? We can talk then. I'm so happy!"

Jesus, Didi thought. She hadn't heard her parents this happy in years. Not only were her parents thrilled, her boss was kowtowing to her, and it didn't hurt that Bruno was ruggedly handsome and, evidently, rich! What harm could there be in getting to know him, while vacationing on a beautiful island?

There was only one last question to answer: what to wear to Bermuda?

Chapter 5

Bermuda Love Triangle

Sunday, January 18, 1998

Joey Robbins was enjoying his first trip to Bermuda. He had travelled to exciting venues in his fifteen years as a baseball scout: Louisville, Dallas, Walt Disney World, San Diego, and San Antonio. During the year, however, when he was not hobnobbing with team executives at ritzy convention centers, his days were spent in dusty towns, dirty travel lodges, and lonely restaurants; traveling the boring miles on old-world buses, crowded trains, and endless car rides looking for the next great ballplayer in small town U.S.A., or in the baseball hotbeds of the Dominican Republic, Panama, Puerto Rico, and Venezuela. Once a year, however, the Chicago Cubs, his major league employer, brought him to the Winter Baseball Meetings, where he and fellow Chicago scouts could discuss the kind of prospects the organization was looking for, both for major league and minor league operations. This year's baseball meetings were being held in Bermuda at the elegant five-star Fairmount Southampton resort, from Sunday, January 18, to Sunday, January 25.

The major league meetings were the reward for those cold, lonely nights on the road without friends and family, cavorting with some strangers who knew no English, or others who you wished knew no English. One thing they did seem to know was the universal language of baseball.

On Sunday morning, Joey, who had checked in the night before, woke up in his king-size bed. Emerging from underneath the clean satin sheets and comforter, he gazed around his second-floor ocean-view room. It was loaded with luxury: an eight-hundred-square-foot suite, complete with a forty-two-inch HDTV LED television screen; full service bar; Internet access; Jacuzzi built for two; a glassed-in shower with a rain faucet showerhead; signature shampoo, mouthwash, bath and hand soap, body lotion, and conditioners; a full-sized window overlooking the Atlantic Ocean and Southampton Beach; and a $200-per-day meal expense account to be used for room service or any of the ten restaurant/bars adjacent to the resort.

Slipping on the full-length cotton robe with the embroidered Fairmount initials, Joey opened the venetian blinds and was welcomed by the blue expanse of the Atlantic Ocean. His eyes were immediately drawn to the horizon, where two ships journeyed on the water's edge—one a cruise ship, the other a freighter.

The temperature was an unusually warm seventy-five degrees. Smaller sailboats and yachts littered the waters between the horizon and the shore; swimmers bobbed up and down in the water as the waves pounded the shoreline. Joey scanned the beach. He watched a long-legged blonde in a thong bikini and oversized sunglasses wading in and out of the waves as they struck the shore. Occasionally she bent down and picked up a shell or stone. Joey couldn't take his eyes off her. He was enchanted. He pondered what it would be like to be with such a beautiful woman. Finally, he sighed and turned away. His first meeting in the Roosevelt Room was a half-hour from now, and he had yet to shower and collect his notes. Reality's battering ram shattered fantasy's door; why would that lovely creature want to be with a $60,000/year balding baseball scout with nothing to offer but a Sammy Sosa autographed baseball?

With six hundred rooms and a convention center that housed fifteen hundred attendees, the hotel was filled to capacity. Joey reached the meeting room in the same manner in which the president of the United States reached the podium in the Senate chambers before his "State of the Union Address." Joey was stopped every few steps by a familiar face; he shook hands, slapped backs, or whispered into the ears of owners, club executives, ball players, scouts, prospects, exhibitors; an endless stream of baseball humanity. Finally, placing his laptop down where the Chicago contingency was concentrated, he attended breakfast in the open veranda where eggs Benedict and mimosas were being offered by the servers with delightful British accents. As he lifted the mimosa glass off the tray, he caught a glimpse of the same willowy blonde on the beach that he had seen from his window moments before. It appeared, however, that she was not a guest of the hotel, for she was making her way up a wooden staircase heading to a seaside home, a few hundred yards from the hotel grounds. His daydream was interrupted by a call to order for the morning gathering.

The assembly was the official welcoming kickoff reception for all the club's attendees. After introductions of dignitaries on the dais, a syllabus of the week's meetings was distributed. The three most important functions were to discuss rule changes impacting the game, labor agreements between players and owners, and player movement from one club to the next. It was in this last capacity that Joey Robbins was brought to Bermuda. No one in the Cubs organization had a keener eye for the assets needed for a prospect to become a valuable part of the organization.

Many intangibles make it difficult to determine whether a player has the "it" factor when it comes to making a minor league club, let alone the majors. Coordination, along with timing, bat speed, and arm extension. Is he fast or a plodder? Does he know how to hit the corner of the base as he's heading for the next base, or does he step on the middle of it? Does he have soft hands on defense, or a brick for a glove? What about his throwing arm? Is it strong? Is it accurate? Is the kid committed to the game, or is he in it for the money? Does he play with 110 percent reckless abandon or does he try to save himself from injury? What is his personality? Is he a troublemaker or a team player? Does he have incredible family support, or is he surrounded by a posse that uses his fame for their success and ability to get women? Is he the best player available, or is he impossible to sign to a contract? If he's a high schooler, does the ballplayer want the college experience before starting his career? When the final determination was needed, the Cubs organization usually came looking for Joey Robbins to make the call.

Joey's agenda was the same at this meeting as it had been for the last several years. When the welcoming speeches were finished, the Cubs troupe retreated to the owner's suite, where specific goals were addressed. In attendance were Victor Gant, the Chicago Cubs president from the *Tribune*; Paul Rosello, the Cubs president of baseball operations; Mark Schwartz, general manager; Santiago Velendez, director of amateur and professional scouting; and the club's sixteen scouts, of which Joey Robbins was now the senior member.

After opening remarks by the front office personnel, Gant and Rosello left the room to attend the league meetings for owners and club presidents. Schwartz, Velendez, and the scouts were left to hash over the information on hundreds of players in their laptops. Each was to present a PowerPoint presentation of the prospective player or players to the group with the biggest upside. The meeting ended when it was determined what holes needed to be filled for the major, the minor, and rookie leagues clubs. If a left-handed relief pitcher was needed to round out a club, the scouts hashed out who they believed to be the best prospect available, weighing all of the previously mentioned intangibles. Once determined, the recommendation was passed up the chain to the G.M., whose job it was to procure the player.

The less-experienced scouts worked collectively in their assigned meeting room. Joey Robbins preferred to work alone. As head scout and the final voice presenting to his superior, Santiago Velendez, Joey had to get it right. The last thing he wanted was to be influenced by some twenty-two-year-old hotshot scout wanting to make a name for himself, willing to take a chance on a ballplayer because he had a "gut" feeling. Most scouts with gut feelings found themselves gutted and out of baseball within a year of discovering the .224 hitter they put their trust into. No, Robbins had his own system, unshared and unseen by others in the business, which increased not only his value, but his mystique.

What the Cubs execs and fellow scouts were unaware of, however, was that Robbins had spent the last month evaluating and refining his recommendations and players for his ball club. He already knew who he would be recommending so there was little left to do for him on this archipelago but explore.

Bermuda consists of more than 140 islands. It is twenty-two miles in length and only two miles wide at its widest point. Many of the islands are uninhabited rocks. With a land mass of only twenty-one square miles, Bermuda is one of the smallest countries in the world, smaller than Liechtenstein but larger than territories like Monaco and Gibraltar.

It was on this island, one of the smallest countries on the planet, that Joey Robbins, level-headed, at the top of his field, well respected by his peers, would make the largest mistake of his life.

Making his way to the veranda, Robbins picked up another mimosa and headed down the creaky staircase to the pink sandy beach surrounding the Fairmount's back porch. Taking off his Bacco Bucci sandals, he pushed his toes into the warm sand, which felt like silk beneath his feet. He looked in both directions, as if wondering which way to go, but Robbins had predetermined his course; the direction of the staircase the long-legged blonde had ascended.

Determined to use his plethora of scouting skills, he was hoping to find out if the "prospect" was as good-looking as he had hoped. Strolling casually, allowing the cool Atlantic waters to submerge his feet, Robbins slowly meandered down the beach, picking up a shell or two, until arriving at the wooden steps leading to the house at the top of the dune.

"What kind of person lives in a home on the ocean?" Robbins wondered. "And why do they always have a beautiful girl at their disposal? Maybe it's her parents' home."

Stopping for a moment at the base of the steps, Joey gazed up the walkway from the beach, unable to see anything but a never-ending staircase. Curious, he had to see more. Ignoring the generic "No Trespassing" sign, Joey climbed the first forty steps, which dead-ended into the hillside. A dirt path continued to the left, elevating another twenty to thirty feet. There, another staircase awaited him. After escalating to the next level, a spectacular house overwhelmed his view. The Olympic-sized infinity pool, with its white trim and bright blue water, was the closest structure to the beach, overlooking the ocean view from the cliff. Blue and white striped lounge chairs populated the concrete deck surrounding the pool, with teak patio tables strategically placed between.

Beyond the pool, approximately one hundred feet, was perhaps the finest oceanside home that Robbins had ever cast his eyes upon. This Tuscan-inspired palazzo had to be at least fifteen thousand square feet. Three stories of glass windows revealed marbled, winding staircases through the center of the structure. Palm trees lined the outside of the home, with elaborate automatic night lighting to showcase the house. Fifteen-foot arched entrances spanned the south wall of the home, facing the waterfront. Through the windows, he could see Bianca tile floors and huge marble fireplaces. Double fountains embellished the glorious grounds, which had walkways made of Boston brick pavers.

"I'd love to see the inside this house," Robbins fantasized, "but how?" Maybe Victor Gant, the president of the Cubs, knew this gentleman, and could get him an invitation, even arrange a meeting. Or perhaps the invitation he wanted the most was from the lovely blonde he had seen climbing the stairs moments before.

A sense of panic suddenly hit Joey Robbins as he stood inches from the infinity pool.

"What the hell am I doing?" Joey mumbled out loud. "I'm representing the Chicago Cubs on beautiful Bermuda at the winter meetings, I'm married to an amazing woman, I have twin boys, and I'm fricking trespassing on these grounds. All because of an incredible, insatiable urge to see a sexy woman who would probably have me arrested on sight!"

As reality set in, Joey turned around and rapidly retraced his steps down to the beach, hoping no one had seen him on the property.

* * *

Almost no one had, with the exception of one person with a keen eye for such indiscretions and detail: Carlos "Tex" Perryman. Tex, a newsman for the *Chicago Daily News* since

1965, was covering the winter meetings for his newspaper. He knew the staircase Joey Robbins was descending from was not part of the estate of a wealthy franchise owner, a ballplayer, a local politician, or even the wealthiest of agents in the sports world.

While Perryman talked politely to an eager, young writer who had recently accepted his first job covering the Williamsport Cubs in the New York-Pennsylvania League, Perryman could not help wondering what Joey Robbins had in mind in visiting the house next door.

Perryman politely excused himself from the young scribe and ambled toward Robbins, who was now nonchalantly making his way back to the Fairmount, as if he had just been for an innocent walk on the beach, pondering the meaning of life.

Everything about Perryman was genuine Chicago, except for the largely misleading appellation "Tex," a name he picked up as a five-year-old when his father decided his little boy bore a resemblance to the country singer Tex Ritter. As for his real first name, "Carlos" was a mild tribute to Cuba, based on his mother's conviction that she had been conceived in that tropical paradise shortly before the family departed to make its fortune in America. Neither Texan or Hispanic, Tex Perryman traded on his faux ethnic credentials to ingratiate himself into more places than he would have had he decided to use his middle name, Jeffrey, as he was instructed to do by his first editor.

"Is that you, Joey?" Tex exclaimed.

"Hey, Tex, how the hell are you? When did we see each other last, at the World Series?"

"No, actually it was when we had that really big story to cover," he said sarcastically. "You know, when Jose Rivera announced his retirement last year from managing the Cubs."

"Gosh, that's right. Hey, man, after fifty years on the road, Jose deserves to be able to spend a little time with his family."

Tex continued. "How is your family these days?"

"Well, the boys, as you'd expect, are rambunctious as hell. It's tough to expect Darla to raise them when I'm out on the road all year long. They're seventeen years old, and they don't have an "A" between them, but they sure have a few other letters, like DWI and DUI."

The two men laughed. "Speaking of letters, Joey, let's talk about the letters WTF."

"WTF?" Robbins puzzled.

"Yes, WTF, like what the fuck were you doing at Bruno Discenzo's house before?"

"Who?"

"Bruno Discenzo, the hit man for the Maravelli family. He lives next door to the Fairmount on the beach right over there."

"I swear. I had no idea that . . ."

"What were you thinking?"

"Honestly, I saw this cute girl go up the stairs and I was a little curious what she looked like, that's all. I didn't realize I was trespassing on Discenzo's property."

"Well, you'd better have a good story about why you went up there, or you'll have more to do with him than you bargained for."

"Christ! It was an honest mistake. I'll tell him I got lost looking for Victor Gant or something."

"Joey, Discenzo must have a hundred cameras on his grounds. He'll have seen and studied your every move."

"Why?" asked Robbins.

"Why? Why! Because people are always hunting him, that's why. The man's killed half of Chicago, for Christ's sake. He doesn't give a shit about you and your little scouting career. Once he IDs you, you'd better have a damn good reason for looking for him."

"But I wasn't looking for him."

"Maybe you weren't, but Discenzo's not going to believe that. You better think of a good reason why you were there because you sure don't want to tell him you were following a girl, do you?"

"Hmm, I see your point, Tex. Listen. I owe you. I don't care want it takes, but if I get out of this, I owe you big time. Okay?"

"That's how this all works, Joey. I'll settle for some inside scoop for the newspaper on who the Cubs are seriously talking to and looking at here at the meetings this week."

The men headed back to the hotel.

"Look," Tex continued, "you're not stupid. You'll figure this out. You'll have to lay low and think it through, then stay calm when he comes looking for you."

Tex watched Robbins hurry back to the Churchill Room. He probably thought there was safety in numbers with his fellow scouts. Poor guy, Tex thought. Unaware of Bruno Discenzo's history, it was a false sense of security.

Chapter 6

April 5, 2013

"What'll it be today, handsome?" asked Julie McGovern, the waitress at the Old Town Tavern on West Elm Street.

Slats studied the menu, as if he were going to find something new. Though the menu offered close to fifty dishes, he invariably ordered the same five or six meals. Slats was a cardiologist's dream. His favorites were the bucket of ribs, the bacon double cheese mushroom and grilled onion burger with fries, the fish and chips, the B.L.T., the corned beef on rye with mustard, and the New York strip steak. Occasionally, one of his favorite entrées was the special of the day, which guaranteed the order. Today's Friday special was the fish and chips.

"The $5.99 special, I guess."

"What a surprise," she answered, as she cracked her gum. "And to drink?"

"Diet Coke."

"Now, you know we only have Pepsi."

"Then Diet Pepsi, please."

It didn't seem to matter where he was. If he ordered Pepsi, the bar had Coke, or vice versa. And though he'd eaten at the Old Town Tavern over a hundred times in the last year, he still managed to get it wrong. Every single time.

The tavern was privately owned by restaurateur Ricky Gage. Slats had been a frequent customer, both before and after his divorce. It was here that he succumbed to alcohol's advances. For the last eleven months, at Slat's request, Ricky had instructed his bartenders and servers not to serve the officer alcohol, no matter how much he begged.

Aside from the tavern's proximity to his apartment, which was right around the corner, the main reason Slats ate at the establishment now was Julie. The tavern had twelve plasma flat screens stationed in every possible location, but Slats ignored the televisions when he had a view of Julie's derrière walking away from the table.

Every screen had the Cubs on today. They had suffered another loss to start the season 0-5. After dropping their first four games to the New York Mets at Wrigley Field, the Pittsburgh Pirates beat the Cubs 4-0, holding them to three hits in a game called after five innings due to an unexpected April snowstorm. All signs pointed to another losing season. Why should this year be different than any other year? After all, the Chicago Cubs had not won a World Series Championship since 1908, the longest drought in the majors.

Chicago had its champions in the three major sports. The Bulls and Michael Jordan won six NBA Championships, the Chicago White Sox had three World Series rings, and the Chicago Black Hawk possessed four Stanley Cups in their storied history. But 105 years had passed since the Cubbies won their last World Series, which was four years before the *Titanic* sunk! Theodore Roosevelt was the outgoing president, and the Model-T was in its first year of production. With a universe and planet in constant chaos ever since, only the Chicago Cubs provided stability and consistency in the big scheme of things.

Three days had passed since the murder of Ted Banks, and the police were still searching for their first clue. News of the murder barely made a dent in the press. Chicago had seen more than fourteen thousand homicides in the last twenty-one years; one more was hardly newsworthy. The grizzly details of the murder had been withheld, which made it even less remarkable.

Yet to Grodsky, this murder was different. Slats used to have a nose for mysteries such as these. It was how he had built his reputation. But years of alcohol abuse had given him anosmia, which was a loss of smell. Eleven months sober after his latest relapse, though his senses were still blunted, he knew trouble was lurking in the shadows of Chicago. It's just that there was no scent to follow.

He was interrupted by Julie as she brought his diet Pepsi to the table.

"So, tough guy, you miss me?"

"How can I miss you when I'm here every night?"

Though it had been almost eight years since his divorce from his wife, also named Julie, Slats had not got past it. Dipsomania ruined their marriage, and his wife hated him for that. But even though Slats still held a torch for his ex-wife, he enjoyed gazing at beautiful women, and waitress Julie was all of that.

Slats had only dated a handful of women since his divorce, if you could call them dates. Most were with waitresses when he was sober or prostitutes when he was stoned. The women he coveted were good looking, young, and sexy. They also had to be on the same page as Slats regarding relationships—not interested in commitment.

Julie fit his profile. Now that he was sober, they had hooked up a handful of times in the last few months. She even had one extra quality that separated her from the other women—her name. He could yell out her name during lovemaking, and she wouldn't know it was ex-wife, Julie, he cried for. For the others not named Julie, it was usually a show-stopper.

* * *

Julie McGovern was thirty-two years old and a looker. She was also loyal, hard working, and extremely independent. Raised by her father when her mother left at age six, she took over the duties of the household early. Cooking and cleaning were expected. As she got older, shouting matches with her father usually ended in a multi-night sleepover at a friend's house. When her pocket book emptied, she returned home, enduring her old man's verbal abuse. He was not a bad father, but he was armed with little skill in the areas of love, praise, or encouragement. Julie accepted this in exchange for food and shelter. Besides, at least he did not abandon her like her mother. Raised with so little affection, Julie had formed a bubble around her that was not to be intruded upon by any man. Though many had tried, few were able to thaw her cold shoulder.

Except for Slats. His rugged good looks made him easy on the eyes, and despite his gimpy knees and lack of exercise, his physique was still formidable. But he was emotionally out of shape. He reminded Julie of a puppy in need of love. Though it was clearly understood he did not want to be in a long-term relationship, that he still had feelings for his ex, the only man who could pop Julie's bubble was Slats Grodsky.

"Coming over tonight?" Julie asked.

"When are you getting off?"

"About a half-hour after you come over," was her sexy response.

Slats laughed. "How can I refuse that offer?"

————————————————————————————————

As Julie was beckoned to another table, Slats perused the bill, which was $9.47, and dropped an extra $20 for Julie's tip.

"See you in a few," Slats said, touching her arm as he walked by.

"Bring a movie," she yelled as he walked out the front door into the evening flurry.

Slats decided to take the long walk around the block before going home and check out the newly renovated apartment building on North Clark Street. The complex, built in the 1920s, was in desperate need of a facelift, and the recent makeover was phenomenal. Now that it was finished, everything else looked timeworn, but within two years, there was no doubt the entire block would be transformed. This was how it was done in Chicago, a block at a time.

The apartment complex, despite its new splendor, was not the most notable story on the street that evening.

"Dibs," the age-old practice of reserving parking spots after a blizzard, had returned to the Chicago streets. Like animals marking their territory, residents had placed wheelbarrows, lawn chairs, and long metal tables where their cars once were to preserve their parking spots till they returned.

"Dibs" was illegal by city ordinance, but legislators and law enforcement showed sympathy for the people who dug their auto out of a drift, only to lose their parking space to another driver, even though they were ignoring the law.

Slats walked past one such argument.

"Hey, you moved my lawn chairs. That's my spot. Move your car out of there right now!" yelled the dibs driver.

"Screw you; no one can have a space on the street all for themselves. You wanna spot? Go pay for one in a garage."

"How do you want your car keyed, asshole, with one line or two?"

"Try it, and I'll get your ass hauled away for vandalism."

A few people who were digging their cars out began gathering around the spot grabber and, finally, intimidated him into moving his car.

"Screw you," the space stealer shouted as he got in his car and pulled away. "Hope your cars are swallowed by a sinkhole!"

There were daily reports of tires slashed and windows broken on space stealers' cars when they moved someone's personal property from the parking spot. Since law enforcement could not prove who performed these acts of vengeance, space stealers were usually left with hundreds of dollars of repairs and no one to blame it on but themselves. They would not make the same mistake again in the future.

Slats sympathized with those digging out their cars. As a young police officer, there were many times Slats had thwarted a crook, only to watch another cop get credit for the collar.

"Maybe the police department should have a dibs program," he thought.

Slats hurried home to change for his rendezvous with Julie. He opened his mailbox and was checking the mail when his cell phone rang. It was Brainard.

"Slats, Pearson needs you back to work. You know that murder Rocky called you to the other day? We have another one at 19 West Rice Street, off North Homan. Same M.O., only this time it's a woman."

Slats happened to know the area. From North Dearborn Street, it was about seven miles due west on West Chicago Avenue, a right turn onto North Long, then a left onto the one-way West Rice.

"On my way, Charlie."

Slats glanced at his car, which was parked in the street. You could only see the front windshield. The rest was buried by snow plows and snow drifts.

"Uh, hey, Charlie, any chance you can pick me up on the way?"

Chapter 7

April 5, 2013

The second murder took place in the Fifteenth Police District in Chicago. Though he never worked in the district, Grodsky had visited the area many times. Within the Fifteenth was the Austin Career Education Center, an alternative high school where he had placed many juveniles to demonstrate there was a better life course than delinquency. Many youths dropped out, but for the few who remained, it was life altering. Slats was proud of those graduates.

The house they were responding to was around the corner from the school. Slowly flashing their badges from their unmarked car to the officers manning the roadblock, the two detectives weaved their way through the parked patrol cars on the street. The illumination from the rotating flashing beacons was more reminiscent of the light and sound exchanges from *Close Encounters of the Third Kind* than of a murder scene.

"Can I help you gentlemen?" Detective Parnell Jones questioned, stopping them at the door.

"Grodsky and Brainard. We're from the Eighth," Slats answered. "Heard about this and was told to come down here to help out."

Jones turned to his partner and asked, "Since when do we ask the Eighth for help? Don't you guys have the most robberies of all twenty-five Chicago districts so far this year?"

Grodsky, absorbing the crime scene details over the detective's shoulder, simply stated, "No, we're only eighth in robberies. But we're first in burglary and property crime."

Charlie, more insulted than his partner, had to put the officer in his place.

"Officer Grodsky here helped examine the exact same murder four days ago on North Rogers."

Jones's attitude warmed a little. "Heard about that. Sorry, man." He nodded toward the house and motioned them in. "Let me tell you what we know. The woman's name is Patricia. Perp exited the house through the front door and left it open. Matter of fact, it was jammed open, as if they wanted someone to see it. Lady across the street thought it was strange for Patricia to have the front door open during a winter storm and tried to call her but got no answer, so she called 911. Her story holds up. Her phone number is the last one on caller ID. Later, when we called in the details, we got a call from the Seventeenth, who said they were sending a detective. Your station must have picked it up as well. You got here before they did."

"Actually, the Seventeenth called our captain who then notified me to get my butt over here," Slats corrected as he walked around the body. "Is there another entrance to the house?"

"Yes, but the backdoor is locked, and there are no footprints in the snow leading to it. No forced entry from windows either. Apparently, they entered through the front door. We're checking house to house to see if anyone saw anything. So far, all we have is the corpse."

"You know," Slats paused, "if they entered the house before the snowstorm started, their footprints are covered. If there's an imprint, maybe the prints will freeze. Make sure to cordon off any grassy areas. We may get lucky when the snow melts."

"Good idea. I'm on it."

"Is she married?" Charlie asked.

"Yes, husband's been notified and is on his way. Works a late shift at an insurance company call center about forty-five miles south of the city. They have two kids. One daughter, married, lives in Milwaukee, and one son, still in college. University of Rochester, I believe. They've been notified as well."

Slats and Charlie went over the details as they saw them, and how they mirrored the first murder. Victim tied up in a chair in front of the television, channel on the same station that carries the Cubs games, throat slashed, no prints, no murder weapon, no witnesses, and a pristine Chicago Cubs hat on the victim's head.

Since none of the details of the first murder were released to the public, Slats and Charlie grasped what this meant. A serial killer was on the loose.

Slats called Commander Pearson to confirm the specifics of the murder.

"Grodsky, I'm calling the police commissioner. No doubt he'll assemble a unit tomorrow to handle the investigation. I'm going to recommend that you be part of the team."

"Not sure that's a great idea, Chief. After the dressing down I got from him after my last rehab, I'm not sure he wants me on the force at all, let alone on a specially convened team."

"Let me handle that. I know you're the best man for the job. I'll remind him of what you've done for this city. I'll guilt and shame him 'til he puts you on it."

"Are you sure you weren't raised by a Jewish mother?" Slats asked his black commander.

Slats, half Jewish and half Polish, knew all about Jewish guilt.

"The Jews don't own guilt, but they did perfect it. Get some sleep, Slats; you're going to be busy tomorrow."

"Night, Chief."

As a trio of policemen came back into the room with a forensic specialist, Slats and Brainard bid farewell and headed back to Slats's apartment.

"Shit!" Slats cried, as he realized he had stood up Julie. Hoping she was not upset, he dialed her phone.

"Hi. This is Julie. I can't come to the phone right now. Please leave a message at the beep. If this is Slats, don't leave a message and don't call back. BEEEEEP."

"Julie, it's me. I'm truly sorry. I was called away on a late night homicide, got wrapped up in it, and forgot to call."

Brainard was mimicking his partner in the background, as Slats continued talking to the machine.

"Please don't be mad. It's my job. These things happen to me, and I hate it as much as you do. Believe me. I would have rather—Brainard! Shut up!—been with you tonight rather than where I was and what I saw. I'll see you at the tavern. We'll talk. Goodnight."

"Since when does a waitress pussy whip Slats Grodsky?" asked Charlie.

"Hey, she's a good kid, and I'm trying to do the right thing. It's called growth, Brainard. Like you standing up to your father-in-law. But it's hard to do the right thing in this job when shit comes at you from all angles."

"Whatever. Hey, not to change the subject, but have you ever had the feeling someone's watching you? Like you're being tailed?"

"I've had those vibes for a long time, Charlie. How long have you felt it?"

"How long have you been working here?"

"Ever see a tail?"

Brainard's cell phone rang.

"No, just a feeling," Charlie answered before taking his call. "Hi, honey."

There was indistinguishable yelling on the other end of the phone. Brainard moved the phone away from his ear until the screeching ceased.

"No, I'm taking Slats back to his apartment, then I'll be home. No, he's not drunk. No. We were at a crime scene. Yes, yes, I will. Love you."

"Meow," Slats purred.

Chapter 8

Bermuda Love Triangle

Monday, January 19, 1998

Joey Robbins awoke to knocking sounds. It was 3:00 a.m. Damn, he thought; he must have forgotten to turn on the TV sleep timer. He always set it for ninety minutes, giving him enough time to fall asleep before the television turned off. Left alone with his own thoughts, Robbins laid in bed for hours. With the TV tuned in to a shopping channel or some other mundane show, sleep descended on him within minutes.

Fumbling for the remote control and pushing buttons, growing ever more alert, Robbins realized that the television was not on. Someone was knocking on his hotel door. He grabbed his robe from the bedside chair, tied the robe's cotton belt in a half-knot, and stumbled to the door. He gazed through the peephole, rubbed his sleepy eyes, and looked again. Though the face was unfamiliar, Robbins had a bad feeling it was the one mug he was hoping never to see—that of Bruno Discenzo.

Joey opened the door. Bruno, accompanied by two well-built men in sweatsuits, stood at the door, in a knee-length cashmere overcoat.

"May I come in?" Bruno politely requested.

"Uh, yes, yes, of course, Mr. Discenzo."

The three men entered the room. One of the sweatsuit studs closed the door and remained there, standing guard.

"Good, Mr. Robbins, so you know who I am."

"Yes, sir, of course, Mr. Discenzo. I mean, everyone knows who you are."

Bruno looked around the room and cast his eyes on the writing desk situated against the side wall.

"Please, sit with me," Discenzo said to Robbins, motioning toward the desk.

Bruno parked himself in the soft leather chair complete with armrests and castors. The man not standing guard at the door pulled over a wooden chair from the kitchen dinette and gently eased Robbins into the chair.

"Mr. Robbins," Bruno started.

"Please, call me Joey."

"Okay. Joey, please excuse me, for I insist on being direct and completely understood when I speak so there can be no miscommunication, capiche?"

"Absolutely," Joey said, squirming in his chair.

"Are you nervous about anything, Joey?" Bruno asked.

"No, sir, I mean, well, I guess it's a little unnerving to be awoken in the middle of the night and to be sitting here like we are now, and I'm not really sure why this is happening . . ."

"Oh, but, Joey, I think you do know why I'm here, don't you?"

The man behind Robbins vigorously straightened Joey's chair, to remind him honesty was going to be his best policy.

"Does this have anything to do with my going up your beach steps?"

"Yah see, Eddie?" Bruno said to the man standing behind Robbins's chair. "I told you, this guy is a very smart man."

Bruno continued, "So, Joey, why were you snooping around my property?"

"What? Snooping? No, no. I wasn't snooping. It wasn't like that, Mr. Discenzo."

"No? So, then who sent you?"

"Huh? No one sent me . . ."

"Eddie, maybe Joey's not as smart as we thought after all."

Eddie put his hands on Robbins's shoulders as Bruno continued.

"You do realize I have cameras on the grounds that caught your every move. I haven't seen anyone move that fast since I was chasing little Tommy McNish with a machete. Remember that, Eddie?"

Eddie nodded with approval.

"Mr. Discenzo, I work for the Chicago Cubs, and I'm down here at the winter meetings . . ."

"Joey, Joey, Joey. I know every fucking thing about you. Who you work for. Where you live. Your wife's name. Your kids' names. I even know your little fucking dog's name. What I don't know is," Bruno said, now raising his voice, "what the fuck you were doing at my house?"

Robbins's earlier conversation that afternoon with Tex Perryman on the veranda had convinced him to come up with a plausible, air-tight excuse. After thinking it through for a few hours, he had one ready. He had hoped he would never have to use it; now he had to put it into action.

"I was bringing you tickets to the Chicago Cubs opener. I overheard that you lived next door to the Fairmount, and knowing you're from Chicago, I thought you might enjoy the tickets. But then, when I got to your pool, I started to think that maybe I should contact you first, because I didn't want you to think I was some punk trying to break into your house, and I started getting nervous so I turned around and left. I didn't think I was going that fast, but maybe I was with all those crazy thoughts in my head. I'm sorry. I should have called you or wrote you or contacted someone who worked for you. I wanted to be hospitable to someone from Chicago, you being down here and all."

"Okay, okay, slow down. You're talking faster than you were walking. You know, Joey, I know you're not a bad guy. Like I said, I had you checked out. I believe you are telling me the truth."

Bruno waved at Eddie, who then removed his hands from Robbins's shoulders.

"So, Joey, when is this game?"

"The opener is April 3 against the Montreal Expos."

Eddie removed a small black book from the pocket of his sweatsuit.

"We'll be in Chicago that week, Mr. Discenzo."

"Excellent! Joey, how many tickets are you planning to give me?"

"Oh, you won't need tickets, Mr. Discenzo. Every year the owner reserves a few of the newly renovated private boxes for the scouts on opening day, and Mr. Gant, the club president, has continued the tradition. I'm allowed twenty guests, not including my wife and kids. The party starts a couple of hours before the game starts. We have hors d'oeuvres, a great menu, unlimited bar, and then we sit back and enjoy the game."

"Well, Joey, I don't want to be a pig and take them all, but I do need to take Eddie and Fredo; did I ever introduce you to Fredo? Fredo, say hello to Joey. Where's your manners?"

Fredo, standing guard at the door, gave an index fingered salute to Joey Robbins.

Bruno resumed.

"And, of course, I will have Didi, too."

"Didi?" Joey responded.

"Yah, that's my ragazza, my belladonna."

Didi. Bruno's girlfriend. Joey's blonde fantasy girl with the long legs and flowing body that he had climbed the beach steps for, if only for a glimpse. This situation was worse than he thought.

"Yes, of course, sir."

"That's all we'll need, Joey. Just the four of us."

"That's great. I'm so relieved. This is all I wanted to do, a friendly gesture to a fellow Chicagoan. I'm sorry I made you worry that this was something much bigger than it was."

Joey stood up, picked up his wallet from the nightstand, and retrieved a business card. He handed it to Bruno, who, without looking at it, immediately handed it to Eddie.

"Call me a day or two before the game, Mr. Discenzo. I'll give you instructions on what gate to enter from, how to get your passes from the ticket office, you know, all the particulars."

Bruno rose. "Joey, I'm sorry to have bothered you in the middle of the night, but a man in my position . . ."

Bruno stopped himself for a moment, and then continued.

" . . . can never be too careful. Now you get yourself some sleep, so you can do whatever it is you gotta do this week. I'll be in touch."

Bruno snapped his fingers. Fredo opened the hotel room door, peeked into the hallway, and gave an all-clear sign. Bruno walked out, followed by Eddie, who closed the door behind him.

Robbins collapsed into a sitting position on the bed. Slumped over, head in hands, he felt every muscle that had tightened up from fear while the thugs were in the room suddenly relax and surrender to gravity. His body shook. He had been on the emotional roller coaster ride of his life: relief that he was still alive, joy that his cover story worked, horror that the Maravelli hit man knew everything about him and his family, and disappointment that he had put himself in this position in the first place.

Now, fully collapsing back onto the bed in a supine position, Robbins, teary-eyed from the terror he had endured, took a few deep breaths, stared at the stucco ceiling above him, and wondered how he'd ever fall asleep again.

He took comfort, however, that even if he remained awake the rest of the night, it was a small price to pay, for at least the worst was over.

Or so he thought.

Chapter 9

Bermuda Love Triangle

Wednesday, January 21, 1998

Joey Robbins never slept after Bruno's impromptu visit. The anxiety that enveloped him wasn't noticeable, for there was always an uneasy energy level at the MLB Winter Meetings. Each word uttered by a club executive or agent was usually dissected by other executives, agents, or media personnel. Cell phones were ringing or dialing all day long. Once Joey and his coworkers began grading players behind closed doors, he put aside his close call with the mob. Joey became immersed in his work, coordinating the efforts of the other scouts' endeavors so they could speak with one voice by week's end.

Each day was more hectic than the day before. As the work load grew, Robbins took his performance to another level; he displayed why he was one of the best in the business. Bruno's intrusion became a distant memory.

Until, two days after the night visit, his cell phone rang. It was Thursday morning at breakfast. The phone said caller unknown.

"This is Joey Robbins. How can I help you?"

An unfamiliar male voice said, "Yo, Joey, hold for Mr. Discenzo."

Robbins felt his heart sink to his feet, and all color leave his face.

"Hey, Joey. I'm sorry to call you at the start of your busy day, but an emergency came up and I am in need of a personal favor, and I know you are the perfect man for the job."

"Do you need more tickets for the opener, Mr. Discenzo? I could see if . . ."

"No, Joey, the four tickets are fine. But I have been called back to Chicago for a couple of days."

"I'm not sure I understand."

"I've got business I've got to take care of back home and need to bring the boys with me. That's going to leave Didi alone in Bermuda, and in the two years we've been together visiting the island, I've never left her alone. I want you to keep her company until I come back. Not the whole time, of course. I understand you'll have to make a few appearances at your conference. I'm thinking, say lunch and dinner, and maybe till 10:00 p.m. or whenever she passes out."

"Mr. Discenzo, I'm flattered that you thought of me to help as a friend, but as you recall, I'm the head of scouting for the Cubs. I'm working one of our most critical weeks of the year. I can't miss these meetings."

"Do we have a bad connection?" Bruno asked, tapping the phone. "Because I thought I was crystal clear about what I need you to do for me."

"Why me? Why not leave one of your men here with her? Why not take her back with you? Why not bring someone in from Chicago to watch her? I'm going to get fired if I disappear from these meetings!"

"Let me put it to you this way because I guess I wasn't making myself perfectly clear. If you don't do this for me, you won't get fired, but you WILL disappear. Do you understand it better now, you insignificant little fuck?"

Robbins sat perfectly still. He looked around him in the restaurant. Everyone was acting as if this were a normal day, not a day when Joey Robbins's life had just been threatened? With just a few words, his whole life had changed. He thought of his wife, his children, his dog, and sighed. "How long will you be gone? Today's Thursday. Our meetings are over on Sunday."

"We'll be back sometime on Saturday. If we can get the early flight from Chicago to New York, we'll be back late afternoon."

With not only his life on the line, but that of his wife and kids as well, Joey realized he had no choice.

"I won't let you down, Mr. Discenzo. But I can't hang out with her here at the Fairmount. I mean, everyone knows me and my wife and all. What would they say if they saw me with another woman?"

"Joey, I don't want to put your marriage or family in jeopardy. I assume you remember where my home is?"

Obviously I do, Joey thought, or I wouldn't be in this goddamn predicament now.

"All you have to do is go over to my home, take her out to lunch, go back to your meetings, take her out again for dinner, and make sure she makes it back into bed before you leave. I trust you, Joey; I know you're happily married, love your kids and your job, and would never let anything hurt or disturb my little Didi."

"Of course not!"

"Then it's settled. She's expecting you by the pool around 12:30 p.m. for lunch."

"Mr. Discenzo, I'll be spotted if I walk over there at lunchtime. Everyone's out on the veranda."

Silence on the line. Joey nervously rubbed his chin.

Bruno came up with a solution. "Here's what we're gonna do. She'll pick you up at 12:30 p.m. at the roadside entrance to the Fairmount. That'll be your meeting place. No one will spot you. From there, you can go back to my place or somewhere of her choosing. You'll do the same thing for dinner. I gave her your cell phone number. Expect a call around noon. I'll make sure I lay out the ground rules for her."

Robbins heard a jet engine humming in the background.

"Joey," Bruno continued, "the plane is about to pull away from the gate. You take care of my girl, and you'll have nothing to worry about, okay?"

"Okay, Mr. Discenzo. I'll wait for her call. Bye."

Joey pressed disconnect on his cell then gazed around the hotel at all the action around him. While there was an intense excitement and glow around the participants of the meetings, extreme sadness cast a dark shadow around him. Somehow he knew this major league baseball winter meeting would be his last.

Chapter 10

April 6, 2013

As Slats entered the high-tech, state-of-the-art police headquarters on South Michigan Avenue, it reminded him of how advanced the police force had become. The building, opened in 2000, replaced the antiquated headquarters three miles uptown at 11th and State Streets. He recollected the old black dial phones at each desk. Dillinger could have robbed a bank in the time it took to dial 312-989-9989.

The new building also reminded him how dangerous the job was. Two glass-encased displays on opposite walls of the circular reception desk housed dozens of silver badges and names. They were a solemn memorial to the officers who had died in the line of duty.

Slats's favorite room was the command center, where Superintendent Dale Randle led the city-wide force. Eight 50-inch screens were mounted in the room. The screens played a combination of live broadcasts, floor plans of buildings, mapping of criminal activity, aerial photographs or videos, cruiser chases, or select webcams throughout the city. The pulse of the command center was at a much higher rhythm than the district stations, much like the pounding of the heart is much greater than the pulse in the wrist. It took a special person to work in the command center. A fast-acting multitasker with a calm demeanor while dealing with crisis was a fitting job descriptor. Though he enjoyed the command center, Slats knew his forte was on the front line in the streets. Viewing a criminal on a television screen was one thing, but facing them in person was another.

The five-story building, almost four hundred thousand square feet, housed over one thousand personnel. The floors had varying levels of security, limiting access to the staff.

Today, Slats was given a security card for entry to the fifth-floor conference room. He entered the elevator, slid his card into the slot, and pressed the fifth-floor button. As the elevator doors opened, he was greeted by two officers who checked his credentials and weapon, then directed him down the corridor to the conference room. The first person Slats met was Superintendent Randle.

"Good to see you, Grodsky. Take a chair. We'll be starting in a moment."

A beautiful, oblong mahogany conference table, large enough for thirty high-back black leather executive chairs, dominated the center of the room. A fifty-inch LED monitor adorned the side wall, with a wireless connection to a laptop at the head of the desk for PowerPoint presentations and direct feeds. Most of the task force had arrived. As far as Slats could tell, one detective from each district was here. Not a woman in the group. Parnell Jones, whom Slats had met the night before from the Fifteenth, also known as the Austin District, was here. So was Rocky Parma from the Seventeenth. Unfortunately, also present in the room were a few others Slats had worked with during his bad years, those years that were far from his finest days as an officer. Kenny Usher, a detective from the Twenty-fifth or Grand Central District, had a bad history with Grodsky; he was instrumental in getting Slats transferred from the Twenty-fifth to the Eighth within a two-week period. The Twenty-fifth, which had been Slats's first assignment as a detective, was represented by Greg Stiffle. Three years his senior, Stiffle had been his teammate in that Rodgers Park

District for over twenty-two years. Stiffle had seen the best, and the worst, of Slats Grodsky. Theirs had been more than a working relationship. Holidays were spent with each other's families; they also vacationed together. The relationship began wearing thin in the last four years of their tenure, both personally and professionally, conspicuously due to the other partner Slats had decided to work with. The partner Stiffle referred to as Al Cohol. Finally, there was Cliff Zeigler from the Seventh, who spent four tumultuous years with Grodsky in the Englewood District. In the beginning, Zeigler had been fired up to work with his idol, but elation soon turned to disappointment. Covering for Slats on countless sleep-ins and crawling out of bed to make middle-of-the-night pick-ups from bars or drunk tanks were enough to knock Slats off the pedestal on which Zeigler had placed him. Shoddy report writing and inferior police work seemed to keep more bad guys on the street than off during Slats's tenure in the Seventh. In a "last straw" moment, they came to blows one night after Slats took $50 from Zeigler in a bar bet. Following a number of beers and vodka chasers, Slats boasted he could do between three and four hundred pushups within five minutes. When Zeigler laid down his fifty-dollar bill, Slats got down and did four perfect pushups. The group around the bar chuckled. Slats's four pushups *did* fall between three and four hundred. But Zeigler wasn't laughing. He wanted his money back. When Slats refused, a fistfight ensued. They never talked civilly again.

"Listen up," Randle screamed over the chatter. "By now, you know why we have assembled this task force. Gentlemen, we have a serial killer in our midst. In front of you on the table are packets containing the following: details of the first two murders and the names of the victims. Also, the cell phone numbers and e-mail addresses of each member of the task force. Make sure you enter these into your cell phone and laptops.

This will assist you in acquiring real-time information from your colleagues on this team. Any questions so far?"

"Do we have a motive?" someone blurted out.

Randle looked at the group assembled around the table. "Not yet, but as you'll see in the report, the Cubs must be connected; I believe that's where we'll find the key."

"Are the feds planning to horn in on the kidnapping action here, Chief?" asked Rocky Parma.

"No, Rocky, the FBI is not interested in our case. They haven't got the time or the resources. These days they're chasing terrorists and leaving the murders to us. Loosely defined, kidnapping is the taking of a person against his or her will, usually to hold the person in confinement without legal authority for a ransom or in the advancement of another crime. These are not kidnappings; they are murders. The only facts we know for sure are these two murders have the same M.O., and in all probability are being done by the same person or persons. Anyone else?"

No one raised a hand.

"Good," he continued. "The information on the screen on the wall behind me is the same intel that's in your packet. So far, we have found no personal connections between the first two victims, but we will need someone in this room to continually monitor the victims to be sure they're not linked. And make no mistake, ladies, there will be more. There may be a pattern for these killings, but as of yet, it is too early to identify. All we have to go on at this point is that the perpetrator ties the victim up in front of a television set, which is tuned in to the Cubs channel, places a Cubs hat on the victim, then slits the victim's throat."

"Shit, Chief, half of Chicago wants to slit their own throat after watching a Cubs game," one of the detectives interrupted.

Laughter permeated the room.

"Silence!" Randle bellowed. You think this is funny?"

The room quickly quieted down.

"The coroner's report on both victims supports the hypothesis that they were watching the Cubs on TV. The time of death is consistent with the broadcasts times. We have no leads presently, but we've got to find out why the Cubs are involved. Who could be responsible for these crimes and why? What's their purpose? We'll write down all possible viewpoints and assign each of you to follow one of these angles. So who wants to start?"

The ideas came in a flurry, and Randle's secretary Gloria entered them into her laptop: an angry relative, psycho neighbor, a street vendor selling Cubs paraphernalia, the owner of the Cubs, a recently fired employee, a disgruntled player who was injured or released from the team and never treated fairly, a psychopath, the station owner or manager of the cable channel that broadcasts the Cubs games, or recently released prisoners who have moved back to Chicago in the last six months.

"You guys have informants on the street. Use them. We'll try to keep the specifics of the murders out of the papers as long as we can. Be tight-lipped as you go about your business. Try not to tip your hand to the individuals you are conversing with. Before you leave this room, report to me and Gloria. For those of you who gave us an idea and you want to follow that lead, we'll log it. We'd rather you pair up with someone in this room, but if you want, you can work with your partner back at district. For those of you who did not come up with suggestions, we'll assign you one. One more thing. As you all know, Mayor

McBride's campaign promise was to decrease crime to ensure safer streets and a safer Chicago. He is all over me on this, so I'm going to be breathing down your necks to solve this as quickly as possible. Now let's get moving. Let's get this guy off the streets."

The detectives in the room quickly scurried about, looking for someone to team with. Everyone avoided Slats, and he found himself alone in the corner. Slats headed toward Gloria and Superintendent Randle.

"I'll take Rance Hellsome," Slats muttered.

Randle looked at Gloria, then back to Grodsky.

"That's gonna be sensitive Grodsky; why don't you partner up with Jones and work the street vendors?"

"I would like to take Hellsome, sir; he was my idea. And I'd appreciate working with my partner back at the Eighth, if it's okay with you."

"We don't know Rance Hellsome or his organization that well. A word of advice: tread lightly. He's only owned the team for a year. But one thing we do know. The Cubs are a sacred treasure to the citizens of Chicago. I can't have you going in there with guns blazing and accusations flying. Do I make myself clear?"

Randle's stern warnings were usually reserved for a rookie cop, not a twenty-eight-year veteran, especially one of Grodsky's pedigree. Randle did not know the Grodsky of days past, the cop who was once the pride of Chicago's finest. Randle knew only of the drunk in rehab who was now back on the beat. Sensing Randle's reluctance, yet thirsting for the need to reestablish his name, Slats reassured his superior.

"I promise, sir, he won't even know I'm investigating him. I do have experience at this, Chief. If you give me the opportunity, you won't be sorry."

Randle silently studied Slats. Slats knew that what Randle saw currently was not what he saw two years ago when he first met the scruffy detective in a drunk tank. This Grodsky appeared to be rock solid. That other Grodsky was a crushed pebble.

"What's your angle?"

"Finding out who hates the Cubs, or him, or both. Something along those lines, Chief."

"Grodsky," Randle sighed, "don't make me regret this."

"You won't. Thanks, Chief. Pleasure seeing you, Gloria."

Temporarily forgetting the pain in his hip and knees, Slats briskly exited the conference room before Randle could change his mind.

"I'm finally on a blockbuster case again," he reflected privately, as he placed his call to Charlie Brainard back at the Eighth District.

"Charlie. What are you doing now?"

"Reports. Why?"

"Pick me up at headquarters downtown. We've got work to do. And bring my umbrella. It's under my desk. Yah, it's been pouring all day. I'll fill you in about my meeting along the way."

Chapter 11

April 6, 2013

"So, Slats, you ever been to the Cubbies headquarters before?" Charlie Brainard asked.

"Nope."

"Me neither. I've always wanted to, but I never thought it would be on a mission like this."

"Well, I guess we get to pretend we're in fantasy camp for detectives."

Brainard eased his standard issue Ford sedan into a "No Parking" spot too convenient to pass up. No one ticketed a Homicide vehicle, not even the meter maids and masters who reported outside the regular departmental hierarchy. It wasn't done. Not that they didn't get in trouble for it.

Entering Wrigley Field from North Clark Street by the advance ticket windows, Slats and Charlie were stopped by security. They identified themselves.

"Yes, sir," said the uniformed security guard who manned the information desk. "May I see your IDs? Formality. You understand."

The credentials were flashed.

Conscious of Slats's warning to be discreet, Charlie spoke in slightly hushed tones, careful to avoid drawing attention, "We're here from the CPD. No one is expecting us."

"Right this way, detectives," said the elderly guard, whose badge identified him as Edgar. Deferring slightly to the police with a nod of the head, Edgar led them into Wrigley Field and the official headquarters the Chicago Cubs Baseball Club.

Slats and Charlie followed Edgar through the main concourse and up the ramp to the second-level offices.

Slats pondered the irony of the challenge facing the man they were about to see. Rance Hellsome was a self-made software mogul, successful at everything he touched. Infused with an ego large enough to fill Lake Michigan, a year ago he had overwhelmed the *Chicago Tribune* with an offer the previous owners couldn't refuse—one billion dollars, the most money ever paid for a major league franchise. This was a man who aspired to leave a legacy in Chicago synonymous with the Wrigley family, owners of the Cubs for six decades. He was determined to end a championship drought of over a hundred years.

While most of the administrative offices were in trailer-like buildings on the outskirts of the stadium, the owner's office was positioned above the main concourse, looking directly out over home plate. Above the door in front of them was the brass-lettered sign that read *The Chicago Cubs Baseball Club.*

Edgar pushed through the door, and they entered a miniscule, marble-tiled reception area. He said, "Elaine, these gentlemen are here to see Mr. Hellsome on official police business."

"Oh, I'm sorry. Mr. Hellsome is in a meeting. I'll let him know you're here as soon as he's done. Please have a seat. The session should only be another five or ten minutes."

"Since the game's rained out, maybe we can go on a tour later," said Brainard, taking a seat beside Slats in the comfy leather chairs in the reception area.

"What do you want to know about this place, Charlie? I've been to a few hundred games at Wrigley," Slats declared.

"Okay, we'll play twenty questions and see if you get the answers right."

"Do you know the answers to the questions you're about to ask me, Charlie?"

"No, but I trust you, Slats."

"Go ahead. What's the first question?"

Brainard pondered. "Why do they call Wrigley Field the 'Friendly Confines'?"

Slats shook his head. "Sometimes, man, it's hard for me to remember that you didn't grow up in Chicago, considering that you've worked here for about ten years and have had season tickets to Bears games and watch the Sox play and all. You'd think some of this would have sunk in through osmosis by now. Anyway, former Cubs player and Hall of Famer Ernie Banks used to call Wrigley Field the 'Friendly Confines' because of the friendly fan support in a ballpark confined and surrounded by row houses. He also coined the well-used phrase, 'Let's play two!' Something harder, Charlie."

"Ernie Banks. Banks, like the first dead guy. Next question. What's White Flag Day? I hear people say it, but I'm embarrassed to ask what it means."

"That's white flag time at Wrigley, doofus! In 1937, two years before *Gone with the Wind* won an Oscar for best picture, P.K. Wrigley, the son of William Wrigley, rebuilt the bleachers and scoreboard with a masthead on the top. Ever since, when the Cubs win, they fly a "win flag," which is white with a blue W, and when they lose, they fly a "loss flag," which is blue with a white L. In the old days, the colors of the flags were different. Now on double-headers two flags are flown . . ."

"Okay, got it," cried Brainard. "Here's your next one: when was Wrigley Field built?"

"That's easy," said a voice behind Brainard. "The park was built in 1914 for a whopping cost of $250,000 by a gentleman named Charles Weeghman, and it was called Weeghman Park. From 1920 to 1926, it was called Cubs Park, and since 1927, it's been called Wrigley Field."

As Brainard turned to see who was talking, Slats rose and thrust out a hand to the handsome, suave, and impeccably well-dressed man.

"Hello, Mr. Hellsome, it's a pleasure to meet you." Hellsome shook first Slats's hand, then Brainard's.

"Good afternoon, officers. Elaine said you wanted to speak to me?"

"Perhaps we could discuss this in your office?" Slats said.

The three men walked into the owner's suite. As Hellsome rounded his desk, Slats and Brainard each took a seat in front of a huge cherry desk. Pictures of past owners, presidents, Hall-of-Famers, team pictures, bats, gloves, balls, and trophies bejeweled the walls and glass cabinets. It looked more like the Hard Rock Café than the corporate office of the owner of the Chicago Cubs.

"I'm a fan, what can I say?" exclaimed Hellsome, as he reclined in his chair, noticing how the two detectives were staring at the memorabilia.

"So when are you going to change the name to Hellsome Field?" Brainard inquired.

"That will never happen, son, not on my watch. I may own Wrigley Field, but it belongs to the people of Chicago. It's as much a part of the folklore of this city as the Water Tower or Sears Tower.

"You mean the Willis Tower?"

"Okay, that was a poor example. Look, I don't want to change Wrigley Field's name for money or naming rights, or to satisfy my ego. But, I'm sure you didn't come here to talk about this dribble, did you?"

"No, sir. We are hoping you can give us some information that may be useful to our latest investigation," Slats said.

"Investigation?"

"There's been a homicide recently, and we have few leads. We're checking into anything found at the scene that might be relevant. One such item was a Cubs hat. We don't know if it is significant or incidental. Still, we'd like get a look at your personnel files and cross-check to see if there is any connection between your employees, players, or coaching staff and the victim. It's the way we do things—you know, narrow down the choices through the process of elimination."

"So you're saying that's all you have to go on? A hat?" Hellsome, his face reddening, leaned toward the two detectives. "Can I ask you both a question?"

"By all means, Mr. Hellsome," said Charlie.

"Do you think I am an imbecile? The police are going to send two dicks to the owner of the Cubs seeking answers because a person died with a Cubs hat on his head?"

"I never said they were wearing the hat," corrected Slats.

"What's going on here? If you have something to say, by all means, out with it," demanded Hellsome.

Slats tried to calm Hellsome down.

"Mr. Hellsome, it's routine. We only need to see the personnel files."

"Not until you tell me the whole truth."

"We can get a court order if we have to," bluffed Grodsky.

Hellsome reached for the phone on the desk and pressed the intercom button.

"Elaine, please contact our lead counsel and have him . . ."

"Wait a minute, Mr. Hellsome, there's no need for that," Slats maintained.

"Elaine, hold that call for a second."

Charlie looked at Slats and shrugged. Slats nodded.

"Mr. Hellsome, you're right. There is more to the story than what we've told you."

"Mr. Hellsome?" squeaked Elaine on the intercom.

"Never mind, Elaine." Hellsome disconnected the call and glared at the cops. "Go on."

"There have been two homicides, not one, and both victims were wearing a Cubs hat when we found them. It appears that it's the same murderer. What we don't know is why he's chosen the Cubs as a symbol. It could be metaphoric, vengeance, or coincidence. We don't have enough to go on yet. Maybe it's a hate crime."

Hellsome's eyes narrowed.

"Hate crime? Hate who? The Cubs? A player? Me?"

"We don't know. That's why it is important to see those files. It may lead us nowhere, or we may get lucky and . . ."

Slats paused in the middle of his explanation. Suddenly, something Charlie said earlier in the reception area rang a bell. Slats turned to his partner, "Charlie, that was brilliant."

"What'd I do?" asked Brainard.

"When we were talking about Ernie Banks, the Hall of Famer, you said Banks, same name as the first victim."

"You think there's a link between the names of . . ."

"That's exactly what I'm thinking, Charlie."

Grodsky pivoted back toward the Cubs owner.

"Mr. Hellsome, did a person with the last name of Moriarty ever play for the Cubs?"

Chapter 12

Bermuda Love Triangle

Wednesday, January 21, 1998

Precisely at noon, Joey Robbins answered his anticipated call.

"Hello?"

"Is this Joey?"

"Yes, it is. Is this Didi?"

Silence.

"Hello, Didi? Are you there?"

"I guess Bruno told you I'd be calling," she finally answered in a low voice that seemed sad and depressed. "I was told to meet you today, but I'm sure you'd rather be playing baseball than to be with me."

"He did tell me you'd be calling, Didi. Only I don't play baseball; I work in the business. I'm a scout for the Chicago Cubs. I'm finishing up a meeting now. I should be able to meet you at the street entrance to the hotel drive by 12:30 p.m."

"I'll be driving a black 1998 Cadillac Seville. I'm blonde, I'm . . ."

"I know what you look like. I saw you on the beach a few days ago. But you don't know me. I'll be the forty-four-year-old with a New York Mets hat on."

"I thought you said you worked for Chicago. Why are you going to wear a New York Jets hat?"

"Uh, that's a Mets hat, and I thought I'd go undercover. This sneaking around stuff is all a little new to me."

"Sneaking around stuff. Cute. Hardly what I'd call it, but okay. I'll be there soon."

Funny, a few days ago Robbins would have given his left nut to be with this girl. Now, he wished he was home with his family, hanging out, watching an old black and white Dick Powell movie on AMC—even though he hated black and white.

"Listen, guys," Robbins said to his fellow scouts. "Something's come up, and I have to check into it. It could be a blockbuster, but I don't want to make a big deal about it yet. If Velendez comes looking for me, tell him that, okay?"

"Who is it, Joey?" asked Sam Leary, one of the scouts in the meeting. "After all this work we're compiling, you're not stashing someone behind our back to make yourself look good, are you? A good stick? A pitcher? What?"

"I promised I wouldn't talk, and I won't 'til the time is right. I need you to cover for me. Please!"

Robbins checked his watch. It was 12:35 p.m.

"Shit!"

First day on the job, and he was already keeping the girlfriend of Chicago's most famous mobster waiting.

Joey closed his laptop, placed it into its protective carrying case, and slid out of the meeting room. Looking left, then right, he exited the building from the side entrance, avoiding the crowded hallways and lobbies of the Fairmount Southampton. The last thing he wanted was to be seen or stopped for conversation.

Rounding the last turn in the driveway, Joey spotted the Seville along the soft shoulder of the street. He slowed his gait and approached the car, pointing to his Mets hat. Didi, cell phone to ear, hit the door unlock button. She closed her phone.

"I thought you were standing me up. I was calling Bruno to tell him."

"God, no!" Robbins cried. The sweat from his quick pace had made his face glisten, as well as darken spots on his Ralph Lauren polo shirt.

"Relax," Didi said with a smile. "I was leaving him a message that I hoped his flight was okay."

Joey slid into the passenger seat and closed the door in the same motion. Looking around the well-appointed car, the first thing he noticed was the darkened glass to prevent outsiders from looking in. The second thing he noticed was Didi. From his first few days on the island, he had already adjusted to the driver being in the right side of the vehicle and driving in the left lane—the opposite of how it was done in the States. Bermuda was an old British Colony, and driving on the left side of the road was a British custom. It was said that Napoleon changed most of the world to right-handed passage. Supposedly, it changed because Napoleon was left-handed, so his armies had to march on his right so he could keep his sword arm between him and any opponent.

"Where are we headed for lunch?" Joey asked.

"I thought we'd go to the Coral Reef Café at the Pompano Beach Club. It's close by and one of my favorites for lunch."

"I don't think so," Robbins said. "The winter meetings filled the Fairmount Southampton, and the overflow went to the Pompano Beach Club. No, we need to go far, far away."

"This island ain't that frickin' big to go far, far away. What about the North Rock Brewing Company?"

"Too close to the hotel. It's a paparazzi watering hole."

"How about the Primavera Ristorante?" said Robbins, checking the map. "This place looks far enough away."

"Oh sure, Bruno's favorite Italian restaurant on Bermuda. Good choice."

"Actually, it's perfect. They know you and him, but I won't know anyone. If anyone asks, I'm your brother—no, I'm too old—tell them I'm a friend of Bruno's, which I guess I am."

"Oh, you ain't no friend. You're like me. You're exactly like me. You're like all Bruno's friends," she said, letting go of the steering wheel long enough to make the quotation mark sign as she said the word "friends."

She didn't have to explain further; Joey knew exactly what she meant. It was clear Bruno forced his friendship on people. What wasn't clear was what happened to the friends Bruno tired of.

The restaurant was five miles away. Traffic stalled at many of the intersections along the way, but the thirty-five-minute trip seemed to last even longer. The two did not talk. Robbins looked out the windows, giving the impression he was catching the sights on both sides of the vehicle, but when he looked to his right at the driver side, pretending to look at the scenery, he was only looking at Didi.

"My God, she's gorgeous," he thought. She was shaped like a model: five feet nine, rail thin, 120 pounds, clad in a loose-fitting blouse that exposed her superb cleavage. She wore an expensive jeans skirt, but if it was priced by the yard, she was severely ripped off. The short skirt rode up her thighs, and her legs seemed even longer than when he first spotted her on the beach, no doubt due to the four-inch heels she was wearing. She wore no jewelry, other than the three-carat rock of a diamond on the fourth finger of her right hand, oversized sunglasses, and red nail polish with little British flags painted on them. Her face was indeed as beautiful as he had hoped. Her skin, golden from the sun, perfectly complemented her long, flowing blonde hair. And that fragrance. Robbins didn't know names or smells of perfume, but whatever she was wearing was absolutely intoxicating! He caught himself wanting her even more than when he saw her on the beach. She only had one flaw: Bruno.

The valet recognized the car immediately as they pulled into the restaurant parking lot from Pitts Bay Road.

"When may we expect Mr. Discenzo?" the valet asked politely, opening the door for Didi.

"Keep an eye out for him; you never know," Didi said with a smile.

She leaned toward Robbins and whispered, "Sneaking around stuff."

He chuckled.

Before entering the old establishment, Robbins did a 360 to take in the beauty of Hamilton Harbour, awash in sailboats, and the pink-colored Fairmount Hamilton Princess Hotel.

"Pink looks great in Bermuda; not so nice in Chicago," said Joey before realizing Didi had already entered the restaurant.

The eatery was old-school Italian. Joey joined Didi at the hostess kiosk, and they were led to a small table in the corner, near the kitchen and away from the windows.

"Your usual table, Miss Lecate," said the young lady. "Would you like the wine menu?"

"No, house red will be fine."

"And for the gentleman?"

"I'll have the same, thank you," said Robbins.

A server appeared with water, another with bread and butter, and another with a plate that was swiftly filled with Primavera's special dipping oil for the bread.

"Bruno's a great tipper," Didi said, explaining the first-class treatment by the restaurant staff.

"Why are you stuck in this table by the kitchen? You can't see anything from here," whispered Robbins.

"Lots of reasons, I guess. Bruno loves to go into the kitchen. It's a hobby of his. He thinks it's romantic back here, because when it's crowded, we can still hear each other talk. And . . ."

Didi's next statement came from a colder, darker place.

"He doesn't sit by windows. Something about sight lines and rifles. When he's back here, he can see who's approaching. Sometimes we leave through the back door in the kitchen instead of the front door. He says it's good to not have the same routine."

Robbins took comfort in knowing that Bruno had a weak spot for fear as well, but it was misplaced comfort. Bruno was simply following his training. The man was afraid of nothing.

It was dark in the back of the restaurant, far away from the windows, and yet Didi still wore her sunglasses.

For the next few minutes, there was an awkward silence. Didi didn't look at the menu; she already knew what she was ordering. Robbins ducked his head and pretended to study the menu. He was uncomfortable and unable to relax.

"What's good here?" Joey asked Didi.

"What do you eat—creamy dishes, salads, seafood, pasta?"

"Cheesy pasta, I guess."

"Get the Risotto al Taleggio. It's the best."

Joey looked up and saw the waiter waiting. "The Risotto it is then," he said.

"Do you want a side salad, sir?" the waiter asked.

"No, thanks," Joey answered.

"Miss Lecate, the usual, I presume?"

"Yes, Franklin, that'll be great."

The waiter gathered the menus from the table, and another minute of stillness ensued.

"The usual?" Robbins asked.

"The mixed field greens with a balsamic vinaigrette. Bruno doesn't want me to gain any weight. He says I'm perfect just the way I am."

On this subject, Bruno and Joey could see eye to eye.

"How did you guys meet?" Joey continued.

"In an Italian restaurant in Chicago."

"How long have you been together?"

"About two years," she said unemotionally.

"What's with all the one-sentence answers?"

"Am I doing that?" she retorted.

Didi, who had been answering all of Joey's questions without actually looking at him, turned to him, placed her index finger vertical to her lips and then surreptitiously pointed to a few places around the room and under the table. Joey was not slow on the uptake. This table was bugged, and cameras were in the corners of the restaurant walls. Joey glanced around and got up from the table, pretending to study a few pictures on the wall. When he returned to the table, he remarked, "Yes, the artwork here is good." He thought of the lack of conversation in the car; it was probably bugged as well.

Into this uneasy silence came their food and wine. As they began eating, once again in silence, Joey's mind drifted back to the winter baseball meetings. What am I going to tell them? They think I'm working on a hot prospect, not hot pasta!

"I've got to make a call, Didi," said Joey. "How's the reception here?"

"Look around. People are on their cell phones," she said dryly.

Without excusing himself, Robbins dialed William Condor, an agent he had worked with numerous times. Most baseball executives hated dealing with Condor, due to ridiculous demands for money and long-term contracts for his stable of aging and frequently injured players. He was known in baseball circles as the "Vulture," a nickname he was quite proud of.

Robbins's call went to voice mail.

"Billy, Joey Robbins here. We need to talk. Call me back when you get this message."

Robbins disconnected and saw Didi watching him.

"Baseball business. Had to call an agent about a player."

"Whatever," Didi shrugged.

As lunch was being cleared, Joey checked his watch. It was 2:30 p.m. He'd been away from his scouts for two hours. Looking at his cell phone, he saw multiple missed calls, calls he had to return, but the conversations would take hours. Hours that Bruno insisted were to be spent with Didi.

Robbins motioned to the waiter.

"Check, please."

"It's been taken care of, sir," was the waiter's response.

He glanced at Didi, saw her lift a hand languidly as if to say "what did you expect," and wished he could see behind those dark glasses.

"It's what he does," she explained.

Following Didi out of the restaurant, Robbins realized he was in a different world, where someone paid for all your meals but also listened in on all your conversations.

On the steps of the restaurant, Didi paused, "Joey, can we walk outside for a few minutes? I love feeling the breeze off the water and looking at all the sailboats, don't you?"

Sensing that she was looking for a place to talk to him privately, without bugs and cameras, Joey agreed.

"Yah, that's fine. I want to check out the boats in the marina."

The valet approached and offered to get the car.

"Not yet, thanks. We're going to look at the marina. I'll be right back."

Joey and Didi walked toward the quay.

"Where's the beach?" Joey asked.

"Mostly on the southern side of the island. Pretty much all marinas and boardwalks here."

Confident enough that she was out of range, she began to speak. Within minutes, she opened up like a can of beans.

"Joey. You know," she hesitated, "I haven't been allowed to speak to anyone or be with someone else without Bruno around. He must really like you."

"If this is liking me, I'd hate to think of what being on his bad side means."

"Why, is it so bad to be with me?"

"Didi, the work I am doing this week for the Cubs is critically important. I need to be with my staff. If I weren't working, and if I weren't married, I could think of no one else on earth I'd rather be with than you. I mean that."

"I understand the work part, but I'm not buying the marriage part."

"Why? You don't know any happily married couples who love each other?" Joey probed.

"No, I don't actually. Look, if I told you I wanted you and came to your room at the hotel, are you saying you wouldn't have me? I've seen how you've been looking at me. Girls know these things, even if they pretend not to be paying attention."

"Jesus," he thought. "She's seducing ME!"

"Well, I didn't exactly say that I don't find you excitingly desirable," he uttered to Didi. "But you are who you are, this gorgeous goddess of a woman tied to a hit man, a man who has threatened me and my family. And I am who I am, a middle-aged married man with two kids and a job that needs me right this minute. Right now, as a matter of fact," he said, looking again at his watch. "Besides, why me, of all people?"

She removed her sunglasses and looked directly into his eyes.

"Do I really need a reason?"

Her words were lost as he examined her face. Now he understood why she wore dark sunglasses in a car with tinted windows and in a dim corner of the restaurant. The sclera, the white part of her right eye, was completely red, as if a blood vessel had burst. The swollen eyelid, bruised eye socket with fluid build-up under the eye, red sclera; Joey knew what this meant.

"I'm Bruno's trophy girl. I can't escape that. I'm also his sex slave and punching bag. He set my family up in cushy jobs making lots of money for doing almost nothing. They love him! I have to pretend I love him in front of my family. What they don't know is if I ever try to talk to anyone about him or try to leave him, he'll see to it that my family will die, one by one, in front of my eyes, right before he kills me."

"He told you that?"

Didi nodded.

"Didi, I'm sorry. Having had my own little chat with Bruno, I understand your fear. But why are you telling me this?"

"Because I don't believe I'm going to live very long, considering my associations, and one time before I die, I want someone to make love to me and make me tingle with excitement, instead of feeling like a cheap whore that's being raped. I think you're a decent guy, and I see how you look at me, and I know you want me, too . . ."

"Didi, I can't do this!" Joey pleaded.

"Yah, actually you can. I'm yours for the taking. We just have to find a place. It's not like I'm going to talk about it."

"I'm sorry. It's absolutely out of the question. There is no negotiation on this. I want to, but it'll never happen."

"You're right—and wrong. There's no negotiation, but it will happen."

"Huh?"

"You can't refuse me, Joey," she paused, "or I'll tell Bruno you put your hands all over me and tried to fuck me."

Robbins stared at her in shock. She was blackmailing him? He wanted to be angry with her, but how could he? She was a victim, just like he was. He suspected once she had been a nice, innocent woman who probably worked an ordinary job. She would have been flattered at Bruno's attentions, at first, and then when she saw the trap closing, it would already be too late. The Didi of long ago would never have considered blackmail and getting her way by force. That was Bruno's method. Bruno had made her into a desperate, sad woman.

"Didi, please . . ."

She turned away and headed back for the car.

"Come on, Joey, we're going to look for some hidden property on this island. That should be easy for a scout to do, shouldn't it?"

"Please, Didi," Robbins begged as he pursued her from behind, but she waved him off, refusing to answer. It was sinking in that he had no option.

"I'll tell you what," he said, resigned to his fate. "Take me back to the hotel. Let me work with my team for a few hours. I promise I'll look on a map and find a quiet spot for us to be together."

The valet, seeing Didi and Joey heading back from the marina, had the Seville ready and waiting. Sliding in, they began the silent drive back, in much lighter traffic. They arrived back at the hotel entrance at 3:45 p.m.

"Meet me here in three hours," Didi said.

Robbins was emotionally exhausted and at a loss for words.

"Okay," was all he could muster.

Joey headed up the long drive to the hotel and was met in the lobby by two of his subordinates.

"Velendez is looking for you, and he's pissed!"

"Where is he?" Joey asked.

They pointed to the bar. Joey sheepishly looked into the bar, saw Velendez, and decided that attack was the best policy.

"Santiago, why haven't you been calling me back? Goddamn cell service here. I've been trying to reach you all afternoon. I've been in touch with the Vulture, and we may have our utility first baseman, pinch hitter for next year. But I need to make sure you're okay with me pursuing this."

Velendez checked his phone, but seeing no messages, swore at the cellular service as well, only in Spanish.

"What have you got?" he asked Robbins.

"We all know that Sammy Reeves is a year or two away from being our starter at first base. We need a right-handed power hitter who can fill the gap 'til Reeves is ready. What do you think of Clay Vaughn?"

"Vaughn?" laughed Velendez. "He's one of Condor's guys. You pissed away the afternoon chasing Vaughn? Too expensive. He played well last year when he was healthy; Condor's gonna want the moon. Besides, Vaughn only played half the year due to his, what, fifth or sixth knee surgery? The only cartilage that guy has left is in his nose!"

"That's the point, Santiago. I'm sure I can get Condor to the table to talk to Schwartz, within reason. If he's signable, we could have him split the time with Billy Brell, who proved he's all glove and no hit last year. If we face a righty, we can always take Josh Green from behind the plate and stick him at first, and play Nick Romaro behind the plate."

"Seriously? This is what you've been doing all afternoon?" Velendez responded.

"I've thought of almost nothing else," said Robbins. "I want your blessing to explore the possibility."

Velendez, on his third Absolute on the rocks, swirled the ice in his glass a few times, scrutinized Robbins's face, then looked back into the glass. Was the vodka making this conversation make sense, or was it the other way around?

"Okay, see if you can get him to the table. But only a one-year deal with incentives. Maybe this could fill some holes for us and give us the flexibility we're looking for. When he played, Vaughn played well. If we could squeeze that out of him again, who knows? But if the money's out of line, I need you back in that room tomorrow. Do I make myself clear?"

Try as he might, Joey couldn't remember the last time he was threatened and/or blackmailed three times in the same day.

"I promise you; I can make this happen."

Joey's attack had worked. By putting Velendez on the defensive, he had covered for his disappearance with Didi for the day and bought himself some time for tomorrow, possibly the entire day. All he needed to do now was to sway William Condor.

Robbins entered the Churchill Room where a handful of scouts were drinking coffee and telling road stories. As they greeted Robbins with "where the hell have you been" expressions, Joey filled them in on his discussion with Velendez.

Robbins pounded his fist on the table.

"I'm on this and will make it happen. I want you guys to concentrate on these things while I'm away tomorrow: young players for our farm system with an emphasis on pitching, veterans looking to stage a comeback who will be willing to accept a minor league contract and Triple-A assignment, and back-end bullpen help for the parent club. Once I've finished this deal, I'll be back to help with the rest. Hopefully, I can wrap it up tomorrow. Tell the rest of the guys when they get back from their breaks. Got it?"

Responding to Joey's exhilarating passion, the scouts nodded to each other in approval, opened their laptops, and began scouring the names on their lists.

Joey had just bought himself time to figure out how he was going to handle Didi.

As Joey rode the elevator to his floor, his cell phone vibrated. It was a voice message from Loren Conroe, Joey's oldest and dearest friend. They shared a bond that dated back to elementary school in Omaha, Nebraska.

It was a simple message: "It's Loren. Call me."

Joey left Nebraska bent on seeing the world; the job with the Cubs had allowed him to do that. Loren, on the other hand, never left his home state. He attended the University of Nebraska in Lincoln for undergrad as well as dental school. Upon graduation, he returned to Omaha to start his oral surgery practice.

Though separated for twenty-six years, their relationship was still intact. They called occasionally to catch up and reunited whenever Joey's travels brought him back to Omaha, mostly when he was scouting the Omaha Royals, the Kansas City Royals Triple-A team. Joey and Loren were football and baseball teammates in high school, and in those days, sports and girls, in that order, were what high school was all about. The minor league team began play in 1969 when Loren and Joey were high school sophomores. The Royals were a perfect venue to escape the pressures of high school, the war in Vietnam abroad, and the racial unrest affecting the country at home. Joey Robbins fell in love with the team and decided to enter the world of sports right then and there at Johnny Rosenblatt Stadium where the Omaha Royals played. That the team finished first in their division and went on to become league champs in the playoffs in their first two years in existence only fueled the fire and passion for Joey to follow his future into the baseball world. The two buddies passed their baseball love down to their sons.

Joey exited the elevator and called Loren. As Joey entered his suite, Loren answered.

"Hey, Loren, it's Joey."

"Hi! How's Bermuda? How's the weather? You having a great time?"

"A little hectic, I'm afraid. This year's meeting hasn't been my favorite."

Though they didn't talk often, when they did, they tended to have hour-long conversations. Knowing he had to meet Didi soon, Joey told Loren he couldn't talk long.

"I'm about to go into a meeting, Loren. Anything important?"

"Is everything all set up for Billy?" Loren asked.

"Yah, it's done. All he has to do is go through the tryout Tuesday, and he'll get assigned to the rookie league. Have him see me afterward, and I'll take care of the details. After that, Loren, the rest will be up to him. "

Unlike most major league clubs, the Cubs frequently held open tryouts for those with professional aspirations. Tuesday's tryout was in New Castle, Delaware, on the Wilmington College campus, five miles outside of Wilmington.

Joey knew of Billy Conroe's talent. He was a great high school player. But many great high school players washed out in college. Fewer than 0.001 percent of kids who played baseball in school made it to the majors. Even if you were lucky enough to make a minor league club, only about 10 percent ever made it to the majors.

"Thanks, Joey. You've gone above and beyond."

Joey brushed off his friend's gratitude. "Hey, I've known Billy since he was in diapers. I'd like to see the kid make good, too. I'll keep you posted."

As Joey hung up, he thought about his last chat with Loren at Thanksgiving. It was an awkward conversation. "Well, actually, I'm calling for a favor," Loren said. "It's about Billy. Since graduation last June, Billy's been playing ball on amateur teams trying to keep sharp, waiting for a tryout for a big league club. But no one's interested in him. Joey, you know how good he is. He batted almost .500 in high school against top-flight completion, for Christ's sake. But he's small, only five eight and barely 140 pounds wet; he's not getting a chance. Other guys with half his talent are getting a shot simply because they're bigger. He'll grow, Joey. I did but not until after high school. He's lost, Joey; he needs a foot in the door. He's not working. Baseball is all he thinks about. If he gets into the system and can't make the grade, he'll be able to move on. I know my boy; if he never gets a shot, it'll kill him. Joey, is there any way you could get him on a team in the Cubs organization? It doesn't have to be with the Cubs. Maybe you could talk to other scouts about him. I've never asked you for help until now. But who else can I turn to if not you?"

Though he knew spending club resources on an unproven, unseen, unwanted ballplayer was crossing the line, Joey could not turn his back on his friend. Thinking back to that conversation, it was the only time in his career as a scout that he agreed to do something he was ashamed of.

Now, on Bermuda, months later, Joey found himself in an uncomfortable situation again, only this time much worse. The comparison of pulling a few strings for Loren Conroe's kid versus betraying his family and Bruno with Didi was like comparing the illumination of a light bulb to that of the sun.

Joey looked at his watch. It was 6:00 p.m. He had forty-five minutes to study a map of Bermuda to find a restaurant and remote spot where he and Didi could get it on.

And then, maybe he could move on.

Joey thought of his flight to New York on Sunday. It couldn't come fast enough.

Chapter 13

April 11, 2013

The task force was pouring over new information gathered in yesterday's homicide as well as data compiled from their inquiries since the first meeting at Chicago HQ five days ago. Mayor Ramsay McBride, anxious to assess progress on the case, also sat in on the meeting.

Superintendent Randle launched the meeting with the latest development in the case.

"Quiet down. Mayor McBride, we are honored with your presence here today. We know the pressure your office is under, and we are doing everything we can to catch this killer and help make this city a safer place to live. Gentlemen, our latest victim was one Albert Bonds at 323 North Post Place, right here in our own goddamn Central District. We have the same method of operation, only it occurred in an apartment building instead of a single dwelling home. Escaping unseen must have been difficult. As was the case in the previous two deaths, Mr. Bonds was tied to a chair and faced a television tuned to the Cubs channel. He had a single slash wound across the jugular vein causing him to bleed out. He was wearing a Cubs cap. Residents in the complex have been interviewed. Incredibly, no one saw or heard anyone or anything unusual."

The detectives began firing off questions.

"Who found him?"

"Mr. Bonds worked part-time in a dry cleaning store," Randle said. "When he didn't show up for his afternoon shift, the owner called him. When there was no response, he contacted the building super, who had a master key. As per regulations, the super called 911, and he and the responding patrolman entered the apartment, where they found Mr. Bonds."

"Have all three Cubs caps used in the murders been the same style cap?"

"No."

"Any prints on the cap?"

"Another negative. No prints anywhere. We do, however, have some new dope. After the first two murders, Charlie Brainard suggested that the first victim, Ted Banks, had the same last name as a past Cubs player. It was confirmed that the second victim, Mrs. Moriarty also shared a last name with an ex-Cub. The latest murder seems to emphasize that this premise was indeed correct; Mr. Bonds has the last name as Bobby Bonds, also an ex-Cub."

Mayor McBride stood up. "I'm sorry, Dale, I have to leave. I like what I'm hearing in this room, but let me be clear. You better find whoever is responsible for these murders, or heads are gonna roll . . . and one of them won't be mine!"

The detectives exchanged glances. Not a word was spoken as the mayor and his lieutenants filed out of the room.

Randle continued, "We've been warned. Men, we're certain there are other patterns that we haven't discovered. We now have the full cooperation of the Cubs organization based on the Bonds murder. The club's historians and statisticians are working on this with us. Employees are talking with the police, and background checks are underway. Grodsky, you had something to add?"

"Thanks, Chief. While there's no forensic evidence of value, the murderer is leaving us clues. Finding a pattern in the last name of the murdered victims is another one to add to the Cubs cap, the television station being watched, and throats slashed in the same manner. We must dig harder to decipher other clues, ASAP. I think we're looking at the worst mass murderer in Chicago since Richard Speck, and whoever it is could become the biggest of all-time if we don't . . ."

"Drink up!" interjected Greg Stiffle, Grodsky's old partner from the 24th.

"Stiffle!" yelled Randle. "And all of you! We're a team, working for Chicago. I won't tolerate any shit on this task force, or you'll find yourself on the outside looking in! We owe it to Mr. Banks, Mrs. Moriarty, and Mr. Bonds. That's my first and last warning. So far, Grodsky and Brainard have come up with the connection to the ex-Cubs players' names. Anyone have something constructive to add?"

The mumbling in the room turned swiftly to silence with continual stares from Randle.

"Get on the street and find some damn evidence. And not a word about this to anyone, do you understand? The last thing we need is a press leak. We're adjourned."

As Slats walked past the chief, he offered, "Thanks, Chief."

"Don't thank me, Grodsky. It's your own damn fault these cops think you're still unreliable. And since we're being totally honest, Pearson talked me into putting you on the task force. But if you keep doing good detective work and stay sober, you'll win back their respect—and mine."

Slats nodded in acknowledgment, walked down the hall, and called his partner. In the elevator, he quickly recapped the meeting for Brainard.

"What do we do now, Slats?"

"Charlie, I'm getting a call on my other line. How 'bout I call you back?"

Slats pressed the answer call key on his phone.

"Slats. Tex Perryman here. We need to talk."

Tex Perryman, the reporter who helped Slats crack the Bermuda Love Triangle case in '98 and stave off a gang war, always had Slats's attention. He had earned it. Slats decided to kill two birds with one stone.

"How about the Old Town Tavern in thirty minutes?"

"Meet you there."

Slats arrived at the tavern ahead of his appointment with Perryman. It was not quite the 11:00 a.m. opening time. Slats knocked on the door.

"We'll be open in five minutes." It was Julie's voice behind the door.

"This is the police. Open up."

"Come back when you're more responsible."

"Don't make me tear this door down."

Slats pounded harder; he heard arguing in the restaurant. When the door swung open, Slats was greeted by Ricky Gage, the owner of the tavern, not Julie.

"She's pissed," said Gage, stating the obvious.

"You'd make a fine detective, Ricky."

Slats walked to the bar, where Julie was busying herself with stacking beer glasses, wiping down a perfectly clean bar countertop, and priming the tap for the draft beer.

"Come on, Julie, I was called away for a homicide. When I'm called, I have to go, you know that."

Julie continued wiping the counter, as if no one was talking to her.

"Look, let me make it up to you. We can go out on a real date to a real restaurant. Afterwards, we can go back to your place and I'll do what I do best: I'll vacuum, do the dishes, dust the apartment, and when the weather changes, I'll even do the windows."

The corner of Julie's lip began to rise, as she found herself surrendering to his charm.

"Maybe when you're done doing that stuff, you can do me," Julie tantalized.

"It's been a long time since I've done this with someone, Julie. And I'm screwing things up with us at the same time I'm on one of the biggest cases of my career. I know I want to be with you and no one else. You're good for me. I know that. And I want to do what's right for you as well. But I can't choose when I'm needed. It's the job. If you don't want any part of that, I'll understand. The job ruined my last relationship. I promised myself I wouldn't put anyone in that position again unless they can handle it."

Julie walked around from behind the bar and strolled up to Slats.

"Oh, shut up already," she said, wrapping her body around his. She gave him a long, warm loving hug.

Someone cleared his throat. Slats turned around, his arm still around Julie's waist. There was Tex Perryman, the reporter. "Slats, did you have an appointment here today, or did you come here especially to make up with me?" asked Julie, eyeing Perryman.

"Well, uh, I came early to have a private moment with you, but I'm not off-duty, Jules. I'm still on the job."

Julie pushed away from Slats and started toward the bar. Slats signaled "I'll be with you in a moment" to Tex. He grabbed Julie by the arm and spun her around into his arms.

"Why don't you call in sick tonight?" he whispered.

"I can't," she replied.

"Why not?"

"Cuz I'm already at work, you big lug." Finally, she smiled at him, and he breathed easier. She playfully smacked him on the chest. "Call me later. And this time, don't forget!"

Julie grabbed a towel and returned to the bar to begin her shift.

Slats motioned for Tex to follow him. "Tex, you're way too prompt."

"Let's go, Slats. I've got some serious questions to ask, deadlines to make, and I need answers."

The two men headed for a corner booth for privacy. The lunch crowd would soon trickle in.

"How long did you think you were going to keep this quiet?" Perryman began.

"Keep what quiet?"

"Three homicides, for Christ's sake."

"Oh. Those. For as long as possible, I imagine."

"Cut the crap, Grodsky, you owe me."

"Come on. I've paid you back ten times over by now. We're in over our heads, Tex, and we need full cooperation of the newspapers and airways."

"How 'bout this. I'll tell you what I've heard, and all you gotta do is confirm it."

Slats was more than slightly curious about where the reporter got his information. He nodded in agreement to the proposal.

Perryman took out a notebook and pretended to study it, as if he didn't already know the details. "Three murders in ten days. All by the same person. Random acts of violence with a purpose, the way I understand it. It all points to a serial killer."

"Where are you getting this from?"

"So it's true then? Well, you better fill in the blanks for me, Grodsky. This is going public soon. The circle of people who know is growing larger. Printing the story is not going to hamper your investigation. I got it first, dammit, and I'm going to break it unless you give me a reason not to."

This was a big story, but how big it was to become would have shocked even a veteran newsman like Perryman. He had seen and covered most of the big stories in Chicago from Speck to the gang wars to the Bermuda Love Triangle Case, the salacious affair that owed its name to the reporter's fecund imagination.

Even though the demographics said there was a nationwide reduction in crime, killings of every kind remained a staple of big city life and, consequently, a regular topic of big city headlines. Slats knew Perryman seethed in disgust at the need for one more headline screaming out the news of another grisly murder, but he also had a clear-headed view that this nasty murder was big news.

Slats was pondering his next move, when Julie arrived at the table to take their order.

"What'll you have, gents?"

"I'll have the cheeseburger, medium well, on a pretzel bun. Can I have the coleslaw instead of the French fries? And my friend, the cop, he'll have a B.L.T."

Slats heaved slightly at Perryman's attempt to remind him of his ball and chain. B.L.T. The Bermuda Love Triangle. Yes, Perryman still expected payback thirteen years later.

"Cheeseburger, coleslaw, and B.L.T.," repeated Julie. "Anything to drink?"

"Diet Pepsi," Perryman said.

"How often do you come here?" Slats asked Tex.

"First time, actually, why?"

"Never mind. Julie, I'll have the same."

Julie laughed as she returned to the kitchen to place the order.

"Well?" continued Tex.

"Okay; all right." Slats rubbed his face. He didn't like this conversation one bit. "Tex, your intel is correct. And, yes, it could be a serial killer. But you can't lead with this story yet."

"Why is he killing them?"

"We don't know why. And we don't know how many are involved."

"Cut the crap. It's one guy, and you know it. It's always one guy. How does he kill them?"

"I'm not at liberty to say. He's leaving clues, but we haven't decoded them yet. No prints of any kind, no witnesses either. We're at a standstill. If the public gets this story, it's gonna be bedlam."

"If not now, when?" asked Perryman. "I've got a responsibility to my paper and the people. They have a right to know. No, Slats, I owe it to the people to let this story be heard. It may save lives."

"Your paper, your paper, your paper. What's so frickin' holy about your paper? Let's be honest; you want a story that'll get you back to the front page. But you could also chase the killer away."

"Gimme a break. You know as well as I do these guys want their story told on the front page. Look. You're giving me nothing to go on. He's got to be leaving clues of some kind. All these schmucks do. Throw me a crumb. Maybe I can help you figure this out. Maybe I could help push the envelope."

"Tex, I'm going to ask you nicely. Give me a few more days on this. If anything else should happen, I'll call you. I agree with what you said. If anyone runs this story, it should be you."

Slats offered his hand to the reporter. "Deal?"

"Sorry, Slats. I promise nothing. I won't be able to sit on this story."

Julie brought their meals, and the two of them watched her walk back to the kitchen.

"Damn, Slats, that's one amazing ass."

"As they say, it takes one to see one," Slats countered.

Chapter 14

April 12, 2013

Blinded by the morning sun filtering through the windows, Slats could not find the ringing phone. When the ringtone stopped and went to voice mail, Slats stopped searching the covers.

"Shouldn't you be answering your calls?" asked Julie.

Disorientation vanished. Slats rolled over, realizing he was in Julie's bed.

"Hey," he said.

"Hey. Last night was amazing. You sure know how to show a girl a good time."

"It's in my DNA. And it didn't hurt that I aced all my anatomy and physiology classes in college."

"So you meant what you said yesterday?"

"I'm here, aren't I?"

Julie began stroking his arm.

"You know, there've been a few times when you were here but not here, if you catch my drift."

"I'm picking up what you're putting down. Yeah, that may have been true, but that was then. This is now."

"What time is it?"

Slats fumbled for his watch on the nightstand. It was 8:00 a.m.

At 8:01, the phone rang again.

More alert, he found the cell phone under the sheets and fumbled to answer it.

It was Brainard.

"Good news, bad news, buddy. Good news first. I set up a meeting at Chicago Lawn at 9:00 a.m. with one of the stat guys from the Cubs. Says he has info that might be important."

Grodsky was already sitting up on the side of the bed, pulling on his socks and pants.

"Okay, Charlie, I'll see you at nine. Wait! What's the bad news?"

"Don't take the Dan Ryan or Stevenson. Accident has it bottlenecked."

"Okay," Slats acknowledged.

"Oh, yah. One more thing. Perryman broke the story. Front page headlines."

"What! That asshole! I begged him not to."

"Holy shit! Tell me it wasn't you he named as his unknown police source."

"What did he write?"

"That there have been three murders, and it appears to be the same man committing them. Thank God, you didn't tell him anything else. Randle's gonna pop a cap in your ass when he finds out it was you."

"Hold it right there, Columbo. I didn't tell him a thing. He came to me with the story. He already had his facts but wouldn't tell me where he got the scoop. One thing I know about Perryman, though. He'll go to lock up before revealing his source. It's his best quality. He may be an asshole, but he's no rat."

"Are you sure about that?" Brainard said as he hung up.

No, Slats couldn't be sure of anyone anymore. Not even himself.

"Gotta go?" Julie sighed.

"Yah, Jules. But if you want to know what I'm up to, buy a paper. That reporter I was with in the tavern yesterday broke the damn story. Front page, Charlie said."

"I take it that's bad."

"Bad enough."

Grodsky, looking for his shoes, found them in Julie's hands. He reached for them, but she wrapped the shoes up under the sheets with her. "Come on," he said. "Give 'em up. I have to go."

"Nope," she smiled. "Last night you gave me your heart, but today I want your 'sole'."

"Cute, real cute."

He leaned over, gently kissed her on the lips, then the neck. Then he wrestled his shoes away by tickling her until she let go.

"No fair, you cheated," she laughed.

He looked directly into her eyes and said seriously, "Not on you I won't. Ever."

He kissed her good-bye and headed for his meeting at Eighth District.

Drive talk radio was ablaze with questions about the maniac roaming the Chicago streets. Police and city officials were vilified by commentators, fueling the ire of listeners.

Grodsky finished his trek to the station and fought through the line of reporters trying to score an interview with Commander Pearson or detectives with knowledge of the murders. Grodsky had seen this before. First came the reporters followed by citizen groups, all hounding the police for information, a scoop, justice.

"Grodsky!" Pearson shouted from his office. "In here. Now!"

Crap! I'm in for it now, he thought, as he entered Pearson's office.

"I don't care how long it takes; I want you to find the asshole who leaked this story to Perryman. That pissant reporter won't divulge his source, even with the threat of a court order. So the force is gonna do their own digging 'til we find the squealer."

"Okay, Chief," he affirmed with a sigh of temporary relief. "It had to be someone on the task force. I'll work that angle from the inside."

"Good. Oh, and Brainard told me to tell you he's in the interrogation room."

Pearson glanced into the open room outside his office and saw two reporters asking a beat cop questions.

"Get them out of here!" he bellowed, arms flailing and spit flying.

Grodsky beat it for the interrogation room, where he found Charlie and Edward Jablonski, one of the Chicago Cubs statisticians. Charlie introduced them.

"Mr. Jablonski? Thanks for coming down today." Slats shook Jablonski's hand.

Charlie said, "Mr. Jablonski was just explaining what he does for the Cubs." Grodsky nodded and took a chair next to Charlie and across from Jablonski.

"As I was telling Officer Brainard, basically, I pore over the volumes of material compiled on each ballplayer and create a comparative catalog for the team, making it easier to evaluate the talent."

"Comparative catalog?" Grodsky asked.

"Correct. We compare players not only within our organization, but also with players on other franchises. We break down all positions: hitting, fielding, and pitching. The usual baseball stats, batting average, RBIs, runs scored, steals, home runs, doubles, triples, walks, slugging percentage, innings pitched, shutouts, and saves, those are so old school. Some of the newer statistics developed by the analytical geniuses of the '80s and '90s are even more precise and relevant."

Indeed. There had been an explosion in the field of statistical analysis in baseball in the last twenty years. Entering a baseball fantasy league a few years back, Grodsky needed an advantage over the other players, so he read about the works of Pete Palmer, Dick Cramer, Bill James, Steve Mann, Nate Silver, and their contributions to the new era of baseball statistics. Stats like on-base percentage (OBP), on-base plus slugging (OPS), value over replacement player (VORP), slugging times on-base

(SLOB), walks and hits per innings pitched (WHIP), strikeouts per opponent plate appearance, walks per opponent plate appearance, and groundballs as a percentage of all balls hit into play (QERA) all helped measure a player's worth—his value as a player and as a trading piece in the future. Many of these stats were used for or against a player in salary arbitration cases.

"Do any of these new stats pertain to our case?" asked Grodsky.

"No. Not at all. I'm explaining some of the things I do. I analyze numbers and patterns. And I believe I've found a few twists for you to consider. You already know about the name of the victim being an ex-Cubs name. Let's review some other details. First, the Cubs lost each game the day a murder occurred. Will someone die if the Cubs win?"

"Don't know the answer to that one."

"Second, the murders have occurred on the opening game of a series."

"Really? Didn't recognize that."

"Third, the Cubs have only played home games. You may want to keep an eye on that to see if any murders occur when the team is on the road."

"Didn't see that coming either, did we, Charlie? Anything else?"

"If more murders occur, I might be able to identify other patterns."

"Let's hope there won't be a long-term need for your services, Mr. Jablonski. But if you identify anything else, please call us immediately, okay? It could be nothing—or it could be vitally important."

The three men rose. Grodsky thanked the statistician again, and Brainard showed him the way out. Watching them walk to the elevator, Grodsky reflected: victim wearing a baseball cap, tied up, watching baseball game, first game of each home series, Cubs lose, victim's throat slashed. If Cubs win, do victims live? Could it be that simple?

The clues, like murder victims, were beginning to pile up, yet much was still missing.

Chapter 15

Bermuda Love Triangle

Wednesday, January 21, 1998

Didi leaned over to kiss Joey hello as he entered the car. Joey tried offering his cheek, but Didi would have none of it. Instead, she cupped his face with her hands and kissed him gently on the lips. Her intoxicating perfume wove around him. He almost reached for her flowing hair. She seemed even prettier than when he had seen her just three hours ago.

"So, where we going for dinner?" she asked.

"Is there any part of this island you've never seen?" Joey probed.

"We've never been to the part of the island on the other side of the airport."

"You mean Saint George's?"

"Yah, that's it. We never go there. I think we drove through it once when Bruno was thinking of moving and looking for property. But he didn't want to be on that end of the island, so close to the airport noise and all."

"Perfect. We'll go to a restaurant you never get a chance to eat at. I found just the spot."

Joey gave directions, and Didi drove the length of the island, past the Bermuda International Airport to Saint George's. It was not awash with restaurants, let alone Italian restaurants, so Bruno never frequented the area. And there was no surveillance equipment at the Old Mansion Tavern. The ambiance, the wine, the meal, and thoughts of sex with Didi made Joey tingle with excitement, despite all his misgivings.

"If I'm going down, I'm going down in style," he murmured under his breath.

"Joey, I was thinking. We can't drive to a remote place. Bruno must have a tracking device on the car. He knows where I am all the time."

She had a point. In fact, perhaps he had added a tracking device to her cell phone as well. If anyone knew how to use the technology, it was an ex-Air Force Special Ops/CIA operator like Bruno.

"Okay," he said. "Here's what we're going to do. Leave your cell phone in the restaurant's bathroom. He'll think we're still here in case he's tracking you. We'll leave the car parked in the lot and take a long walk to the ocean's edge. I'm sure we'll find a private spot. When we're done, we'll come back, grab your phone, and drive home. If he asks why we were here so long, tell him we had shitty service, and that you never want to come here for dinner again."

The reviews he had browsed on Internet about the restaurant were spot on.

Everything after dinner went according to plan. Leaving the restaurant and following a nearby path to the beach, the two walked for a quarter mile on the sand till they found a patch of grass in an undulating field adjacent to the beach, surrounded by brush. Instantly locking their lips, Didi soon found Joey's tongue caressing her mouth. Didi began unbuckling Joey's belt while Joey caressed what he discovered to be Didi's firm implants. Tearing at each other's clothing, they stood naked in the moonlit sky. Melting into the ground as one, Joey could feel Didi surrender underneath him as he entered her. Their first encounter ended quickly, as the excited Joey could not contain himself.

"Don't worry about it, honey." Didi stroked him. "Next time will be longer; much, much longer."

And indeed, it was.

Spent from their hour-long tryst, they retraced their steps back to the restaurant, retrieved their phones, and began the long, silent drive back to the Fairmount Southampton.

Afraid to say anything romantic as they pulled up to the hotel entrance, Joey said, "I'll meet you here again tomorrow at noon."

She nodded in approval, whispering, "Sounds good."

As Joey headed up the concrete driveway, he heard footsteps behind him. Turning quickly, he realized it was Didi, no more than three feet behind him.

"Tonight was amazing, like I always dreamed it would be," she smiled.

"I know. It was insane. It'll be even better tomorrow, knowing what we know now."

"And tomorrow won't be our last night together. I've been thinking. I need you to do one more thing for me."

Still feeling happy from their encounter, Joey teased, "What do you mean? Toys, bondage, anal?"

"Who do you think you are, Bruno?" she reprimanded, backing up as if Joey were serious.

"Come on, I'm kidding. I'm totally smitten by you. You have to know that by now. Look at all I'm risking for you. Don't be upset. I'll do anything you want."

Making sure no one was watching, she snuggled close to Joey and grabbed his crotch with her hand. Pulling Joey in closer, she squeezed his package hard enough so he could not pull away without pain. She gently whispered in his ear, "I want you to kill Bruno."

Joey's heart would have dropped to his feet, had her hand not been in the way.

"You've got the wrong guy, babe. I'm a scout, not a murderer."

"I figure I've got one or two years, maybe five tops, before he dumps me for a younger girl. And when a hit man dumps his girlfriend, it's in concrete shoes. No, you are going to figure out a way to off him, or I swear I'll go to the hospital and tell them I was raped tonight. I've got your DNA all over me, inside and out. And then, my sweet lover, you will never make it off this island."

Oh my God, I'm an idiot, he realized. She didn't love him. She didn't even like him. How could she? She was putting him in a position to kill or be killed.

"Did you ever want me at all, or were you setting me up?" he questioned.

Didi released her grip and smiled slyly. Laughing, she turned back toward her car.

Taking about twenty steps, she turned around and stated, "You've got a day and a half to figure it out, Joey. He's smart, so you better be smarter."

Didi disappeared into the darkness. Soon, Joey might be doing the same thing. Permanently.

Chapter 16

Bermuda Love Triangle

Sunday, January 25, 1998

Damarco Maravelli was still in shock twenty-four hours after he had been notified of Bruno Discenzo's passing. Losing Bruno as well as Eddie and Fredo in the auto accident in Bermuda had spun Damarco into a depth of depression he had never experienced. Not even for his own brother. His aunt Sophia and uncle Carmine had adopted Bruno, and being the same age, he and Bruno had been more like twin brothers than cousins.

Damarco summoned the family to Biatelli's for a meeting. They needed to hear what he had learned. When the last *paisano* entered the dining hall, Mark Anthony tapped his water glass to request silence. Damarco, with a heavy heart, slowly pushed himself out of his chair. He stood, looking down the long string of tables that had been pushed together. He sat at the head of the family and the organization.

"Thank you all for coming so quickly."

He paused. The words were choking him.

"Two days ago, our beloved Bruno sat right here at this table. And now he is gone." Handkerchiefs were being pulled from pockets, tissues snatched from purses. Some in the family had actually had feelings for Bruno. Many were afraid of him. No matter which it was, they all sensed change coming, and change could take on an ugly face in the Maravelli family. Damarco continued, "We were notified yesterday that Bruno, Eddie, and Fredo, who left Chicago for Bermuda Saturday morning, were killed in a car accident after arriving in Bermuda. The police investigation was prompt and short. It has already been closed, citing it as a horrible, unfortunate accident."

Damarco stared down at the table for a moment, as if gathering himself. A hush fell on the room.

When he lifted his head, there was tears on his cheek. He said, "This was no accident. Last week, our *intelligenza* discovered the identity of the man who killed Bruno's family when he was a boy. I verified this information, which was sensitive because of who the man is and who he works for. When I confirmed the evidence was correct, I contacted Bruno late last Wednesday evening. This was why I brought Bruno home. To tell him in person.

"Knowing this could cause a problem for the family, Bruno asked for my blessing. How could I refuse my *fratello*?" Damarco went on, "Does the name Gino Aroletti sound familiar?"

The room buzzed. Of course, they knew the name. He was the first cousin of Dominic Aroletti, the Don whose family runs all the operations in the south side of Chicago.

"It was Gino who killed Bruno's sister, father, and mother, right before his eyes. On Thursday, Bruno paid Gino a visit and avenged his family, after thirty-one years. A day and a half later, Bruno was taken from us.

"One hour ago, I had a sit-down with Don Aroletti. He swore no one in his family had killed Bruno. He was upset with his cousin, who shamed and embarrassed his family with his actions. Don Aroletti said Gino had admitted to him long ago of the atrocities that Gino laid at Bruno's feet; Don Aroletti told Gino that one day he would not be able to protect him. Sure, Don Aroletti was upset that Bruno took his revenge, but understood, and assured me that there was to be no retribution to our family; that Gino's sacrifice was to be the only bloodshed between our families."

Slamming the side of his fist into the table, Damarco said, "Bruno, Fredo, and Eddie are dead forty hours after Gino is killed? Don Aroletti has lied to my face and disrespected our family. He and his family will pay for those lies. I want everyone here to move their wives and children out of Chicago. Take them out of harm's way. If Aroletti wants a war, then, by God, he's got it. Tomorrow night, I want the members of the war council at the restaurant by 9:00 p.m. On Wednesday, we will finish the war Don Aroletti has started."

With a wave of his hand, Damarco cut the tension in the room and dismissed his family. All that was heard was chairs scraping the wooden floors and the scurrying of footsteps out of the restaurant. There was no calling off this war. As far as the Maravellis were concerned, it was already on.

Chapter 17

April 15, 2013

It was late afternoon when the task force reconvened at Central HQ. Protest groups were still parading in front of the South Michigan Avenue entrance from early morning until late evening. Now in their fourth day of picketing the police department, sympathizers brought food, water, signs, and the latest information; replacement demonstrators took turns relieving fellow marchers. Police pushed their way into the station through the chanting crowds carrying signs: "We Have a Right to Know," "We Pay to Have a Say," and one apparently borrowed from the last abortion rally, "Protect Our Children." The crowd was mostly female and hostile.

David Locke, Superintendent Randle's chief of staff, was handling meetings with dissident groups and reporters. His actions afforded Randle the time to address the task force four floors above.

"We're awaiting on Rick Nardi from the 19th. A fourth victim was found alive about an hour ago and was taken to Kindred Hospital. Nardi and his partner have been at the scene and the hospital, and are on their way here to fill us in."

Cliff Zeigler yelled across the table to Matt Jasper.

"I told ya', this team is cursed."

"Screw you," Jasper answered. "There's no such thing as a curse. It's an excuse for losers."

"Ask Grodsky about it. I heard all his bullshit for four years. Come on, Grodsky, you're the expert on Cubs trivia. Tell Matt why the Cubs will never win a World Series."

Slats looked around the conference table. Friend or foe, all eyes were now fixed on him, waiting for Cubs gospel. Slats said, "I don't think we have time for all the stories."

Rocky Parma egged him on. "Come on, Slats. Tell 'em a few until Nardi gets here."

Slats shrugged his shoulders. Maybe they all needed a little entertainment, a little relief. "Okay. In 1945, William 'Billy Goat' Sianis, owner of the Billy Goat Tavern, bought two tickets to the Cubs-Tigers World Series game at Wrigley—one for him and one for his goat. The Cubs were up two games to one at the time. The ushers, with the owners backing, refused to let Billy into Wrigley Field with the goat. It was reported that Billy was so upset he said, 'The Cubs ain't gonna win no more. The Cubs will never win a World Series so long as the goat is not allowed in Wrigley Field.' The curse was in place. Sure enough, the Cubs lost the series to Detroit and haven't won one since."

Several members of the task force, including Randle, chuckled.

Slats continued, "When the *Tribune* bought the Cubs in 1984, they invited Sam Sianis, Billy's son, and his goat to the opening game ceremonies in an attempt to lift the curse. But 105 years since their last World Series Championship, they are still cursed."

"Go on, Slats. Tell 'em about the cat," Zeigler blurted out.

"There was a black cat that gave Ron Santo and the rest of his teammates the evil eye in Shea Stadium in a game against the Mets. The Cubs lost that game and seventeen of the next twenty-five games to finish eight games behind New York."

"Sounds like the Cubs have a problem with animals," someone joked.

"Not to mention their fans," Rocky Parma said.

Slats nodded. "You're talking about Bartman. It was 2003. the Cubs were beating the Florida Marlins at home in the playoffs until Bartman interfered with a catchable pop foul near the stands by third base. The Cubs ended up losing that game and the playoff series."

"How does he know all this crap?" Matt Jasper asked his fellow cops.

"Sorry. I'm still not convinced. I said it before, and I'll say it again: excuses, excuses, excuses."

Randle just grinned and pulled a vibrating phone from his pocket. It was a text from his chief of staff.

"Nardi's on his way up," Randle said. "Before he addresses the force, remember, from now on we'll use the back entrance. It'll be kept off-limits to nonpersonnel. We don't need to be caught up in the distractions occurring in front of the building. Don't confront those uninformed dissidents outside. I need you clearheaded and focused. In the long run, they want the same thing we do—a resolution to this case."

When Nardi entered the room, all eyes turned to him. Randle relinquished the floor.

"We finally caught a break," Nardi said. "Eighty-seven-year-old Lydia Bosley was overtaken by our attacker and tied up in her living room chair in front of her television. She's one lucky lady though. As the game was ending, Mrs. Bosley's niece came over to drop off groceries. With her hands full, she rang the doorbell with her elbow, but when Lydia didn't answer the door, the niece put the groceries down, used the key Lydia had given her, and entered the premises. Her arrival must have spooked our perp, who missed his mark on Lydia's jugular vein. He was able to escape undetected out the backdoor. The niece called 911 and applied pressure to the neck wound. Paramedics arrived on the scene seven minutes after the 911 call, stabilized Mrs. Bosley, then transported her to Kindred Hospital. The surgeon repaired the slice in her neck; she's in critical but stable condition. My partner is outside her hospital room waiting for her to wake up. Guards will be stationed outside her room 24/7. The doctors gave no timetable, but, based on past experience, we're hopeful we'll be able to talk to her in the next four to six hours. We're anticipating she'll be able to tell us more about her assailant. I'm sure I left out quite a bit, so I'll open it up for questions."

The questions came out faster than ammo from an M-60 machine gun.

"What was her address, and is her last name the name of an ex-Cub?"

"293 West Nelson Street. Someone call the Cubs to confirm the last name."

"Is she married?"

"Husband deceased. Lives alone."

"Did the niece get a look at the intruder?"

"No."

"Was Mrs. Bosley wearing a Cubs hat?"

"Yes. Sorry, forgot to include that."

"Was she knocked unconscious by the intruder?"

"We were unable to examine her. We'll have to check with the surgeon. They were concerned about saving her life, so we don't have the full report yet."

"Did the Cubs lose today?"

"Yes, at Wrigley."

"Was it the first game of a series?"

"Yes, with the Colorado Rockies."

"So was it an accident that this lady lived?"

"We don't know for sure, but, from his brief yet lethal history, it appears the perp may have screwed up."

"Any prints found at the scene?"

"Not yet, but the forensic team is over there now, hoping to find something relevant."

"Did we cordon off the area?"

"Yes, but apparently not in time. A sweep of a ten-block area in every direction came up empty. We're checking the neighborhood for active surveillance cameras as well."

"Does the press know about this?"

"Due to the blockade and sweep of the streets, they're aware of a crime but don't know the specifics. I suspect they will know soon. Our position is to acknowledge the attack, but do not, I repeat, do not release details of the attack to anyone outside this room unless you have the authority of Superintendent Randle."

Rocky Parma hung up his phone and spoke.

"Cubs said there was a Thad Bosley who played for them from '83 to '86."

As the questioning ceased, Nardi finished up.

"Let's hope Lydia can give us more to go on. I'll text the group as soon as she's awake and able to answer some questions."

After dispersing from headquarters, the members of the task force headed back to their districts to debrief their fellow officers. Two hours turned into four, then six. There was still no word from the hospital, and the men, hoping for a more detailed plan of attack, were uneasy with their unproductiveness.

Back at the Eighth, Brainard had an idea.

"Why don't we order a pizza? We always get busy when food's delivered. Doesn't it seem like a busload of people are outside waiting for the food to arrive, follow it in, and are determined to keep us from eating it?"

"Yes, the pizza bus," another patrolman offered.

"I don't think it works if you try to plan it, but go ahead," said Slats. "What have we got to lose?"

Three hours after the last bite of pizza was consumed, all was still quiet in the district. And there was still no word from the hospital.

"I told you," Slats said. "You can't fool the gods. They screw things up when they're good and ready. I'm going home to get some sleep. I'm exhausted. We'll fight the fight tomorrow."

Slats checked his answering machine upon entering his apartment. Both messages were from Julie, but 12:30 a.m. was too late to return the call. Too tired to brush his teeth, Slats removed his clothes and crumpled into bed.

At that precise moment, a text came in from Detective Nardi.

Lydia Bosley was awake.

And, thanks to the hospital gods, so was Slats.

WARREN FRIEDMAN

Chapter 18

April 16, 2013

Grodsky entered Chicago Lawn at 7:30 a.m. without his usual six hours of sleep. After Nardi's first text, Slats, anxious to hear Lydia Bosley's account of the attack, had found it impossible to sleep. The next text at 3:00 a.m. was disappointing.

"No recollection; patient still in recovery."

Nardi's 6:00 a.m. text contained a surprise. When Lydia did not wake up after surgery within the allotted time frame, the anesthesiologist was concerned. Verification of the pre-surgical anesthetics quantities used on Mrs. Bosley confirmed she should have been unconscious for no more than six hours; she was out cold for nine. A toxicology report was ordered, which revealed trace amounts of midazolam, a presurgical medication used for inducing sedation and amnesia before medical procedures. The only problem was the hospital did not administer midazolam to Lydia Bosley before surgery.

The anesthesiologist theorized the attacker must have drugged Mrs. Bosley with an injection of midazolam. Given intramuscularly, the dose would take effect in fifteen minutes resulting in total amnesia of her ordeal. Nardi contacted the coroner's office and ordered an additional test on the first three victims for midazolam. The original reports had been delayed due to new construction and remodeling of the coroner's lab, so all blood samples and tissue had been sent to an outside laboratory. Results from those tests would not be known for an additional twenty-four to forty-eight hours.

Nardi also notified the DEA and Illinois State Board of Pharmacy to investigate if doses of midazolam had been reported missing by pharmaceutical companies, wholesalers, physicians, or pharmacies. If the attacker used an industry standard five-milligram dose, one package was enough to produce the desired soporific effect in one hundred victims. Those agencies acknowledged, however, that it was near impossible to uncover the theft of one box of midazolam. From past cases and the wealth of history in drug diversion, it was more likely the midazolam was obtained at a less secure site such as a doctor's office or clinic. That is where the two agencies decided they were going to appropriate their time and resources.

"You look like shit, Slats," said Brainard.

Slats had been motionless, deep in thought for almost ten minutes, staring at his overdue phone bill, with his elbows on the desk and biting down on his index finger. Without warning Grodsky leaped from his chair, grabbed his coat, and yelled at Brainard, "Come on, Charlie, we're leaving."

"Where to?" Charlie probed.

"To Kindred Hospital. We need to talk to Lydia Bosley'"

"Well, it beats sitting here watching you stare into space."

The eighteen-mile ride from the Eighth District to Kindred Hospital North on West Montrose Avenue went smoothly as traffic was light. Lydia Bosley was brought to Kindred Hospital because it was the closest hospital with an emergency room. But Kindred Hospital North was not a typical hospital. It was a long-term acute care rehabilitation hospital for those with complex illnesses needing specialized attention. Considering her advanced age and type of wound, Mrs. Bosley had landed in the ideal infirmary for her recuperation.

Charlie kept checking the rearview mirror.

"See something?" Slats asked.

"No, but I'm getting that feeling again, you know? Like we're being tailed."

"You haven't been cheating on your wife, have you? Maybe it's Chief Pearson keeping a close eye on his son-in-law."

"Ha, ha, ha. Very funny. Forget I mentioned it."

Precautions were taken to protect Lydia. She was under an alias at the hospital. Guards were posted outside her room on the fourth floor, which was located next to the nurse's station. Everyone entering her room had to show ID and sign the guard's manifest.

"Names, please," said the police guard.

"Grodsky and Brainard. You'll find our names and badge numbers on the task force sheet."

"Yes, I see it. Sign in please."

The men entered the room to find Lydia Bosley sitting in her bedside chair eating breakfast. She looked remarkably well considering her age and her tribulations during the last twenty-four hours. As was standard protocol, senior partner Grodsky asked the questions while junior partner Brainard transcribed.

"Hello, Lydia, I'm Detective Grodsky. This is Detective Brainard. Sorry to bother you; we know you've been through a lot. But I'm hoping you could answer a few questions for us."

"I've already told the other policemen everything I know. It's all so fuzzy."

"What was the last thing you remember?"

"I was drinking tea and watching the Home Shopping Channel. I remember wanting to buy a necklace—I think it was onyx—and I got up to get my credit card out of my wallet. The next thing I knew I was in the hospital. I've told that to everyone. I don't understand why you all keep asking me the same questions."

"I'm sorry, Mrs. Bosley, I agree with you. The police do tend to ask the same questions. Let me ask you something different. Are you in your home most of the time?"

"Except for visiting the doctor, I was home all winter. I used to love the snow when I was younger, but I hate the winters now. My niece takes me out in good weather to my favorite places: Lincoln Park Zoo, Navy Pier, Natural History Museum. I enjoy watching the crowds. I have to use my wheelchair; I can't walk very well, and all those places seem so big now!"

"Can you think of anything strange that has happened to you in the last few months?"

"What do you mean strange?"

"You know, someone soliciting at your door, or vandalizing your property?"

"No, I don't think so. I've had a few hang-up phone calls, oh, but everyone has those. I guess they had the wrong number. Is that what you mean?"

"Exactly. Anything else you can think of?"

"Not really."

"Lydia, sorry to disturb you. I hope you feel better. We'll catch the person who did this to you, I promise."

After signing out on the police officer's log, Grodsky turned to his colleague.

"Charlie, find out what her phone service is. See if you can get a record of her incoming calls in the last six months. Maybe this guy called to make sure she'd be home at specific times during the day. If we can cross off the numbers of her friends and family, that might trim the list to a few phone numbers. And if any of those calls were under thirty seconds, maybe we can trace them to a number that could lead us to the guy casing the old lady. We'll need to do the same thing with the other victims as well."

"Good thought, Slats."

"Charlie, once you and I catch this guy, all those assholes messing with us can stick it where the sun don't shine. We'll be back on top, looking down."

"You do realize I've never actually been on top yet?" answered Brainard.

"Well, strap 'em up, Charlie. It's going to be a hell of a ride."

As Charlie dropped him off at the Old Town Tavern, Slats had his old bounce back in his step. He felt his mojo coming back and was feeling rather proud of himself. Proud that he may have found a way into the killer's world which others had missed. Proud that he was a key figure once again in a significant investigation, not a grunt lending support. Proud that he may still have "it" after all.

Chapter 19

Bermuda Love Triangle

Sunday, January 25, 1998

"Slats," Stiffle yelled. "Cowboy on line one."

The phone call interrupted his study of the Green Bay-Denver Super Bowl game to be played that evening. Green Bay, the defending NFL champs, was an eleven-and-a-half-point favorite with MVP Brett Favre leading the way. Wildcard entry Denver had John Elway, Terrell Davis, and the league's top offense but had lost four times before in the Super Bowl. Slats was loyal to any NFC team versus the AFC in the Super Bowl. Still, it was hard to root for Green Bay, the Bears' arch rival. He put down the paper to cover his naked knees and lap and yelled through the stall door.

"Be right there."

Murphy's Law. It always seemed to happen. If food was brought in, all hell would break loose and no one could eat. If a pretty girl came in, someone blocked your view. Or if you went to the crapper, someone always called you on the phone.

Back at his desk, he pulled the phone to his chin, "Slats here."

"Slats, it's Tex Perryman."

"Hey, Tex, what's up?"

"I'm in Bermuda covering the winter meetings for the newspaper. Something's wrong down here. Terribly wrong. I can feel it in my gut."

Newspapermen and cops have one thing in common: gut feelings.

In his early years, Tex had seen and covered most of the big stories in Chicago, from serial killer Richard Speck to the gang wars. Now, at fifty-four years old, Tex was covering softer stories—elections, sporting events, and entertainment news— as the paper restructured under yet another young editor.

"What is it, Tex?"

"Bruno Discenzo was killed yesterday in a car wreck."

"I know," retorted Slats. "Read about it in your newspaper this morning. Sorry that scumbag and his two friends are dead. It makes at least 190 of my files on him at headquarters obsolete, and I'm . . ."

Tex interrupted. "I don't think it was an accident."

That gave Slats pause. "What makes you say that? The police report seemed pretty specific. I believe their words were 'tragic accident'."

"Ever heard the name Joey Robbins?" Tex queried.

"Can't say I do," Slats said, starting to turn his attention back to the sports page.

"He's a baseball scout for the Cubs. I saw him hanging out with Bruno's girlfriend at the baseball winter meetings in Bermuda this week."

"So? Sounds like he's lucky he wasn't killed."

"Don't dismiss me. I saw him coming down the stairs from Bruno's estate, which was located next to our hotel on the day the baseball winter meetings started. I confronted him, and he said he wanted to see the girl's face, went on about how pretty she was. I warned him that it was Bruno's house. A couple days later, I heard he disappeared and his boss was looking for him for almost three days—the same three days Bruno was back in Chicago. The minute Bruno came back to Bermuda, Bruno's ticket was punched. Doesn't that seem odd to you?"

"So you think he was banging Bruno's broad, and then this scout, a guy that assesses baseball players for a living, killed one of Chicago's most notorious hitmen and his two bodyguards? No wonder you're doing restaurant reviews, Tex."

"If you don't want to look into it, fine. I can call someone else. But I've never steered you wrong yet, have I? The old Slats I knew cared about putting bad guys away, even if they killed other bad guys."

Slats could feel Perryman's disdain as he hung up. He was an excellent journalist with a nose for trouble. It was not his fault that he was unappreciated by editors half his age who pointed to him as part of the problem rather than part of the solution. More often than not during his career, it was Tex who had broken a story, examining obvious signs that were missed by untrained, unobserving eyes. That included the eyes of the police force.

Slats sighed and leaned back for a few minutes in his swivel chair with his hands clasped behind his head. Straightening his chair, Slats reached down and opened the bottom drawer in his desk. Rustling through the papers in the drawer, he retrieved an old address and telephone notebook.

He scribbled down a phone number from the book and two others he found on the computer. Three calls would clarify Perryman's tip. The first was to the Chicago Cubs. The second was to the Bermuda Police Department. The third was to an old informant, Golly Satchow.

"Chicago Cubs Front Office, how may I help you?" said the nasal, friendly voice.

"This is Officer Grodsky from the Eighth District Police Department. Do you know if the Cubs keep fingerprints on their employees?"

"You're in luck. HR is closed but someone from the department is in the building as we speak. Let me connect you. I'm sure she'll be able to help you, sir."

"Chicago Cubs Human Resources, this is Barb Urso. How may I assist you today?"

"Hello, Barb. This is Officer Grodsky of the Eighth District Police Department. Who can I talk to about whether the Cubs keep fingerprints on their employees?"

"That would be me, officer; I'm the HRIS coordinator."

Slats new the initials. Human Resource Information System Coordinator. It was her job to protect classified material.

"I need a set of prints from a few employees. Do I need to pick them up in person?"

"No, sir, we can fax them to you. All I'll need is your fax number. Whose prints will I be sending?"

Slats did not want to tip his hand.

"All the scouts that were at the Fairmount Southampton for the baseball meeting in Bermuda."

"Yes, sir, I will get that list and send it over as soon as possible. Did they do something wrong?"

"I doubt it. We're clearing up a little mishap at the hotel, and I want to rule everyone out, that's all." He rattled off the fax number.

"Got it."

"Thanks, Barb." He hung up, spun his chair to face his partner Greg Stiffle, and briefed him on Perryman's suspicions.

"Sounds like a long shot to me," Stiffle said.

"Yeah, but Perryman's usually solid. Let's check it out, anyway," Slats said with a shrug. "See if there's any automotive background in Joey Robbins's past; high school car class, brother who owns an auto dealership, anything."

"You got it," Stiffle nodded.

Slats decided to call the Bermuda Police Department last, after he received the fingerprints. Next to contact was Golly Satchow.

As usual, Grodsky got the answering machine. "Golly, this is Slats. Meet me this afternoon at the usual spot, 2:00 p.m. And Golly, don't be late."

Slats held his informants in high regard as sources of information, if not as human beings. They gave him bits of junk that on a good day might be useful in making a connection, a collar, or a case. Golly Satchow embodied the extremes of the type. Submissive, scruffy, clever, he was loyal to Slats for dozens of legal favors, great and pedestrian.

Two hours later, Slats rounded the corner of Madison and South Wabash, nearly bumping into his informant. "Golly, Officer Slats, what are you doin' here today?" said Golly.

"Morning, Golly. I've missed you these past weeks. Isn't a man allowed to cultivate his friends? I'm here to cultivate you, Golly."

"One time you cultivated me by planting weed. So, with all respect Officer Slats, may we use another figure of speech?"

Both men roared with laughter at the exchange. They continued around the corner together, walking at a leisurely pace, away from the El line for a few blocks east on Madison, then south toward Grant Park. They finally settled on a bench that was protected from the noise of the street and shaded by a giant sugar maple tree. Slats's mood abruptly morphed from light-hearted friend to stern father.

"Golly, what can you tell me about Bruno Discenzo?"

"Better get your Kevlar dusted off, Slats, cuz it's gonna get ugly around here soon."

"How's that?" Slats queried.

"You're kidding right?" answered Golly.

"Come on, out with it. I swear to God, I don't have time for your games and riddles."

"Man, you cops must have your head so far up your ass you don't hear or see nothin'."

Knowing Golly's past, Slats took a veiled shot and laid it out on the line.

"I saw enough to see you buying smack this week. Care to see the video down at headquarters?"

"Fucking cops. What're they paying you guys for? You don't know shit, do you? Bruno Discenzo put down Gino Aroletti, then got wacked the next day. Now the Aroletti family and the Maravelli family are going to war. The mob's got M-16s and AK-47s, and you've got what, .9mms and .45s? Water pistols, man. I'd stay out of the way if I was you."

But if Tex Perryman was right, the Aroletti family wasn't to blame for Bruno's death. Did the Arolettis or a Cubs scout kill Bruno? What Golly was telling him seemed reasonable, even more feasible, but Slats could not be sure. He left Golly staring at the pavement, mindlessly watching two ants fighting for the same scrap of food.

This was the way they always met. Out of the blue, in and out in a minute. But for a man whose senses were not always in full operation, Golly had learned to be a world-class listener. The ears of this junkie heard the music of the streets, and he had heard enough melodies to be sharp instead of flat.

Chapter 20

Bermuda Love Triangle

Monday, January 26, 1998

Slats plunked down in his chair and took off his watch. It was a Movado, given to him by his wife as a thirty-fifth birthday present. It was an expensive yet simple watch, which was Julie's taste. But Slats was a complicated, multitasking man, and initially wanted a watch that gave more information than the time of day. He even argued about it with her. Julie reminded him he already knew every trivial thing there was to know. He needed something in his life that could be mindless. Originally he despised the Museum Watch simplicity, defined by a single gold dot symbolizing the sun at high noon and hands suggesting the movement of the earth. But after two years, Slats was beginning to appreciate the beauty of its minimalism.

It was too late to admit it; Julie was right.

It was 3:15 p.m. on the watch, which would be 5:15 p.m. in Bermuda. Grodsky had received the fax he had requested from the Cubs. He had procured the fingerprints of all of the Chicago Cubs' scouts, but needed only one set—those of Joey Robbins. Within minutes, Grodsky transferred Robbins prints to the national and international fingerprint database. Now, these prints could be matched from anywhere in the world.

Slats reached for the phone and dialed the Bermuda Police Department.

Waiting for the connection to go through, he saw Commander Sam Pearson was about to leave the station. He heard Pearson say, "What's Grodsky up to, Stiffle?"

"Calling Bermuda, I think."

Great, Slats thought. I'm in for it now. Pearson made a beeline for Slats.

"That's right," Slats said to the official in the Bermuda Police Department. "The prints are in the database. You need to sweep the following: Bruno Discenzo's home, railings on the staircase to the beach, his cars, and, if you can find out what clothing Didi Lecate was wearing over the last few days, check those for prints as well. I need to know if there is any evidence that could prove an affair existed between Joey Robbins and Didi Lecate. No, I don't mean to insult you; yes, of course, you were trained like I was; no, I'm not a control freak. We just have some information that this might not have been an accident and want to make sure."

Slats sighed and rubbed his eyes. "We don't believe Didi cooked, and they wouldn't have eaten at Joey's hotel. They had to eat or drink somewhere on the island where they wouldn't be spotted. If you have the manpower, can you go to the restaurants and flash their picture to the waiters, bartenders, maître d's, and valets to see if they saw the couple together? One hundred and fifty restaurants in Bermuda?" Slats said with disbelief.

"Come on, you can probably cut that in half. I doubt they went to any fast food joints. Bruno wined and dined this chick. Chances are they were going as far away from the hotel as possible to avoid being discovered together by any of Robbins's coworkers. Please, as many as you can. You will? Thanks. Oh, and one more thing. Any chance I can have this info back by tomorrow?"

Slats moved the receiver away from his ear to avoid the screaming. When the noise stopped, he talked again.

"I know, I know, but it's important. You've got to try and get as many people on this as you can. We're about to have an all-out mafia war in Chicago at any moment, and if Robbins did this . . ."

Slats moved the phone away from his ear again.

"Look, I know our gang war is not your problem, but you said my theory was possible. I can't come out there myself. I need your help. Please. Yes, anything, even if you think it's insignificant. Thank you. I'll be in touch."

Slats looked up at Commander Pearson, whose face was slowly turning red.

"What?"

"Do you know how much that call cost the department?" asked Pearson.

"You're joking, right?"

"It was unauthorized, and it's coming out of your pocket, not ours."

"Let me get this straight. You'd rather have a mob war than spend thirty dollars on a phone call?"

As Pearson turned to leave, he muttered, "Mob war."

Stiffle wheeled his chair over to Grodsky's desk.

"Talk to me, Slats. What's up?"

"My snitch told me the Maravelli and Aroletti families are going to shoot it out on the streets of Chicago in the next day or two on the heels of the deaths of Gino Aroletti and Bruno Discenzo."

"I thought Bruno died in an accident?"

"That's what the Bermuda police wrote in their hasty investigation, but the families aren't buying it. And frankly, I'm not so sure either."

"Why? Everyone said it's an open-and-shut case."

"It's hard to believe the accident report, based upon what I've learned. I believe Bruno was whacked; the better question is who did it? I don't agree with the Maravelli family. I don't think the Arolettis had Bruno killed. I received a tip from Tex Perryman."

"The reporter?" Greg asked.

"That guy has a nose for this shit, and he thinks a scout for the Cubs and possibly Bruno's girlfriend did this. If so, a lot of people are going to die for no reason. If that's true, we've got to stop this war between the families before it begins."

"Would it be so bad if the bad guys killed each other?"

"Innocent bystanders, Stiffle, innocent bystanders. Come on, we're going for a ride. We need to buy some time."

The eight-and-a-half- mile ride from the Eighth District headquarters to Biatelli's Ristorante on West Taylor Street in Little Italy took Grodsky and Stiffle about twenty minutes. They arrived at 6:30 p.m., the height of the dinner hour. Most of those eating in the restaurant were familiar faces to the two policemen.

"May I help you gentlemen?" asked the maître d', who without delay sized up the pair as cops.

"Table for two, please," stated Stiffle.

"I'm sorry, sir, we have a three-hour wait."

Slats looked around at the plethora of empty tables.

The maître d' didn't bat an eye. "All of the tables are reserved, sir."

"That's okay. We're here to see Damarco Maravelli," Slats replied.

"Do you have an appointment?"

Slats and Greg flashed their badges.

"I'm sorry, these badges could be counterfeit. I'll need more proof, sir."

Stiffle hated it when people doubted his credentials. Forgetting where he was and now angered by the maître d', he leaned over within a few inches of the man's face and said, "I've locked up four of the goons in this restaurant. Why don't you ask them if my badge is real?"

Mark Anthony, Damarco's brother, was sitting at the closest table. Stiffle's tough demeanor made him rise from the table to help the maître d'.

"It's all right, Mario," Mark Anthony said, placing his hand on the man's shoulder. "I know these men. They are who they say they are."

Mario nodded and went back to his station to attend to the next guest.

"Please, don't scare the patrons," he said, looking at Stiffle. "We want them to come back."

He turned his attention to Slats.

"So, you want to see Damarco?"

"Yes, we would," answered Slats.

"He's unavailable at present. Perhaps I can be of service to you in place of my older brother. After all, I am the consigliere of the family business."

"This has more to do with life and death rather than business," said Stiffle, "though I suppose in your business they are one in the same, eh?"

"Anything you need to say to my brother you can say to . . ."

"Okay, Mark Anthony, we get it," Slats interrupted. "We know of the bad blood between your family and the Arolettis. We also know that in the not-too-distant future a number of people are going to die needlessly. I agree that Bruno's death was not accidental, but I have solid information that the Arolettis may not have put a contract on Bruno. We are here to save lives for both families, not to cause trouble or scare patrons. But I need more time, at least another day to follow up a lead. I promise, as soon as I know what is happening, I will call the Don immediately. Can you give him that message for me?"

"I don't know of this 'war' you are talking about, but yes, I will relay your message to Don Maravelli. Now if you'll excuse me, I must get back to my guests."

* * *

When Slats and Greg exited the restaurant, they took Slats's unmarked '97 Grand Prix back to the station to wait for word from Bermuda.

Slats's phone rang, and he glanced at the clock on the wall. It was 11:11 p.m. Seeing "11:11" on a clock has different meanings around the world. Theories of spiritual significance or paranormal activity are attached to the numbers. Many see it as a good luck sign and "make a wish." There were no such good vibes for Slats. Two years prior, he had to put his little Maltese Cody to sleep on 11/11. Whenever he saw that time on the clock, and it usually came up about three times a week, the moment in the vet's office was all he could think about. Today, however, his mind was on Bermuda. Maybe he was finally moving on.

"Grodsky here."

"Good evening, Officer Grodsky, this is Inspector Emanuel Solomon of the Bermuda Police Service. I have news for you."

"Go on," Grodsky begged, realizing that it was now 1:11 a.m. in Bermuda.

"Number one, we did find Mr. Robbins's prints in all the places you had requested. We also found semen stains on the jeans skirt of Ms. Lecate, which was quite a surprise to our forensic team, I might add. We found the skirt in the Discenzo mansion. We'll have to collect a DNA sample from Robbins to see if it's a match. Second, his prints were found not only on the staircase leading to the house from the beach, but also in the house foyer. Apparently, he never drove a car owned by Mr. Discenzo, but his prints were found on the seat belt, dashboard, and door on the passenger side of the vehicle often driven by Ms. Lecate. And lastly, we have word that Ms. Lecate and Mr. Robbins had dinner at a restaurant in Hamilton, though we had to pay for that information. I'm assuming the Chicago Police Department will be willing to reimburse us for that intel?"

"If not, I'll do it myself," said Slats, scribbling notes in his notebook. "I'm already paying for the phone calls."

"That is all we know so far. A team has been going over the carnage at the scene of the car crash to determine if it was an accident, but nothing unusual has come to light so far."

"Have you located Ms. Lecate or Mr. Robbins?" Slats asked.

"No, sir. The baseball meetings at the Fairmount Southampton have ended, and Mr. Robbins has left the island. Our research says he landed in New York, rented a car, and is apparently making his way toward New Castle Delaware, where he is holding an open tryout for ballplayers at Wilmington College. I don't know where he is staying, but now that he's in the States, you may be able to track him by his credit card."

"And Didi Lecate?"

"I'm afraid she has disappeared. She may be on the island still, but then again, maybe no. We have no knowledge of her leaving the island, by sea or by air."

"Do you have her cell phone number? Maybe you could track her from that?" Slats responded.

"Already thought of that, sir. No, she is no longer using that phone."

"Any chance you could find out if she opened an account with another service with a disposable phone?"

"We've been looking, and we will verify with the providers on the island."

"Thank you, Inspector Solomon, these details will be invaluable. Any chance you'd move to Chicago and work here with us?"

Solomon laughed.

"Nooooo, sir, I hate cold wind, and I hear you have an abundance of it in Chicago. But if you care to move to Bermuda, you can stay with me. We already have fifteen relatives in our house, so what's one more? Good night, Officer Grodsky."

"Goodnight, Inspector."

"Well?" asked Stiffle.

"Robbins and Didi were definitely having an affair. Semen was found on her clothing. Their prints are all over the house and the cars. They were identified from photos at one restaurant," Slats went on. "I'm sure there would be more evidence if we had more time. Robbins is back in the States, and Didi has gone underground. Knowing she's not living in that palatial mansion by the sea tells me she's guilty as sin and doesn't want to be visited by any of Bruno's compadres."

"If we could just get to Robbins," muttered Stiffle.

"Actually, we can. He's on his way to Wilmington College in New Castle, Delaware, for an open tryout for the Cubs. Got a glove, Greg?"

"Hey. You were the athlete, not me. Why don't you try out?"

"You think Pearson will pay for a ticket to Delaware?"

Stiffle turned and looked toward Pearson's office.

"Shit. He ain't here, but I'll lay ten to one odds he won't approve it."

Slats checked online. The closest airport to New Castle was Philadelphia International Airport.

"Got it," Slats said. "Here's a direct roundtrip flight to Philly for $500."

"Or it's a 761-mile, thirteen-hour drive. I hate flying."

"Thirteen hours? Are you crazy? We need every hour we can to get this war stopped."

"Okay," Greg continued. "I'll call the chief about the flight because there is no way I'm spending $500 of my own money to go talk to a dickhead who's banging one of the best-looking broads on the planet. I have better ways to torture myself, even if you don't."

"Call him now, Greg. This flight leaves at 6:00 a.m. tomorrow morning from O'Hare, and lands in Philly around 9:00 a.m. Also, see if you can get a squad car waiting for us to take us to New Castle. We can take the 7:40 p.m. flight back to Chicago tomorrow night, which comes in at 9:00 p.m., and if things go as planned, we'll be coming back with Robbins in the seat next to us. I'll tell you this. I'm going, with or without the department's money."

Slats leaned back in his chair and listened as Stiffle tried to talk the chief into approving the expenditure. Stiffle was a debater with attitude, and he didn't mind going up against the old man. Pearson seemed to like his spunk. Greg looked pleased upon hanging up.

He walked over to Grodsky's desk and leaned over with a sly smile on his face.

"Pearson okayed the flight—for you only."

"So, why are you so happy?

"Are you kidding? He wasn't going to let either of us go. That I got one of us a flight is a win."

"Congratulations, Greg. Look what happens when you stand up to the old man. Some day you might be running this department, and I'll be able to say I knew you when."

"You'd better get out of here and pack a bag. And don't forget your spikes and glove."

Slats took his advice and headed home to catch a few winks. Hopefully tomorrow, he'd catch more than that.

WARREN FRIEDMAN

Chapter 21

April 25, 2013

The Cubs were at home after playing two road series in seven days. They split the two games against the Atlanta Braves and won one of three from the Florida Marlins. This brought their overall record to 6-12, tied for fifth place in the National League Central. Only the hapless Pittsburgh Pirates, at 3-15, were worse.

The only thing good about this road trip was there had been no more murders.

The task force was still looking for leads from the first three murders and the botched attack as they braced themselves for the Cubs return. Superintendent Randle addressed the troops.

"I think we should assume the statistician—what's your name?"

"Jablonski," the Cubs employee stated.

"Jablonski may have been correct. The Cubs lost the first game in each opening game of their away series against the Braves and Marlins, yet there was no attack or murder reported matching our slasher's M.O. We have to assume until proven otherwise that the murders are targeted for home games only. This means we'll have our hands full this week, men. The Cubs will be home for two series before heading to Milwaukee. Jablonski, do you have something to add?"

"There are over 2,500 players who have worn the Cubs uniform, and in this city of three million people, there are over 155,000 people in Chicago that have the last name of a Cubs ballplayer. From what I've been told, we have about 13,500 officers on the police force in Chicago, which means that at any given time there are about 6,700 off duty, 6,700 on duty, and out of that number about 4,000 patrolling the streets."

"So what Jablonski is trying to say," Randle interrupted, "is that a stakeout of people with a Cubs name is impossible. We are trying to identify potential victims, but each officer would be responsible for almost forty citizens. And that's assuming patrolmen had no other duties, which is not the case. The reality is, gentlemen, we have an imposing task. We've made progress, but we're going to have to narrow our potential victims list down a hell of a lot more if we plan on catching this killer. Okay, anything else?"

Grodsky raised his hand, a cell phone plastered to his ear.

"Uh huh, yep, okay. Thanks, Charlie," Slats turned his attention to his boss. "Chief, we're tracking down a lead as we speak. Last week Lydia Bosley told us she received hang-up calls days before her violent assault. Phone records revealed eight calls of less than fifteen seconds in length from an unknown number over a three-month period. The phone company has finished triangulating the last call and mapped it for the location of the cell phone. Detective Brainard called and said squad cars are on their way to the location right now. This could be the break we are looking for."

"Why weren't we notified of this? I thought we were sharing information," growled Randle.

"Trying to be a hero again, Grodsky?" said Greg Stiffle.

"I thought this was a team, not an association of rogue operators," added Cliff Zeigler, addressing the force.

"Typical Grodsky. He steals credit from the task force as easy as he steals someone's girlfriend," said an angry Kenny Usher.

Grodsky held up us his hands for attention. "Terrific. I've heard from my ex-partners, anyone else? Look, I'm sorry, I thought Brainard called it in, and he may have thought I called it in. I'm on the team; I'm not looking to be a hero, okay, Greg? The task force can take full credit if this pans out. And Kenny, let's keep our personal life out of this, okay?"

Grumbles swept through the room.

As squad cars raced to the location, the group waited for a report. Several cast frowns in Grodsky's directions and shook their heads. He didn't care what they thought. He would do whatever it took to catch this killer, even stepping on a few toes.

Nearly ten minutes passed when the call came in to Superintendent Randle, who was pacing in the hallway.

"Yes, I see. Thank you, officers. Good work," praised Randle, returning to the conference room.

"False alarm. Turns out the cell phone belonged to Lydia Bosley's eighty-four-year-old senile cousin, who called her a few times by mistake then hung up. The phone calls were displayed in the call history. That's it. Meeting's over. Let's get back out there. Grodsky, you stay here. Everyone else—dismissed!"

If anyone looked at Grodsky with disdain, he didn't notice, for his eyes were looking down at the table. When the room was cleared, Randle pulled up a chair next to him and spoke in a hushed tone.

"Look, what you did, that was a good piece of detective work. Everyone in this room missed it, and they are the cream of the crop. I know you're trying to win back their respect, but it blew up in your face. You have got to work with the group, not against it, whether the information was accidentally omitted or not. When you sneeze, I want to hear about it. Thanks to your little stunt, I'll be doing damage control for the next few days covering your ass because, from what I saw, not many in this room want to work with you right now. And Grodsky, this will be the last time I get your back. Do I make myself clear?"

"Crystal, sir. It won't happen again."

"Fine. That's the end of it. Go on. Get out of my sight."

Slats had been around long enough to know that with this bunch of cops, this was not going to be the end of it.

Just last week, Grodsky thought he had "it" back. And he did. Unfortunately, the "it" started with "sh."

Chapter 22

April 26, 2013

Slats was at his Chicago Lawn District station desk when the call came.

"Paybacks are a bitch, aren't they?" said the caller.

Grodsky looked at the phone then put it back to his ear. "Who is this?"

"It's Rocky."

"Sorry, Rocky. Didn't recognize you."

"Hey, I'm calling to let you know about the latest living victim and the task force meeting."

"Another living victim. That's good, I guess. What meeting?"

"The one you obviously didn't get a call to attend today. You pissed off a lot of guys down here, Slats, going on your own with the cell phone thing. Zeigler's been in charge of notifying the group, and he conveniently left your name off the list. Don't worry though; Randle laid into him about it. He won't pull that again. Randle told me to fill you in. Got a moment?"

"Sure. Go ahead, Rocky." Slats took out his notebook.

"Cubs beat the Padres yesterday, but I'm sure you know that. Bottom line, the statistician got it right. Cubs lose, victim dies; Cubs win, victim lives. This guy is blackmailing the Cubs for wins."

"It's the only thing that makes sense."

Rocky added the obvious, "Lydia Bosley was damn lucky when her niece came over. The Cubs lost that game; she was supposed to die. The guy blew it."

Slats noticed the other clue.

"The guy? So the perp's male?"

"According to yesterday's victim, Eric Chance. Lives at 795 North Sutton Place. Chance was drugged but definitely remembers a man's voice. He says the guy was five ten, two hundred pounds, and wore a mask to hide his face and gloves. He was waiting for Chance behind the apartment door and clubbed him on the head. Chance was tied up when he came to. That's all he can remember, but that's pretty good stuff."

"North Sutton Place. That's about five minutes from my apartment."

"You live in the Eighth? That's Matt Jasper's district. Anyway, the rest pretty much follows the same script we've seen: no prints, no witnesses, Cubs hat on victim, first game of a series, victim drugged and tied up watching the game, yada, yada, yada. When the Cubs won, the perp told the guy it was his lucky day and left. Walked right out the front door, leaving the guy tied up."

"Did the task force talk about anything else?"

"Yah, one more thing. It should be obvious that if we want to keep people alive, the Cubs need to win their first game of every series. We are going to try to get the support of Major League Baseball, the other clubs, and the umpires to make sure that it happens. Randle has designated me and Greg Stiffle as the point persons for two separate delegations. Stiffle is going to Major League Baseball's front office in New York to discuss our dilemma with the commissioner and whoever's in charge of the umpires. My group will be working with the Cubs to let the players and execs know what's at stake, what we're up against, and to see how we can work with their organization to win, upgrade the talent, things like that. Since you've met with Hellsome already, I placed you on my team."

"You realize you're talking about fixing games. The last time that happened was also in Chicago, and it didn't work out too well."

Slats was referring, of course, to the Chicago Black Sox scandal of 1919 when eight players admitted to throwing the World Series to the Cincinnati Reds.

"Yah, I know," Rocky continued. "It's gonna be tough getting baseball to back us on this. It's 11:30 a.m. We have an appointment with Hellsome at 2:30 p.m., after which we'll have to address the players. How about meeting at Wrigley at, say, 2:15 sharp? Bring Charlie."

"Charlie won't be able to make it. He's in court."

Charlie Brainard, the lead officer in the Marathon Gas Station beating case, was finally listening to the sentencing of the thug convicted of the crime.

Slats's cell vibrated. It was Tex Perryman. The call went to voice mail, as did all of Perryman's calls since their last meeting. Things were bad enough within the task force for Slats. If anyone found out he had talked to Perryman at the time he broke the original story, Slats would be run out of town.

"See you there, Rocky."

There was one person, however, Slats did want to call. He had not talked to Julie since she started cooking classes at Le Cordon Bleu College of Culinary Arts three days ago. Slats called her on speed dial. Strange, he thought, that it was no longer necessary to memorize phone numbers, yet his head was filled with phone numbers and other trivial facts from the past. He knew, for example, that the penny whistle was the name of the instrument used in the theme song of the *Titanic,* but had no idea what Julie's number was. Or that Ryne Sandberg was the MVP of the National League in 1984, batting .314 with 200 hits, 19 home runs, 19 triples, 114 runs, but didn't know his daughter's phone number either. With the advent of computer and cell technology, many people, including Slats, were learning where to get the information rather than learning the information.

Grodsky got her answering machine.

"Hi, Julie, it's Slats. Calling to see how you're enjoying culinary school. Notice I didn't say, 'What's cooking, Julie?' Anyway, I know our schedules have been crazy, and we've been missing each other lately, so I was hoping maybe we could hook up later if you're free. I know you love my stories, so I'll be happy to tell you about Merkle's Boner. Give me a call. Miss you."

Julie enjoyed being in Slats's company, and wanted him, but didn't need him. She was fiercely independent. This pained him because it was exactly those same traits that caused his divorce. Now, after years of therapy, years of learning how to be a partner instead of being apart, he was dating the mirror image of his former self. Slats decided he was going to ask his therapist for a partial refund.

Slats got to Wrigley Field in time to find Rocky waiting for him by the ticket window with another familiar face.

180

"Hello, Edgar," said Slats.

"Good to see you again, Officer Grodsky. Do you have a new partner?"

"No, Charlie's busy today. This is Rocky Parma. Rocky, Edgar."

"Good meeting you, Edgar. We're here to see Mr. Hellsome."

"Yes, sir. You're on my list. Right this way."

"How old are you, Edgar?" Slats inquired as they walked toward the offices.

"Seventy-four years young, Officer Grodsky."

"And they didn't make you retire?"

"No, sir. Matter of fact, they got some ushers in this place even older than me. 'Course, they got to sit down on a stool the whole game now. But we're all part of the folklore of Wrigley, as much as that ivy on the outfield wall. They gonna let us work here 'til we die."

"Let's hope you see a championship before that happens, Edgar."

"Maybe this season; team's looking pretty good."

Within a few minutes, the two detectives found themselves outside the owner's office.

Elaine, Rance Hellsome's secretary, also recognized Slats.

"Mr. Hellsome is waiting for you. I'll take you in."

Elaine held open the office door. As Slats and Rocky walked in, Hellsome was looking out his window at the field and motioned for the two to join him.

"Quite a sight, isn't it, gentlemen? I get a thrill every time I look out at it. Of course, it would be better if we were winning."

"Well, sir," said Rocky Parma, "that's actually why we're here."

"It's the murders, isn't it?"

Slats spoke. "I think we should sit down. It's time we told you everything we know."

* * *

Until now the owner of the Cubs knew only what the press had published besides the sliver of information he had gleaned from the first meeting with Brainard and Grodsky a few weeks earlier. At that time, he recalled, there were two murders and a few facts about the names and the caps. For the next half-hour Grodsky and Parma took Hellsome through the entire case start to finish, with every last detail, including the police pilgrimage to Major League Baseball's New York offices.

Hellsome, stunned at this news, slumped dumbfounded in his chair. The men sat silently for a few minutes as the owner tried to assimilate what he had been told.

Rocky and Slats looked at each other as Hellsome punched a button on the phone and said, "Elaine, ask Mark and Franklin to come to my office immediately, please?"

As they waited for Mark Schwartz, the president of baseball operations, and Franklin Izant, the Cubs general manager, to arrive, Hellsome looked at the detectives.

"We have no time to lose. My executives will handle upgrading the talent. I'll get on the phone with the commissioner and see where we stand with his office. I'll be honest with you. I'd be surprised if his office helps us. The integrity of the game is of the utmost importance, not only to him, but to all of us."

Hellsome looked at his watch. It was a few minutes past 3:00 p.m.

"The players should be arriving about now. I'll have Edgar escort you to the locker room to meet with Cahill and his coaching staff; I want you to explain the situation to them. I'll let my manager know you're coming. I'll be down when I'm done speaking to the commissioner. I want to be with my team when Cahill breaks the news."

"Of course," they said in tandem.

* * *

As Grodsky and Parma were leaving the office, they passed the two Cubs executives who had been summoned. As they left the office, they heard Hellsome say, "Fellas, call your families and tell them you won't be home for dinner. . ."

Edgar and the detectives meandered to the bowels of the stadium and into the small yet modernized locker room.

"Manager Cahill, this is Officer Parma and Officer Grodsky from the CPD," introduced Edgar.

"Rance said you were coming. Please, in my office."

Manager Doug Cahill peeked into the locker room looking for his assistant coaches.

"Hey, rook," Cahill shouted at rookie David Sampson, the starting right fielder for the team, "round up the assistant coaches and get them in my office ASAP. Also, I want to know the minute all the players have arrived."

As Sampson took off, Slats walked around the locker room for a few minutes, gazing at its décor. He was astonished at its simplicity and size.

"I'll bet some of the guys on the club have had larger locker rooms in the minors."

"True," Cahill responded as all the assistant coaches began filing into his office, "but when they get to Wrigley, they understand the link this ballpark provides between the past and present, both with players and fans. It's a privilege and a responsibility they don't take lightly."

"I'm glad to hear you say that, because that's never going to be more tested than now," said Rocky, closing the door behind the last assistant coach.

The detectives took turns filling in the coaching staff with what was to befall them. The ten-minute, closed-door meeting was interrupted by Sampson knocking on the glass door, mouthing the words that the players were all here.

"Let's get this over with," the morose manager said, pointing to the locker room.

Cahill and his staff entered the locker room. Slats and Rocky followed, taking positions at the back of the room.

Cahill whistled. "Listen up. Everyone take a seat by your locker. I want complete silence and no screwing around."

The players complied, sensing a major announcement. When the manager assembled the troop together hours before a game, the news was generally a proclamation of a trade or a death in the Cubs family. None of them were prepared for what they were about to hear.

"What I am about to say is for your ears only. It is not to leave this room. If I find out you have discussed this with anyone—wives, girlfriends, buddies, your mother even—I will Super Glue and pine tar your ass to the bench."

Cahill looked his players in the eyes. He had their full attention. Rance Hellsome entered the room quietly and stood behind his manager, who continued to speak.

"Almost every single time I've stepped onto a baseball diamond, from little league to the pros, I've enjoyed being part of this game. We all do. That is one of the bonds that tie us. I said almost every single time, because there are days when the joy of playing this game is temporarily taken from us, when playing baseball seems insignificantly small compared to a death in the family, or tragic world events. September 11 was one such time; the earthquake during the World Series between the Athletics and Giants in 1989 was another. Still, we go out and play this game, even with a heavy heart, in the hope we can help someone heal in some small way."

Cahill, heart pounding and voice weakening, paused. He was visibly fighting for his composure.

"Today we have learned that we must play baseball under circumstances that no other player has ever had to deal with. The police have informed us that on the opening game of each home series we play, a man breaks into the residence of a person here in Chicago. What happens to these people when they're abducted is classified. The bottom line is this: When we win, the victim lives. When we lose, the person dies."

Silence. Shock. The players looked at each other.

"Is this a joke?" someone asked.

"Skip, we're six and thirteen," whispered one of the stunned players. "How many people have died?"

Cahill took a deep breath. "We're one and four in opening games. Three people have died so far. It should have been four, but the guy botched one attempt. Men, we have twenty-one more home series on our schedule to play. Hopefully, the police will catch this guy. But until that time, it is paramount that we win the opener of those series. I'm not going to lie to you; we do not have the luxury of losing. For this squad, this organization, these games have truly become life and death. The Chicago police are asking for everyone's cooperation: the umpires to call the games in our favor and the opposing team to make an error or bad pitch at a critical moment. Representatives of the Chicago police force are in New York and are having discussions with the commissioner's office as well as the umpires about fixing these games."

"Fixing games?" one player moaned. "We can't do that."

"I know. It's extreme, it's something we all despise, but people are dying," the coach said.

The rookie Sampson said, "I don't want to win on some trumped-up call."

"Look, the police have put in their request. It's not likely the league and the umpires are going to rig games. So it is our burden, our charge, to win. This may dictate changing personnel on the roster, which will unfortunately affect some of you on this ball club. We hope the police will catch this guy before he kills again. But if not—I'm not going to kid you—every one of those opening series games is going to be extraordinarily intense. Someone is going to live or die because you struck out or walked a batter. If anyone in this locker room is not up to this challenge, I need to know. We will give you some time to think about this, and I will talk with each of you individually to get your thoughts."

Cahill looked to the detectives, coaches, and Hellsome.

"Does anyone have more to add?" No one stepped forward. "If not, I'll see you guys on the field. Let's make it two in a row today."

The players remained in their metal folding chairs in front of their lockers, not knowing what to say. Matt Bailey, one of the team captains, finally dragged himself out of his chair to speak.

"Guys, we know what we have to do. We're going to have to be mentally and physically sharp. We're going to require rest and relaxation, sleep, and no distractions in our personal lives. As captain, I'm going to ask that we all follow the same curfews we followed in spring training. I want everyone in here four hours before game time, and no clubbing after the games; go straight home after every game until this is resolved."

Nick Cade, one of the co-captains, agreed and weighed in. "Let's increase our fielding reps, batting reps, spend more time in the weight room, work more on our communication on the field for cut-offs and infield plays. Whatever it takes to get better, let's do it; and let's do it as a team."

"Man, I didn't sign up for this shit," exclaimed pitcher Cameron Fox in disgust.

"Shut up, man. How do you think I feel?" worried backup first baseman Vinnie Thompson. "Some asshole killed somebody because I grounded into a double play in the opener."

The previously harmonious squad was quickly becoming unglued. The quiet locker room erupted.

Heads whipped around as a cat call whistle from Doug Cahill, now standing on a chair.

"Shut the fuck up! This is how you're acting? After two minutes? Are you kidding me? Fox, in my office. The rest of you, get out there and take it out on San Diego."

Rocky Parma and Slats Grodsky exchanged looks.

"How are we going to keep people alive with that shit going on?" Parma said.

"Inside or outside the locker room?" Slats retorted.

Chapter 23

Bermuda Love Triangle

Tuesday, January 27, 1998

"Officer Grodsky? I'm your escort to New Castle," said Billy Osborne, a patrolman with the New Castle, Delaware, police force. "We're more than happy to oblige your department. It'll only take us about thirty-five minutes, straight south down I-95."

"How fast is it if you have your siren on and lights flashing?" Slats asked.

"Will the extra few minutes make a difference, sir?

"No, my arrival will be a surprise, so I suppose not."

The squad car entered the freeway and, with lights flashing but siren off, was soon up to a comfortable cruising speed of eighty-five miles per hour.

"Ever been down here before?" asked Osborne.

"Not really. Sorry to admit. Been to New York a few times, DC, and Baltimore, but not to Philly or Delaware, except maybe driving through it. You from the area?"

"Yah, born and raised in Dover. Got my BS degree at Delaware State University; lived at home. Shit, I even work near home. Is it weird that I've lived within a fifty-mile radius my entire life?"

"No," said Slats. "I lead a similar life in Chicago."

Slats phone rang. It was Stiffle.

"Hey, Slats. Nothing in Robbins's past remotely tied to automobiles, from a dealership to a junkyard, and anything in-between. He's an expert at renting them, though."

"Thanks," Slats answered. "I'm on my way to New Castle now. I'll get back to you."

Slats had hoped Robbins had remarkable acumen in cars and the ability to rig a car to cause an accident. He was wrong.

"So where are we headed on campus?" asked the Delaware cop.

"Not sure, really. The Cubs tryout is somewhere on campus, but in this weather, I doubt they'd be outdoors."

The average temperature for Delaware in January was forty-three degrees. Today's high registered at the Philadelphia Airport was thirty-three degrees, and the rain hadn't stopped since Slats landed.

"Wilson Field is where the baseball team plays, but it's too wet and cold to be out there today. I'm sure they'll be at Pratt Gymnasium. They have an indoor batting cage and room to do sprints and agility drills."

Soon they were on the Wilmington College campus driving past the empty baseball field. Officer Osborne drove to Pratt Gym and parked his vehicle.

"I'd appreciate it if you'd accompany me inside," requested Grodsky to his driver.

"Sure."

They entered the building and followed the squeaking tennis shoe sounds of the MLB hopefuls to the main gym.

"Over there," Grodsky said to Osborne, recognizing Joey Robbins from pictures he had seen.

Making their way to the other end of the gym, dodging ballplayers and baseballs, they came to a stop next to Joey Robbins, who was timing players as they ran sprints and typing journal entrees into his laptop.

"Good job, Hanks. You too, Conroe."

"Joey Robbins?" Slats raised his voice.

"That's me," Robbins said without looking up from his computer. "You're late. Get a key for a locker from Sam Leary over there. Report back here when you're dressed, stretched, and ready to go."

"Sorry," continued Slats. "I'm about fourteen years past my prime. But I am here to see you."

Robbins lifted his head and noticed Slats and the uniformed policeman.

"I'm kinda busy, fellas. Anything important? Did I park in the wrong spot? I can have my car moved if that's the problem."

Osborne stood with arms folded across his chest.

"Actually," stated Slats, "what we need to discuss is going to require quite a bit of time."

Joey Robbins was starting to pay more attention although he was pretending that he wasn't, Slats thought.

"Can you guys come back around seven? We'll be done evaluating most of the guys by then. I can't take a break right now."

"Well, I'm afraid you'll have to," Slats interrupted, flipping out his badge, "because you need to come with us."

Robbins stopped his computer entries.

"You're not getting it. I can't leave. My boss is the Chicago Cubs. I'm conducting tryouts for our minor league system. I have a million things to watch for. I'm their top scout. A couple of these players could be a major leaguer one day."

Grodsky persevered.

"I am a scout of sorts myself, only my players end up in the pen. And I don't mean the bullpen."

Robbins now looked scared, and the two cops sensed it.

"I need to talk to you about the disappearance of Didi Lecate and the accident involving her boyfriend, Bruno Discenzo."

Slats watched closely for a response. He thought he saw a slight twitch of the lips, a small widening of the eyes.

"What could that possibly have to do with me? I don't even know them," Robbins said.

"You don't know Didi Lecate and Bruno Discenzo?" Grodsky persisted.

"Everyone in Chicago has heard of Bruno Discenzo."

"What about Didi Lecate?"

"Lecate?" Robbins shook his head.

Slats made a tsk sound. "First lie, Mr. Robbins. You can come with us to New Castle headquarters on your own volition, or I can handcuff you and haul you away in front of all these recruits. It's entirely your choice."

Robbins closed his computer and stared at the two cops for a few seconds. Slats knew what was running through Robbins's mind, what runs through any perp's mind: how do I get out of this?

"Sam," Robbins shouted to another scout. "Take over for a while. Something has come up, and I need to talk to these officers. Run the rest of the drills and log the results into my computer for me, will ya?"

Slats whispered to Osborne. "Do you have an IT guy at your HQ?"

"Absolutely. If he's not there, I can do whatever you need. My minor was IT in college, so I can find what you're looking for if it's there."

"Sorry," Grodsky said to Robbins. "We're going to need your computer as well."

Joey Robbins tried to argue with them, but in the end, Joey and his computer came along.

"Do me a favor, Billy," Slats said to his fellow officer as they escorted Robbins out of the gym. "Call ahead to New Castle HQ and book us an interview room."

The ride was short and soon Robbins was in a private cross-examination room with the standard two-way mirror. Grodsky, Billy Osborne, and the New Castle police chief peered at him through the glass.

Grodsky turned to his two fellow officers before entering the room to interrogate a fidgety Joey Robbins. "This should be short. We had this guy checked out back home. He's clean as a whistle. He should roll in no time at all."

Slats entered the room and walked up to Joey, who was sitting in the plain room, on a plain chair, behind a plain desk.

"Normally, I'd dance with you for a while, but I haven't got the time. All hell is about to break loose back in Chicago, Joey, and I'm afraid it's your fault. So, I'll get right to the point. I have no idea how a guy with a great job, great wife and kids, who has won the love and respect of family, friends, and coworkers, could possibly get caught up with Bruno Discenzo, the most notorious hit man this side of the Mississippi. In your own words, Joey, tell me what happened?"

Robbins, still in shock, tried playing the denial card. "I don't know what you're talking about. None of this is making sense. Maybe someone gave you wrong information and is setting me up, you know, to take the heat off of them."

"Cut the crap, Joey. Most of the punks that end up in this room are career criminals, and I know that's not the case with you. Something is different; something doesn't add up. So help me understand, and I'll make sure to stand up for you at your trial."

"Honest, I'm a scout for the Chicago Cubs, I don't know . . ."

"Didi gave you up, Joey."

Slats was bullshitting him, of course, but since it worked with hardened criminals he was sure it would succeed with Robbins, who was simply the wrong guy at the wrong time.

"What?"

"Don't try to be coy with me, Robbins. We have your prints all over Bruno's staircase . . ."

"I can explain that."

Slats plowed on. "Prints in his house and prints in his cars. You've been identified escorting Ms. Lecate into restaurants. According to your fellow scouts, you were missing for three days from the winter meetings, important meetings, Joey. Oh, and did I mention the semen stains on Didi's jeans skirt? Wonder if it'll match your . . ."

"Oh my God, oh my God," declared Robbins. "Yes, I had an affair with Didi Lecate, okay? My wife doesn't know. It's the first time I did anything wrong in my life. I lied because I'm so ashamed. You would too if you didn't want your wife to know. But since when is it a crime to have an affair with a beautiful girl?"

"Do you think Didi loves you, Joey? Is that it? Because she gave you up a few hours ago. How does it feel to be the fall guy in a murder?"

Joey jumped at the word "murder."

"Officer Grodsky," a voice thundered over the PA in the room, "could you step outside for a moment?"

"I'll be right back." Slats left Robbins alone.

"What's up?" Slats asked.

Osborne smiled. "Robbins wiped the search engine on his laptop clean by deleting temporary files, history, and cookies, but the IT guy was able to duplicate it from the hard drive.

Robbins searched the Internet for ways to create a car accident. Quite a coincidence, isn't it?"

"Billy, can you do me one more favor? Book another seat for my flight to Chicago. I'm going to be taking Robbins back with me and booking him as a co-conspirator in Bruno Discenzo's murder. Extradition won't be a problem, will it?"

"No problem. I know the state officer in Dover. I'll expedite the paperwork for you. As for the flight, I'll call the airlines myself. Continental Airlines, right?"

Slats nodded and then reentered the interrogation room where Joey Robbins awaited.

"I think I need to see a lawyer," Robbins declared.

"No, I *know* you'll need to see a lawyer. We just lifted incriminating searches off your computer's hard drive, Joey. The kind of information that will make a jury go 'aha'. Come out to the hallway. You can use the phone there. You'll want your lawyer to meet you in Chicago because that's where I'm taking you."

"But the tryouts—the Cubs—my family—what'll they say?"

"Didi screwed you twice, Joey, so to speak."

"That goddamn bitch. She was blackmailing me."

"I think you're going to want your lawyer present."

Robbins, realizing his entire life's work and family life were about to go down the drain, hung his head and cried. Between the tears, he vomited in the wastebasket. After Slats gave him tissue to wipe himself clean, he began filling in the blanks for Slats. What he was doing in Bermuda. How he came to Bruno's attention and how Bruno threatened him and his family. How he had to babysit for Didi during Bruno's business trip to Chicago. How she used her body as well as her threats to get him to do anything for her, even murder. Lastly, how he researched rigging the brake and steering system to fail, how he worked on Bruno's limo in the cloak of darkness while it was parked in a so-called security zone at the airport, and how he paid off the night watchman to let him into the lot.

When he was finished, Officer Osborne came in, read Robbins his Miranda rights, and then led him to a cell. Others in the department worked on the extradition papers so Grodsky and Robbins could make the evening flight back to Chicago.

"Poor guy," Osborne said. "I'll give you ten-to-one odds he dies in the joint within two years. If Don Maravelli's arms are as long as you say they are, there will be no jail in this country that will keep Robbins safe.

"Fewer than that if we don't keep him in isolation."

Slats placed a couple of calls while the New Castle police worked on Robbins's papers. One was to Greg Stiffle, and one was to Chief Pearson.

By 6:20 p.m., Slats and Robbins were at the airport gate. It was dinner time. Slats had one last call to make, and he knew where Mark Anthony Maravelli was dining.

"Biatelli's Ristorante, are you making a reservation?" said the voice on the other end of the phone.

"I need to speak to Mark Anthony."

"I'm sorry, sir, he's in a meeting."

"Tell him it's Slats Grodsky. He's gonna want to hear what I have to say."

"One moment, sir."

197

Nearly two minutes went by until Slats heard another voice on the phone, the one he was hoping to hear.

"Officer Grodsky, this is Mark Anthony. I'm listening."

Chapter 24

Bermuda Love Triangle

Friday, January 30, 1998

Slats was working on a report at his desk at Eighth District headquarters when the command center began to stir. He looked up to see six men in suits and overcoats heading his way. Officers in the room cleared a path for the visiting party, which fanned out in front of his desk. Recognizing the man in the middle of the cluster, Slats slowly rose from his chair. The man, clad in a full-length beige cashmere coat, was Damarco Maravelli.

"Officer Grodsky."

"Don Maravelli, it's good to see you. Please have a seat."

Maravelli looked from the old rickety wooden chair to Slats and waited.

Noticing the Don's disapproval, Slats motioned to Stiffle, who quickly wheeled a leather chair over to Grodsky's desk.

Damarco Maravelli sat while the others remained standing, surrounding him; two facing Slats and three facing the other officers in the room who had stopped working to watch the spectacle.

The Don spoke.

"I cannot tell you how grateful I am that you found the *assassino* that murdered Bruno, Eddie, and Fredo. Bruno was my *fratello, my buoni amici*. Mark Anthony told me how you were concerned that we might choose to blame the Aroletti family for Bruno's murder and retaliate. Though I assure you that was never the case. But had such an event taken place . . ." he shrugged his shoulders. "You have saved numerous lives. For your concern for both my family and the Aroletti family, I am eternally grateful."

"We still have unfinished business, Don Maravelli. We have not found Didi Lecate. She seems to have disappeared."

"Yes," the Don said, as if he knew something Grodsky didn't. "I am aware that she has vanished."

The Don stood and walked around Slats's desk to where Slats was now standing as well. Damarco placed his arm around him and whispered into his ear.

"I swear to you, on my father and mother's grave, on my children's lives, and on my children's children's lives, that as long as I live, as long as YOU live, I am forever in your debt. I do not know how or when, but someday, I will repay you for what you have done for the Maravellis."

The Don bowed his head to Slats then turned and left the building, once again surrounded by his men.

Still standing, Slats was absolutely speechless, as were the other officers in the room.

Greg hurried over to Grodsky.

"Well, what did he say to you?"

"I'm not exactly sure," Slats responded, wanting to keep the whispered words to himself. "It was all in Italian. It sounded friendly, though. Beautiful language, Italian is."

Commander Pearson, the one man missing at HQ during the Don's visit, entered the usually noisy room and found the silence unsettling and disturbing.

"Who died?" he blurted.

"No one, sir," someone in the room responded.

"Then get back to work, you cocksuckers."

The room once again filled with familiar clatter as the men picked up where they left off before the Don and his entourage had come calling.

"You're supposed to be protecting the city," Pearson continued to rant. "Who the fuck is going to protect anybody if it's not you? The mafia?"

While other officers and secretaries around him pushed papers and tried to look busy in front of the chief, all Slats could do was stand there, motionless and smiling.

Chapter 25

April 26, 2013

Cornelius Mayfield knew the points he wanted to make to his fellow umpires. He knew the order of priority. He knew the areas of vulnerability. He also knew that he was prepared to change his views almost instantly. In fact, he wasn't quite sure what he believed. All he knew for sure was what he had been told by the Chicago police and the baseball commissioner in the commissioner's office. And he wasn't pleased.

Mayfield had been promoted to vice president of umpiring by William Calabrese III, commissioner of baseball, two seasons ago, and had worn the mask for twenty-three before that. A burly man with the bulk to argue eye-to-eye with the protein-enhanced behemoths of the modern game, he was respected by his peers, the players, and the owners as a solid professional, the kind of umpire who was essential to the game. If his eye-hand coordination hadn't been acute enough to let him play the sport he loved, at least his eyes were good enough to earn a reputation as the master of the strike zone. All agreed that Ted Williams would have deferred to his calls.

With a heavy heart, Mayfield began.

"This conference call will be called to order, but I must inform you that there will be no record that we have talked. No notes are to be taken, no minutes will be prepared, no report will be issued, and unless compelled to testify under oath, we are all to deny that we have discussed today's topic. Any questions?"

A voice filtered through the speakerphone.

"Fine, Conny, but can you fill us in a bit on why we are not having the meeting we only appear to be having? I mean, you've got the eight national league crew chiefs assembled on two hour's notice using some special secure lines hired by a fictitious outfit, Carling Enterprises, and we all have games we need to prepare for. So, what's going on? Is this related to negotiations on our contract, the players' association agreement, contraction, the All-Star game assignments, or what?"

"Let me try to explain. And when I finish, I am afraid we can't really have a discussion. But you need to know what I expect from each of you. We are talking about more than balls and strikes, fair or foul, safe or out."

When Mayfield completed his short summary of the recent events in Chicago, there was total silence. There had been no need for him to preempt discussion because his normally verbose colleagues had been rendered speechless. They needed time to digest the impact of what they had learned. After all, what could they say after hearing about the three game-related murders, one attempted murder, one kidnapping and release, the plea for help from the police, and most alarming, the role they were about to play in this unfolding saga.

Mayfield cleared his throat and continued, "We have the full support and resources of the commissioner's office on this. I hope you'll join me in praying there will be a quick resolution to these murders, a prayer for the police, a prayer for the victims, and a prayer that we are doing the right thing as well. That's it, gentlemen. Let's go play ball."

Mayfield turned to Commissioner Calabrese, Detective Stiffle, and the rest of his party who were listening to the call. Calabrese, sensing Mayfield's discomfort, tried to reassure him.

"Corny, I know you're opposed to this decision, but as I told you in my office, once the murderer is caught, these games will be replayed if the schedule allows, or expunged if it does not. We will not allow fixed games to count in the standings."

"And as I told you in your office, sir, how will you explain this to the bettors that lose money on these games in Vegas, or to the millions of fantasy baseball owners who have collective millions riding on these games? How will you explain it to Pete Rose, or the grandchildren of the Black Sox that fixing games are tolerable under certain circumstances? No sir, as promised, I will preside over my crews during the crisis, but when this sordid business comes to a conclusion, you will have my resignation on your desk."

"Corny . . ." Calabrese said, but Mayfield was already storming out of the room. The commissioner sighed, interlocked his hands behind his neck, and stared at the ceiling. Detective Stiffle placed his hand on Calabese's shoulder.

"When he thinks it through, he'll be okay. Commissioner, for what it's worth, I'm truly sorry we have put you in this situation. We don't know what else to do, to be honest with you."

"It wasn't you who saddled us with this predicament, officer; it was the murderer. We must always remember where to lay the blame. In the meantime, our office has done all it can, detective. The umpire crews working the first game of a Cubs home series will have a wider strike zone when the Cubs are at bat, and a close call on the bases might go in the Cubs favor.

205

My staff is in touch with the other ball clubs playing at Wrigley this year, and we're working on acceptable baseball solutions for them."

"Acceptable baseball solutions?"

"Well, we have given the other clubs a number of options. We've asked that they alter their pitching rotation so the Cubs won't see the best pitchers. Perhaps their best hitter will have a minor injury and be scratched from the lineup that day. Maybe the catcher will let the Cub's hitters know what pitch is being called. It's a lot easier to hit when you know what pitch is coming. Outfielders might accidentally miss their cutoff men to allow a Cubs runner to advance. Those are the variables we're looking at."

"And they can do that without tipping it off to the public?"

"Look, our men are ballplayers and umpires, not actors. Let's hope they can pull it off."

The commissioner's secretary interrupted the men.

"Mr. Calabrese, the owner of the Mets is on line one."

"And so it begins. I'm sorry. I must take his call. If there's nothing else?"

The detectives shook their head.

"Good luck, gentlemen. Let's pray you apprehend this man as soon as possible."

When the commissioner left the conference room, Stiffle turned to the group that made the New York trip.

"Anyone feel good about this?"

Not a word was said as they headed for the airport for the return flight to Chicago.

WARREN FRIEDMAN

Chapter 26

Bermuda Love Triangle

Tuesday, January 27, 1998

"Okay, guys. Everybody in," said Sam Leary, who had taken over the tryout when Joey Robbins left the building with the police.

Most major league clubs sent scouts to one large combine, where team representatives watched and evaluated talent. The Cubs were one of the few major league teams to hold their own, private, open tryouts, as many as twenty in some years, for major league hopefuls. Many of them were set up by Joey Robbins. Today's tryout, at Wilmington College, was a convenient site for ballplayers to access from Richmond, Virginia; Philadelphia; Washington, DC; Baltimore; New York; New Jersey; and, of course, the large state of Delaware.

Leary continued, "Today, we had a chance to assess your abilities. We timed your speed in the sprints; watched the pitchers throw their pitches and gunned their speed; gauged the arms of catchers, infielders, and outfielders as they threw to the designated bases; and saw you hit in the cages. I have a file on each of you; what your strengths are and what we feel you need to work on to get an invitation from a big league club. I will give you a copy of this report so you know where you stand."

Leary looked at the young men as they nervously awaited their name to be called. He pushed on.

"Make no mistake about it. There are some talented ballers in this gym. I appreciate the commitment you all made to get here today. I want to thank you for coming. But at this time, we are only able to offer one of you an invitation to the Cubs. Pedro Gonzalez, congratulations."

So many downcast faces as first, but then the group began to applaud for Gonzalez.

"Pedro, come see me after we're done. To the rest of you, read our report. Take it to heart. Work on your weaknesses, but don't forget to keep enhancing your strengths as well. If you are serious and remain dedicated, if you improve on the areas we mentioned in your report, major league baseball will find a spot for you. It's an old cliché, but it still holds true. The cream always rises to the top. Thanks again for coming, boys. Good luck."

The boys, tired from the paces they were put through, tired from the crashing adrenaline rush, and now disappointed from the comments from Leary, lined up for their reports before exiting the gym.

"Excuse me, Mr. Leary?" a young man inquired.

"Yes?"

"I'm Billy Conroe."

"Good job today, Conroe. You're one of the few players I believe has a shot at making a club. Let's see," he said, looking up Billy's report. "Here you are. You need to bulk up a little, maybe another ten to fifteen pounds. Get a little stronger. Make it all muscle. It won't hurt your speed or range. But it'll help your arm strength and bat speed a lot. If you do that, you'll have a better shot."

"I was to report to Joey Robbins. He said he had a spot for me in the rookie league."

"He said that, huh?"

"Yes, sir. So you see if you could get him on the phone . . ."

"Sorry, kid. Maybe you were in the cages at the time, but you're obviously unaware that Joey Robbins left here with the police. I'm not sure what happened, exactly. Don't know if someone died or if he had unpaid parking tickets. What I do know is I haven't been able to contact him for the last four hours."

"Well, what am I supposed to do?" Conroe asked. "I drove here from Omaha for this shot."

"Wow. That's real dedication, young man. I'll add that to my report. How far is that?"

"It's twelve hundred miles. Twenty hours of straight driving time. I had to do it over three days though, because my car ain't in the best shape."

"That's unbelievable. When Joey calls, I'll discuss it with him. In the meantime, stick around town if you need to, or go home, boy, start lifting weights. I'm sorry. I don't know what else to tell you right now."

* * *

As Leary turned away to gather his gear, Billy Conroe couldn't believe this was happening.

Having gone through the paces of an eight-hour tryout, Billy was dog tired and hungry. Driving off campus, he pulled off the South Dupont Highway and into the parking lot of the

SDH Bar and Grill. The cheeseburger and fries were delightfully greasy, blending well with the thirty-two ounce, $2.50 draft beer special. Since refills were only $2.00, Billy hydrated with three more before calling it a day.

Grabbing quarters in his pocket, Billy called his dad from the pay phone in the bar foyer.

"Dad, it's Billy."

"Hey, rookie, how was your first step toward the majors today?" Loren's smiling voice came across the line. Loren had told his son that his pal Joey would take care of him, as promised.

"Dad, he wasn't there at the end of the tryout. The scout I talked to said Mr. Robbins was hauled off by the police for some unknown reason, and the other scout didn't know anything about me. I don't get it, Dad. I thought it was a done deal."

"Son of a bitch!" screamed Billy's dad. "I don't believe this! Billy, look, I'll find out what happened. I'm sure Joey will clear up this misunderstanding with the cops and the tryout and make things right. I'll get in touch with him. Son, go back to the motel and wait for my call, okay?"

"Okay, Dad. Talk to you later."

Staggering slightly to his car, Billy was glad his Econo Lodge Motel was only two miles down the road. All he craved at this point was to go to bed and put the most disappointing day of his life behind him.

Chapter 27

April 26, 2013

Slats got to the Old Town Tavern in time for Julie's evening shift. It had been days since he'd seen her, and he longed for her. Since his divorce, Slats had spent the last six years distancing himself from emotional ties, but he was drawn to Julie like a moth to a flame. He hadn't felt this way since courting his ex-wife in college. Was it the sex? The fifteen-year age difference? Had she sparked some primitive need of belongingness? Did it really matter why? She had awakened a part of his life that had been comatose, and he was enjoying the renaissance.

Looking out the window, sipping his Diet Pepsi, he noticed Julie jaywalking across the street approaching the restaurant. Out of nowhere a pickup truck sped by, obstructing Slats's view. When it passed, she was gone. Did it hit her? Leaping from his seat, Slats bolted to the front door. He discovered Julie wasn't in a hit-and-run accident or the recipient of the pickup's front grill; instead, she was on the receiving end of a handsome young man's lips. It turned out the only casualty was Slats, the victim of a hit-and-run heart.

"Thanks for walking me to work," she told the good-looking young man.

"My pleasure, mademoiselle. I'll see you Thursday," he answered back.

Julie turned to enter the tavern and saw Slats standing at the front door.

"Hi, handsome. Have you been standing there long?"

Slats instinctively reached for his phone and showed it to Julie.

"Long enough. I stopped by to see you but got a call. Gotta run to the station."

"You know, whatever you saw, that wasn't what it . . ."

"Julie, it's okay, you don't owe me an explanation. Hey, I'm late. I'll call you," he said, quickly sprinting around the corner on his aching knees.

"Grodsky, goddamn it, get back here," she shouted, but to no avail.

* * *

Julie entered the tavern.

"Hey, honey," greeted Ricky from behind the bar. "Did you see Slats? He left without paying for his Pepsi."

"Uh-huh. He saw me kissing my gay cooking instructor good-bye in front of the restaurant, then ran off like a little kid."

Julie hung up her coat in the back room, then came back to the bar.

"Ricky, Slats has been coming here for years. Do you know what happened to him?

"What do you mean?"

"Don't play innocent with me. Why'd he start drinking? What happened between him and his wife? He won't talk about it with me. He shields his past better than a stealth fighter hides from radar."

"Don't know if it's my story to tell, Julie. If he doesn't want to talk about it, you should leave it at that."

"Come on, Ricky, maybe if I understood where he's been, I could help him a little. For instance, what parents name their kid Slats?"

"No one. That's not his real name. It's an acronym from his drinking days. I gave it to him. Gotta be at least ten years ago. I didn't know his name at the time. He showed up every day and drank the same thing in the same order: **S**toly with a **L**ime, followed by an **A**mstel beer, then a **T**equila **S**our. Get it? **SLATS**. I made it up so I could remember what to serve him. One day, a few detectives came in looking for Detective Grodsky and asked me if I had seen him. 'Oh, you mean Slats!' I said. That nickname permeated through the police department. No one knows his real name anymore, which was—say, I never did know his real name. Anyway, he sobered up that time, but started drinking again before and after his divorce. That's when he hit bottom."

"Well, that's a start. Maybe I can learn more with a trip through time."

"How so?" Ricky wanted to know.

"I'll look up some old articles on the computer. His partner told me Slats was Chicago's Top Cop twenty years ago. His name must have been in the papers. Or remember that fella he met here a couple of weeks ago? Slats said he was a reporter. Tex something or other. I heard the guy making a joke about a B.L.T. I'll look into that. I want to learn more about him."

"You know what they say. Be careful what you wish for. It might come true."

"Meaning?"

"Meaning what if you find out something you didn't want to know?"

"I guess we'll see, won't we?"

Julie couldn't wait 'til tomorrow, excited about starting her detective career in the morning.

Chapter 28

April 27, 2013

Julie opened her laptop and began her quest for newspaper articles. Her search engine quickly directed her to newspaperarchives.com, a comprehensive list of thousands of articles from a vast array of newspapers. She paid the nominal fee for entry to the site and began searching Chicago papers. Typing in the letters "BLT" shed clarity on a previously fuzzy subject.

"Ah, Bermuda Love Triangle," she murmured and began an hour-long journey into the dark story of Bruno Discenzo, Joey Robbins, Didi Lecate, and the detective who solved the murder and prevented a mafia war, Detective Grodsky.

"He was a frickin' hero," she said out loud. "You had life by the short hairs. What went wrong?" She dug on.

Most of the *Chicago Daily News* articles covering the BLT were written by Tex Perryman. Julie changed the search from "web" to "images" and typed "Tex Perryman" in the search line. The screen loaded thumbnail pictures of the man who lunched with Slats at the Old Town Tavern. She scribbled his name on a sheet of paper. If anyone knew the scoop on Slats, it would be Perryman.

Continuing to scroll through the journals, she stopped to read a story from 2003. Grodsky was working the Rogers Park

District when 911 calls came streaming in. Someone with a rifle was on a shooting spree in the Loyola University Student Union.

Grodsky was the first officer on the scene. Students and faculty were fleeing the building. Most were uninjured, but a few were tending to bleeding wounds. Entering from the West Loyola Ave entrance, he found three students bleeding and crying for help at the top of the stairs, felled by gunfire as they attempted to exit the building. Grodsky assured the students help was on the way. One of the students was shot in the leg, bleeding profusely from a leaking femoral artery. Grodsky used his own belt as a tourniquet to stop the bleeding and save the student's life. Leaving the young man in the care of fellow students, he entered the lobby and saw the assailant standing alone by the south entrance of the student union. White, early twenties, wearing a hooded sweatshirt, jeans, and combat boots, he carried an AK-47 assault rifle with enough ammo for a few hundred kills.

Grodsky placed his back against a support pillar and checked the chambers of his outmatched .38 DA/SA Smith and Wesson special to assure he was fully loaded. First in his graduating class in weaponry and sharpshooting, he maintained that lofty position through semi-annual shoot-out competitions. Now, in this precarious situation, he prayed his accuracy would make up for what he lacked in firepower. Peeking around the corner, the hooded attacker was reaching for another cartridge to reload. Taking a deep breath and cocking the hammer on his pistol, he stepped into the open and, with a two-handed grip, unloaded his six-gun on the assassin. Five of the bullets hit their mark, ending the student union carnage. Officers and emergency medical crews quickly followed, taking twenty-eight shooting victims to the hospital, eleven of which were eventually transferred to the city morgue.

Grodsky was hailed as a hero, saving not only the life of the bleeding student he encountered, but countless more, by taking out the shooter before additional lives were lost. The next few weeks found stories of his heroism in newspapers across the country, as well as *Newsweek* and *Time* magazines. Reporters camped outside the Rogers Park Precinct, hoping to interview the Toast of Chicago. Most did, as Grodsky was accommodating to all requests. He even appeared on *Nightline,* ABC's half-hour nightly television newscast.

It wasn't until the final autopsy reports were filed a few weeks after the shootings that Grodsky's world began to unravel. One of the dead was a two-year-old girl, shot in her mother's arms. Stumbling upon the screams of those fleeing the building as she walked on the courtyard path behind the student union, the mom attempted to run for cover, away from the student union's southern entrance where the man was standing. The single bullet that pierced the child was fired from a .38 special revolver. The only .38 special fired that day was in the hands of Officer Grodsky. The one round from Grodsky's gun that had missed the assailant inadvertently ricocheted off a metal door frame and landed in the infant's chest cavity.

Despite the revelations brought about by the autopsy report, Grodsky was still a hero in the eyes of a grateful Chicago. The press labeled the child as a victim of friendly fire, whose blood was on the hands of the rampaging murderer, not Grodsky. Further attempts to interview Grodsky, however, were rebuffed by the officer, and over time the story eventually faded.

Julie pushed herself away from the computer. Unable to ebb the flow of tears, she heaved uncontrollably as she wept for her friend and lover. Ricky was right when he talked of being careful what you wished for. She regretted investigating Slats's past.

How would she face him knowing this information; information that Slats had gone to great lengths to hide? One look into her eyes might reveal her awareness, an innocence gone forever. Should she confront him and make him face the truth, or should she leave his ghosts in the past?

Unquestionably, she had uncovered the source of Slats's pain, known previously only to those close to him. Tex Perryman was surely one, as was ex-wife Julie. Most of the officers Slats worked with in those years had either retired from the force or moved away, leaving Slats in an environment of unsympathetic cops who only knew his existence as an alcoholic or as a recovering alcoholic.

Closing the door on his personal life and his heart allowed Slats to be less vulnerable and to maintain his sanity and sobriety. The last time Julie had seen Slats, however, he ran from her like a humiliated schoolboy. Had she unknowingly opened the door? Was he more susceptible to demons from his past? It appeared to Julie that he was, albeit ten years later, still reeling from the anguish inflicted from that lone stray bullet. No, she would bottle her knowledge, throwing it into the sea of despair, hoping that one day, as he walked the sands of isolation, he'd find it, open it, and reveal to her the man he used to be.

Julie was also uncomfortable that she had discovered his real name. A name few people around him knew. A name no one called him. A name he avoided like the plague. A name that linked him to a time he perceived as darker, shameful days. This, too, would be her secret.

Chapter 29

April 30, 2013

Playing with more determination and a refined sense of purpose, the Cubs won all four games of the San Diego series, improving their record to 10-12. No one in the organization could guess how the team would respond under pressure, knowing that a life lay in the balance. To that end, the front office sought to acquire battle-tested, major league veterans. Optimism for the team's immediate future increased as General Manager Franklin Izant acquired left-handed power pitcher Manny Garcia from the Houston Astros. Garcia, 18-11 last year for a team with a losing record, had a 3.24 ERA, logged 210 innings, and recorded 203 strikeouts. Garcia, who joined the club before yesterday's game, was penciled into tonight's lineup card as the starting pitcher. After his team's lackluster start, Izant was following through on his promise to do everything within his power to make this year's team more competitive and hinted that he had even more changes in store. Little did anyone know these changes were born from the impetus of a murderer more than from management's true sense of commitment to their fans.

Tonight's 7:00 p.m. game was against the Arizona Diamondbacks, losers of four straight ballgames. A Cubs sweep of the three game series could vault the team into sole possession of fourth place in the Central Division. Winning three games in a row gave the team confidence that they could compete. Playing a team on a losing streak added to their self-assurance.

Having the commissioner, umpires, and opposing team in their back pocket was their insurance policy, at least for tonight.

Following the direction of co-captains Cade and Bailey, the players arrived at Wrigley early for their pregame rituals. Garcia, tonight's pitcher, was going through his usual Pilates stretches. Tony Damato ate exactly twelve honey mustard barbeque wings. Utility infielder Jake Uhl smoked a Cuban cigar in his car in the parking lot, listening to Crosby, Stills and Nash on his Nano iPod. Mike Garrett played Spider Solitaire on his laptop. Each player, in his own way, was getting ready for the game.

"Hey, rook, where's the Krispy Kremes?" asked Duncan O'Neill. Each year a rookie was the designated "Donut Man," whose duty was to pick up two dozen donuts for the team before every game. This year's honor belonged to David Sampson. Over the course of a 162-game season, this amounted to almost $2,000 worth of donuts, a paltry figure compared to Sampson's $414,000 minimum salary.

"Bring me a chocolate-covered glaze," yelled Vinnie Thompson from the trainer's table.

To Manager Doug Cahill's ears, the boys seemed loose. Too loose. He would have to put a stop to that, he thought. Cahill walked the full length of the locker room, down and back, before offering his feelings.

"Don't think because you have the blessing of the league that you can walk onto the field tonight and beat the Diamondbacks. If you play without a 110 percent effort, you'll be wrong. Dead wrong. You need to play this game tonight with a sense of urgency. If you make three or four errors, even the umpires won't be able to save your back end. Somewhere in this town tonight, a man is going to be holding someone hostage, threatening to kill them. That person will be terrified, unable to know what we know about the outcome of tonight's game. Let's jump out to an early lead. If the game is close in the last inning or two, if we screw up, things could go wrong. Do not, I repeat, do not let that happen. Someone is unwillingly putting his or her life in your hands tonight. Major league baseball is putting its reputation and credibility on the line for you as well. We will not let them down. I want to see good at bats up there tonight. Infielders, watch that ball into your gloves, make your throws, make sure you've got your signs down pat, and get the outfielders throwing to the correct base. Outfielders, hit your cut-off men. Tonight's battery, get the scouting report on Arizona's hitters and make sure you're on the same page as to how you're going to pitch them."

Cahill grabbed a pumpkin seed from his jacket, cracked it, and spit out the shell before continuing. "Anyone treating this like an exhibition game will be made an example of, I promise you. Do I make myself clear?"

A few of the men answered, "Yes, sir."

Raising his voice an extra few decibels, Cahill let loose. "I said do I make myself clear?"

"Yes, sir!" everyone responded in unison.

"That's better. Now let's go get 'em."

The players ran down the tunnel to the dugout and out onto the field for calisthenics and practice. The Cubs, as usual, took the field first, an hour before the visitors. Assembling at home plate before beginning practice, the players decided to say a prayer for the person they labeled "The PIC of the day." PIC was an acronym which stood for The **P**risoner **I**n **C**hicago.

* * *

Tonight's PIC was Audrey Anson of 2995 West Pierce Avenue, seven miles from the ballpark. A pharmacy technician, she left Walgreens on West Belmont Avenue after her 9:00 a.m. to 3:00 p.m. shift and headed to her step class around the corner at XSport Fitness Gym on North Central Avenue. The pretty, red-haired, thirty-one-year-old single female had joined the gym in January to fulfill a New Year's resolution, which was to lose the fifteen pounds that had attached itself to her butt, belly, and thighs over the last few years. Four months and seventy classes later, the transformation was complete, validated by her new wardrobe and male groupies at the gym. Audrey, though, had a secondary goal—Steve Abel, her step class instructor. Steve, a ruggedly handsome forty-plus ex-athlete, juggled his time between the $25 per class job as a step instructor and his $325,000 law practice. Now divorced, Steve had Audrey in his sights as well.

"Good class today, Steve," Audrey offered as she toweled off, walking past his podium in front of the class.

"Thanks. You know, with that new body of yours, you might need an escort home. There's a killer on the loose, you know."

"What makes you think I didn't drive here?" Audrey asked. "Besides, how do I know you're not the killer?"

"I saw you walking down West Belmont on my way to the gym."

"So you're not a killer; you're a stalker?"

"I'll tell you what. Let me take you home, and if I kill you, I promise XSport Fitness will give you a full refund on your gym membership."

"How can I refuse that deal? How 'bout I take a quick shower and meet you in the front in fifteen minutes?"

"Wow, a girl who can get ready in fifteen minutes. You're looking more like a real keeper. See you soon."

True to her word, she met Steve in the lobby within her self-imposed time frame.

"Love your car," Audrey said as the two walked toward a hunter green Corvette.

"Thanks. So where to?"

"Do you know where Humboldt Park is?"

He nodded.

"Good. Go south on North Cicero then east on West North Avenue. Turn right when you see Dunkin Donuts, then left on West Pierce. I'm the first small brick bungalow on the right. The address is 3012. It's about five miles, okay?"

"Well, all right then."

After navigating through the twenty-minute drive, Steve pulled up in front of Audrey's home.

"Wanna come in?" Audrey inquired.

"Boy, I'd love to, but I've got to pick my son up from my ex-wife's house. If I'm late, she punishes me by not letting me see him. Can I have a rain check, say, next week after class?"

"Sure. Next week it is," she said, exiting the Corvette. She leaned back into the window, revealing more than cleavage.

"I'm gonna hold you to it. In the meantime, thanks for the protection."

Steve bit on his finger and growled in anticipation of next week's date as he motored off, soliciting a laugh out of Audrey.

She turned, headed up the sidewalk, gym bag in hand. She entered her house through the front entrance into a darkened living room. As the door closed behind her, she leaned over to turn the switch on her table lamp.

An arm suddenly grabbed her across the waist from behind, pulling her in tightly against a powerful body; the other hand covered her mouth. Terrified, Audrey squirmed and struggled to free herself but was up against a much stronger force. Though unable to see her attacker, the mirror on the other side of the room revealed a masked man.

"Stop fighting me or trust me, I'll hurt you," the voice from behind said.

As she relented to his tight grip, he loosened his hold around her waist for an instant. A few seconds later, a needle pierced her deltoid muscle.

"There you go, Audrey. You're so pretty. I was hoping we could have some fun before the game, but we're running late. You'll be falling asleep for a while, but when you wake up, we'll watch the Cubs game, okay? While you were exercising, I got everything ready in the den. Let's head over there, shall we?"

* * *

On his way to pick up his son, Steve Abel couldn't stop thinking about Audrey. "What an idiot I am! How could I drive away from that?" Scolding himself, he quickly circled the Corvette around the block and found an open parking spot in front of her house. He would have to explain to his ex-wife that he was stuck in traffic and would be about a half-hour late to pick up his son. He locked the car and headed up the sidewalk to the concrete front steps.

As Steve was about to knock on the wooden door, his phone rang.

"Dad, where are you?" said Steve's son, crying. "Mom's having a bird. I thought you were taking me to the Cubs game?"

"That's tonight? Oh my God, I'm sorry, son. I forgot the game was tonight. I'm running a little late, but I'll be there in twenty minutes. Tell your mom I'm on my way."

Steve sheepishly turned and ran back to his car, hoping Audrey had not seen him through the window. Whether she did or didn't, however, he'd call tomorrow to explain.

* * *

Both Audrey and her captor heard the screen door open and squeak, alerting them to someone's presence at the front door. They froze halfway to the den. Audrey's body stiffened as she tried to scream. The man behind her slapped a hand over her mouth.

They waited.

When the unexpected visitor turned around and left, the kidnapper returned to his routine of tying his rapidly weakening victim to a wooden dining room chair. The midazolam injected a few minutes ago was now working its way into Audrey's bloodstream. The man ran the edge of the hunting knife across her breasts, down one leg and up the other. At this point, he knew she was unsure of reality, drifting from twilight to deep sleep, where she would remain until the seventh inning.

The television station began its broadcast of the game.

"Good evening sports fans and welcome to Wrigley Field, where your Chicago Cubs meet the Arizona Diamondbacks in the twenty-third game of the 2013 season. This National League

broadcast is brought to you by WGN, Chicago's Official Summer Baseball Station. Tonight's game pits two teams heading in opposite directions. The Cubs have won four straight, while Arizona has lost four straight. I'm sure Chicago fans are hoping to see both streaks hit five. We've got a beautiful night for a baseball game. Game-time temperature is sixty-eight degrees. So sit back, relax, and get ready for Chicago Cubs baseball."

As the dog on the commercial was getting his owner a cold beer from the refrigerator, the masked intruder cut a hair on Audrey's head to test the sharpness of his knife. His quest was to propel the Cubs to become World Series champions, only killing when he was forced to by a Cubs loss. The blood of his victims, he believed, was on the Cubs and their organization, not him. He was rooting for the Cubbies and hoped he would not have to kill Audrey. But as the game began, he told the drugged Audrey, "It's out of my hands now."

* * *

Across town at the same time, another man's fate was also out of his hands.

"It's about time you called me back. What are you, twelve years old?" Julie asked Slats.

"Emotionally, maybe I am. Look, I'm sorry, Julie. I got your message and your explanation about your cooking instructor. I don't know what to say. I'm a shit."

"No, you will have to do better than that. You're so closed off, Slats, and I always give you a pass on it. But no more. I won't accept your apology until you tell me what you were feeling."

"This is hard for me, Jules. I haven't let anybody in for so long, I forgot what it was like to care about someone. But I care about you—a lot. I didn't want to throw my heart back out there only to have it crushed again. When I saw you kissing that guy, I was jealous, and guess I overreacted to the situation. Now I know the truth. My heart is . . ."

"Where are you?"

"Look out your window."

Julie pulled back the blinds to see Slats standing on the curb, looking up at her.

She walked over to the intercom and pressed the buzzer to let him in.

When Slats reached the top stairs of the third-floor walk-up, Julie was waiting at her door.

"I've missed you," she said.

"I've missed you, too."

Awkwardness held the two apart, until Julie spoke.

"So, you were going to tell me about Merkle's Boner," Julie said, looking down at Grodsky's crotch. "Is that some sort of code name for it? Or should I be calling him Mr. Merkle?"

"No, Merkle's Boner was a baseball play in the . . . oh, never mind."

They embraced, locking lips gently while moving inside the apartment. Tender turned titillating as Julie unbuttoned his shirt. He pulled her camisole over her head, throwing it onto the floor. Julie unbuckled his belt and pulled him toward the bedroom with it. She pushed him to the edge of the bed and removed his shoes, allowing his pants to fall to the ground.

Watching her step out of her jeans and before she could pounce on him, Slats grabbed the cable remote and turned the Cubs game on.

"Mmmmm, how romantic," Julie purred, now sitting on Slats as he lay in a supine position.

"Research," he smiled.

She reached behind her back, unsnapped her bra, and threw it onto the TV.

"Research these," she said.

* * *

It was not until the seventh inning that the first controversial play occurred. Max Neyland, the Cubs play-by-play announcer, was calling the game.

"The score is five to nothing Cubs, top of the seventh. Garcia has been masterful tonight up until this inning. He retired seventeen of the first eighteen batters he faced. And the lone hitter before this inning reached base on a blooper to the opposite field. Garcia may be tiring, however, giving up back-to-back singles and a walk to the first three hitters in the seventh. Righty Clark Nelson and lefty Steve Camp are up and throwing in the Chicago bullpen. Coming to the plate with no one out is cleanup hitter Jorge Ramirez, a lifetime .385 hitter with the bases juiced. Outfield is deep and straight away. Garcia looks in for the sign. Here's the windup, and the pitch is outside ball one. Recapping, the Cubs took command of this game in the fourth when they scored five runs in the inning as eight hitters made it to the plate, the final blow being a three-run, bases-clearing home run by left fielder Nick Cade."

Ben Fair added his usual color.

"That shot travelled 455 feet down the left field line, almost hitting the 460 sign on the rooftop across the street. I mean, it got out of here like a bullet."

"Here's the next pitch to Ramirez. It's over the outside corner of the plate for a strike. That one hummed in at ninety-four miles per hour."

"Garcia's ball isn't moving as much as it did in the earlier innings, and that's why he's suddenly hittable," added Fair. "Another sign he's getting tired."

"Bailey's calling for a fastball inside. Let's see what Garcia does with the pitch. Here it comes. Ramirez sends a grounder into the hole. Carrasquillo dives to his left and spears it. He hops back to his feet, his only play is to first, and he's safe. No! The umpire calls Ramirez out! Wow. The Cubs got a break on that one. We'll see it on the replay, but it sure looked as if he was safe at first."

"Oh, yah, he took a full step past the bag before Garrett even got the ball. Ramirez is going nuts. He's in ump Leland Farinacci's face."

"Here comes the D'Backs manager Skippy Henson onto the field, and he's absolutely livid! A few of the D'Backs have come out to drag Ramirez back to the dugout, but he'll have none of it. And there it is. Farinacci just tossed Ramirez out of the game. Now Henson's getting the thumb as well. Holy cow!"

The television was temporarily muted by the gloved hand in the den.

The melee on the field had piqued the curiosity of the man watching the game with Audrey Anson.

"Tell me, sweetheart, what's going on over at Wrigley? You don't think the umps are trying to help the Cubs, do you? Trust me; no one blows a call that bad!"

231

The question was rhetorical, for Audrey was ill-equipped to answer any question at this point in her revival. Still glassy-eyed and not much of a baseball fan, she knew little of the intricacies of the sport. She was not even clear-headed enough to be fully aware of the terror confronting her. The binds of the rope were tight, as was the gag in her mouth, yet she showed no signs of a struggle against them.

"Trust me, I'm keeping my eye on you," her assailant yelled at the television as he paced back and forth.

He picked up a pillow and threw it, breaking a dish on the living room buffet table.

"A lot more than dishes are going to be damaged. If you start fucking with me, you're going to be fucking with them," he screamed, pointing at Audrey.

The game continued without incident, and though the D'Backs made it close by scoring three more runs, the Cubs prevailed 6-4.

"Sorry about your broken plate, Audrey," the masked man said to the now wide-awake, wide-eyed captive.

"Can you understand what I'm saying?" he asked her.

She nodded.

"Tell them I'm onto them. The umps better stop blowing the calls. Tell them not to fuck with me. Got it?"

Again, she nodded.

With that, he stole into the night, leaving Audrey tied to her chair.

Chapter 30

May 1, 2013

Slats was at the firing range with Charlie when his phone vibrated. Even when not necessary, he found himself using the vibrating option on his cell phone more often. He had long since lost the higher frequencies, partly from aging, partly from listening to Led Zeppelin through Koss headphones, and partly from the 153 decibels generated from his S&W .38 revolver in the firing range. Despite wearing headsets or ear plugs on the range, most cops had a partial hearing loss after thirty years on the job. At least that's what they told their wives when not responding to requests of folding the laundry as they watched a ballgame.

"Got a call," he yelled to Charlie as he pointed to his cell. "I'll meet you outside."

It was Chief Randle. Grodsky returned the call from his car. That way, he could eat his lunch while listening. When the chief was finished talking, Grodsky grilled his boss similar to the tuna sandwich he was eating.

"The girl is fine? Good. And they're sure about the name? Okay. Can we narrow down the potential victims from that? Who was the guy in the Corvette anyway? Oh, I see. Well, thank God, the Cubs did their job. Right. You got it."

Brainard finished shooting and found his partner in the parking lot.

"Who called you?"

"Randle," Slats answered, staring out into space.

"Well?"

"Sorry, Charlie."

"If that's some sort of reference to your Starkist tuna sandwich . . ."

"What? Oh, the old commercial. Ha! No. Randle was filling me in on the latest abduction in the Twenty-fifth District."

Grodsky thumbed through the notes he made during the conversation with Randle.

"Let's see. Girl's name is Audrey Anson. Found when she didn't show up for work at Walgreens and didn't answer the phone. Neighbor was her emergency contact. She had a key to the Anson house. She saw a guy drop her off around dinnertime. Turned out to be her aerobics instructor who had the hots for her. His alibi checked out. All the usual evidence on this: Cubs cap, drugged with midazolam, tied to a chair to watch the game, has a name of a past Cub, first game of a home series, Cubs won, she's alive. But get this—we have a new clue. Every street name is the name of an ex-major leaguer. Rogers, Rice, Post, Nelson, Sutton, and Pierce. Jablonski from the Cubs confirmed it. He is certain there is significance to the street number, but he hasn't figured it out yet."

"Wow," Brainard said. "Can the names be matched up by computer, you know—Cubs-named victims living on streets with ex-major leaguer's names?"

"I asked Randle the same thing, and he said it can, but the list is too large to be helpful. There're about forty thousand combinations."

"Why don't we send out flyers to the forty thousand and tell them not to be home during the first game of a home series?" Brainard asked.

"Actually, Charlie, that was brought up by the task force, but it was vetoed. A few of the guys were for it, but most were against it, including me. What if the murderer is one of the names on that list? Maybe he planned it that way. Then he'd be alerted to what we are doing. Second, many of our addresses are old, and up to one fourth of the list may have moved. Also, and perhaps most significantly, once the killer finds out what we're up to, he could simply move his kidnappings to another day, or on away games. He's playing a game with us, and we are slowly figuring it out. We are getting closer to him, albeit one abduction at a time, and no one wants to have to start over by tipping our hand."

"Yah, I guess that makes sense," Brainard concurred.

"So Jablonski is soliciting help from his colleagues around the league to figure out what the address numbers mean. The first address was 512 North Rogers Street, and the victim was Ted Banks. Ernie Banks had 512 career home runs. No one thinks the street numbers and home run numbers are a coincidence, but they can't find a correlation with the other numbers from the other victims. Once they figure that out, we might get our potential victims list down into the hundreds instead of the thousands. Same thing with the ex-major leaguers' names and street names. Even when we figure that out, we still might be missing a vital clue."

"So, what do we do now, Slats?"

"Let's go view the tape of the girl's deposition when she was in the hospital."

"Where at?"

"Grand Central."

"Grand Central. Grand Central? Kenny Usher's district? Shit! Are you kidding me? Seriously? Slats, I really don't think . . ."

"Thanks for the concern, Charlie. It's okay. We've been in the same room together a few times now, and he's over it."

"Slats, he's far from over it. Last I heard if he'd have been on the firing range with you, he would have used you as the target."

"That's ridiculous. When did you hear that?"

"Yesterday."

"Oh."

"Well, I'll simply tell him I'm there to invoke step eight of my twelve-step program."

"Which is . . ."

"Make a list of all the people I have harmed, and be willing to make amends to them all."

"Do you mean it?"

"Sure. Why not?"

"Did you forget what went down between you two?"

How could Grodsky forget?

In 2011, Slats's low performance ratings, illnesses, sick days, and mysterious disappearances tried the patience of his partner of four years, Cliff Zeigler. The final blow leading to their irreversible incompatibility as partners developed over the fifty-dollar push-up bet. Slats was eventually transferred to the

Twenty-fifth District and unwillingly teamed with Kenny Usher. The same Kenny Usher who was Slats's childhood friend from elementary school through high school. The same Kenny Usher who was Slats's best friend, roommate, and fellow classmate at the University of Illinois Chicago. The same Kenny Usher who vowed to put a bullet in Grodsky's back if he ever saw him again.

Ten-year-old Slats and Kenny first met at a summer day camp in Deerfield, Illinois, and carried that friendship into high school, though they were fierce adversaries on the football gridiron. Both were straight A students as well as exceptional two-way football players for their high schools in the Central Suburban League; Grodsky at Niles West High School in Skokie and Usher at Highland Park High School. Forming a pact to push each other to become first-team all-league, the boys attended a three-day football camp in Urbana-Champaign on the University of Illinois campus the summer before their senior year. The camp was designed to increase the players' skills, but it was also a showcase for college coaches looking for the next Heisman Trophy candidate.

Both boys had terrific senior seasons and, true to their bond, ended their high school football careers as first-team all-league All-Stars, Slats on offense as a halfback and Kenny as a linebacker on defense. Despite success on the football field, Slats and Kenny had no desire to play ball in college. Kenny aspired to be a Marine; Slats longed to be a cop. The two argued the merits of each. Kenny wanted to see the world, help save oppressed people by toppling evil regimes, and serve his country. Slats wanted to know why Kenny wanted to save people who, in his opinion, hated America. Instead, he wished to serve the citizens of this country by keeping them safe. After months of debate, Slats convinced Kenny to delay entering the Marines for a year and room with him at UIC.

Though the young men lived in Chicago, each chose to live on campus for the full college experience. Rooming together on south campus in Thomas Beckham Hall, they even enrolled in the same classes so they could study together. At some point during freshman year, one of their classmates dubbed them "the twins." That friend was Julie Hanson, a freshman from Austin, Texas. Julie sat in front of the boys in geology, but by the middle of the year found herself sitting between them, garnering the attention of both. By the end of the year, other students were calling them "the triplets."

Kenny and Slats were crazy about Julie. At five feet seven and 110 pounds, Julie resembled a runway model. With sparkling blue eyes, straight, flowing blonde hair and incredible, mesmerizing good looks, Julie was the campus magnet; men were always attracted to her. Kenny and Slats became Julie's bodyguards, delighted to hone their police-type skills and ward off admirers and potential suitors.

Slats was gregarious and the life of any party, but inexplicably shy and insecure when alone in the presence of a woman. Kenny was exactly the opposite; more reserved in a crowd, but always the ladies' man. Though Julie loved them both, Julie slowly gravitated to Kenny's wit and charm. Recognizing the dynamic involved, Slats took a backseat in the threesome's relationship. Quietly suffering as he watched his best friend fall in love with the girl of his dreams, Slats sought solace in his studies, making it his goal to graduate in three years instead of four. Hanging out with Julie and Kenny was too painful to the soul. Mercifully, a fateful day in June changed their simpatico forever.

Slats was home, studying for his last final of the semester in biochemistry, when he heard pounding on the door. It was nearly one in the morning.

"Julie?" he said, opening the door. "What's wrong? Is Kenny okay?"

"Screw Kenny," Julie blurted, choking on her tears.

"Come in. What's going on?"

"When did you know? Why didn't you tell me?" she shouted.

"Tell you what? What are you talking about?"

"I'm talking about Kenny backpacking through Europe this summer and signing up for a study abroad program next fall in St. Petersburg, Russia. Russia!" she ranted, plopping down on the couch. Slats scurried to find Kleenex tissues for his best friend's girl.

"He's never so much as hinted a word about it," Julie said tearfully. "Never mentioned it to me. Not once. Don't pretend he didn't tell you. I know him. He tells you everything."

"I swear, I had no idea. Honest. He never told me either."

Slats paused.

"I will say this. Ever since Kenny and I first became friends, he talked of nothing else but joining the Marines so he could travel and see the world. This doesn't surprise me at all. I was the one who talked him into coming to UIC. Now leaving you, that surprises me."

Julie sniffed. "He lied to me. I don't feel I know him at all."

Slats sat next to Julie and handed her the tissues. She tried desperately to hold back the tears, but could not. As she sobbed, Slats moved closer and put his arms on her shoulders, turning her upper body toward him, sliding his hands down her arms to hold her hands.

"Listen, I know Kenny loves you. He probably didn't know how to tell you he wanted to leave, that's all. It's not as if he won't come back. I mean, it's only a four-month program, right?"

"No," she cried. "He's leaving after school's out. He'll be gone for seven months. I love him, you know? I don't want him to go. What if he finds somebody else?"

"He's not going to do that. You're the nicest, smartest, and prettiest girl in the world. Who could he find to compare with you?"

Julie, emotionally vulnerable, stared at Slats. Slats suspected Julie was beginning to put the pieces together, especially why he had stopped hanging around her and Kenny. He sought to diffuse the moment and divert her attention from him.

"When is he planning on leaving?" he asked.

"Friday."

"This Friday? In three days? Are you frickin' kidding me? Let me call him. Maybe I can talk some sense into him. I've done it before; I can do it again."

"No, he has to do what's in his heart. I'm not going to stand in his way if it's what he wants. I'm not going to be the bitch that won't let him live his life. I don't want him taking it out on me thirty years from now that I didn't let him go to Europe or Russia."

Julie was regaining her composure. The two friends sat on the couch for a minute, looking at each other in awkward silence.

"I'd better go,'" Julie said, breaking the stillness.

"Yah, I should finish memorizing my notes," Slats countered. "Got an eight o'clock final."

Slats walked her to the door and gave her a comforting, compassionate hug.

"It'll be all right, Julie. You'll see."

Still in his embrace, she looked into his eyes and kissed him on the cheek.

"Thanks. You're a good friend."

Julie turned and walked away.

He closed the door and said aloud, "I'm not so sure about that."

Completing his final exam the next morning, Slats decided to wait for Kenny to contact him. It was early Thursday morning when Kenny used his spare key, letting himself into Slats's bedroom, where he was still sleeping.

"Hey, buddy, you up?" Kenny inquired as he sat down on the bed.

"I am now."

"Did Julie tell you?"

Slats wiped the sleep from his eyes and sat up.

"A better question is why didn't you tell me?"

"Easy, Triple G."

"Huh?"

"Groggy Grouchy Grodsky. I'm sorry I didn't tell you, believe me. But you talked me out of joining the Marines to come here, and I figured you'd try to talk me out of leaving again. So I decided not to tell you 'til the last minute. I'm weak in your presence."

"And what about Julie?"

"She understands me. She knows I need to go. I don't want to have regrets in my life, and this has been eating at me for a long time. I can't be whole until I finish this journey. Julie will wait for me, and when I return, I'll be a better man and a better boyfriend. But that's another thing I need to talk to you about."

"What's that Kenny?"

"There are a lot of guys who are going to see Julie alone and try to pounce on her while I'm gone. You'd be doing me a big favor if you'd hang out with her—like a big brother."

"As a big brother? You know something, Kenny, I don't think that's a good idea. Why don't you graduate and then both you and Julie can travel the world. I don't think you want me to . . ."

"What are you afraid of, man? It's only seven months. Remember when we went to the Journey concert and I was puking my guts out afterward? Doesn't that seem as if it was yesterday?"

"Yah? So?"

"Well, that was over seven months ago. See, I'll be back before you know it. Please, I'm begging you."

"When are you leaving, tomorrow?" Slats asked, trying to change the subject.

"Changed my plans. I'm leaving this afternoon. I don't want a farewell party, you know? I don't want a long, drawn-out cry. Short and sweet. Less pain that way. So promise me you'll take care of her."

"I'll do my best, okay?"

"Cool. That's all I can ask. Look, I'm gonna book. You take care of yourself, too, okay? I know you want to graduate and all, but you need to get laid, too. I'll have Julie take care of it."

"Excuse me?"

"She's got tons of friends. I'm sure she knows someone who wants to hook up with you."

"Oh, yah, whatever."

Kenny stood up and headed for the door.

"You're a good friend, Triple G."

Just like that, Kenny was gone.

The triplets were left to their own devices for the summer. Slats enrolled for a full course load, Julie went home to Austin, and Kenny gallivanted across Europe. It wasn't until late August, when the fall semester began, that Julie and Slats reconnected. It was an uncomfortable meeting in the student bookstore.

Julie was talking to a girlfriend in a long queue, waiting to buy her books.

"Hey," Slats said.

"Hey," she replied coldly, before resuming her conversation with her girlfriend.

Slats continued walking, but upon seeing Julie, forgot what he had come for. He picked up a book in the corner of the store, pretending to be interested.

"You didn't call all summer."

He turned to see Julie standing behind him.

"I know. I'm sorry. I'm not good at long distance. I got wrapped up in school here, and the next thing you know it was fall."

She was not impressed with that explanation, so he pressed on.

"What do you hear from you know who?"

"Oh, he's having a great time, but it's rather expensive to call from Europe, so we talk once a week, on Sunday mornings. Texas and Illinois mornings. You?"

"Nope. Haven't talked to him all summer. Been pretty much a loner."

Julie softened her voice. "So what's going on here? Are you mad at me? Do you not want to be friends with me?"

"What? Of course not! I'm not mad at you. I had a heavy class load, that's all. Of course, I want to be friends with you. I mean, I'll never stop being your friend. I thought about you all the time."

"That's good," Julie smiled, "because you're taking me out to dinner tonight to make it up to me. Make it expensive. We'll catch up on the last three months."

"Sure," he answered. "That'll be great."

The two rekindled their friendship at the pizzeria, talking about summer and Kenny. Over the next few weeks, when they weren't in class, they were together, studying, frequenting museums, attending school sporting events, and working out at the gym.

One evening, watching a romantic comedy at the movie theater, Julie instinctively grabbed Slats hand during a tender scene and didn't let go. When they realized they were still holding hands long after the scene had passed, they looked at each other and knew what it meant without a word.

"Get a room," someone shouted while they embraced and kissed. Embarrassed, they left the theater and spent the rest of the evening in Julie's apartment, making hot, passionate love throughout the night.

Three months later, when Kenny returned from Russia, he arrived at Slats's apartment with a baseball bat. By then, Slats had changed the lock on his door.

"You backstabbing asshole!" Usher yelled as he beat away on the door. "You're dead, Grodsky, do you hear me?"

Slats was not in his apartment at the time; a neighbor filled him in on Kenny's threat. When Slats entered his apartment, he found Usher also had heaved a rock through the bedroom window, spewing glass over the bed and floor.

Julie eventually diffused the situation, taking full responsibility for their failed relationship, though she insisted Kenny do the same. His inability to communicate long distance, as well as his decision to leave in the first place, were the driving forces between the split, not Kenny's best friend.

Usher's friendship with Grodsky was over, that much was clear. The two never spoke again—until the police department's ill-fated attempt to pair them together in the Twenty-fifth

District over the Christmas holiday weekend, 2011. Though Usher did not put a bullet into Grodsky as promised, he refused to work or drive with Grodsky. He visited his captain daily with transfer papers, threatening to leave if Grodsky stayed. On the twelfth day of Christmas, Grodsky was transferred to Chicago Lawn to work with his current partner, Charlie Brainard.

As Grodsky pulled his car into the district parking lot, he noticed the baseball fields directly across the street in Hanson Park and wondered if Kenny still had his baseball bat.

"Can I help you?" the unfamiliar officer at the front desk asked Grodsky and Brainard.

"We're from the Chicago Cap Murder Task Force," Charlie answered. "We're here to see Detective Usher."

No one had actually labeled the task force or the murders 'til now, not even the press. But it was a name that stuck from that moment on.

"He's not here, but said if anyone from the task force should come by, I should give them this."

The officer reached into a drawer and pulled out a pile of CDs labeled "Audrey Anson" and gave them one of the copies.

"Thanks. Got a computer for us to view this?" Charlie asked.

The officer pointed to a vacant desk. "Knock yourself out."

The pair hurried over to load the CD. Watching intently, the detectives learned nothing new from the first video file of her statement. The second file, recorded two hours later, revealed a more composed Audrey Anson adding more substance to her statement.

"I know I said I thought he intended to rape me, and the doctors did find those red scratches on my chest and legs, but the more I play it back in my head, I'm not sure he meant that at all."

"Can you recall what he said, Miss Anson?" asked the district attorney.

"I think he said, now don't quote me on this, I was still foggy at the time. I think he said, fuck me—no, fuck them. I don't know who he was talking about. He was angry, that's for sure. Waving his knife at the TV."

"Do you know what upset him? Do you remember when he said it?" the DA inquired.

"No, I have no idea why he said it. But it must have happened late in the game if I remembered it, you know? I dunno. I was asleep most of the game 'til the last three or four innings. Something woke me up. A noise, glass, or a window breaking."

"Yes, you did have a broken plate in your dining room, Miss Anson. We found a pillow from your couch near it. That must be what you heard."

"Oh. Well, I'm sorry, that's all I can remember. I wish I could have seen more, heard more, but . . ."

The CD stopped.

"What do you make of that, Slats?"

Grodsky was sure it could only mean one thing.

"Shit. He knows."

"Huh?"

"Charlie, has Usher posted anything to the task force yet?"

Brainard checked his e-mail. There were no posts.

"Nothin' there."

"Okay, see if you can get him on the line. I'm going to call Randle to see if he received Audrey's updated testimony."

Both men left the building and placed their calls from the sidewalk. Moving in different directions for a few minutes, both returned to the precinct's front door as their calls ended.

"Usher didn't answer," Charlie said. "Left him a voice mail."

"Not surprised he didn't answer, Charlie. He knows you're my partner. Talked to Randle, though. He's going to call Stiffle, who's handling the Major League front office and the umps."

"I'm not sure that I'm following you, Slats."

"Look. Late in the game the umps blew a call at first. Remember? Our killer saw it and got pissed off. That's probably when Audrey heard him swearing and breaking the dish."

"So Cap Killer suspects major league baseball is protecting the Cubs?"

"I think so. Stiffle will stress to the league that the umps can't blow a call that blatantly, or it will cost us a life."

"But if the killer's intent is to have the Cubs win, what's the difference if they have a little help?"

"This jerk is evidently a purist. He wants the game played according to the rules—for the Cubs to win fair and square. He wants to be responsible for the Cubs playing at a higher level, not the league. One more obvious blown call by the umpires and our mystery man may take it out on his next victim. When that happens, the umps will back off and the Cubs will be on their own trying to save lives."

"Shit."

"You can say that again," confirmed Slats.

"Shit."

Chapter 31

May 17, 2013

Three more abductions occurred over the next fourteen days. There was Geraldine Jenkins, the sixty-nine-year-old retired school teacher, widowed at the age of twenty-four, never to remarry. David Hands, the fifty-year-old aluminum casting foundry worker, devoted husband and father of twin boys. And lastly, twenty-seven-year-old Shareta Collins, who graduated from the Loyola of Chicago School of Law less than a year ago and was a new hire at Steinberger, Wien and Evans, LLC. All three had two things in common. First, and most obvious, they were all held against their will by the same psychopath using the same M.O. Second, each kidnapping ended in a Chicago Cubs victory. Unfortunately, that is where the similarities ended, for each experienced a different ending to their ordeal.

Born in Baltimore, Maryland, Geraldine Jenkins was thirteen years old when her family moved to Washington, DC, in 1957. The teenager entered Anacostia High School six years after the Supreme Court's 1954 landmark decision in *Brown vs. Board of Education.* The Supreme Court found black schools, including those in Washington, DC, to be segregated, overcrowded, and lacking in adequate educational materials. The High Court stated that school segregation violated the Equal Protection and Due Process clauses of the Fourteenth Amendment. In 1955, the court ordered desegregation "with all deliberate speed." The demographics in Anacostia were changing from white to black in the '50s due to three events: construction of the Anacostia Freeway, creating a barrier that pinned the Anacostia neighborhood between the freeway and the Anacostia River; numerous public housing apartment projects built in the neighborhood; and white flight to the more affluent suburbs. Though the neighborhood was becoming predominantly black, the Supreme Court's ruling guaranteed an integrated learning environment in Anacostia High School. In this nurturing atmosphere, Geri, as her friends called her, became class valedictorian and earned a scholarship to the District of Columbia Teachers College.

In August 1963, Geri was one of a handful of Anacostia High School graduates invited to meet the Reverend Martin Luther King minutes before his "I Have A Dream" speech from the steps of the Lincoln Memorial. Among that group was her future husband, Pastor Jeremiah Jenkins, from Chicago, Illinois. Two years later, they were husband and wife, living in Chicago, preaching, teaching, and living a fulfilling life together in troubled times. In the spring of 1968, however, after the assassination of the Reverend King, riots broke out in the ghetto on Chicago's West Side. Reverend Jenkins, who had gone to the neighborhood to help diffuse the situation and calm the residents, lost his life attempting to save an elderly man from a burning building, three days before his wife's twenty-fourth birthday. Devastated by his death, Geri never remarried. Staying close to Jeremiah's family, she resumed her teaching career in Chicago until retiring in 2001.

When news of her abduction and subsequent release on May 3 became public, flowers and tributes accumulated on the front lawn of her home at 167 South Robinson Street from well-wishers touched by her story. Left alive because the Cubs had beaten the Houston Astros, Geri became a media favorite. Uncharacteristically, she embraced her fifteen minutes of fame. When her backstory came to light in the press and the corridors of City Hall, Geri received a key to the city soon after her recovery.

David Hands was born, ironically, August 28, 1963, the same fateful day that Geri and Jeremiah Jenkins met in DC at the Reverend King's speech. A lifelong Chicago resident, David was probably one of the few people in Chicago who could say he had never left the state of Illinois. The oldest of seven children, he dropped out of school at the age of sixteen to help support his family when his father died suddenly from a heart attack. When he turned eighteen, the foreman at the aluminum casting foundry, who was a close friend of the family, hired David at the plant. By his twenty-first birthday, David had taken his father's place on the line, and it soon became apparent to David why his father had died. His duties included maintaining the foundry furnace temperatures, feeding aluminum scrap into the furnace, and pouring molten aluminum into dies. The foundry was a hot, nonclimate-controlled building, where workers had to lift fifty- to seventy-five-pound bundles of aluminum repeatedly. If your family had a history of heart disease and you worked in the foundry, you weren't saving for retirement.

David worked at the foundry for thirty-two years but rarely took vacations or a day off. When he did, it was usually to go to his aunt's vacation property on Lake Michigan in Waukegan. As a child, his father used to take the family fishing on the shoreline. His dad used to say, "Give a man a fish, feed him for a day. Teach him how to fish, feed him for a lifetime." David heeded that advice and saved every penny with the intent of sending his children to college, giving them the gift of opportunity that was unavailable to him.

David Hands was bound, gagged, and drugged on May 9 during the first game of a series featuring the Cubs and the Los Angeles Dodgers. It was the same day his wife and children were visiting the college campuses of Indiana University and Butler University. Though the Cubs crushed the Dodgers 11-3 that evening, David became the fourth fatality of the Chicago Cap Murderer. His kidnapper did not check David's drug allergy history, which included midazolam. Suffering from anaphylactic shock, David died within minutes of the injection.

Shareta Collins was a legal prodigy. Her father was a district judge in the Northern District of Illinois; her mother lead counsel for Abbott Laboratories. While her childhood classmates brought frogs, watercolor pictures, and old coins to show and tell, Shareta brought gavels, judges' robes, and stenographs. Instead of reciting fairytales as an assignment, she delivered the Gettysburg Address verbatim or quoted closing arguments from specific cases of Clarence Darrow or Louis Brandeis. This loquacious child hit her stride in high school, winning the IHSA Debate Championship with her debate partner and gaining entrance into the National Honor Society. And though she never played upon her good looks, Shareta was crowned homecoming queen by her classmates. As an exclamation point to her high school career, Shareta won the coveted Banneker/Key Scholarship to the University of Maryland, which provided the full cost of tuition, mandatory fees, room and board, and a book allowance each year for four years. Only two students were chosen for this award each year. For Shareta, it was not enough to finish her law school career at Loyola summa cum laude; once again she graduated first in her class. Not unexpectedly, Miss Collins was highly sought-after by all the top law firms upon graduation. Steinberger, Wien and Evans, one of Chicago's oldest and most influential firms, managed to bring Shareta into its fold. It helped that her father started his profession in the same firm.

Sitting upright in her hospital bed, three days after the May 16 victory against the San Francisco Giants, three days after being held at knifepoint, three days after being raped by the man holding her hostage, Shareta was awake but unresponsive. The damage done to her physically was healing, but the mental scars were not. This promising young barrister was suffering from post-traumatic stress syndrome, and it was unclear if she would ever fully recover from the ordeal. Trauma doctors were already counseling her parents on the possible risk factors of depression, alcohol abuse, drug abuse, eating disorders, and suicidal thoughts and actions.

The police were no further along in finding their man than they were two weeks prior, but with the help of the Cubs staff, they did solve the meaning of the street number, which had eluded them to this point. The brutal, disparaging remarks aimed toward them in the papers and on the air were taking a toll on the force, so any breakthrough on the case was uplifting news.

Once again, the task force convened in the fifth-floor conference room at police headquarters. Superintendent Randle addressed the group.

"Gentlemen, let's review what we know to date. You can follow this on the screen behind me. I took the liberty of using the latest three victims' data as examples."

Randle turned to the monitor and reviewed them one by one.

#1. Victim's name is that of an ex-Cub.

#2. Victim's street name is that of an opposing major league player.

#3. Victim's street number is a career statistic of the Cubs player with the victim's name.

#4. Kidnapping/abduction occurs on the first game of a home series.

#5. Victim is drugged with midazolam.

#6. Victim is tied up and forced to watch game on television when awoken.

#7. A Chicago Cubs baseball cap is placed on the victim's head as a calling card.

#8. If the Cubs lose, the victim is meant to be killed by having throat slashed.

#9. If the Cubs win, the victim is supposed to be left alive.

Example #1

Victim: Geraldine Jenkins, 167 South Robinson Street

Ferguson Jenkins, Cubs player

167 career wins as a Cub

Robinson, last name of a major leaguer

Example #2

Victim: David Hands, 1485 West Armstrong Avenue

Billy Hands, Cubs player

1485 career hits given up as a Cub pitcher

Armstrong, last name of a major leaguer

Example #3

Victim: Shareta Collins, 258 North Carpenter

Ripper Collins, Cubs player

258 career games played as a Cub

Carpenter, last name of a major leaguer

"Any thoughts?"

"We have a first and last name of the old Cubs player associated to each event," said Matt Jasper from the Eighteenth District. "Shouldn't we have a first and last name of the major leaguer whose name is linked to the street?"

"It has to be important, given the killer's trail of clues, but we are unable to solve it at this point." Randle fumbled through his notes. "Ah, here it is. The statisticians have told us there were eight ballplayers named Rice, seven Rogers, sixteen Nelsons, five Suttons, nine Pierces, twenty-six Robinsons, five Armstrongs, seven Carpenters, but only one Post. Wally Post. Obviously, major league baseball is looking into all of these players' names, looking for some tie-in, but as of yet there is nothing to go on."

"What about motive?" questioned Detective Shelly Licker from Shareta Collins' neighborhood station in the Twelfth District.

"Our psychiatrists have pieced together recollections from our victims' testimonies as well as their own professional profiles, and have come up with a working theory which we believe is on target. Our perpetrator is a sociopath who believes his actions are going to transform the Cubs into world champions. Through sheer terrorism—nine abductions, four deaths, and one near-death—he has managed to get the Cubs into first place. He also has inadvertently enlisted all the resources of major league baseball to support the Cubs to ensure they maintain their winning ways. We are not sure how he'd respond to that if he found out. If his goal is to have the Cubs win the World Series, I think he would support it."

"Chief," interrupted Grodsky, "the rape of Miss Collins is a major deviation from our killer's M.O. In the game she was being held, a San Francisco player was called out at home with two outs in the top of the ninth and the Cubs won on that play. I want to go on record that I believe the killer knows the umps are blowing calls in favor of the Cubs—and he's angry about it. Put it together. He suspected foul play during the Arizona game where the umps blew that call at first base and, judging from his reaction, I don't believe he was happy about it. Look at Audrey Anson's statement that day regarding . . ."

"There have been three games since then, Grodsky," sniped Kenny Usher. "The umps had two blatant missed calls during those games, yet all three victims were meant to live. They would have too, if it weren't for the frickin' drug allergy."

Greg Stiffle added his thoughts, "I've been in constant contact with Cornelius Mayfield, the head of the Umpires Association, and he assures me the umps are doing a great job, all things considered. He said the human element that umps bring to the game has always been under scrutiny, but he's convinced no one could ascertain those games were slanted in the Cubs' favor. Grodsky, as usual, you're headed down the wrong path."

"Well, Shareta Collins and Audrey Anson might not agree with you," Slats persisted.

"A broken dish? A broken dish!" said a few of the men simultaneously, breaking into a round of laughter. Slats, elbow on table, rubbed his forehead with his fingers and thumb while his colleagues roared in hysteria at his expense.

"Simmer down," Randle chimed in. "Let's solve this thing before we end up the laughingstock of Chicago. Dismissed."

While the officers filed out of the room, Grodsky remained seated, checking cell phone messages. Tex Perryman had left another text, a daily occurrence since their last meeting at the Old Town Tavern, on April 11, five weeks ago. He was also leaving phone messages at the precinct and at Grodsky's apartment. Had he known Slats was living at Julie's the last few weeks, he would have left messages there, too. Slats turned off his phone without responding to the scribe.

An article on the murders and abductions had appeared somewhere on the front page every day since April 12 when Perryman broke the story. Reporters were scuffling to find information from victims' relatives, neighbors, hospital personnel, and ambulance drivers, because police had issued a gag order on its officers. Reporters knew a serial killer was on the loose, one who had allowed some of the victims to live. What the journalists wanted to know was why. The police beseeched the victims not to discuss their torment with the press; the press urged them to talk. Both sides claimed they would be saving lives. Both sides, however, were wrong. There was only one true lifesaver in this nightmare: the Chicago Cubs.

It was two in the afternoon when Grodsky entered the Old Town Tavern. Julie was waiting to meet him for lunch in his favorite booth with a guest. Tex Perryman.

Slats sat next to Julie and kissed her hello, then picked up the menu, ignoring the newsman.

"Do you know there's a man sitting in your booth?" he asked Julie.

"We're friends, "said Perryman. "And unlike you, she's a good friend. I know you think I'm a little slow on the uptake, but based on the unanswered text and phone messages, I kinda guessed before coming here that you wouldn't talk to me. I'm only here out of respect for our past relationship and as a courtesy to let you know what I'll be writing about tomorrow."

Perryman slid the article across the table to Slats, who put down his menu and read the story.

"You can't print this."

"I can, and I will. Good to hear your voice, by the way, Slats. See ya around."

Tex excused himself from the table and walked away. Julie grabbed the sheet of paper away from Slats and read it:

CHICAGO MURDERER A BUZZ KILLER

The abductions and murders that have shaken Chicago in the last month have stolen the thunder from the first place Chicago Cubs. Unnamed sources have confirmed a serial killer is stalking and kidnapping Chicago Cubs fans after a Cubs loss. When asked about the details of the crimes, Superintendant Dale Randle of the Chicago Police Department replied, "No comment."

The article went on to list accounts of what the paper knew on each crime. There was no mention of the last two victims, but no doubt their story would be discovered and told in the next few days as well.

Julie grabbed Slats's hand. "This is going to create mass hysteria in Chicago."

"And terrific ratings for the Cubs on radio and TV," he replied aloud.

"Come on. You don't think . . ."

"You know what, babe? It's exactly what I'm thinking. They were on our list of suspects from the beginning, but the dicks covering it never found a tie-in and could have dropped the ball. There's motive. As far as I'm concerned, everyone involved with the Cubs and the stations are suspects until proven otherwise. What if a station manager's salary is predicated on the station's Nielsen ratings? Or the ticket sales manager's bonus on the attendance at Wrigley Field? It's a different world than the one I grew up in, Jules. I don't put anything past anybody."

"What are you doing now?"

"I'm calling Charlie. I'll have him check out the radio and cable stations again, and I'm going back to Wrigley to talk to someone in ticket sales. Someone who has nothing to gain by increasing ticket sales. See you at home?"

"Okay."

"By the way, what did Perryman mean when he said you're friends?"

"What?"

"Perryman. What did he mean by that?"

Julie said, "I, uh, remembered his face when you two met here last month, and we talked for a few minutes after you left. About you, mostly."

"Really? What did you say about me?"

"Come home early and we'll discuss it in bed."

"It's a date."

He gave her a quick peck on the cheek and headed out into the gray Chicago afternoon.

Chapter 32

May 17, 2013

Grodsky knocked once again on the Addison Avenue door.

"Hello, Edgar. Doesn't Mr. Hellsome ever give you a day off?"

"I'm telling you, the man works me like a dog. How you doin', Officer Grodsky? You here to apply for a job? May as well, you're here almost as much as I am. Does Mr. Hellsome know you're coming?"

"Actually, I need to see someone in ticket sales."

"Well, Officer Grodsky . . ."

"Call me Slats."

"Well, Officer Slats, I can call Mr. Fazio, the vice president of ticket sales and service, or Mr. Radnor, the assistant director of ticket services. They're both here today. We've been awfully busy around here, being in first place and all."

"It's great, isn't it? I'm here regarding a small detail. No sense in bothering the V.P. I could see Mr. Radnor, if he has the time."

"Right this way, Officer Slats."

Inside the ticket office, Radnor was looking over a computer printout when Edgar interrupted.

"Mr. Radnor, this is Officer Grodsky from the Chicago Police Department. He'd like to ask you a few questions if this is a good time."

"Good a time as any," he responded. "Thanks, Edgar. Office Grodsky, is it? How can I help you?"

Slats pulled out a sheet with the nine Chicago Cap victims' names and handed it to Radnor. "I was wondering if any of these people show up on your master ticket list, your database, or mailing list, whatever you might have."

"Hmm, let me take a look. Why do you think they'd be on our list?"

"Call it a hunch. We're crossing T's and dotting I's, ruling out everything we can."

"Let's look at our existing season ticket holders first." Radnor checked the names alphabetically. "No, not one came up. Now let's check the master mailing list. Theodore Banks. Yep, he's here and the next one also. Let's keep going. Well, how about that, they're all in here. But I have to say, so is 30 percent of Chicago."

"Who has access to this computer?" Slats asked.

"Who? All of us," Radnor responded.

"All of you in the ticket office?"

No," Radnor corrected. "All of us in the Cubs organization."

"To the best of your knowledge, have your computers ever been hacked into?"

"That, I can assure you, has never happened. We have two firewalls for protection and encryption software for good measure. What are you suggesting—that someone in the organization is killing people on our list?"

"No, of course not. We're simply looking at every angle. Since most of Chicago is on this list, it's not surprising to find the names, is it? I doubt it means anything at all. Thank you for your time, Mr. Radnor."

"Pleasure. If you need to get hold of me, this has all my contact numbers," he said, handing Slats a business card.

Slats tucked it into wallet, wished Radnor a good day, and left the office. Outside the stadium, Grodsky dialed his partner.

"Charlie? Did you get anything with the broadcasting stations? No? I didn't think so. Why? Because I believe the killer is someone within the Cubs organization. Meet me back at the precinct. I'll tell you all about it there."

The half-hour ride to Chicago Lawn went quickly, as Slats called in his findings to David Locke, Chief Randle's chief of staff. Arriving at the station, Slats found Brainard at his desk and pulled up a chair.

"Charlie, here's the deal. The Cubs mailing database contains about a third of Chicago's residents. Yet all nine of our victims' names are in the database.

"What are the odds of that happening, Slats?"

"There are 2.7 million people in Chicago proper, according to the latest census. The Cubs have around 30 percent of those people, about 850,000, in their database. So you'd expect about 30 percent of our victims, maybe two or three names, to turn up in the database. For all nine names to show up is highly suspect. My instincts tell me the killer is in the Cubs organization. Everyone in the organization has access to that database—all the names of the victims. We know our guy has be a baseball aficionado to know all the major league and ex-Cubs ballplayers, stats, and God knows what else that we haven't discovered yet. One of these employees must have a financial motive, Charlie. You've gotta admit, it makes sense."

"Actually, it does. You should report it to the task force. Remember what happened last time you . . ."

"Yah, yah, already took care of it. Thanks for having my back, though. There are 142 employees in the Cubs front office, from the chairman of the board to the organist. I made the recommendation to the superintendent that we put a tail on each one of them on the next pertinent home game; that's the twenty-second against the Cards."

"What did he say?"

"Don't know yet. I told the chief of staff. I'm waiting for word on how to proceed."

"What should we do next?" Charlie asked.

Slats picked up the newspaper and opened it to the crosswords.

"Charlie, can you give me a four-letter word for 'evidence'?"

"Sorry, Slats, I haven't got a clue."

Chapter 33

May 22, 2013

It was 11:15 a.m., two hours before game time at Wrigley Field. A Cessna 185 dragged a "Go, Cubs, Go" banner above the stadium as Chief Dale Randle and Cubs owner Rance Hellsome reviewed last-minute security details in the owner's loge before the 1:20 p.m. contest with the St. Louis Cardinals.

"Rance, I can't tell you how much we appreciate your understanding and cooperation today. I realize the suggestion that someone in your organization might be responsible for these crimes is hard to wrap your head around, but one of our officers is convinced it's the case."

"Dale, I'm going to be honest with you. The people in this organization are family. And there's no way one of our family members is a killer. I can vouch for each and every one of them. I've only agreed to this charade because you're so desperate, and the public is scared. This escapade will prove you and your detective wrong. Then you can get your head out of your ass and find the real killer."

"I understand your anger, Rance, but you know, every killer has a family, too. Hey, I hope for the Cubs' sake we're wrong. Let's agree that at least we will be able to rule them out, okay? In the meantime, assembling the entire front office here for today's game saved our department valuable time and manpower. I thank you; we all thank you, for that."

Hellsome nodded. "All but three should be here, according to our club president's report. Let's see, one of our board of directors is in London, but Interpol confirmed his presence there. We have a scout at the hospital; his wife is having a baby. There's a patrolman at the hospital to verify that, right?"

"Right. We also know about your assistant trainer tearing his Achilles tendon in the Rockford Marathon last weekend. We have a man outside his home as well, but I bet the poor bastard can't run very fast on crutches."

"Uh-oh," Hellsome said, reviewing the sign-in sheet. "I better call Schwartz about this."

"What's wrong?" Randle inquired.

"Nothing, I'm sure. Vic Gallagher hasn't shown up yet. He's our chief financial officer. I know he got the memo."

"Let me take care of it," Randle said, dialing his chief of staff.

"David, it's Dale. Who's tailing Vic Gallagher? I'll wait. What'd he say? Gallagher's still home? He called in sick? No, everyone else is accounted for. Thanks."

"I'm impressed, Randle. You had eyes on everyone, didn't you?"

"Sorry, Rance. We can't afford any mistakes. Your employees don't know we're tailing them. Anyway, Gallagher called in sick. Someone forgot to log it when he called in."

Hellsome checked his watch.

"Why don't we head over to the Stadium Club where you have my staff corralled?"

Rance pushed the intercom button.

"Elaine, do we have the police escort in the office? Yes? Thanks. Tell them we're ready."

As they left Hellsome's office to walk to the Stadium Club, around twenty reporters were waiting for a sound bite from the owner. Tex Perryman's newspaper article on May 18 had stirred up the press. Officers politely parted the sea of questioning reporters to make a path for Randle and Hellsome.

"How does it feel to be playing in life and death games?" one reporter shouted at them.

"Do you have any leads?"

"Any regrets about buying the Cubs, Mr. Hellsome?"

"Can you confirm if the next ten games are sold out?"

"Who are you paying to keep you in first place?"

The pair crossed the threshold of the restaurant without satisfying any of the reporter's inquiries. The Stadium Club, with a maximum occupancy of two hundred, was the perfect venue to host the front office staffers. Police secured the exits, keeping staff in and reporters out. The Stadium Club was used as a distinctive setting for events ranging from rehearsal dinners to unique receptions, and this gathering was no exception. Knowing the police and paparazzi presence would rattle the employees, Hellsome eased the tension in the restaurant with a surf and turf buffet, to be washed down with beer, wine, and liquor flowing freely from the bar.

When the game started, a few thousand fans stood outside Wrigley. Whereas football tailgaters were routinely raucous and inebriated, the spectators in the parking lot today were eerily subdued, hanging on to every pitch and every word from the multiple radios blaring out the play-by-play. The game held the same fascination that drew onlookers to a freeway wreck. People felt history in the making and wanted to be part of it, blood or no blood.

It was the fourth inning when Randle got the call. While listening to the caller on the other end, he motioned for Hellsome to come join him.

Randle held the phone to his chest and repeated his officer's report to Hellsome.

"Rance. Vic Gallagher left home, and he didn't go to Wrigley."

"Please tell me he went to the doctor," Hellsome said.

"His car's parked on 2385 North Lynch Avenue. Been there for over an hour. The house belongs to Elizabeth Alexander. Does that name mean anything to you?"

"No, but her last name is the same as Grover Alexander, an ex-Cubs pitcher, and the street name Lynch could be a major leaguer."

"Great Scott!" Randle screamed. He put the phone back to his ear, repeated the information to the detective tailing Gallagher, and yelled "Code Two" into the receiver before disconnecting the call.

"Our man is calling for backup. We'll have a SWAT team there in less than an hour. The responders will run "Code Two"—no lights or sirens. We don't want to alert Gallagher we're coming. All we can do now is wait."

The task force was also alerted, and those who couldn't head to the scene in the Jefferson Park District waited anxiously for word that the killer had been caught. Grodsky and Brainard, who had been assigned to the game at Wrigley, were deployed to the North Lynch address, which was less than twenty minutes from the stadium.

Patrol officers silently secured the perimeter of the block and kept surveillance on the address. Members of the task force had received permission to take over the house four lots away from Miss Alexander's residence to use as a temporary field-op center. Gary Stevens, the task force detective from the Sixteenth, was already running the command post when Brainard and Grodsky arrived.

"He still in there?" Brainard asked Stevens.

"Yah. Hasn't moved. SWAT will be here sooner than we thought. ETA any minute."

"Any noise from inside the house?"

"Nada. But at least we know she'll be alive till the end of the game. What bothers me is that the guy changed his M.O. and raped his last victim. Look at this photo of Miss Alexander. She's a good-looking broad. I'm afraid she could be getting raped right now as we speak. We should move in now."

"We should wait for SWAT," Brainard piped in. "You know Randle's saying, 'The needs of the many outweigh the needs of the few, or the one.'"

"Actually, that was Mr. Spock in *Star Trek: The Wrath of Khan,* 1982," said Slats.

"Whatever," said Stevens. "SWAT's here."

The doors on the black modified van flew open, and the armor-clad team poured out onto the street. Strategy was discussed on the ride to the hostage site, so upon debarking from the vehicle, the officers took their assigned positions. The van and its high-tech surveillance equipment became the new HQ for the operation.

Stevens approached the SWAT team leader.

"Hey. Stevens, Sixteenth District. How long 'til you'll be in place to move? You know the last victim was raped before the game ended."

"We know. We'll be operational in two minutes," the captain said. "We're running thermal images on the premises to see how many people are in there and where they are."

The captain held up his finger to stop conversation so he could listen to the voice from the van speaking into his earpiece.

"Captain, two images, second floor, southwest room."

"Good job, Frankie."

"One more thing, Cap. Both images are horizontal."

"Crap." The captain spoke into his microphone. "Everyone in position?"

"Affirmative."

"Let's go."

The SWAT team formed a snake line by the side door of the house. Quietly jimmying the door, the team entered and quickly advanced to the upstairs bedroom door. The point man, with shield in place and M-9 drawn and aimed forward, entered the bedroom when one of the other officers opened the door. No less than seven team members flooded the room, all screaming and yelling to disorient the criminal.

"Freeze," the point man shouted, putting a gun to the man's head.

"Don't move or you're a dead man," yelled another cop.

"Don't shoot!" yelled the naked man in the bed.

"Ma'am, are you Elizabeth Alexander? Are you okay?" asked the cop.

The naked woman beneath the naked man was shrieking and could not speak.

Vic Gallagher was pulled off the woman and forced face down on the floor with his arms twisted behind his head and a SWAT member's knee in his back. He was crying. After several seconds, upon police insistence, his howling ceased. One of the officers spoke into his mic.

"Cap, we've got two warm naked bodies here. But something ain't right. I'm bringing him downstairs."

A SWAT member checked the man's crumpled clothing on the floor for weapons. He found none.

"Put these on, pronto."

"There's some mistake here," whimpered Gallagher. "My wife is going to kill me if she finds out about this."

"Ma'am," asked the officer, "Get dressed. We'll wait outside your door."

Shoeless Vic Gallagher was dragged down the stairs and pushed into a living room chair. Waiting to interrogate him was an intimidating group, including Brainard and Grodsky.

Stevens was the first to speak.

"We know who you are, Gallagher. We've been watching you since six this morning. We know you called in sick at work. We know what you had for breakfast. We know when you took a shit. What we don't know is why you are here? What was your goal?"

Wiping back the tears, Gallagher slowly pulled himself together with a few measured breaths. Gathering courage, he answered the question with a touch of sarcasm.

"Are you kidding? Look at me. I'm a middle-age, balding, slightly overweight man totally infatuated with that gorgeous creature with the unbelievable body. I'm invisible to almost every young girl. Do you know the only kind of young girls that talk to me? Prostitutes, or restaurant hostesses that say, "Your table is ready now, sir." Elizabeth is crazy about me. I'd be crazy to not want to tap that."

"So, you decide to rape Elizabeth and then kill her? Just like you've been methodically killing people in Chicago over the last two months?"

"What? What are you talking about? The only one that's gonna get murdered is me. Oh my God, you can't tell my wife about this. Please, don't tell her about this. She'll kill me."

"Mr. Gallagher, we've already received a court order to search your house for evidence linking you to the murder and abductions of nine people. They are probably rifling through your home right now."

"Oh God! She's going to find out about the affair for sure. I'm dead. I'm dead!"

"Sir," an officer interrupted Stevens, "may I speak to you a moment?"

"I'll be back in a minute, Gallagher. You better get your story straight."

The captain turned to his inferior.

"What do you need?"

"We've been talking to Elizabeth Alexander upstairs, sir. Mr. Gallagher and Ms. Alexander are having an affair. They've been meeting at her home for nearly seven months. She showed us her journal. The only thing Mr. Gallagher is guilty of is adultery. And I'm not sure if catching two adults screwing is under SWAT team jurisdiction. And this guy? He's more afraid of his wife finding out about his love tryst than our accusing him of mass murder. No way he's our man, Cap."

"I'll take that under advisement. This whole operation was bullshit! Book him anyway and get him downtown."

The captain then called Chief Randle and explained to him what went down in the sting.

"Yes, sir. Of course. Thank you, sir. Who? I'll get him."

The captain looked in the direction of the detectives.

"Which one of you is Grodsky?"

"Right here. Why?"

"Randle wants to talk to you."

Slats reluctantly took the phone from the captain, understanding he was about to get an earful. If there was any comfort in this day at all, it was that the Cubs rallied from a 2-0 deficit to win 3-2. At least some lucky stiff was alive tonight thanks to the victory.

At least, that's what he thought.

* * *

In the eighth inning, center fielder Rick Elliott of the Cubs hit a towering foul ball down the left field line with two men on base, a foul ball that was declared a three-run homer. Home runs are the only play reviewable by instant replay in baseball, and the television station replayed it from every angle. Though the hit was a good two feet foul from every angle, the replay umpire still called it a home run. A call that was obviously wrong to even the most casual observer. But William Matthews and his uninvited guest were not casual observers. Not this day.

"Billy, Billy," the masked man said to the unfortunate man tied in a chair with a Chicago Cap on his head. The man with a dishrag stuffed halfway down his throat.

"Son of a bitch! I didn't want to believe it. But it's true, isn't it? Look at that replay. Even the announcers agree it was foul by plenty. That was foul, wasn't it?"

Matthews, gagged and tied, nodded vigorously in agreement.

"Major League Baseball must want you dead, Billy. I warned them to play the game honestly, to let the Cubs control their own destiny, but nooooo. They had to rig the competition, didn't they? Well, we all know that's unacceptable, Billy. That's not how baseball is supposed to be played. Trust me. One cheating scandal for Chicago is enough. The Cubs must win their games with dignity, or you all will have died in vain. They'll understand the message when they find you, Billy. Thank you for your part in helping to make the Cubs world champions."

Chapter 34

June 3, 2013

And as life slowly drained from Billy Matthews's body, so too did Slats Grodsky's position on the task force simultaneously go down the drain.

The closed circuit video conference via Skype between the CPD Task Force and Major League Baseball Headquarters was hastily put together by baseball's executives in New York. The results of the high-level summit between Commissioner Calabrese; Cornelius Maxwell, the head of umpires; and the thirty representatives of all the major league franchises had facilitated this call.

The commissioner kicked off the meeting.

"Chief Randle, members of the task force, Cornelius. First of all, I want to thank each and every one of you for your hard work and dedication to the great citizens and fans of Chicago and the fans all across America. It is because of professionals such as yourselves that we enjoy freedoms in this nation unparalleled by any other country in the world. As we all know, we were forced to play a role in this delicate drama by a madman intent on carrying out his diabolical plan to propel the Chicago Cubs to a World Series championship. We were fish on his line, and while we aided the police investigation in an attempt to buy time to locate him, he played us hook, line, and sinker.

"At the end of April, roughly six weeks ago, this office grudgingly agreed to allow the umpires to make close calls that favored the Cubs and to have opposing teams sit key personnel during Cubs games for the purpose of creating an advantage for the home team. We all agreed that saving lives was paramount. However righteous our decision was, it now appears it was the wrong one. Not only did we compromise the integrity of the game, we failed in our mission to protect your citizens. It is with much sadness and regret that I have to inform the CPD that we are immediately ceasing all cooperation in this matter. I must make this point clear. The Chicago Cubs are on their own from this moment forth. The Chicago police are going to have to solve this crime against humanity and against baseball so we can return to the point where it's about the game. We wish you Godspeed, gentlemen, and hope that someday soon you will catch this perpetrator of evil. Cornie, do you have something to add?"

The head of umpires cleared his throat. "I do. Thanks, Commissioner. The request by the police department to tilt games in the Cubs' favor was unprecedented. When I look back at our original decision, I am actually embarrassed that we agreed to participate. We explained that our umpires were not actors. Luckily, we did not need to interfere with 99 percent of the plays on the field. But when we did, it was a disaster. It is not easy to blow a call in the heat of battle with forty thousand in the stands, instant replay scrutinizing every play ad nauseam, and two to three million watching the game on television. Indeed, blowing the calls like we did opened us up to intense criticism. Commentary talk shows blasting our officiating on ESPN, FOX news, MSNBC, CNN, and other channels has crippled our effectiveness. The crew that caused the death of that young man is absolutely heartsick. They've all had to receive post-event counseling. We train our crews to be unnoticed participants on the field, but now we have lost our invisibility cloak. The game itself, not the umpires, should determine the victor. We owe that to the players, the fans, and the owners—past, present and future. It sickens me that a person may die due to a Cubs loss. But what do we tell the fan who bet on St. Louis to beat the Cubs and we pulled their star pitcher and hitter from the Cubs series and they lost a few grand? Maybe that guy's life depends on the Cubs losing. It's a no-win situation. That's all I have to say."

Commissioner Calabrese thanked the chief umpire. "We have discussed this with every National League team as well as the American League teams that will play the Cubs this year in interleague play. The franchises still expressed an interest in making favorable trades with the Cubs up until the July 31 trading deadline, but as we stated, they will no longer purposely bench a player in a Cubs home series. They reminded us, however, that there are several All-Star quality ballplayers in the last year of their contracts. Assuming the Cubs are willing to part with some of their young talent in their farm system for these first-tier players, that scenario could help stack the Cubs with talent. Of course, those players will be free agents at the end of this season, so the Cubs may only get their services for the remainder of this year. Each and every representative was in agreement at this point. We've done all we can, and now we must put this in the hands of the CPD and God."

"Commissioner," said Greg Stiffle, "I know that I speak for the entire Chicago Police Department when I say it has been a pleasure working with you and Mr. Mayfield. We appreciate all you have done in trying to save lives here in our town. We will continue to pool all our resources in an attempt to close this chapter and bring this murderer to justice."

"One last thought," interrupted the commissioner. "If nothing else was accomplished, at least the members of the Cubs family were exonerated. That was a grave concern of mine, so thank you for great police work in that area."

Greg Stiffle dared not tell the commissioner that the man responsible for that, Slats Grodsky, had been suspended from the task force for what Calabrese was calling great police work. Some of the officers in the room looked down in their notes, some looked at each other, and some, such as Stiffle, Zeigler, and Usher, quietly snickered to themselves, refusing to respond to the comment.

"CPD at its finest, sir," said Randle. "Thank you for the compliment. Have a good day. Signing out."

"Can you believe that horseshit?" laughed Usher. "Good police work my ass. Ask Mrs. Gallagher if her husband feels exonerated."

The others joined in.

"Knock it off!" shouted Randle. "Have any of you come up with one theory or lead for us to act on?"

The room quieted down.

"I'm sick of your axe grinding. You're the Chicago Cap Task Force, not the Kick-Grodsky in-the-Balls Task Force. Start acting like professionals and do your goddamn job! Christ!"

Randle threw his arms in the air and stormed out of the conference room.

"Guess this meeting's over, guys," said Chief of Staff Locke.

Chapter 35

June 6, 2013

Slats stretched his body as he lay in bed and guessed the time to be 5:30 a.m. Rarely off target by more than a few minutes, he played this game every morning. Alarm clocks were set, but an alarm clock was never necessary in the apartment of a Grodsky. Waking in the morning at a precise time was a family trait, inherited from his father and grandfather. As he sat up on the side of the bed and rubbed the crust from his eyes, he peeked at the clock and nodded in approval: 5:37 a.m.

Charlie Brainard once told Slats that he had seen prison cells that were better decorated than Slats's apartment. Indeed, the dwelling he awoke to these days was a far cry from the beautifully kept home in the suburbs he once shared with his wife and daughter. At the time of their divorce, Julie had taken the decorator-picked furniture, art, china, and cutlery from the home, leaving her rehabbing husband with post-college remnants that had been stored in the basement. These select gems were from his early depression era—a double bed without a frame; a spool from the telephone company that doubled as a table; an old oak wine barrel; rusty knives, forks, and spoons that weren't much better than plastic; and a twelve-piece china set that was missing half its pieces, sold as a special companion set for $12.99 when a new set of towels were purchased in a grocery store sale.

The plaster-walled one-bedroom, one-bathroom apartment was dark and stark. There were no paintings on the walls; no pictures frames on display. Shades, not curtains, were the window treatment. There were two folding-door closets, in the bedroom and off the bathroom. The bathroom consisted of an old pedestal sink, above-sink mirror with medicine chest, and standard toilet. The bathtub, once porcelain white but now stained to tan, had black mold on the caulking in the corners where it attached to the wall. A few of the black and white tiles on the floor were gone, casualties from numerous plugged toilet episodes.

The living room centerpiece was the sleeper sofa couch on the opposite wall from the entertainment cabinet, housing the only new item in the flat: a thirty-six-inch flat LCD television.

A bookshelf divided the dining and living room areas. The shelves neatly housed forty books that included a few of Slats's prize possessions: biographies of Churchill, Roosevelt, Lincoln, and Kennedy. Larger books, including historical accounts of the Civil War, World Wars I and II, and the Roman and Greek Empires, lay on their side. The white kitchen cabinets and cupboards were mostly bare. Bowed wooded shelves held dishes, glasses, a George Forman grill, and not much else. The gas stove, oven, refrigerator, and dishwasher that came with the leased space were old but serviceable.

The only other items that stood out were the wall phone in the kitchen, the answering machine on the barrel, and the two pole lamps that gave the apartment its only artificial light.

Julie initially promised to help Slats clean, paint, and decorate. The more time she spent in his apartment, however, the more her promises centered on a new strategy—slash and burn.

His psychologist once told him that his meager trappings were more about self-punishment than indifference, and when he felt better about himself, his lifestyle would change. Case in point: Slats purchased his television after he started dating Julie. He hoped there would be more positive changes on the horizon.

Sitting on his tattered couch the last morning of his two-week leave of absence, a punishment levied by the CPD until Internal Affairs could review his body of work on the Chicago Cap Killer case, he perused the *Chicago Daily News* account of the latest abduction three days ago.

CAP KILLER FINDS RUSH HOUR

Damian Rush, of 1076 W. Palmer St., the latest prey of the Chicago Cap Killer, spoke for the first time since his June 3 kidnapping. Rush gave a chilling account of a crazed masked man, armed with tranquilizers, rope, gloves, a large hunting knife, and a Chicago Cubs cap . . .

The first-place Cubs were now 38-20, about to embark on a ten-game road trip after today's home game against the Cincinnati Reds. The police were no closer to solving the crimes than they were sixteen days ago, the day Vic Gallagher was found in a love lock with Elizabeth Alexander. But one thing had changed, which made their undertaking a little more challenging. Tex Perryman and the rest of Chicago's media had now uncovered every detail of the killings and abductions and were sharing it with Chicago in the papers. Every local talk show, newscast, and water cooler conversationalist was reconstructing and dissecting the story. Blogs dissecting the case filled the Internet, and national network news reporters were roaming the streets of Chicago seeking opiners. Churches led prayer services for the victims. Neighborhoods formed community watch groups. Inner city gangs and newly formed vigilante groups patrolled the streets. Tickets for Cubs games were a valuable commodity. Chicago had gone viral, and Slats was on the sidelines, albeit temporarily.

It had been almost eight years since Slats had taken time off. And that was twenty-eight days at Hazelden, the substance abuse addiction treatment center in Chicago. At the time, his life had spiraled out of control. Unable to cope with the accidental shooting death of the two-year-old at the Loyola Chicago Student Union, Slats drank himself into oblivion. Hazelden was his second and final rehab stint. Therapy sessions with his psychiatrist helped develop a healthier outlook on the accidental shooting. He had also reached out to the mother of the dead child, receiving absolution and sympathy from the forgiving Christian family.

Unfortunately for Grodsky, he received no such amnesty from his own family. The long hours and danger of the job had worn his wife down. Each time a policeman was killed in the line of duty, Julie confronted her husband, asking him if a desk job might be more suitable for raising a family. Slats laughed it off, explaining it was better to live a life wrought with danger than to die behind the desk. As the years and police burial processions rolled by, each phone call to their home created a synaptic symphony, driving Julie to Valium, Xanax, and Ambien. By the time the profession Slats loved turned against him, culminating in the shooting death of the toddler, Julie reluctantly had one foot out the door. After months of doing the right thing for her husband by delivering dutiful support and loving care, her reward was infuriating tirades and drunken stupors. So, after months of mood swings, relapses with alcohol, and noncommunication, Julie, his college sweetheart, girl of his dreams, and wife of nineteen years, moved out during Slats's stay in Hazelden, taking Ava with her. While Slats sat introspectively in his rehab room, divorce papers sat in his mailbox at home.

Ava, an eighteen-year-old clone of her mother at the time of separation, had her own issues with her father, who had missed countless dance recitals, gymnastic events, track meets, and parent-teacher conferences. Though there was never any question of his love for Ava, his absences at the milestones of her young life had led her down a path of inner rebellion against her father. Ava also picked up on Julie's resentment of a cop's life by listening in on her mother's phone conversations, as she complained to family and friends. Her ire finally boiled over at her high-school graduation, which Slats missed because he was in Hazelden at the time.

As Slats learned in therapy, he allowed Ava to slip away out of guilt. He had taken the life of someone else's child, so punished himself by pushing his own child farther and farther away. If those parents were to be denied the pleasure of watching their daughter grow up, so would he. Slats did not drink because he wished to die. He simply yearned to check out for a while and then return when the pain subsided. He eventually realized his pain would not disappear but could be managed. Yet, by the time he wrapped his brain around that awareness, he was all alone, unable to make amends with his girls.

Though her parents desperately tried to persuade her to return to Texas, Julie took a job in an Arlington Heights dental office, resisting the move back home to Austin. Two years later, Julie married her boss the dentist, cementing her roots in Chicago.

Ava matriculated to the College of Wooster, a beautiful eighteen-hundred-student liberal arts college in Ohio, an hour's drive south of Cleveland, majoring in psychology with a minor in anthropology. Her independent study, a year-long senior project unique to Wooster, culminated in the research paper, "Police and the Family that Bleeds for Them," which placed first in the Psi Chi/ J.P. Guilford Undergraduate Research Awards competition. The award came with a one-thousand-dollar prize.

Upon graduation, Ava returned to Chicago to enter the PhD program in counseling psychology at Loyola University. While working in a residency program at the Jesse Brown VA Medical Center, Ava dated and eventually married Geoff Gleeson, an orthopedic surgeon in the United States Army who had completed two tours of duty in Iraq and three in Afghanistan. He was due to start his next and last tour in July at the U.S. military hospital in Bagram, Afghanistan.

Slats had yet to meet Major Gleeson. On the biggest day of his daughter's life, her wedding day, Slats was not invited. On the night of her nuptials, he was knocking down a TV dinner in the dark, his thoughts wandering back to Ava's preschool years and how she used to dress up for her pretend wedding, with Daddy walking her down the aisle. Julie and he had laughed as Ava tripped and contorted in Julie's heels. Tears flowed down Slats's cheeks that night, at the realization that it was Ava's step-dad, not her real dad, giving his daughter away. Those were the last tears he cried.

If it's true that hate is the closest thing to love, Julie must have still loved Slats, but her anger toward him dampened Ava's love for her father. It wasn't that he didn't try to reach out to his daughter after Hazelden. Abusing police protocol, he obtained his daughter's cell phone number and left messages offering dinner invitations for reconciliation. Though the dinner R.S.V.P. had not yet been returned, she did leave a text one day stating she was not ready to rekindle her father-daughter relationship.

Slats finished the Perryman article and peered out his window into the Old Town neighborhood. Among the passersby were a father and an elementary school-age daughter, holding hands as they walked across the street. Feeling melancholy, Slats looked around the apartment to locate his cell and texted his daughter.

"Very sad right now. I miss being in your life. Like I've told you in my letters, I'm so sorry I disappointed you. I hope one day you'll forgive me. Love, Dad."

As he finished his text, the house phone rang. Slats let the answering machine pick it up.

"Hey, Slats. It's Charlie. Chief wanted you to know you're clear to report to the station tomorrow morning. Randle should be calling you, too. He's reinstating you to the task force. When the smoke cleared, they determined you followed a plausible lead. They said it was ultimately Randle's decision to call SWAT, and he based it as much on a conversation with Rance Hellsome as he did with your investigation. So your slate is clean, partner. Congratulations. See you in the morning."

How ironic, Slats thought. Internal Affairs, the department that struck fear into the heart of most cops during an investigation of their actions, had once again been Grodsky's champion. Cleared after the Loyola shooting, cleared after Greg Stiffle accused him of drinking on the job when it was determined he had vertigo, and now this.

To celebrate his last day off, he joined the throngs of runners and walkers along the western shores of Lake Michigan. His two-mile walk ended purposefully at the Jay Pritzker Pavilion at Millennium Park to hear a medley of Mozart and Strauss concertos, performed by the Grant Park Orchestra. Slats knew almost every work of the composers, and today they were playing some of his favorite pieces.

During Mozart's Piano Concerto No.21, Andante ("Elvira Madigan"), Slats cell phone vibrated. It was a two word text from Ava.

"What letters?"

Chapter 36

June 19, 2013

It was a typical morning in the life of a serial killer, though there was nothing typical about this serial killer. It was 5 a.m., and the sun was beginning its ascent. Walking to his fiftieth-floor apartment window atop 215 West Washington Street overlooking the Loop, he stretched his arms over his head, bent to touch his toes, and circulated his torso until the sun had fully breached the horizon. The aroma of the Starbucks blend coffee waiting for him in his Cuisinart Brew Central wafted through the apartment. He proceeded to the kitchen, poured a cup of java, collected the *Chicago Daily News* at the front door, and settled into his balcony lounge chair.

Few people lived this life of luxury. His eighteen-hundred-square-foot penthouse suite had three bedrooms, two-and-a-half baths, and a balcony, but that was just the beginning. Stainless steel appliances, floor-to-ceiling windows with unbelievable views of the city, granite countertops, utility room complete with modern energy-sparing washer and dryer further described this millionaire's suite. The building contained an attached, enclosed parking garage; fitness club with every machine and weight set available; twenty-four-hour-per-day doorman; dog run; landscaped green roof with pool and grill region; state-of-the-art media room; clubroom featuring billiards and game tables; business center and library; and a twenty-four-hour emergency maintenance service.

Finished with the paper, he cut out articles relating to the abductions and pasted them into his scrapbook. Each victim had his or her own unique volume, neatly placed on the bookcase shelf in the spare bedroom that was used as command central. An eight-by-ten color photo of each past and future victim was framed and hung on the west wall. There were twenty-six pictures in all, one for the first game of each home series. Number twelve, Carlos Santo, at 66 South Phillips Avenue, would be visited today. Like all the others, underneath the framed picture was a bio and description of the victim's movements on a daily and weekly basis. Initially, seventy-eight potential targets were identified before choosing the finalists. Only the easiest prey was chosen. Mandatory criteria included work schedule, relatives at home or at work, age, height, weight, if they were a registered gun owner, access to and escape routes from the target's home, visitors, etc.

Carlos Santo was a hit-and-run accident victim now confined to a wheelchair, unable to offer much resistance. Divorced, he had three possible visitors. Most prominent was the cleaning lady, who was not due until Thursday, five days from now. Both sons lived out of town, and they were not the kind to casually pop in to visit Dad from Los Angeles or Boca Raton. And, of course, the victim had to have a name similar to an ex-Cub, have a street number that matched a Cubs career statistic of that player, and live on a street with an ex-major leaguer's name.

Next on the morning agenda was a workout in the fitness center on the fourteenth floor. At 6:30 a.m., a cute curvaceous redhead in a skimpy leotard led the aerobics class, appropriately named "Body by Christy." The high-impact class was heavily populated with young to middle-aged women. The handful of middle-aged men participating in the early morning class tortured their bodies for the reward of watching beautiful bodies bouncing to the fast-paced music mix of the instructor.

"Hi, Lucky. How's the knee today?" Christy asked the man.

Few knew his name. Members of the fitness class had nicknamed him "Lucky," a name that caught on with the apartment tenants. The moniker was bestowed upon him after he told and retold the story of surviving a horrific car crash as a teen. His nickname, however, more accurately referenced his premium elite status as a card-carrying member of the lucky sperm club. At the time of the reading of his father's will nearly a year ago, Lucky was living in the Washington Park ghetto, working part-time as a short order cook. Within a month after his father's entire seven-million-dollar estate had been transferred into his name, he was living in the penthouse.

"My knee? Still hurts, but not enough to keep me out of your class, Christy," he replied. "Of course, I suppose the ibuprofen, glucosamine, and Oxycontin help a little."

"Really? And just how would a guy like you know where to find glucosamine?" Christy joked, knowing all along that Oxycontin would be the drug most difficult of the three to obtain.

Lucky took his place in the last row as the music began. Though it was a high-impact aerobics class, a few, such as Lucky with medical conditions, did the movements in low impact. The last row was reserved for beginners, gimps, and perverts. Lucky was all three. And more.

When the hour-long class finished, the attendees schmoozed for a few minutes before making a mad dash to the showers and then to work. Lucky, on no such timetable, spent his time flirting with Christy.

"So, what does a retired person do after class?" Christy asked.

"Oh, I read, volunteer, and prey."

"Do you pray and volunteer at a church?"

"No, I don't believe in going to church. I do my own kind of preying," he said, knowing she would not pick up on the double entendre, but feeling liberated that he could tell the truth in a twisted way. "As for volunteering, presently I'm working with a group of people who are, to be frank, pretty much losers. I'm trying to change their attitude and teach them how to be, well, winners."

"Kinda like a motivational speaker?"

"Yah, I guess you can say that."

"That's really cool. Do you think I could watch you work one day?"

"I'm not sure that's a good idea. We use a one-on-one method, and there can be no distractions. And I spring new techniques on clients from time to time when the situation calls for it. I swear this one girl didn't know what got into her."

"Maybe you can show me that one day?"

"Why, it would be my pleasure."

"And you think I'd benefit from your training?"

"Honestly, you are already the kind of person I try to teach my clients how to be—driven by their goals. You also have what I can't teach. Good looks, good personality, great body."

"You're sweet. But so far my life's a bit of a mess. Divorced. Single mom, two jobs . . ."

"Trust me, that'll all change for you. Your makeup is that of a winner. One day you will be highly successful and extremely content with your life."

"You think so? Gosh, it's so hard for me to see that right now."

"Christy, I know what I'm talking about. Trust me."

"Thanks! It means a lot to have someone believe in you. Oh my. Look at the time. Gotta go. See ya."

With no reason to stay now that Christy was leaving the building, Lucky headed back to his penthouse. It was time to study his afternoon mark: Carlos Santo.

Home security was important to Lucky. He had replaced the standard apartment door and frame with a precision-engineered, high-tech, heavy-duty steel door frame and door jamb reinforcement shields. Complete with two deadbolt locks, the door was virtually impossible to kick in. After entering the suite and locking the front door, he proceeded to the bedroom he fondly called "The Cave"; it also was under lock and key with the same kind of security door. Two 13-round Beretta semi-automatic handguns with multiple rounds of ammunition adorned the inside wall adjacent to the door.

Routine was equally significant. He needed a structured day, leaving no chance for error, either from omission or haphazard planning. Each element of "abduction day" had been meticulously scrutinized before it was entered into the "client" jacket. First item on the itinerary after the fitness center workout and subsequent shower was verifying the breakfast meal. He chose a different and distinctive restaurant in the Loop for breakfast each day of the week. Saturday was a bacon, caramelized onions, Gruyère cheese omelet at the Atwood Café; Sunday, Bahama pancakes at Beef and Brandy; Monday, stuffed French toast at Eppy's Deli; Tuesday, shrimp and cheddar cheese grits at Heaven on Seven; Wednesday, Italian eggs Benedict at the Lockwood Restaurant; and Thursday, grilled strip steak and eggs at the South Water Kitchen. Today was Friday, which meant breakfast at IPO, where he'd order the chorizo and chicken breakfast burrito.

Next item on the list to review was the driving directions to and from the victim's house. A quick check of traffic.com provided real-time updates on traffic conditions. Malfunctioning lights, road construction, accidents, back-ups, parades, and marathons were obstacles to be avoided at all costs and were circumvented by choosing alternate routes.

Parking near the chosen address was vital. Finding a parking spot in Chicago was an art form, and Lucky took it to the next level. In choosing his victims, ample, available parking spaces were mandatory. Usually, though there were exceptions; if an area was sparsely populated or totally void of parking spaces, a new pigeon was picked. Verification required a drive-by months prior, followed by periodic spot checks in succeeding weeks to avoid a mishap.

Once parking was settled, a foot route to and from the car was mapped out during the morning and evening hours to avoid deterrents such as porch-sitting cigar smokers, backyard dogs, swimming pools, barbed wire fences, and brick walls.

Subtle pictures were taken of the home or apartment building that housed his intended target. Doors, locks, hallways, windows, window treatments, sewer passages, and rooftop entry were all taken into consideration. If possible, floor plans were accessed off the Internet.

Time of entry was also critical. Was the victim home, or on the way home? Were there maids, neighbors, repairmen, deliverymen, friends, family members, or pets to be accounted for?

Last was a checklist of supplies needed for the operation. Knife, disposable cell phone, rope, prefilled syringes with midazolam, surgery slippers to prevent footprints, wire cutters, mask, latex gloves, gag rags, break-in tool kit, condoms, smelling salts, and, of course, a Chicago Cubs baseball cap. Items that weren't carried on his body were stowed in a reusable Jewel-Osco green shopping bag. A large bag of potato chips was placed over the villainous items to give the appearance of a full bag of groceries.

Satisfied he had mastered the rudiments of today's undertaking, Lucky hopped in the shower, where he continued to replay the events of the day over and over in his mind. Toweling off, he headed to the walk-in closet off the master bedroom, where his hand-picked wardrobe, consisting of nondescript blue jeans, gray shirt, dark socks, and sneakers, waited neatly on a cherry wood clothes valet stand.

Lucky packed the equipment in his bag, which he would return to pick up after breakfast. He locked up "The Cave" and locked down the fortress. En route to the restaurant, his single-mindedness allowed him only to focus on the next task at hand. That scrumptious chorizo and chicken breakfast burrito.

Chapter 37

June 19, 2013

With their ten-game road trip, the second longest of the year, now concluded, the Chicago Cubs found themselves alone atop the National League Central Division with a record of 44-24,five-and-a-half games ahead of the St. Louis Cardinals. Wrigley Field was packed to its standing-room-only capacity of 42,157 every game. The players were aware, however, that the fans had a dual motive for coming to the games. A win was nice, but this year transcended baseball standings. Specific home game victories meant a life was spared, and every victory brewed confidence in the Cubs' kettle. Attendance rivaled the 2008 season in which the Cubs drew more than 3.3 million fans. Given the grotesque circumstances and press surrounding it, this year's attendance figures weren't surprising. Equally unsurprising were the one hundred thousand plus fans surrounding the stadium in the restaurants, bars, and surrounding streets. With limited parking available, fans poured off the El Red Line and found refuge in the establishments around Wrigley. Murphy's Bleachers, Captain Morgan's, Casey Moran's, Cubby Bear, John Barleycorn, The Irish Oak, Guthrie's Tavern, The Full Shilling, Sluggers, Goose Island, Yak-Zies Bar and Grill, Mullen's, and Bernie's were more populous than some small towns in America, at least on game day.

The Wrigley Rooftops were top heavy. Corporations and large groups had snagged the last open rooftop seats on West Waveland and North Sheffield Avenues. Prior to the 1980s, the thirteen residential buildings on Waveland and Sheffield accommodated a total of twenty to thirty fans per game on their rooftops who watched the Cubs games for free on folding chairs. As the Cubs' fortunes rose, formal bleacher seating began to appear on rooftops and rooftop fans were charged admission. In 2002, the Cubs franchise sued the facilities, as they saw this as pirating their copyrighted game product. Threatening to place a "spite fence" to prevent free viewing of the games, eleven of the thirteen rooftops worked out a financial agreement with the Cubs, who now received 17 percent of the gross revenue for their official endorsement.

Wrigley has always been known for its party atmosphere. Most years, the second biggest draw to Wrigley was the beautiful, young, thinly clad, tight-bodied women frequenting the park. Called by one writer the "Playboy Mansion of the East," Wrigley was the best pick-up spot in the nation for five months of the year, when the young women descended. Like salmon swimming upstream to spawn, few singles left Wrigley without a handful of phone numbers. The ladies displayed their inventory in the bleachers with a South Beach attitude, watched by millions at home and away through the WGN cameramen, making Cubs games a combination game-reality show for the viewing audience. Usually, if the Cubs were losing by the seventh inning, a mad dash was made to the bars around the field, where men and women began discussing baseball terminology in a different way, as in Meat Loaf's "Paradise by the Dashboard Lights." This year, with a life on the line, even young horny fans stayed glued to their seats until the last out. Not that they cared who the Cubs were playing.

Today's opponent was the Florida Marlins, a National League expansion team established in 1993. Chicagoans were envious of the upstart franchise that had won two World Series in its brief eighteen-year history. This year, the squad was buried in last place in the NL East, fourteen games behind the

Philadelphia Phillies. Still, as any sports fan understands, any team can win on any given day.

And though the Marlins were short in tradition, baseball was steeped in tradition and could bridge the gap. Take, for example, the "Star-Spangled Banner." Though the 1918 World Series took credit for the first playing of the national anthem during the seventh-inning stretch, the song had been performed at opening day ceremonies in Philadelphia as early as 1897 and 1898. The tradition of performing the "Star-Spangled Banner" before every baseball game officially began during World War II.

Then there's the ceremonial first pitch, a longstanding ritual in baseball, where an honored guest throws a ball to signify the end of the pregame activities and the start of the game. The ball was originally thrown from the stands, but now the guest toes the rubber on the pitcher's mound and throws the ball to the catcher waiting at home plate. Honored guests have been celebrities, former ballplayers, politicians, company sponsors, or a fan who won the honor. President William Howard Taft started the American tradition in 1910 by throwing out the first pitch in Washington, DC, at a Washington Senators game on opening day. The first ceremonial first pitch ever thrown, however, was in Japan by Prime Minister Okuma Shigenobu in 1908.

The anthem and first pitch are only two of many traditions attached to Wrigley. The white flag designating wins and losses is unique to Wrigley. Fans frequently bring "win" flags to home and away games. Another custom is the song "Go, Cubs, Go," sung after each Cubs victory.

A new practice started a few years back. As Cubs players take their position in the field before the start of the game, ball boys and ball girls bring a baseball and pen to the fielder, who signs the ball which will be auctioned for charity.

The tradition of throwing a home run ball back onto the field when it was hit by the opposing team started in Wrigley Field. It began in the late '70s to early '80s after the stage play *Bleacher Bums* became popular in Chicago. The fans continued the practice because it's "cool" and because there is pressure from the other bleacher fans to make sure they throw it back.

Perhaps the most well-known tradition attached to Wrigley is the singing of "Take Me Out to the Ballgame." Harry Caray, the fabled Cubs announcer, started the tradition in 1982, and it's been a staple during the seventh-inning stretch ever since. Since Caray's death in 1998, former players and celebrities have been invited to lead the song for the crowd. A caricature of Caray is painted on the glass above the announcer's booth. While attendees at other ballparks politely sing along with the crowd, the Wrigley faithful throw themselves into it as if auditioning for a spot on *American Idol.*

Today's crowd was no less boisterous. By vocalizing their support of the Cubs, the hometown fans were trying to make a difference in the game, either by their decibel level or by heckling the opposing team. And if they could help the Cubs win, they'd be saving a life somewhere in the city.

Another tradition was evolving in Wrigley and ballparks across the country, at least for this season. At game's end, both teams gathered on the infield and prayed to the God of their choice on bended knee to help protect those in danger from this horrible menace.

Yuki Takayoshi, a thirty-six-year-old pitcher acquired by the Cubs from the Yokohama Bay Stars in the Japanese Central League, was today's starting pitcher. Takayoshi had been lights out since joining the Cubs a week after they added All-Star pitcher Manny Garcia to the roster. His herky-jerky motion, ninety-two-mile-per-hour fastball, and full command of a slider, curve, and change-up had National League hitters way off balance. In his eight starts, the former Japanese League All-Star hurler was 6-1 with one no-decision. Teamed with Garcia, who was 7-1 in his short stint with the club, management had put together a formidable pitching staff. Adding power hitting center fielder Rick Elliott to the middle of the lineup gave Cubs pitchers enough run support to compete in every game.

Today's evening game advanced to the fourth inning with the home team ahead 3-0. It was then that the unexpected rainstorm hit the Chicago area, forcing a ninety-minute rain delay.

When play resumed, Takayoshi's arm had stiffened, and he was not the same pitcher he had been in the first four innings. Florida used his misfortune to its advantage and jumped on him for four runs in the fifth inning. It remained 4-3 heading into the bottom of the ninth.

"Tonight's ninth inning trivia question was: What does the rooftop sign AC0467105 stand for? Well, the AC stands for After Championship, the first two numbers are the number of years since the Cubs won their division, the next two numbers are the number of years since they've played in a World Series, and the last three numbers are the number of years since the Cubs won a World Series. If you got that question right, you have way too much time on your hands," said announcer Ben Fair.

"Thanks, Ben. Things are not looking good for the Cubs," stated his colleague Max Neyland. *"Due up in this half of the inning are the seven, eight, and nine hitters. Collectively, they are batting .212 against Steve Fritz, the Marlins right-handed*

closer. No doubt we'll see a pinch hitter for relief pitcher Brad Pott, as Mota and Camp are warming up in the bullpen."

"*The Cubs need base runners,*" piped in Fair. "*But they've only had two players reach base since the rain delay, and none have reached scoring position.*"

"Charge" played over the speakers, and the crowd responded in unison, rising together as left-handed hitter David Sampson dug into the batter's box.

"*There's a weak grounder hit toward second. The pitcher scoops it up and throws out Sampson by plenty. Wow. Sampson swung on the first pitch. When you need to reach base, you've got to take a few pitches. I'm sure he'll get an earful from Cahill in the dugout about that.*"

"*You're right, Ben. That was a classic rookie mistake.*"

"*Coming to the plate is Frank Petronsky. He's one for three tonight against Marlin pitchers.*"

Each pitch had crowd noise rising and falling like a rolling coaster. The next pitch must have crested Mt. Whitney, for the noise was deafening.

"*Ball four!*" screamed Neyland. "*Boy, Petronsky's eye is amazing. He may only be batting .242, but that's his fifty-second walk of the year, which leads the majors. Here comes Jarod Johnson out of the dugout to bat for Pott. With one out, the sacrifice has been taken out of play. Cahill has to be looking for a hit from Johnson, who bats from the left side of the plate. The crowd is imploring Petronsky to steal, but you can't afford to run yourself into an out in the ninth inning.*"

"*You're right, Ben. Cahill may be afraid to hit-and-run as well because Johnson isn't the best contact hitter on the . . . look out! Ouch. Fritz hit Johnson in the hip with a fastball. Boy, that had to hurt. The gun measured it at ninety-seven miles per hour."*

"No way was he purposely throwing at him, though. Not in this situation. Looks like Johnson's okay. He's shaking it off and heading toward first. That'll put a runner in scoring position for the Cubs with two on and only one out, and it'll bring up lead-off hitter Nick Cade. Listen to this crowd."

Indeed, the fans had been on their feet the entire inning and were drowning out the organ music.

"Here's the windup and the throw. It's in the dirt and rolling to the backstop! Both runners move up, and the crowd is going nuts!"

"Fritz looks shaken out there, Max. Now he's gonna have to walk Cade to load the bases for the force or the double play. And he's going to be facing the Cubs' hottest hitter today. Stepping up to the plate is Tony Damato, who's three for three with a walk."

"Fritz looks in. Here's the windup and the pitch— swwwiiiing and a miss, strike one. He was trying to hit one onto Waveland Ave with that swing. Fritz looking in again to get the sign. Damato is ready. Fritz goes into his motion. Here's the pitch. There's a line shot up the middle into center field for a base hit. One run is in. Johnson is rounding third and heading home. Here's the throw to the plate, it's got Johnson beat, he slides feet first and— the catcher can't hold onto the ball. Johnson scores! The Cubs win! Cubs win! Cubs win!"

It was as if the Cubs had cemented the World Series championship, yet it was only the sixty-eighth game of the season, with ninety-four more games yet to be played. Tony Damato was mobbed by his teammates as a few hundred fans streamed onto the field, despite the best efforts of the police and field security. Those who remained in the stands yelled, whistled, applauded, and gave each other high-fives. Car horns honked throughout the city, which was ablaze in excitement at the come-from-behind victory. Five-year veteran Tony Damato was the star of the game with the first walk-off hit of his career and appeared to be the happiest guy in town. In fact, there was one person more pleased with the victory than Damato.

Carlos Santo.

Chapter 38

June 20, 2013

Carlos Santo was alert, recounting last night's ordeal to Greg Stiffle from his hospital bed at Roseland Community Hospital as Grodsky and Brainard waited at the nursing station. As part of his penance, though absolved of any wrong-doing by superiors and Internal Affairs, Grodsky was not allowed to interview suspects or victims, or to be interviewed by the media, without another task force member by his side. This was at the insistence of the task force. This was subject to change, according to Superintendent Randle, but for now, Slats was happy to be back on the biggest case in Chicago since Speck, or maybe Capone. Somehow, some way, he'd win back the respect of his fellow officers.

"You know, I've tried not to bring it up again, Slats, but I'm sure someone is following us. I felt it in the car driving here."

"Can it, Brainard. Unless you see something or someone, I'm sick of hearing about it."

The two paced the hallways together for a few minutes without speaking, ignored by three other task force members also walking the hospital wing floor.

"Wow, this is an old hospital," said Brainard.

"Yep," Slats answered. "Opened in 1924."

"It was a throw-away comment, Slats. I didn't really want to know about this hosp…"

"This area was actually settled by the Dutch in the 1840s. They called it 'Hope' back then, but then changed it to 'Roseland' in the 1870s."

Charlie Brainard rolled his eyes and headed down the hallway, out of earshot from Grodsky's history lesson, which was interrupted by Stiffle's emergence from Santo's room.

"Well?" they asked.

"Let's go to the visitor's waiting room down the corridor," Stiffle answered gruffly. "I'm not going to spill my guts in the hall."

When the last man filed in and shut the door, Stiffle began.

"Carlos Santo is a fifty-six-year-old white male. Lives on the first floor of a six-story apartment building. He's divorced; two sons live out of town. His hips were shattered in a hit-skip accident in 1996, and he has been confined to a wheelchair ever since, though he does have feeling in his legs. He's self-sufficient but has a woman come in once a week to handle cleaning and shopping chores. About 6:00 p.m. he heard a noise from the bedroom. When he wheeled over to take a look, he was overtaken by a masked man who dragged him out of the wheelchair and stabbed him in the neck with a sharp object. He remembers waking up in his wheelchair around 9:00 p.m., tied and gagged, and the intruder was still there, bitching and moaning about the rain. The rain delay must have prolonged the process, so his drugged victim regained consciousness a lot sooner than expected. Apparently the perp doesn't want his victims to remember too much. From details of our previous cases, the victims were regaining consciousness somewhere around the seventh or eighth inning, and by the time they'd shake the cobwebs off, the cutthroat would be gone.

"Santo woke up in the fifth inning. He spent a good deal of time with this guy since the game didn't end 'til 11:00 p.m. He was forced to watch the Cubs game and was told he'd die if the Cubs lost. Needless to say, he was scared shitless when they were losing. I mean, the poor man peed and shit his pants in the ninth inning. Santo said the man told him they were both lucky guys, then he left. The apartment has no camera capability, but we're checking nearby convenience store and gas station surveillance cameras for activity two hours before and one hour after the game."

"Did Santo give us anything we don't know on our man?" asked Brainard.

"Umm, yes, said he's about five eight or five nine in height. That's how high his kids' pictures are mounted on the wall. Also, Santo is brilliant with American dialects and says the man we are looking for is not a native of Chicago, definitely not an East Coaster or a Southerner, but maybe from Kansas, Missouri, Nebraska, or Iowa. The man's a regular Henry Higgins."

"Did Santo remember anything else besides being told he was lucky?" Shelly Licker asked. "I mean, he was awake for two hours with the guy. Did they talk?"

"He recalled the guy saying 'trust me' a lot, which he thought was weird, considering the guy drugged him, tied and gagged him, and was planning on killing him if the team lost. Hardly the kind of guy you'd trust. The doctors said it's possible Santo will remember more in a day or two, but not to count on it."

The room was silent.

"Okay. The press is going to be all over our ass tomorrow. Remember, we have one spokesperson: Chief of Staff Locke.

If reporters ask you about the case, refer them to Locke. We speak with one voice, and that voice is his and his alone. As my Uncle Barney used to say, I have two little words for you, just two little words. No, and comment. Everyone on this force should memorize 'no comment'. Okay, I'm done and heading home. If I were you, I'd do the same."

The task force team members filtered out of the hospital. As Slats drove through South Chicago, he noticed the numerous overturned, burnt-out cars, remnants of yesterday's post-game victory festivities. This kind of celebration was first attributed to the 1984 World Series after the Detroit Tigers beat the San Diego Padres and violence broke out in the streets. Cast as one of the top ten ugliest sports riots of all time, most people believe that riot kicked off what we see today as victory celebrations. Slats vividly recalled the picture of a happy fan holding a Detroit Tiger World Series pennant over his head in front of an overturned, burning Detroit police car. He wondered what Chicago would be like if the Cubs won the World Series. He laughed out loud as he thought of a plausible solution; controlled celebrations in each neighborhood with a designated junker that could be turned on its roof and set on fire. Each fan could throw a log on the fire to participate.

Someone else would have to bring up that suggestion because Slats figured correctly his peers would insist he be committed to a home. Not for the burning car idea; more likely for the notion that the Cubs could win the World Series.

Chapter 39

June 28, 2013

Slats waited nervously in his booth at the Old Town Tavern, checking his watch and the front door every thirty seconds. Ava was running about fifteen minutes late for their first reunion in nearly six years. With her would be her husband, Major Geoff Gleeson.

Julie snuck up behind him as he fidgeted with the six-sided standard issue salt shaker on the table.

One of his favorite tricks for Ava when she was a child was to pour salt on the table, then balance the shaker on one of the bottom edges, so it would come to rest on an angle instead of upright. Once the trick was completed, he took a pinch of salt and threw it over his left shoulder for luck. To win his daughter back, he'd have to create a little more magic today.

"Why did you do that?" Julie asked.

"Do what?"

"The salt over the shoulder thing. You got me full of salt. Did you know I was standing there?"

"Sorry, Jules. It's an old superstition that the devil sits on your left shoulder and a guardian angel on your right shoulder. Spilling salt was considered bad luck as far back as Roman days because salt was a rare and valuable commodity. Throwing salt over the left shoulder and into the eyes of the devil keeps him from seeing that you did something wrong."

"It figures you'd know that."

"So, tell me, what shoulder were you behind?"

"Your right shoulder, of course."

"Ahh. So you're my guardian angel."

"Nervous?"

"Are you kidding? I'm petrified. What will I talk about? What will I say?"

"Just be yourself, Slats. That'll be good enough."

Slats chose the meeting place with Ava. Having a familiar setting and Julie nearby bolstered his confidence for the encounter.

Julie looked out the window.

"There's a soldier outside. Is that her? Oh my God, I think that's her. Slats, they're coming in."

"What the hell are you so nervous for? You're supposed to be my rock, remember?"

"I'm excited for you, that's all. I'll go bring them over."

Julie hustled over to greet the couple at the hostess kiosk.

"Hi. Are you Ava?" Julie asked.

"Uh, yes. How did you know?"

"Your dad is here. Follow me please."

Julie led them to the corner booth, quickly retreating to allow the trio space for their private reunion. Slats slid out from his seat and stood next to the table when they approached.

His instinct was to pull Ava into a bear hug. He restrained himself. Though she had come to reconcile, the ice from years of noncommunication had not yet melted. Ava, with arms hugging her sides, turned her body sideways, which allowed for a less intrusive hug. Respecting her body language, Slats backed away, then just stood and stared at her for what seemed to be a minute or two.

"Dad, this is Geoff."

"Geez, I'm sorry, Geoff. Where are my manners? It's been so long since . . ." He extended a hand to her husband. "It's a pleasure to finally meet you."

"Likewise," the major responded.

"Look at you," Slats continued, turning his attention back to Ava. "You're as beautiful as your mother. Wow. It's like 1986 all over again. Come on. Sit down. I have so much to ask you."

The young couple slid into the booth, opposite Slats.

"So how's your mother?"

"Do you really want to know?"

"I wouldn't have asked if I didn't care."

"She's good. Real happy, you know? Steve has a great dental practice, and they have a gorgeous home in Arlington Heights. They travel a lot. In fact, they were on a Mediterranean cruise about two weeks ago."

"That's good. You're mom deserves it."

"He pretty much works eight to five. Mom still works in the office three days a week. She doesn't cook much anymore. They eat out a lot. Hmm, let's see, what else? She got a new BMW 750i."

"Does she ever say anything about me?"

"Not too much. Once in a while she'll ask if I've spoken to my asshole father yet."

Slats looked down, and began to fidget again, this time with his napkin.

"You said you wanted to know," Ava said.

"No, it's fine. Seriously." Slats paused, looking at Geoff. "I understand you did a couple of tours in Afghanistan."

"Yes, sir. I'm going back in a few weeks for another six months. It'll be my last tour of active duty and then I'll be going into private practice."

"Really? Doctors still do that?"

"Yes, sir. A lot of my colleagues are working for hospitals these days, but after three years of army hospitals, I'm going to try private group practice for a while. A chief resident I used to work under has offered me a position in San Antonio, and I'm going to take it. Ava and I . . ." he trailed off to look at Ava as she gave him approval to continue. "We'll be moving there next spring when I get discharged."

Slats feigned surprise.

"Why Texas? Why not stay here? I'm sure you have contacts, don't you?"

"Well, the biggest thing is that the liability insurance in Texas is about one-fourth the cost of what it is in Illinois, and that's a lot of money to a private practice."

"Ava, what does your mom think of you leaving?"

"She's totally okay with it. She'll come down a couple times a year; I'll come back a few times. It'll be all right."

Julie came over to the table.

"So, Slats, aren't you going to introduce me?"

"Uh, Ava, Major Gleeson, this is Julie."

"It's nice to meet you. I've heard so much about you. So, do you kids know what you want yet?"

"Diet Coke for me, please; Geoff?"

"I'll have the same," Geoff added.

Julie looked at Slats and smiled.

"Is Diet Pepsi okay? We don't have Coke."

"Yes," Ava said, noticing the eye contact between her dad and the waitress. "Pepsi is fine."

"How 'bout you, handsome?" Julie asked Slats. "The usual?"

"Thanks, Jules, that'll be great."

As Julie left to get the drinks, Ava squinted at Slats.

Slats quickly said, "Aren't you going to order something to eat?"

"We already ate, Dad."

Slats looked confused.

"I thought we were meeting for lunch?"

"Sorry, Dad. We can't stay that long. Besides, I thought our first visit should be short, in case it was a little weird."

"What if it was a good visit and not nearly as weird as you thought?"

"Well, then, I guess we could have something to look forward to. Is something going on between you and the waitress? I saw that exchange."

"I've been coming here for a long time, and I always order Coke instead of Pepsi. She smiled because you did the same thing."

"That is so not what I'm talking about. You're seeing her, aren't you?" Ava pressed on.

"Yes, actually, we are. What about it?"

"Her name is Julie, too? That's creepy. That's all I'm saying."

Julie dropped off the drinks before greeting customers at the next table.

Stillness hovered over the table, before Major Gleeson broke the silence.

"Look at the salt shaker, Ava," he said noticing its odd, leaning stance on the table.

"Gee, I wonder how it does that?" she responded, looking at Slats.

"So Ava," Slats said, ignoring her rhetorical question. "Did you finally read all the letters?"

"I did. I was so pissed at Mom. We didn't talk for weeks. But I told you about that on the phone."

"And?"

"And— I'm here, aren't I?"

"I want to be part of your life again, that's all. I want a second chance to do it right this time. I saw this guy once, a motivational speaker, who said the best time to plant an oak tree was ten years ago, but the next best time is today. Do you understand what I'm saying?"

"I'm not an idiot, Dad," Ava said, sounding a bit agitated. "I get the metaphor."

"Ava?" her husband said, sing-songing her name, gently reprimanding her for being sharp with her father.

Ava shook her head, took a deep breath, then slowly let it out, releasing the anger with it.

"I'm sorry. I obviously still have a lot of pent-up anger and frustration over you and me. I'm trying. You have to know. It was so confusing, reading those letters. You were always gone, first physically, then mentally. I thought you hated me, but I couldn't figure out why. I'm still not excusing you, but I understand it, what you went through, a little better at twenty-four than I did at thirteen or eighteen years old. Oh my God, Mom was so angry with you. But she cried and cried over her part in ruining our father-daughter relationship. She promised she won't try to undermine it again."

"Ava, honey," the major said, looking at his watch. "I have to get back to the hospital."

"Sorry, Dad, we gotta go."

"Can we do this again, sometime soon? Maybe even eat something together?

"Sure, Dad, I promise."

"It was good to meet you, sir," Geoff said, as the two men shook hands.

"Ditto. Take care of yourself over there, ya hear?"

Slats stood up, turned to his only child, took her in his arms, and gently kissed her forehead. This time, she offered little resistance, and even wrapped her own arms around his waist.

"Ava, I will never let you down again. Ever. You'll see."

The corner of her mouth rose slightly, yielding the slimmest of smiles.

"See yah soon, Dad, okay?"

"That sounds good. Great, actually. That sounds great."

As she was about to leave through the front door, Ava turned to her father.

"By the way, nice touch with the salt shaker."

Slats watched her and Geoff scurry down the street to catch a taxi.

"Looks like you've got a new friend." Julie said, putting her hand on Slats's shoulder.

"Two friends, I think," he answered.

Chapter 40

July 4, 2013

No day on the calendar represented America better than the Fourth of July. Politicians pontificated about the most democratic and free society known to man. People living in foreign countries viewed it as a symbol of hope for their future. And while Americans treasured it as the day America declared independence from Great Britain in 1776, it was more treasured for the possibility of three-day weekends, travel, barbeques, picnics, fairs, parades, and fireworks. To Chicago Cubs fans, however, it signified the halfway point of the season. At 54-29, the Cubs would start the second half of the season with a ten-game lead over the St. Louis Cardinals.

All elements of the game had come together for the Cubs. It all started in the front office, where they had done their part to bring in three difference makers in All-Stars Garcia, Takayoshi, and Elliott, thanks to some arm twisting and special favors from opposing general managers. On the field, almost every position player and pitcher was having a career year. The Cubs were in the top five in almost every statistical team category and were leading the league in the two most important ones: hitting and fielding.

In 2008, the Cubs set a franchise record in having seven players selected to the All-Star team. To put an exclamation point on the team's excellent first half, that record was equaled by this year's squad. Joining Garcia, Takayoshi, and Elliott on this evening's winning National League All-Star Team were Nick Cade, Matt Bailey, Tony Damato, and closer Ron Allen. The Cubs contingent contributed to the 6-2 victory, as Elliott and Bailey homered and Garcia was named the winning pitcher. The win was important, because it determined which city would have the home advantage in the World Series. If the Cubs were to make it that far this year, they'd be playing four at home and three away should the series go to seven games.

Despite their first place standing in the divisional race and accolades placed upon them, the season was beginning to take its toll on the players. On the field, the players had been responding to the pressure placed on them by the Chicago Cap Killer. Outside the white lines, however, a few were beginning to exhibit strained behavior. It would only be a matter of time until it began affecting their play on the diamond. Psychologists, previously on call if needed, were now a clubhouse staple. Rance Hellsome spared no expense for his players. No less than three shrinks could be found in Wrigley on game day. Two internists were also on hand for good measure. Players were starting to talk about their favorite anti-anxiety medications, like alprazolam, diazepam, or lorazepam, instead of their favorite beer. For those having trouble sleeping, the popular zolpidem was prescribed. Anti-depressants would be the next topic of conversation if the killer wasn't caught soon.

Group sessions, initially held once a week, had now become a daily activity. Players were required to join a get-together at least twice a week, their attendance monitored by management. Players bared their souls in group therapy with many a tear shed. No player wanted to make the error or last out of the game knowing a fan would die as a result of his actions. In uniform, these athletes looked like men. In these sessions, they more resembled scared kids with raw emotions.

Though the entire city was drawn to this year's Cubs games like moths to a flame, one truth still prevailed in the region. North Siders followed the Cubs; South Siders were loyal to the White Sox. Hospitals providing free mental health screenings at makeshift clinics throughout the city reported more patients in North Chicago than in South Chicago. The disparity was due to one truth; White Sox fans hated the Cubs and Cubs fans hated the White Sox. To a White Sox fan, a good day was when the Sox won; a great day was when the Sox won and the Cubs lost. As for Cubs fans, the feeling was mutual. The rivalry began in 1900, back when the American League was founded. Owner Charles Comiskey moved his team to Chicago for the 1901 inaugural American League season and was promptly sued by the Cubs. After negotiations, it was decided that Comiskey could move his team to Chicago, but the team was not allowed to use Chicago in the name and had to play somewhere south of 35th Street. In spite, he named the team White Stockings, which had been the original name of the Cubs in the 1800s. From that first season, fueled by the news media, fans, players, and owners, the city had divided loyalties.

South Siders did not want to see someone die, but it was still hard for them to root for the Cubs. While the Cubs were at war with a murderer, the South Side of Chicago was at odds with itself. Giving in to their morbid curiosity, the majority of White Sox fans eventually offered their support to the Cubs.

Being a policeman did not allow for the same divisiveness accorded Cubs and White Sox fans, though each cop had his or her favorite team. Born and raised in Skokie, Slats Grodsky was a North Sider and Cubs diehard. He was hooked the first time he read New York newspaper columnist Franklin Pierce Adams's poem "Baseball's Sad Lexicon." The scribe wrote it, from the perspective of a New York Giants fan, about the greatest double-play combination in the history of baseball: Joe

Tinkers, Johnny Evers, and Frank Chance, the Hall of Famers who led the Cubs to their last two World Series victories in 1907–08:

These are the saddest of possible words:

"Tinker to Evers to Chance."

Trio of bear cubs, and fleeter than birds,

Tinker and Evers and Chance.

Ruthlessly pricking our gonfalon bubble,

Making a Giant hit into a double—

Words that are heavy with nothing but trouble:

"Tinker to Evers to Chance."

As he lay in bed reading Tex Perryman's latest article on the psychological implications from the Chicago Cap Killer on the players and fans, Slats thought back to his youth, when baseball was purely about baseball. Today's sports page was so inundated with crime he double-checked the headlines to make sure he wasn't reading the crime blotter: a perjury trial for an ex-player who may have lied in a congressional hearing about his alleged steroid use; a player suing his agent over blunders in his contract; court proceedings on the new collective bargaining agreement; three players arrested, one for drunk and disorderly, one for domestic violence, and one for resisting arrest in a barroom fight; a fan suing a ball club after taking a beating from a gang in the stadium parking lot after a game; and, of course, Chicago's kidnapping/murder saga.

"Put the paper down, honey. I can tell you're getting irritated," said Julie, lying in bed next to Slats.

"Jules, I can investigate a triple murder and be completely objective and unaffected, but when I read the sports page and most of the articles are about issues other than sports, I get pissed. Is it frickin' weird that it bothers me?"

"Maybe it's time you stopped reading the sports page. Why don't you check out the entertainment section and find us a movie?"

Slats shuffled the papers until he found the section he was looking for. After looking at it, he threw it down.

"Now what?" Julie asked.

"Every other movie is a vampire movie. What's with the sudden American obsession with vampires?"

"What's wrong? Ah we a wittle cwabby?" Julie said as if talking to a child. "You know what? You're tired. Turn off the light and go to bed. You don't want to be this irritable for your party tomorrow."

"You mean Randle's sixtieth birthday? That hardly classifies as a party. I'll make an appearance out of respect for Dale. Sing happy birthday, have a slice of cake, get a lap dance from the stripper; I hate going to these average run-of-the mill cop parties."

"Stripper? Excuse me? When you plan my birthday party, I hope you'll celebrate it with a little more panache."

"No expense is too great for my girl. I'm going to hire the Chippendale Dancers for you, dear."

"Oh please! Turn off the light and go to bed, would you? It's midnight, and I've got an eight o'clock class."

Slats turned out the light, snuggled next to Julie, and spoke to the back of her head.

"Sorry, but class isn't over 'til this professor says it's over."

"Slllaaats," Julie giggled, taking a peek under the sheets. "Better hurry, looks like the bell's going to go off any minute. Hello, Mr. Merkle . . ."

Chapter 41

July 5, 2013

Slats turned his keys over to the valet attendant hired for tonight's party and entered Rocky's Bar and Grill on West 31st. The owner, a high-school classmate of Superintendent Randle, was thrilled to be hosting his friend's party for the evening. It was standing room only as only fifty chairs were available between the handful of tables in the bar and the beer garden patio.

Grodsky snaked through the sea of blue uniforms and gray suits to the bar in the outdoor patio where Randle was seated.

Happy birthday, Chief."

Randle was glassy-eyed already. Slats recognized the incoherent speech pattern and pegged him one beer short of a twelve-pack.

"Hey, Shlats, glad you could make it. Pull up a chair, have a beer, er, piece of my cake. We've got hot wings, shtuffed peppers, sliders . . ."

"Yes, I saw the spread when I came in. It looks amazing. I'll have some in a minute. I wanted to see you before you forgot I was here. Looks like a great party."

"Have you ever met George? He owns this place. He's my best friend in the whole world."

Randle's stool was spun in a different direction, ending his conversation with Slats.

Mission accomplished, Slats thought. I've made my appearance. Time to hook up with Julie.

"Happy birthday, Chief," he bellowed as he left the patio.

"Where you going, Slats?" asked Charlie Brainard, who grabbed his partner before walking out the door.

"Gotta get home, Charlie. Have a date with Jules. This isn't my thing anymore, you know?" Slats said, pointing to the liquor and beer behind the bar.

Charlie was clearly sloshed as well.

"Oooh, that's right. Sorry, Slats. I didn't mean anything by it. I love you, man."

"I know, Charlie. Who's driving you guys home? You're too drunk to drive."

"We got a limo service, partner. Not to worry."

Slats caught Charlie as he was listing starboard, preventing a collision with one of the servers.

"See you in the morning, Charlie."

* * *

As Slats left, Cliff Zeigler approached Charlie and put his arm around him.

"Where's your partner going, Brainard? He only got here a few minutes ago."

"Oh, he's gonna go see his girlfriend."

"I didn't know he was seeing somebody."

"Yah. She works at the Old Town Tavern. Cute girl. Name is Julie."

"Isn't that his ex-wife's name? That's frickin' spooky."

"Yah, I guess."

Zeigler steered the wobbly Brainard to a table.

"Have a seat, Charlie. We don't get a chance to talk very often. You know, having the same partner and all, we probably have a lot in common."

"You think? Like what?"

"Well, he's a great detective, for one thing," Zeigler said, trying to open Brainard up like a can of beans. "But he does tend to mess up now and then. You know what I'm talking about. Like, I remember this one time we got a call on a '211' in progress. We were only five minutes away from the store, but he took a fifteen-minute shortcut. Another time he went to unholster his gun as he was about to enter a building, but it was lying on his car seat. He had to run back to the car to get it."

The two laughed and laughed as Zeigler, Grodsky's partner for over four years in the Englewood Precinct, told story after story about Slats. All were true but stretched for comedic effect.

"Another two beers here, please," Zeigler begged the server.

"So, Charlie, you got any stories like that? Stories about Slats crack me up."

"Well, we've only worked together for a short while, so I don't have much shit on him."

"Come on, Charlie," Zeigler prodded, looking for material to use against Grodsky. "There must be something. You know, like the cell phone tracing incident, or catching that Cubs executive with his pants down."

Zeigler grabbed Kenny Usher, walking past the table, and quietly motioned for him to sit down.

"Come on, Kenny," Zeigler winked to Usher. "We're recounting Slats Grodsky's Greatest Hits. Charlie was about to share one of his stories."

Usher sat down and put his arm around the back of Brainard's chair.

"Didn't mean to interrupt you, Charlie. Go ahead, I'll tell some of mine when you're done."

Brainard, with a blood alcohol content approaching 0.2 percent, had been stripped of rational thought three beers ago. Unaware of Zeigler's and Usher's ulterior motives, Brainard pushed forward.

"See, I don't think the cell phone tracing was wrong. I thought it was a good lead worth following, even though it didn't pan out."

"But he should have informed the task force," Usher added.

"Well, yah, that part's true. And the Cubs guy," Brainard said, shaking his head and snapping his fingers. "What was his name?"

"Gallagher?" Zeigler offered.

"Yes! That's the guy. That wasn't a bad lead either. I mean, everyone was shupposed to be at the game, right? He was consickulusly, uh, I mean conspicuously missing in action. He could have been the murderer. We didn't know he was only a horny guy thinking with his dick and not his head. But you know what? Not one other guy in that task force has come up with even one lead."

Brainard then held up two fingers before rambling on.

"Slats came up with two leads."

Zeigler and Usher were momentarily embarrassed by the brash young upstart who had his partner's back. True enough. No one on the task force had been proactive on any lead since the case began April 1.

The three detectives were getting bored with the conversation as they finished their beer.

Zeigler pushed back his chair from the table and was about to leave when Brainard spoke.

"The only thing that got me pissed off was his meeting with Tex Perryman."

Zeigler pulled his chair back up to the table. Grodsky's old partners and longtime enemies leaned in closer to Brainard. They spoke simultaneously.

"Excuse me?"

"What did you say?"

"You know the reporter who's writing about the murder?" Charlie continued.

Zeigler nodded. "We got that part. What about the meeting? When was it? What did they talk about?"

"I don't remember, exactly. Maybe after the second murder. No, wait, it was after the third one. I don't know what they talked about. Slats didn't tell me. He said he didn't tell Perryman anything, but the next morning it was splattered all across the newspapers."

Brainard took a deep breath, held up his index finger, and leaned back as if to give the pair even more earth-shattering news.

"I gotta go pee."

Brainard stumbled toward the bathroom like a pinball caroming off bumpers.

Usher looked at Zeigler. "As much as I'd like it to be true, I don't believe he'd tell the . . ."

"I think we found a way to get rid of the bastard once and for all, that's what I think. We should tell Randle," Zeigler said.

"He's in no condition to process this."

"He may not be, but I'm sure there're a few other guys who might be interested to know Grodsky is our leak. Spread the word."

"You know, Cliff, I hate the guy as much as you do, maybe even more. God knows I have more reason to. But Brainard is totally drunk on his ass. He has five brain cells functioning out of a few billion, and he still said that Grodsky didn't tell Perryman anything. Let's confront Grodsky tomorrow about it before going to Randle."

"You going soft on me, Kenny?"

"No way. But my wife is right. I've spent so much time and energy hating him that the hate's embedded in my personality. I'm sick of looking for ways to make Grodsky's life miserable. I should be looking for ways to make me and my family happy. I want to let go already. I've had enough of it. Maybe he told Perryman, maybe he didn't. But it won't come from me."

Usher excused himself from the table.

"Geez, who died and made you Gandhi?" Zeigler exclaimed.

Chapter 42

July 6, 2013

"Grodsky! Get in here, ASAP!" shouted Sam Pearson from his Eighth Precinct office.

"Morning, Chief. I didn't see you at Randle's party last ni . . ."

"Shut it, Grodsky. And shut the door, too."

Slats turned and closed the door. No matter how thick, it did not offer enough sound proofing for the staff in the outer office to be shielded from the conversation.

"Tell me about your conversation with Tex Perryman."

"What?"

"You heard me, dickhead. Seems like Cliff Zeigler told a few of the men it was you who broke the story to the reporter."

Slats was blindsided.

"That's not true. Where did he hear that bullshit?"

"From a reliable source."

"I don't care who his stoolie is. It's not true. I never told Tex a thing. Sure, we met. But he came to me. He told me he was going to break the story the next day and was hoping I'd confirm what he knew. I tried to talk him out of it. That's all. But the story was going to be front page news, whether I talked to him or not."

"That's not how I heard it went down." Pearson paused. "So, why did he come to you?"

"It may be fifteen years later, but the asshole still believes he has some sort of entitlement. He thinks I still owe him for a tip on the BLT case."

"Did you confirm what he knew?"

"Yes, but I asked him to give us a few more days, and not to print it. Obviously, he didn't listen to me."

Pearson swiveled to and fro in his chair, his eyes never leaving Grodsky's. He believed Grodsky was telling the truth, so his next words were painful.

"Slats, I'm gonna lay it on the line. Randle can't stand the divisiveness on the task force. You've become a sideshow, a distraction. A number of the guys don't want to work with you."

"He said that?"

"No more than five minutes ago, before you walked in the station."

"What are you saying, Captain, I'm off the case?"

"Those are Randle's words, not mine."

Slats took a few steps backward as if he were punched in the midsection.

"Look, Slats, for what it's worth, I believe you. But my hands are tied. There's nothing I can do to change Randle's mind. I have to officially notify you that you are no longer a working member of the Chicago Cap Murders Task Force. I'm sorry, Grodsky, but that's how Randle wants it."

Slats stood silently for a moment, staring at the certificates on the wall behind Pearson's desk. Grodsky had many of the same ones. They used to adorn the walls of his home office when he was married but now sat in a storage closet in his apartment building basement. His lifetime of work could've been followed by connecting the encased citations. Had it even been worth the effort? It all seemed so meaningless and pointless now.

Grodsky reached into his coat pocket, pulled out his badge and weapon, and laid them both on Pearson's desk.

"Slats, I get it. I know you're upset. I am not accepting these. Take them back. Go home, take a few days off. Shit, take a week or two. You'll feel differently after a little time off."

"Captain, being a cop . . . it's all I've ever wanted since I was a kid. I was good at it, too, you know? Until . . ."

His voice trailed off as he thought about the young infant felled by his stray bullet.

"Well, I spent a lot of time and a lot of years getting past it. But this? How do I work in the field when I'm constantly being undermined by other cops? They don't have to like me, but do they have to go out of their way to keep me from doing my job? I need their respect at a very minimum. Without that, what do I have?"

"Don't talk crazy, Grodsky. You're the best this department has. You can't let events or people define who or what you are. Only you know what you want and who you are."

"You know, Cap? That's the problem," Slats said as he opened the door. "I don't think I do anymore."

Leaving his badge and gun on the desk, Slats closed the door to the captain's office and walked out of the building. He

looked up at the clear blue sky and wondered, what the hell was
he going to do now?

Chapter 43

July 7, 2013

Slats tuned in to the Chicago news stations hourly on the way to Wisconsin. Yesterday's doubleheader with the Milwaukee Brewers opened a quirky five-game series in four days thanks to an early season rainout. The Cubs won them both, but there was still no word of an abduction or murder on the airwaves. Changing back to his Toby Keith CD, Grodsky turned his thoughts back to his mother and father. It had been over three years since he had visited his parents' retirement home in the Wisconsin Dells. Bored with highway driving, Slats decided to take the more scenic route. After all, what was the hurry? The drive from Chicago was not particularly a long one, four-and-a-half hours, covering 210 miles. It was, however, a lonely one, leaving Slats time to reflect on his conversation with his girlfriend Julie. After leaving his credentials and weapon on Captain Pearson's desk, he had headed to her home for comfort. What he received instead was more than he could stand.

"He didn't get any information from me," Julie had said.

"What?" Slats asked her. "You and Perryman are talking?"

"Now don't get mad. I simply wanted to know more about you, what makes you you, you know? And everyone said he was the only one that knew your past. So I called him and we've talked a few times and . . ."

"Christ! What have you told him? He's probably been playing you like a piano. He's a newsman, goddamn it! Once these guys get their hooks into you, it's all over, don't you understand?" Slats shook his head in disappointment. "What's the use. Did I really think I could have a normal life again?"

No matter how many times he played it back in his head, he saw no possible scenario other than betrayal. He stormed out of the apartment, laying rubber as he peeled away. Slats had only driven a couple of blocks when he saw an open parking spot directly in front of a neighborhood bar. He pulled into the space, but left the car running as he rested his head on the steering wheel.

Slats felt so abandoned. He had lost his position on the task force, his job, and now apparently his girlfriend. His life had once again come to a crossroads. A blinking beer sign beckoned. It would be easy; turn the car off, walk inside, and order a drink. Who would know if he had one drink? Better yet, who cared, he thought.

He had earned the right for self-pity. One singular event, an accident, redesigned his life's map. One road contained a wonderfully happy family secure spiritually, physically, and financially; a fabled career envied by contemporaries; and a content inner being. Forced off that road, Slats now found himself in the belly of his own whale, a Jonah-like journey to the depths of despair.

But there were two voices preventing him from opening the car door. He suddenly knew what to do. He had to follow those voices. To find his way home, he had to get back to his roots. Back to the people who gave him his start, his greatest supporters in a world of doubters. His mother and father.

Bronislaw Grodsky, at age twenty-five, and Esther Lang, three years younger, first met on a refugee ship headed to the United States in 1957. Both had a common bond fleeing oppressive Communist regimes—Bronislaw from Poland and Esther from Hungary. With only the clothes on their back and a few dollars scraped together by family members for their journey, the two sailed across the Atlantic, destination Chicago, sponsored by relatives living in the area. Fate put them together again in naturalization classes as they were studying for their citizenship. Once they learned enough English to communicate with each other, they began to date and, six months later, were married by a justice of the peace. Bronislaw, nicknamed Bennie by his American friends, had apprenticed as a glazier in Poland, so his transition to a local glass company was a smooth one. The young man was the company's hardest worker and soon found himself moonlighting on private jobs at restaurants, gas stations, and homes. The money earned from those jobs funded the college educations of their five children and, eventually, Bennie's retirement.

Esther, who had no skill prior to her arrival in the States, became an amazing cook and baker, though she never worked a day outside her home. Bennie may have been the moneymaker in the family, but it was Esther who told him how to spend it or save it. There was no miscommunication among the children either, for they all knew mother, not father, ran the household. It was a strict, disciplined home whose gift to the world was five successful offspring: Thomas, an orthopedic surgeon at John Hopkins; Robert, a worldwide clothing importer; Elaine, head nursing supervisor at the Mayo Clinic; Nancy, the owner of a small boutique on Rodeo Drive in Los Angeles; and the most decorated police officer Chicago had ever experienced.

Slats pulled his Grand Prix into the driveway, turned off the engine, and stared at his parents' wilderness home. The fifteen-hundred-square-foot pine-wood condo, overlooking the Wisconsin River, had its own private beach and balcony. The two-bedroom, two-bath unit, one of twenty in the planned development, came complete with stone fireplace and cathedral ceiling family room, and was completely furnished with pine tables, pine chairs, and pine bed frames. A pine ladder led to a loft, penned in by a pine railing.

Slats rang the bell and entered his parents' home in the same motion.

"Mom, Dad, anybody home?"

His walk through the house came up empty. Exiting through the back patio door, he followed the stone path down to the gurgling riverside, where his father sat, fishing on the shoreline, across from unique sandstone formations.

"Hey, Pops," yelled Slats.

"Quiet. You'll scare the fish."

"Good to see you, too, Dad."

Bennie stood to greet his son.

"Let me look at you. Oh, you're a sight for eye sores."

"You mean sore eyes, don't you, Pops?"

Fifty-six years later, Bennie still hadn't grasped command of the English language.

"Whatever you say. Come here. Come here."

Bennie wrapped Slats in a bear hug. Though his father was slightly built, he was leathery tough. Glazier Bennie garnered his strength lifting glass panes ranging in weight from fifty to three hundred pounds. He did not lose an arm wrestling match with any of his sons, including Slats, until he reached his seventy-fifth birthday.

Slats pretended to be short of breath.

"O . . . K . . . Dad . . . let go . . . you're killing me."

"Ah, ha, ha, ha, I still can make you squeal like a baby. Come. Grab a pole and fish. We'll talk."

"Where's Mom?"

"She go shopping at Zinkes. She's back soon."

"Mom still walks to the market?"

"It's good for her. She's strong as ox. She goes every day with shopping cart."

Slats picked up another fishing rod near his father's tackle box, hooked a worm, and cast it into the river.

"What are we fishing for today, Pops?"

"Mama wants northern pike."

"Dad, I hate to tell you, but I have no clue which fish is which."

"What, you think I do? You think your mama does? Whatever we catch, it'll be northern pike."

"So Dad . . ."

"Shhhhh. We talk later. Now, we fish."

For the next hour-and-a-half, the two men sat in silence, throwing their lines into the river without a bite. Slats basked in the solitude. Sounds of the city were replaced by crashing fishing lines cast into the river, fluttering bird wings and calls, and the crunching of sticks and leaves by a passing fawn.

At precisely 6:30 p.m., the fish began to hit. Bennie threw the panfish back into the river but kept three of the four smallmouth bass he snagged. Slats had not caught one.

"We're done!" he proudly exclaimed to his son. "Let's eat."

Heading back to the condo, they were greeted by Esther Grodsky at the top of the stone path.

"Oh, my baby," she cried, tears flowing down her cheeks.

"Come on, Mom, don't cry. You should be happy to see me."

"Silly boy. These are tears of joy. Oh, you're joking me. Come, my boychick, come give me a hug."

After a long embrace between mother and son, the trio headed to the kitchen where Esther cleaned and prepared the fish for dinner. Bennie retired to the living room to watch the news.

"So," Esther asked Slats, "you like bass?"

"I thought we were eating northern pike?"

"Pike, shmike, your father doesn't think I know one fish from another, because HE doesn't know the difference. I accept this nonsense so I don't embarrass him."

"Still the diplomat, eh, Mom? Well, I'm sure it'll taste great no matter what kind of fish it is."

"Son," Bennie yelled from the living room. "come look at this. Hurry."

Slats and his mother joined Bennie who was watching the evening news. The broadcast was about the Chicago Cap Killer and yesterday's victim. Slats realized another benefit visiting elderly parents. He didn't have to ask them to increase the volume on the television.

The reporter spoke as video of the home, newly decorated with yellow crime scene tape, flashed across the screen.

"Jermaine Smith, of 458 North Jones Street, was found alive and tied to a chair in his home early this morning by his wife Yolanda. Mr. Smith is apparently the latest victim of the Chicago Cap Killer, the most notorious Chicago nemesis since Richard Speck. Mrs. Smith finished her double shift at Mercy Hospital when she noticed her husband's car was still on the street. He should have been at work. She found her husband in the den and immediately dialed 911.

"Superintendent Randle, head of the Chicago Police Department, admitted his task force, which has been diligently working on this case since the beginning of April, is still one step behind . . ."

"So this is the case you are working on, no?" asked Bennie.

"It's a long story, Pops, but no, I'm no longer on the case. I quit my job yesterday."

"I don't understand," Esther chimed in. "You're a good cop, one from the best."

"It's not about being a good cop anymore. It's hard to explain. Let me start from the beginning."

Slats spent the next half-hour detailing the events of the last couple of months to his parents. He told them about the investigation, his participation on the task force, and his missteps with his colleagues. They listened intently as he spoke about his last conversation with Captain Pearson and, finally, his falling out with Julie.

"First, I'm gonna tell you the easy part," Bennie began. "This girl, Julie. What was her crime? That she talked to the bigshot Texas reporter to learn more about you? Did she say she told him about the case?"

"No," Slats answered. "She denied telling him anything about the case. But she hid their relationship from me. How can I believe her anymore? She said she wanted to know what made me tick. Christ, she could have asked me straight up. I would have told her. And Perryman? I know how that guy works. Once he helps you, he expects something in return."

Mama had to ask.

"Have you ever given him something? Cuz it sounds like what is good for the goose isn't good for the gander."

"Son," Slats father added, "you have more secrets than the government's State Department. You didn't tell us about your divorce for over a year, don't forget. This girl, she's done nothing wrong. You have to make it right."

Slats absorbed his parents' advice and hung his head.

"Second, no son of mine is a quitter. You can catch this killer."

"How, Pops? We only have a handful of clues. The man's a ghost. A brilliant ghost. No one can catch him. Shit, I'm beginning to think Cubs fans don't want us to catch him. Do you know people call radio shows and say that a few deaths in return for a world championship are acceptable?"

Bennie's voice was stern. "Stop it! Quit feeling sorry for yourself. I know how smart you are. You're the smartest of all my children, did you know that? You can figure this out. You can catch him. But not if you're fishing the banks of the Wisconsin River!"

"Don't yell, Bennie. It's no good for your heart," Esther pleaded. "Come, let's eat. Chicago can wait, but the northern pike can't."

Esther winked at her son and whispered in his ear as they walked to the dinner table.

"So her name is Julie, also? That's mishuggah, don't you think?"

Slats put his arm around his mother and squeezed.

"Oy! Don't squeeze so hard. Papa means well. He wants the best for you. Stay as long as you want. Stay as long as you need. It's good to have you home with us, Alexander."

Slats took a step back and smiled at his mom. It had been a long time since anyone had called him by his given name.

Chapter 44

July 10, 2013

The Philadelphia Phillies landed in Chicago to find the Cubs in sole possession of first place, twelve games in front of the Milwaukee Brewers. With a record of 60-30, the 2013 team's winning percentage of .667 was one of the best in club history. Only the old Cubs teams from 1906 to 1910, which appeared in four World Series, winning two, had achieved higher marks. The Phillies, leaders in the Eastern Division, were baseball's hottest team, winning sixteen of their last seventeen games. The 2008 World Series champs were once again loaded for bear, in the hunt for the coveted trophy. This three-game series showcased the two best teams in the majors, and the first game of the series, the "kill game" as the networks were now calling it, would be the second most watched sporting event of the year, trailing only the Super Bowl.

Once again, a circus atmosphere encompassed Wrigley. The story had captured the attention of the entire country. Cameramen and interviewers, denied press credentials to the Friendly Confines for lack of space, overflowed into the street. Hundreds of gatherers were soaking up their fifteen minutes of fame as reporters talked to all comers. Bars and restaurants, unprepared in earlier kill games, had scheduled a full complement of employees to handle the load. Inside Wrigley, security was doubled to meet the expected rush of fans onto the playing field in the event of a Cubs victory. Fans unfurled clever, colorful signs, attaching them to the upper deck and lower deck railings:

Let my

People

Go

Cap

Killer

Sucks

World's

Greatest

Prisoners

Want

Gustice

Now

Eradicate

Sick

Perpetrator

Now

Ushers screened signs for vulgarity, forcefully removing them over the objections of fans in the section. Signs that sided with the Cap Killer or spurred him on to keep pressure on the Cubs to win were torn down as well.

Chicago preached sportsmanship to its fans, but many were unable to channel their fear and anxiety into positive energy due to the magnitude of the event—and the amount of beer they consumed. Fifty raucous fans were removed from their seats before the game had even begun. By game's end, almost three hundred more were shown the gate.

Below the grandstands, athletes from both squads were pacing the tunnels near their locker rooms. A victory would impact the Phillies, knowing it cost a Chicagoan their life, but the onus clearly rested on the shoulders of the Chicago Cubs.

Doug Cahill and Derrick Taylor, today's opposing managers, were discussing the game in the Phillies locker room. As had been his practice since William Matthews was slain despite the Cubs victory that day, Cahill from the Cubs reminded Taylor that the only way the hostage was going to live was for the Phillies to play fair and to play hard. Anything even hinting of an impropriety in the eyes of the killer could lead to a captive's demise.

Rance Hellsome, attempting to mitigate the locker room tension, hired a pair of juggling clowns in the Milwaukee series to provide some levity. Today, a quartet of Playboy Bunnies graced the locker room, a gift from Hugh Hefner. Though the women were a hit in the locker room, and indeed distracted a majority of the players, Hellsome lost points with the wives, who were routinely banned from the locker room three hours before game time.

If proof was needed to verify the importance of this game, it was presented in the pregame ceremonies. Country singer LeAnn Rimes, lauded for her version of the "Star Spangled Banner" at the NCAA Men's Basketball Championship, was on hand to reprise her a capella rendition of the national anthem. The Blue Angels, the Navy's flight aerobatic squadron, flew overhead as the song ended. Ernie Banks, the Hall-of Famer known as Mr. Cub and the man who coined the Wrigley Field nickname "Friendly Confines," was present to throw out the first pitch. As the ball thumped into the catcher's mitt, fireworks lit the Illinois sky.

Though it appeared as if the entire world had tuned in, scores ignored the media extravaganza surrounding the Cap Killer story.

Perhaps they should have paid more attention.

"Thank you, Mr. Terry," said the salesman. "Remember, you'll need to return your tuxedo the day after your wedding."

"We're leaving for Paris after the wedding. Can I have someone else drop it off?"

"Of course. Make sure they bring the ticket so we can credit your account. Hope you have a beautiful wedding day and an awesome time on your honeymoon."

Charles Terry, age twenty-four, was about to wed Greta Van Dorn. Greta was spending the weekend on a spa-cation with her mother and bridesmaids at the Eagle Ridge Resort near Galena, Illinois, leaving Charles time to run last-minute errands.

The resort was replete with spa, championship golf course, stables, wilderness trails, gorgeous grounds, magnificent suites, and gourmet restaurants. But then, the Van Dorns were used to such amenities. Owners of the largest trucking fleet in Illinois, the family was third-generation millionaires. The Van Dorn name could be found on six Fortune 500 company boards of directors in the Chicago metropolitan area, and they had been members of the distinguished North Shore Country Club in Glenview since it opened in 1924.

Charles had not originally been considered Van Dorn material in the eyes of Greta's parents. Graduating from Northwestern with a horticulture degree, Terry was working as an apprentice landscape designer on the Van Dorn mansion grounds when he met Greta. Greta, for her part, had been smitten with Charles the first time she laid eyes on him and purposely planted herself in his sightline by sunbathing in her skimpiest two-piece bikini. The rest was history. Greta campaigned for her man, taking a stand against her parents' objections. Now, two years later and fully accepted and embedded in the Van Dorn family and their business, Terry was daydreaming about his future, grateful for the incredible luck bestowed upon him, as he entered his Old Town apartment.

* * *

Incredible luck is also what Slats felt, reflecting on his decision to visit his parents instead of the sleazy bar he had parked in front of a few days earlier. Four days with his parents in the Dells had been the perfect distraction for Slats. No matter what had happened in the past, his parents always managed to elevate his spirits and sustain his strength. Their belief in him was unwavering. But like a Las Vegas vacation, four days was enough, and Slats was now sprinting back to the city he had run away from.

Speeding past the city of Rockford, Slats fumbled for 720 on the radio dial, searching for the Cubs game. He picked up the announcer's call in the bottom of the third.

"There's a fly to shallow left, Jones has got it and the Cubs are finally retired. But not before they score three more on the home run by Nick Cade. We head to the fourth with the Cubs on top of the Phillies, five to nothing."

Slats's phone was vibrating. It was Julie. With an hour-and-a-half drive still in front of him, this was a good time to mend some fences.

"Hi, Jules, I'm glad you called."

"Slats, are you okay? You like dropped off the face of the Earth, and I didn't like our last conversation. You were so upset."

"I'm better. I'm sorry I said those things to you. They were hurtful and wrong, and you didn't deserve them. I was lashing out at the wrong person. Please forgive me."

"I've been doing a lot of that lately, Slats," she said with a sigh. "Where have you been?"

"It's a long story, but it looks like we have plenty of time to talk about it."

"So, start talking. I'm all ears."

"I've been thinking about you for the last few days, and it wasn't about your ears."

"Oh, Slats."

Turning off the radio, he spun the tale of his adventurous four-day trip to Wisconsin. His parents were incredibly perceptive, as he was finding out. He really could patch up his relationship with Julie. Perhaps he could repair his problems with the job as well. But catch the Chicago Cap Killer? No offense to their optimism, but maybe, just maybe, Mom and Pops had been out in the wilderness too long.

Their conversation continued for over an hour until Julie whispered "shit" under her breath.

"What did you say?" Slats asked.

"I said shit. The Phillies just tied the game."

"What? Cubs were up five-zip last I heard. Let me call you back."

Slats turned the radio on again.

"Listen to this crowd. It's stunned. It's so quiet you can hear the ivy growing on the fence. The Cubs have let a seven-run lead slip away, and the Phillies haven't been put away yet. Left-hander Steve Camp has been summoned from the bullpen to try and douse this rally. Camp has an excellent ERA of 2.34, and has not allowed a run in his last twelve innings of work. Opponents are batting .208 against the Cubs' southpaw as he enters the game with two outs and the bases loaded. Momentum has definitely shifted to the Phillies. I don't have to tell you what is at stake here. Everyone knows it, and you can sense the concern on the faces of the Cubs players. Camp is finished with his warm-up tosses, and stepping to the plate is left fielder Rodney Baker.

"Baker, batting from the left side, is two for three today with a strikeout. The Cubs could sure use one here. Camp looks in for the sign. He's pitching from the stretch, here's the throw, and Baker swings and misses strike one, on a ninety-two-mile-per-hour fastball. Baker was swinging for the fences on that one. Camp shakes off Bailey's sign. Now he's ready. Here's the pitch, and it's fouled back behind the backstop and out of play.

Camp takes control as he jumps out in front to an oh and two count. Outfield is in. Here comes the next pitch and— the ball bounces in the dirt. Bailey can't stop it! It's rolling to the backstop. Here comes the runner from third. Bailey's got the ball, throws to Camp, and— safe at home plate! Phillies take the lead. Holy mackerel, Philadelphia just went ahead on a wild pitch. Oh my. Camp is slamming his glove against his thigh. Boy, is he upset with himself. The runners moved up on the play, so now we have second and third with two out and a one-two count on Baker. Bailey is motioning to Camp with his glove to calm down. Camp is furiously digging at the dirt on the pitcher's mound. Now he steps on the rubber and finally looks in. Camp unleashes and a swing and a miss. Strike three! Wow. That one was clocked at ninety-eight miles per hour. One pitch too late. Well, Cubs fans, we head to the bottom of the ninth with Chicago trailing Philadelphia nine to eight."

As the station cut to commercial, Slats couldn't help thinking of the poor soul being held at knife point, scared for his or her life. He also wondered what the nut-job killer was thinking. Was he ecstatic that the Cubs were losing, or angry? Slats's attention was grabbed by the ending of an ill-timed radio ad for the suicide hotline.

"Are you at the end of your rope? Dial one-pleasehelp. That's 1-753-273-4357."

"Welcome back, sports fans. The Cubs trail nine to eight as we begin the bottom of the ninth. The Phillies closer, right-hander Kwan Lee Tang, will be facing the heart of the Cubs order in Carrasquillo, Elliott, and Bailey. Tang, a junk ball pitcher, is an anomaly as a major league closer. Most closers throw in the mid- to high nineties. Tang's top end is around eighty-eight miles per hour, but he's extremely tough to hit because he has such great command of his pitches and varies his speed exceptionally well. And throw the lefty-righty

matchups out the window with this kid. Righties are batting .213 versus Tang, lefties are hitting only .178."

Slats heard the crowd roar and knew everyone was on his or her feet. He vaguely heard the standard "Charge" billowing from the speakers. The announcers noted that fans were begging the Phillies players to blow the game and pleading for the Cubbies to blow it open.

Danny Carrasquillo, up first and taking all the way, quickly found himself behind with a one-two count. Each pitch was answered by a round of boos from the crowd.

"Carrasquillo turned to say something to the home plate umpire about the location of those last two pitches, but the replay shows both strikes painted the corners. Tang looks in. He shakes off the catcher's sign. Now he's ready. Here's the pitch— there's a long fly to left field. It won't be long enough, however, as Baker hauls it in, and there's one away in the ninth. The crowd tried to will that routine fly ball over the fence with the noise level it generated, but the noise quickly dissipated when Baker reeled it in."

Slats, the cop who could calmly thread a needle as bullets whizzed past his head, the man who could balance on a steel beam twenty floors above ground on a stakeout without so much as a quiver, was having trouble concentrating on driving as he listened to the game. Grodsky pulled his car onto the soft shoulders of the freeway. Taking stock of the emergency lane, he realized he was not the only one on the highway sidelines. Dozens of cars and trucks were stopped, honking in unison to cheer on the Cubs.

Rick Elliott quickly raised the decibel level.

"There's a shot into the gap. It's rolling to the fence, and it disappears into the vines! Elliott is churning for two, and the

ump is going to stop him there. Elliott is on second with a ground rule double. Ladies and gentlemen, it's so loud in the park I can barely hear myself think. The Cubs have something going now as Matt Bailey is stepping to the plate. Bailey is on fire today; three for four with three RBI's and looking to add one more. The Phillies infield has converged on the pitcher's mound, and now here comes the ump to break it up. Bailey taps the dirt from his spikes with his bat and digs in against Tang. Here's the pitch, low and outside, ball one. Bailey steps out, readjusts his batting glove, tugs on his belt, cracks his neck, and moves back into the batter's box. He's ready. Tang looks and fires— there's a grounder to the second baseman. He looks to third but won't have a play on Elliott. He throws to first, and now there's a man on third with two out in the bottom of the ninth. Whoa Nelly, this is going down to the wire.

*   "That's going to leave it up to Mike Garrett, the hard-hitting first baseman. Garrett is two for four with two strikeouts. He looks down to the third-base coach before stepping in and now moves in against Tang. Here's the pitch, and it's a curveball in there for a strike. Garrett didn't offer at the pitch. The crowd is pleading for Garrett to tie it up. I know the organ is playing, but it's hard to hear above the din. Tang unloads— there's a swing and a foul back against the netting behind the plate, and Garrett quickly finds himself behind oh-two. Uh-oh, time-out is called as objects are being flung from the stands onto the playing field. Doug Cahill and the Cubs team are out of the dugout imploring the fans to stop . . ."*

Slats's phone rang.

"I thought you were going to call me back?" said Julie. "I'm so nervous."

"I know. Me, too. I pulled off the freeway to listen to the rest of the game. There're about thirty other cars on the berm besides me. Wait. They're done cleaning up the field. Let's listen."

"After that delay, we're back to playing baseball. Mike Garrett is up with an oh-two count. Tang looks in— shakes off the sign— still looking— he sets, he throws— and— a swing and a miss! Oh no. He missed it. Garrett missed it. He has actually collapsed in the batter's box. He's on his knees with his head in his hands. Mike, it's not your fault. There's only one person to blame, and it's not Mike Garrett. Now Garrett's hitting the ground with his fists. Oh, this is terrible. Tang and the rest of the Phillies are converging on home plate, gathering around an inconsolable Mike Garrett. The Cubs players are coming out of the dugout, stunned at the outcome. Sobbing sounds are emanating from the grandstands. Garrett is on his feet now and is being comforted by the Philly players. They are all in obvious grief. Players and coaches from both sides are congregating at home plate and taking a knee in silent prayer. Oh man, I've never seen anything like this in all my years in broadcasting. Many of these athletes are in tears. It's deathly quiet in the stadium. You may want to say a prayer as well, my friends, so I'll let you listen in silence."

Slats raised the volume of his radio, but heard nothing. Even Julie, still on the other end of his phone, was quiet. Then, a smattering of applause was heard over the airways, which grew exponentially louder; loud enough that Slats toned down the volume back to normal.

"I wish you could see this, sports fans. The crowd is giving these athletes a standing ovation and is cheering both teams as they make their way off the field. Many of the players have their arms around the shoulders of their brothers, trying to comfort them in their anguish. What a display of sportsmanship. I tell you, I've never been prouder of Major League Baseball than in this moment."

"Slats. Are you still there?"

"Yah, Julie. I'm here," he said, as he turned off the radio. "I'm coming home. I'll be there in about forty-five minutes. Don't leave, okay?"

"I'm not going anywhere," she answered, choking back the tears. "Bye."

One by one, the parked cars on the berm reentered the freeway to continue their journey. One by one, cars and trucks turned on their hazard lights and began driving at substandard speeds, as if in a funeral procession.

* * *

People residing in and around the Chicago area, as well as the rest of the country, were mourning in their own way, struggling to cope with the idea that a person, eventually identified as Charles Terry, was murdered because the Chicago Cubs lost a baseball game.

And while Chicagoans reflected on the events of the day, somewhere in the city, a shadowy figure stole into the evening after snuffing the light of another man's soul. Chicago's despair only steeled his resolve. Chicago might be suffering now, he thought, but when the Cubs win the pennant and the World Series, Chicago's suffering will finally be over.

Chapter 45

July 19, 2013

The series against the Philadelphia Phillies exacted a toll on the citizens of Chicago. After the series opener, 1,343 drunk and disorderly arrests were made in and around Wrigley Field, and carousers were hauled off to spend the night in local jails. Unlike previous and similar arrests, however, 1,343 sobered-up drunks were released without charges in the morning, amnesty provided and blessed by Mayor McBride and the city council.

A week after returning from Wisconsin, a week of relationship mending with Julie, a week of self-contemplation, and a week filled with three couch sessions with his psychologist, Slats Grodsky entered the Eighth Precinct headquarters and made his way to Chief Pearson's door.

Pearson, checking e-mail on his laptop, waved him in.

"Cap, I have to tell you that . . ."

"Hey, Slats, how was your vacation?" Pearson responded, as he reached into his drawer and slid Grodsky's badge and weapon back to him over the desk.

"I've got a full caseload waiting for you on your desk, Grodsky. Get to work."

"Yes, sir," said the pleasantly surprised detective, relieved that he didn't have to explain his actions of almost two weeks ago. He gathered his possessions on the desk and turned for the door.

"Oh, and Grodsky?" Pearson continued.

"Yes, Cap?"

"Welcome back."

"Thanks, Cap. Thanks a lot."

Grodsky pulled back the wooden chair to his desk and plopped down to read his newly assigned cases.

"Slats," said the voice behind him sheepishly. It was Charlie Brainard.

"Hey, Charlie."

"Slats. I, uh, I want to apologize for the trouble I caused you. I had no idea Zeigler wanted to use things I told him against you, I mean, I was drunk. I don't remember saying much. But, I guess I must have because . . ."

"Look, Charlie. You aren't the first guy to kick someone in the ass when you're drunk. If anyone knows about that, it's me. Forget about it. I've caused my own problems, Charlie, and I need to take care of them myself. Capiche?"

"Sure. Thanks. Hey, I've got an extra ticket to the Cubs game tonight. Wanna come?"

"I don't think it's appropriate, Charlie, not being on the task force anymore, you know? Besides," Slats continued, pointing to the stack of files on his desk, "your father-in-law has me doing double time now that I'm back from vacation."

"Oh yah?" Brainard said, picking up a few of the jackets and quickly thumbing through them. "I worked on a few of these cases myself while you were gone. Well, if I can help you, let me know. You'll see my entries in the jacket."

Brainard stopped at one report and opened it up.

"Hey, Slats?"

"Yah?"

"You may want to look at this one. This bank robbery case. A guy matching his description shows up every Tuesday night to bowl with his buddies at the Seven Ten Bowling Alley on West 55th Street, and tonight's the night."

"Thanks for the tip, Charlie. Bring home a winner."

Slats triaged the jackets on his desk. Two rapes, three B and E's, one bank robbery, one carjacking, one graveyard desecration of a headstone, one domestic violence report, a lost dog, on and on and on. All were reminiscent of the cases he worked on before the Chicago Cap Killer reared his ugly head. Slats opened the jacket on the bank heist. Brainard was right about the bowler. The composite sketch drawn by the police artist, based on the bank teller and customer descriptions, definitely matched the tip they received on the bowler, right down to the height and weight. He would stakeout the bowling alley tonight. Besides, he had a craving for a Reuben sandwich and chocolate shake, two items that happened to be on the bar menu.

Slats started with cases that could be handled from his desk. A few were handled with a single phone call, but most required multiple calls to set up appointments for depositions and interviews, most of which would be taped at the precinct. Less than a handful of the reports required visitation. First on the list was a quick trip to the dog shelter where he IDed the missing dog. Had the incompetent shelter aide checked the dog's collar upon arrival, he would have found the name, address, and phone number of the owners, saving them anguish over their lost pet and the police about three man-hours.

Next, Slats stopped at the cemetery to take pictures of the swastika spray-painted on a tombstone. According to the groundskeeper, the event happened two nights ago after a torrential rainstorm, yet no footprints were found in the muddy areas immediately surrounding the grave site. He was convinced it was a ghost, and Slats obliged him by noting it in his report. The last stop was a shakedown at an elderly couple's apartment where the wife clobbered her husband with a lamp. It was reported by a neighbor, as these cases usually were, and was triggered by the husband's sarcastic remarks about the burnt macaroni and cheese dinner she had served him. Slats warned her that his next visit would land her in city jail for the night and a $500 fine. He decided to rename the case "Smack and Cheese."

It was 7:30 p.m. when Slats entered the bowling alley.

"Excuse me," Slats interrupted the teen at the desk. "I'm supposed to meet a friend here, but I might be early. What time does league bowling start?"

"Nine o'clock. What size shoes?" was the clerk's response.

"No, no. Sorry, I'm not bowling."

"You a cop?"

"What? Ha! No. Just watching. Getting over a broken thumb. Why are you asking me that?"

"Last three guys in here that didn't bowl were cops."

"Gotcha. Say, you got food here?"

"In the bar down that way. Next."

Slightly annoyed that he was made by a pimple-faced bowling employee, Slats found the restaurant and sat on the bar stool facing the television.

"What'll it be?" asked the bartender.

"Turkey Reuben, chocolate shake, and bring my bill with the food, would you?"

An ESPN baseball classic played on the flat screen TV.

Why in the world was this game on TV when the Cubs-White Sox rivalry was starting tonight, Slats wondered? This was probably the only TV in Chicago that did not have the Cubs game on.

Indeed. This was the series everyone had a name for: the Crosstown Classic, the Windy City Showdown, the Red Line Series, the Crosstown Cup. Since interleague play began in 1997, the series between the two clubs was close, with the White Sox holding a slim 41-38 lead. Tonight's game took on an even greater significance, as it was the "kill game" for the Chicago Cap Killer.

Slats waved over the bartender.

"Can you please change the station to the Cubs game?"

"Can't. Remote's broken, and there's no way to change the station on the set itself."

"Excuse me? So your one-thousand-dollar LCD television only plays one channel? You do know they sell universal remotes, don't you?"

"Take it up with my boss. He'll be here tomorrow afternoon."

Slats peered around the bar. He was not gathering support from the other patrons. They were all bowlers, so they weren't planning on watching the game anyway. Not wanting to make a scene, he quietly began watching the replay of the Chicago Cubs-Montreal Expos game from 1983, which was already in the bottom of the ninth inning.

"Leon Durham singles up the middle, and that'll bring up Ron Cey who's one for three with a double . . ."

Slats took out the composite photo of his suspect, making sure no one saw it. He burned the image into his mind.

"There's a comebacker to the mound. Rogers picks it up and fires to second for the force on Durham. Cey is on first with a fielder's choice. Looks like the Cubs are going to bring out Jay Johnstone to pinch hit for pitcher Bill Campbell, who was hitting sixth in a double switch made by manager Lee Elia in the seventh inning . . ."

Slats looked at his watch. It was close to 8:00 p.m. He waved at the bartender again.

"I'll be right back. Save my seat for me."

Walking up and down the alleys, he looked for his man, but found no one that looked like his drawing. He returned to his barroom stool.

"Johnstone lines out to Tim Raines in left and there are two down in the ninth. Jody Davis is stepping in. He's oh for three with a strikeout . . ."

"Here's your order and your bill, Mac."

Slats dug in. It was the first food he had eaten all day.

"There's a called strike three, and the ballgame is over. Steve Rogers has shut out the Cubs on the first game of the year, three to nothing . . ."

Slats was positive he heard the announcer correctly, but needed reassurance.

"What did he say?" Slats asked to those watching. "The guy on TV. Did anyone hear what he said?"

"Something about Rogers shutting out the Cubs on the first game of the year. Why, did you forget to bet on the game?" the jerk on the next stool said as his buddies howled.

Slats sat stunned for a moment, then took out his pocket notebook on the Cap Killer, thumbing through it until he found the page he was looking for.

Victim #1: Theodore Banks, 512 North Rogers Avenue. First game of the year.

Could it be? He needed positive confirmation from someone with quick access.

Picking up his cell phone, he found and dialed the cell number for Edward Jablonski, the Cubs statistician who had assisted the detectives on the task force.

"Your call has been forwarded to an automatic voice message system. Ed Jablonski is not available. At the tone please record your message. When you are finished recording, you may hang up or press one for more options. To leave a callback number, press five. Beeeep."

"Ed, this is Officer Grodsky. Please call me immediately on my cell when you get this message. It's urgent. Thanks."

Slats couldn't wait for the return call. He was too antsy. What if he was right?

"Anyone know the score of the Cubs-White Sox game?" he blurted out.

Someone checked his smartphone app.

"Two to nothin' White Sox, top of fourth."

His desperation led him to call the only other person he knew who could help him.

"Tex?"

"Well, if it isn't my old buddy Slats. Never thought I'd hear from you again. If it's about Julie, I only met with her because she wanted to know more about you. She's a great gal, Grodsky. Her only flaw is that, for some reason, she seems to be madly in love with you."

"Listen, Tex, it's not about that. Where are you right now?"

"In my office at the paper, watching the game. Why?"

"I need you to look up something for me. Stat. Do you have access to past Cubs games?"

"Yeah." Slats could hear Tex typing. "What are you looking for?"

Slats looked at the next page in his notebook. Victim #2: Patricia Moriarty, 19 West Rice Street.

"I need you to cross-reference any ballplayer named Rice who did something to beat the Cubs in the fifth game of the year."

"Sure," Tex said. "What year?"

"I don't know what year."

"Eat shit!"

"Don't hang up! Tex, it's important. Please!"

Tex captured the urgency in Grodsky's voice.

"Fine! This is going to take me a while."

"We don't have a while. Hurry!"

"Let me call you back."

Slats downed the rest of his food and waited outside the bowling alley for Perryman's call, walking the parking lot perimeter as his adrenaline kicked in. He had circled it three times around when he got Perryman's return call.

"Okay, Slats. I think I found the entry you're looking for. Del Rice of the Cardinals hit a home run in the thirteenth inning to beat the Cubs in game five, back in 1950. What does this mean?"

"Not yet. What was the Cubs record after the Audrey Anson abduction?"

"Audrey Anson? That was April 30. Let's see, they won that game, so they were 11-12."

"So that was the twenty-third game. Need you to check another one, Tex. Any ballplayer named Pierce that beat the Cubs in the twenty-third game of any year."

"You're getting on my nerves. Call you back."

Slats knew Perryman would come back with a positive answer. Three out of three would not be a coincidence. He had now forgotten about the suspected bank robber he was chasing. He did go back into the bowling alley to find someone, however. The guy with the cell phone app was scoring his teammate's strike.

"What's the score now?" Slats asked him as his phone rang.

"Four to one White Sox, bottom of fifth."

"Thanks. Hello, Tex? Give it to me."

"Pitcher Billy Pierce of the Giants beat the Cubs in the twenty-third game of 1962. Grodsky, what's going? What are you not telling me?"

"You'll see in a second. What's the Cubs record at game time today?"

Slats could hear Perryman rustling the paper as he looked for the standings in the sports page before he blurted out the game number.

"The Cubs are playing their ninety-fourth game today."

"Okay, Tex, in the ninety-fourth game of every season in Cubs history since 1900, see if you can find someone that did something to beat the Cubs, and has a name that's the same as a Chicago street."

"You're a lunatic! That's over a hundred games."

"Well then get someone to help you, goddamn it. We can stop the murderer, but we have to act fast. You've got to find this."

"Okay, say I find a name, then what?"

"Then all we have to do is find someone who lives on that street with the name of an ex-Cub, and we'll know who his victim is tonight."

"Do you know what you're saying, Slats? That you know how to catch the killer?"

"We've got it, Tex. We've got the key to the murders. It's been there all along. The victim is the name of an ex-Cub. The street address is a specific career statistic for that player when he played for the Cubs. The name of the street is the name of an opposing player . . ."

" . . . who beat the Cubs on a specific game of the year. Oh my God, oh my God. Grodsky, you're a fucking genius!"

Before Tex disconnected the call, Slats could hear Perryman yelling at other reporters to help him research.

With three reporters and four copy boys helping out, Perryman and his staff checked all the box scores of the ninety-fourth game from 1919, the first year box scores were available online, up to 2013. With each new discovery, Perryman sent Slats a text.

"Cubs were 44 and 50 since 1919 in game ninety-four . . ."

"Found 96 players that significantly contributed to their team's victory over the Cubs in the 50 games . . ."

"16 players with names that are also names of Chicago streets . . ."

"Cross-referencing 16 Chicago streets that have people with ex-Cub names living on them. . . it's time consuming . . ."

Grodsky sought out the man who was supplying him with the Cubs-White Sox score.

"What d'ya got now?" Slats asked.

"Four to two Sox, seventh-inning stretch."

Grodsky's phone rang once again. It was Perryman.

"Grodsky. Found nine streets out of the sixteen that have people with ex-Cubs' names living on the street. Got a pen?"

"Ready."

"Ed Brandt, South Brandt Avenue; Buster Adams, West Adams Street; Junior Thompson, Thomson Drive; Larry Jackson, West Jackson Boulevard; Steve Garvey, North Garvey Court; Kelly Downs, Downs Drive; Tom Browning, East Browning Avenue; Kevin Young, South Young Parkway; Dennis Cook, North . . ."

"Browning? Did you say Browning?"

"Yes. Tom Browning, East Browning Avenue."

Grodsky's heart was pounding through his chest.

"How many people with ex-Cub players names on that street?" Slats asked.

"Uh, one. Gleeson."

Slats stumbled backward against the wall as his body shook with fear. The victim Perryman was talking about on East Browning Avenue was not just any person. The target was Ava Gleeson, Slats's daughter!

"Grodsky. You still there? Grodsky!"

Slats had already hung up and was hurrying to his car. Though there were eight other addresses on Perryman's list, there was no doubt of the target. Thoughts of who he had harmed or arrested in the past were being played back in his head. A relative of the child he had accidentally shot and killed looking for revenge? An ex-con back on the streets? There was no way of knowing until he arrived at Ava's apartment. Assuming he arrived in time. As he peeled out of the parking lot, he turned on the radio to find the game. It was the top of the ninth with two outs, but the Cubs had their last ups, as they were still behind four to two.

East Browning Avenue was three miles and ten minutes away from Seven Ten Lanes. Driving without lights or siren but carefully plowing through stop signs and red lights, Grodsky reached for his phone. He had time for two calls. The first was for backup. The second was to Chief Randle.

"Chief Randle's phone."

"Who is this?" Slats asked. "Where's the chief?"

"Grodsky, is that you? It's Zeigler. We're at the ballgame. Randle's talking to the mayor. I'm taking his calls 'til he's done."

"Cliff. Tell the chief. We figured out the Cap Killer's code. I'm pulling in there now. I already called dispatch for backup. The address is 277 East Browning Avenue."

"Who's we?"

"Tex Perryman helped me with online research of the Cubs. I don't have time to explain it now."

"Why the hell are you even working on this? You were kicked off the task force, Grodsky, or did you forget that? And part of it was because you were in bed with that asshole reporter."

"Cliff, it's my daughter's house. He's after my kid."

"Sure, Slats, like the two times you had it figured out before. Let's see, there was the wild goose chase tracking down a cell phone, and, oh yah, catching that criminal Cubs executive Gallagher having sex with his mistress."

"Goddamn it, Cliff! You hate me. I get that! But this is my kid. Now tell Randle, or . . ."

"Or what? Listen to me, Grodsky; go hand out some parking tickets and let the real detectives handle the murders!" Zeigler shouted into the phone before disconnecting the call.

* * *

Cliff Zeigler's hatred of his ex-partner went beyond normal, way beyond reason. Convinced Grodsky was once again on the wrong track, he made a phone call from Chief Randle's phone.

"Dispatch, you got a call a few minutes ago for backup to East Browning Avenue. Cancel that call please. False alarm."

"Copy that," replied dispatch, noting that caller ID listed the cell phone as Dale Randle's.

* * *

Slats pulled his car into the parking lot at the intersection of South Rhodes Avenue and East Browning Avenue. Making sure his weapon was fully loaded, he jumped from the Grand Prix and lumbered across South Rhodes Avenue. Ava's house was one of only two on the block. It was surrounded by empty parking lots in the front and vacant lots to the rear. With no cover, Slats prayed he had not been spotted approaching the front steps of Ava's house. Never having been invited to his daughter's home, Grodsky circled the perimeter of the bungalow, hoping to gain insight on the floor plan and where Ava would be, but the shades had been drawn on every window. Though help was coming any minute, he also knew the game was almost over. He could not wait for backup with Ava's life hanging in the balance.

Returning to the front steps, he pressed a button on his phone to turn on the backlight. It gave enough illumination to discover what he was looking for in the flower bed behind the juniper shrubs. Picking up the Hide-A-Key fake rock, he scraped off the dirt and opened the bottom to reveal a house key. "Thank God, you take after your mother," he thought. The screen door creaked against his wishes; hopefully, the volume on the television cloaked the sound. The key opened the lock it entered, and the door silently opened, yielding to his pressure. Slats tiptoed into the house, leaned against the foyer wall, and wondered, "Where's the damn backup?"

* * *

Cliff Zeigler grabbed Kenny Usher away from another cop. The two were deep in conversation about the Cubs' lack of depth on the bench.

"Just got a call from your old pal Grodsky on Chief Randle's phone. Did you know the asshole is still working the Cap Killer case?"

"No, I didn't," responded Usher. "What did he say?"

"Wait 'til you hear this. He said he figured out where the Cap Killer was, and was there right now. Oh, and this is the best part. He said it was his daughter's house."

"Christ! I know where that is. That's about twenty-five minutes from here. Let's get go . . ."

"Don't be stupid. Grodsky's a crackpot. I cancelled his backup call."

"You did what? Are you nuts? I swear to God, if you put him or his girl in harm's way—I'll be the one that holds your ass to the fire."

"What's with the one-eighty? I thought you hated the guy? Why do you keep sticking up for him?"

"It's not about like. It's about what's right, you moron!"

Usher ran over to Chief Randle to relay what Zeigler had told him. Randle kept glancing at Zeigler while Usher explained the situation. Randle called dispatch to reissue the backup request.

The superintendent yelled for the detectives who were present at the game to gather round.

"Gentlemen, we have a credible lead of the whereabouts of the Cap Killer. There's a fellow officer on the site now. The address is 277 East Browning Avenue. Let's hope we're not too late!"

"Usher," Randle shouted. "I'm going with you. I hope Grodsky knows what he's doing. This is one devious killer, maybe too much for him to handle alone."

* * *

Alone, and peering around the corner, Slats identified the living room, and ninety degrees to the left of that, the dining room. The broadcast of the game was emanating from a room beyond the dining area, most likely the den. As he was making his move into the living room, he was tackled from behind, both bodies hurtling to the ground. His weapon separated from his grip, sliding to the other side of the room on the hardwood floor. Slats was pinned beneath his attacker when he felt a pinprick to his neck.

Drawing from his training, Slats raised his butt into the air and, with knees firm on the ground, flipped the attacker over his head. Rising to his feet, he kicked the masked intruder first in the stomach, then the head, rendering him motionless. Eager to ID the bastard, Slats removed the mask. It was, however, a face he had never seen before. Turning to the den, Slats saw

Ava gagged and tied to a lawn chair in front of her television. Hurrying to her side, he struggled for a minute as he attempted to free the tightly tied gag from her mouth.

"Did he touch you?" he shouted to Ava.

With the gag still firmly in place, she motioned to her father with her eyes. So frantic to get her safe and untied, Slats missed her silent signal. Once again Slats was body slammed from the side as the man Slats assumed was unconscious struck again. The two fell against the window, pulling the shade off its bracket, exposing the window. Tugging, spinning, and bumping into lamps and tables, the struggling men sent vases, picture frames, and candleholders crashing to the floor. Both men landed solid punches to the body. Slats went for the head and staggered his opponent with a solid left uppercut to the jaw, but it was Slats who began feeling woozy. The room was spinning around him. The Cap Killer regained his composure and forcibly shoved Grodsky to the ground, leaning him against the wall facing his daughter. On his buttocks with legs sprawled out in front of him, Slats was shocked he could barely move.

Knowing Slats had questions to be answered and would soon be unable to articulate them, the Cap Killer wiped the blood from his mouth, then began.

"This is actually better than I had hoped," started the Cap Killer. "You'll probably be asleep in about five minutes, so I better talk fast. My name is Billy Conroe. Does that mean anything to you?"

Slats shook his head no.

"Thought not. Well, while you were receiving awards for solving the Bermuda Love Triangle case, I was lying in a hospital bed fighting for my life. And it was your fault.

Conroe became increasingly agitated as his story progressed.

"You see, I was a baseball player. And trust me; I was supposed to play in the Cubs organization. Oh yes, it was all set up by my dad. You see, my dad's best friend was a scout for the Cubs. All I had to do was show up at the tryouts at Wilmington College, and I was going to be added to one of the Cubs' minor league rosters. It was a rookie league, but it would have been a start. I would've had my foot in the door. I was going to be living my dream. I was destined to play in the majors with the Cubs and lead them to a World Series championship. But a strange thing happened, Officer Grodsky. At the end of the tryout, my name wasn't called. I asked to see the scout that led the tryout but was told he was arrested, and had been forced to leave the campus. The scout's name was Joey Robbins. Does that name ring a bell? Ding, ding, ding— thought so. Well, needless to say, I was not offered a contract. That was your fault, Grodsky. So I got drunk after the tryout. That was your fault, too. Then I wrapped my fucking car around a tree, breaking three bones in my back; both knees; and twenty-eight other bones, tendons, and muscles in my body. And that, you goddamn son of a bitch, was also your fucking fault! So you see, Grodsky, it was your fault my baseball career was over before it began. I sat in that rehab hospital for six months planning how I was going to pay you back. That's when I figured out how I could satisfy both dreams. To lead the Cubs to the World Series and to pay you back for destroying my life."

"The BLT wad firteen years ago," Slats slurred. "Why wait this lonng?"

"Good question, officer, but hardly well spoken. As it turned out, my revenge plan required time and money, two things I was a little short on; that is, until this year when my father died in January. He left me his entire estate. Seven million to be exact, more than enough to put my plan into action. Did I tell you he was an oral surgeon? I cleaned out his office, and trust me, the syringes and drugs came in quite handy, as I'm sure you can testify."

Only then did Slats realize that the pinprick he felt earlier was the fine point of a needle entering his neck, carrying with it a sedating dose of midazolam. He must fight it as long as he could. Please, God, he thought, let me hang on a little longer. At least until backup arrives.

"Now, here we are," Conroe continued. "Together at last. You, me, your lovely daughter, and the Chicago Cubs. Ooh, did you hear that?" Conroe said, pointing to the TV. "Let's listen, shall we?"

Conroe picked up the remote and increased the volume of the television to hear the announcer.

"The crowd has been silenced once again as the Cubs have dropped tonight's ballgame to the Chicago White Sox, four to two. As the players converge at home plate and drop to a knee, let's join them in silent prayer."

Conroe smiled as he heard the final score.

"You know what that means, don't you, Slats? May I call you Slats? It means your little girl here has to be sacrificed for the good of the Cubs organization."

Billy whipped around with a curious stare aimed at the detective on the floor.

"Say, how did you figure out I was here tonight?"

"Fagure it lout?" Slats repeated. He could not let Conroe know he had deciphered the code. Should he die here tonight, the police would catch the bastard during the next kill game.

"You geeve me too much cradit. I'm off the tisk force."

The drug's soporific effect was making it harder to talk.

"I was—bawling alley—came to visit . . ."

"You're not talking too well, officer. But do you really think I'm that stupid? You think I believe it was a coincidence you are here tonight?"

Reaching into the small of his back, Conroe withdrew his hunting knife, displaying it proudly to his captured guests.

With a quick thrusting motion, Conroe plunged his knife into Slats's abdomen. Slats heard Ava's muffled scream.

"Maybe you'll talk to me now."

Slats fell to his side in a fetal position, blood staining his shirt.

Conroe half-circled around his prey.

"I'll bet that didn't hurt as much as it should, you know, all those drugs and all."

As Slats groaned on the floor, Conroe turned his attention toward Ava.

"Hey, better yet, maybe I'll carve up your little girl. Then maybe you'll tell me the truth."

Ava squirmed frantically in the chair as Conroe approached, but made no progress against the pressing rope. Her screams, partly muted by the gag, were completely drowned out by the television.

Handling the knife with the skill of a butcher, Conroe picked off the buttons of her shirt one by one, cut her brassiere in half which uncovered her breasts, and gently pressed the cold steel against her skin without breaking it.

"You know, Slats, she's absolutely gorgeous. It would be a shame to kill her without first tasting her, don't you think?"

Unable to move, and consciousness nearly gone, all Slats could do was pray for his daughter. Tears rolled down the side of his face as he closed his eyes to the terror that lay before him.

"Trust me," Billy said to Ava as he unbuckled his pants and unzipped his zipper, "I may not be your first, but I will be your most memorable."

As his pants hit the floor, the uncovered den window exploded, spraying shards of glass into the room. The single bullet, which had burst through the pane, penetrated Conroe between the eyes. His body swayed before falling backward like a timbered tree. The thud from his head falling hard against the wooden floor startled Grodsky momentarily out of his twilight. Opening his eyes, his vision was now obscured by the motionless, bleeding head of Billy Conroe.

"Avaaaaaa," Slats howled.

Still gagged but screaming to her father, Slats knew his daughter was alive.

"Love you," Slats gurgled, blacking out to the beautiful sounds of sirens in the distance.

*   *   *

Within minutes, officers from the Second District arrived on the scene. Squad cars kept coming every few minutes, until thirty to forty cops mobbed the premises.

"What the hell?" the first officer on the scene yelled as he surveyed the den. With his gun still drawn, he kicked the knife and gun away from the two men lying on the floor. He checked for a pulse on Conroe's neck. There was none.

"This one's dead. Hey, untie her," he said to his partner, pointing to Ava while holstering his weapon. He moved over to Grodsky. "I've got a pulse here. Buddy, can you hear me?"

As he pulled his hands away, he discovered they were painted with Grodsky's blood.

Ava's gag was off.

"That's my dad! He's a cop."

"Shit! Ten-Double-Zero Officer Down. Ten-Double-Zero Officer Down," he repeated into his two-way radio.

"Need an ambulance at 277 East Browning Avenue. That's two-seven-seven East Browning Avenue. Hang on buddy. What's his name?"

"Grodsky. Slats Grodsky." Ava screamed through the tears. "Please. Don't let my dad die. He saved me."

An arriving officer tore the packing off a Hemcon bandage, exposed Grodsky's wound, and applied the dressing. The Hemcon chitosan-based bandage, first used by the military to stop massive hemorrhaging, was now field issue for the CPD.

Ava was freed and ran to her father's side.

"Daddy, please don't leave me. I love you. I'm sorry I pulled away from you. Please. We have so much to live for. I promise I'll always be there for you. I'll never leave you again. Don't go—don't leave me—hang on, Daddy, hang on."

Medics gently lifted Ava to her feet, moved her aside, and began treating their fallen comrade.

While the medics worked on her father, Ava stumbled over to the Chicago Cubs cap lying next to Billy Conroe that was meant for her.

"Here you are, asshole," she said, grabbing the cap and shoving it over his face.

Grodsky was on the gurney and being lifted into the ambulance when Dale Randle and Kenny Usher arrived.

"How is he?" Randle asked the paramedic sitting in the back of the ambulance by Grodsky's side.

"He's got a deep abdominal stab wound; lost a lot of blood. BP is 90 over 50."

"And the girl?"

"She's in shock, but she's going to be okay. Surgeon's waiting. Gotta go."

Randle closed the ambulance door as it pulled away. He turned to Usher.

"Kenny, get me Zeigler on the phone. Now!"

WARREN FRIEDMAN

Chapter 46

Epilogue

October 29, 2013

The 105-year wait was finally over. World Worlds I and II, the Stock Market Crash of 1929, the Great Depression, the Korean War, the Cold War, the Vietnam War, the Cuban Missile Crisis, the Kennedy and Martin Luther King assassinations, the moon landings, the Flower Generation, rock and roll, the collapse of the Berlin Wall, the new millennium; all these events and a million others had come and gone since 1908, the last time the Chicago Cubs had won the World Series trophy. Now there was no need to talk about the drought, the goat, the black cat, or Bartman. The Cubs had finally won it all, besting the Minnesota Twins in the fall classic, four games to two. And now, Cubs fans in Chicago and around the globe could bask in the glory of their beloved team. The Cubs victory march was rolling through the streets of Chicago.

It was one of the largest and longest parades in the history of sports. Twenty-five double-decker buses carried the World Champion Chicago Cubs players, staff, corporate office workers, and, of course, family through the streets of Chicago. Starting at Wrigley Field, the buses circled the streets in Wrigleyville before heading down North Clark Street to a path that emptied into North Michigan Avenue, finally ending at a Cubs rally at Lasalle and Wacker in the Loop. Thousands of supporters lined the entire route from the Friendly Confines to downtown. An estimated two-and-a-half million crazed fans lined the streets of Chicago, hooting and hollering as the buses passed by. Car and truck horns blared; church bells rang; even horn blasts could be heard from the dry-docked boats in the marinas off Lake Michigan. When the bus convoy passed through the downtown skyscrapers' shadows, confetti and ticker tape poured from the sky, riding and twisting in the thermal wind currents up and down the avenues. The noise was deafening. "Cub Luv" was everywhere. Signs adorned business windows, banners flew from buildings, and fans carried homemade and professional signs proudly in the air. Nearly everyone wore a Cubs jersey or the white, blue, and red colors of their favorite team.

The loudest roars of the day were for the grand marshal of the parade, the man whose own career mirrored the storied history of the Cubs. He had been a champion early in his life, only to fall from grace for many years before resurrecting his career and reemerging at the pinnacle of his profession. Sitting on the folded down top of the BMW convertible, with his daughter and ex-wife in the front seat and his girlfriend by his side, Slats Grodsky could not hear himself talk as he waved to the adoring crowd.

"Now I know what Lou Gehrig must have felt like, for I too consider myself one of the luckiest people on the face of the Earth."

"What? I can't hear you," said Julie, his girlfriend, cupping her hand to her ear.

"Never mind, just wave." Slats smiled.

At the end of the parade route, Slats was escorted to the rally podium along with Mayor McBride, Rance Hellsome, his top execs, players, and coaches of the Chicago Cubs team.

"It is with great pride that I stand before you today side by side with the best team in all of baseball—the Chicago Cubs!" the mayor barked as he brought a crying and emotional Hellsome to the microphone.

"No one deserves this more than the great fans of Chicago. On behalf of Doug Cahill and the team, we want to thank you for your years of support, love, and devotion to our organization. This is truly your trophy."

Hugs and tears were shared by the players on the podium, the weight of the season now lifted from their shoulders.

"I want to call Chicago's favorite son to help me present the team with the trophy. Please welcome Officer Slats Grodsky."

The two-minute ovation from players and fans left nary a dry eye. When the applause subsided, Slats took the microphone.

"I am grateful to you for your response, and I am truly blessed. My sacrifice was nothing compared to others in our community. I'd like to take this opportunity to honor those who died or suffered during this season, inadvertently helping the Cubs to achieve their goal. May we please have a moment of silence . . ."

Though the participants on the podium bowed their head in prayer, the clatter from the crowd continued.

"Chicago," Hellsome continued, breaking the not-so-silent prayer by raising the World Series trophy high above his head, "we give you the World Champion Chicago Cubs."

As Cahill and the players began fielding questions from the press on the dais, Slats stealthily moved off stage behind the podium to a smaller press conference.

"I can only take a few questions, but before I do, I want to publicly thank Tex Perryman for his terrific work in helping to catch the Chicago Cap Killer."

"Officer Grodsky," asked the first reporter, "did the police ever determine the identity of the shooter that actually killed the Cap Killer?"

"No, I'm afraid they never did. It was not a policeman, however. They didn't show up until a few minutes after the shot was fired. It was a Good Samaritan, I guess."

The crowd laughed.

"This is your first interview since your stabbing. How are you feeling?" asked another scribe.

"Best I've felt in years. Who needs a spleen anyway?"

"When do you think you'll go back to work?" shot a question from the pack of reporters.

"I'm already working. Yesterday I did two loads of laundry, swept the kitchen floor, cleaned the bathroom, and made spaghetti and meatballs for eight."

"Was this the best case you ever worked on?"

Slats stared his interviewer down.

"No, sir. This was the worst case I ever worked on."

Though the questions were still being blurted out, Slats had had enough for the day.

"Thank you very much. I appreciate all of you as well as all of the citizens in this great city. This is a great day for us all."

The reporters parted, creating a path for Slats as he walked to join his family in the waiting limo parked on the LaSalle

Bridge over the Chicago River. Slats entered the vehicle and slid into the plush black leather seat next to Ava.

"Oh, Dad, I almost forgot. Remember I told you about the company that came out and repaired my den window at no charge the day after the Cap Killer was shot in my house? Well, here, I found their bill, the one you were asking about."

Ava handed her father the statement. It was from Mark Anthony Windows.

Suddenly, the mystery of who shot the Cap Killer was clear as a bell. Mark Anthony Windows, one of the legitimate businesses owned and operated by Damarco Maravelli and the Maravelli family. He tingled with excitement as the answers to all his questions sent chills through his body. Of course! The promise by Don Maravelli in the police station years ago when he vowed to repay Slats for saving countless Maravelli lives after solving the Bermuda Love Triangle case; the feeling of being followed all those times, all those years. There was no doubt in Slats's mind that the bullet that felled the Chicago Cap Killer, saving Ava as well as himself, belonged to the mafia angel whose sole purpose for the last thirteen years was to follow Slats and protect him and his family. Unbelievably, Don Maravelli had kept the vow he swore on his parents' graves and his children's lives.

"Where to?" asked the chauffeur.

"I'm hungry," Slats said. "Anyone in the mood for Italian?"

About the Author

    Warren Friedman lives off the south shores of Lake Erie in Cleveland, Ohio with his wife Geri, where they own and operate Hillcrest Atrium Pharmacy. Having played football and baseball in high school and college before embarking on a thirty-six year career as a pharmacist, Warren now enters the next chapter of his life with his debut novel, The Chicago Cap Murders.

    www.warrenfriedman.com